TEXAS
The Great Theft

TEXAS
The Great Theft

Carmen Boullosa

TRANSLATED BY SAMANTHA SCHNEE

INTRODUCTION BY MERVE EMRE

DEEP VELLUM PUBLISHING
DALLAS, TEXAS

Deep Vellum Publishing
3000 Commerce Street, Dallas, Texas 75226
deepvellum.org · @deepvellum

Deep Vellum is a 501c3 nonprofit literary arts organization founded in 2013 with the mission to bring the world into conversation through literature.

Support for this publication has been provided in part by grants from the National Endowment for the Arts, the Texas Commission on the Arts, the City of Dallas Office of Arts and Culture, the Communities Foundation of Texas, and the Addy Foundation.

ISBN: 978-1-646053-53-7 (PAPERBACK) · 978-1-646053-65-0 (EBOOK)

LIBRARY OF CONGRESS CATALOGING-IN-PUBLICATION DATA
Names: Boullosa, Carmen, author. | Schnee, Samantha, translator. | Emre, Merve, other.
Title: Texas : the great theft / Carmen Boullosa ; translated by Samantha Schnee.
Other titles: Texas. English
Description: Tenth anniversary edition. | Dallas, Texas : Deep Vellum Publishing, 2024.
Identifiers: LCCN 2024029736 (print) | LCCN 2024029737 (ebook) | ISBN 9781646053537 (trade paperback) | ISBN 9781646053650 (ebook)
Subjects: LCSH: Mexicans--Texas--History--19th century--Fiction. | Texas--Ethnic relations--History--19th century--Fiction. | LCGFT: Novels.
Classification: LCC PQ7298.12.O76 T4913 2024 (print) | LCC PQ7298.12.O76 (ebook) | DDC 863/.64--dc23/eng/20240709
LC record available at https://lccn.loc.gov/2024029736
LC ebook record available at https://lccn.loc.gov/2024029737

Cover design by In-House International
Interior layout and typesetting by KGT

PRINTED IN CANADA

Texas-Mexico Border (1859)

Introduction

The spirit of gossip presides over Carmen Boullosa's *Texas: The Great Theft*. Opening the book to its first page, we find "A Busybody's Brief Note." "Let's state it up front, so we don't get muddled: this is the year 1859," it begins. "We're on the northern and southern banks of the Río Bravo, known to some as the Rio Grande, in the cities of Bruneville and Matasánchez. Heading into the wind on horseback we could make it to the sea in half a morning." It is a relief in a strange new novel to know where we are and when. But do we? If we read these sentences again, we begin to see how the matter-of-fact precision of the first—"this is the year 1859"—is, in fact, muddled by the second. How are we on both the northern and southern banks of the Río Bravo (or is it the Rio Grande?), in the cities of Bruneville and Matasánchez at the same time? Before we can figure out how to be in two places at once, we are swept away by the third sentence, galloped from the city to the sea; its cold blue air rises to greet us at the end of a journey we barely register making. Already, we are bewildered— well before the busybody tells us about the thefts and betrayals of the Americans, the gringos who carved the state of Texas out of

Mexico's northern frontier and established the city of Bruneville to protect their invented border.

This busybody sounds suspiciously like our novel's narrator. Theirs is the voice of gossip: plainspoken, vigorous, and combative, a voice that babbles along as a single "we," but in varied tones and tongues. Like a thief, gossip moves swiftly, undeterred by rivers or valleys, indifferent to borders and the hotheads who patrol them. It makes it possible for us to be on both the northern and southern banks of the Río Bravo, in Bruneville and in Matasánchez at the same time. Or rather, it floats us just above the cities, high enough for us to chuckle at their inhabitants, but not so high that we mistake ourselves for gods. We observe the events that launch our story with equal parts excitement and agitation. At high noon, Don Nepomuceno, the Robin Hood of the Rio Grande, tries to get the Sheriff to stop beating Lázaro, an old vaquero who is drunk in the plaza. "Shut up, you dirty greaser," the Sheriff spits at Nepomuceno. The men freeze in a face off—one second passes, then two, then three, then ten, then thirty—until their hands reach for their guns. Two shots are fired. The victim falls to the ground, bleeding. The victor flees, to plot his next move. All this transpires in less than a minute. But it takes the first part of the novel, almost two hundred pages, for the narrator to tell it. The drama is repeatedly interrupted by the story of how the insult—"Shut up, you dirty greaser"—travels across the plains, along the coastline, and up and down the mighty, moody rivers that separate the U.S. from Mexico.

The novel's meanderings remind us that, as with all good gossip, what happened is beside the point. What matters is how it is told. In the beginning, it is easy to track. The insult wings its way across Market Square, carried by Frank, "one of the many Mexicans in the streets of Bruneville who run errands and spread gossip, a 'run-speak-go-tell,' a pelado," a bum. Frank tells the butcher. The butcher tells the chicken dealer. The chicken dealer tells the greengrocer—and from here, the novel begins to tug us in several different directions, to whirl us round and round, until we collapse on both banks of the river, dizzied, confused, and at the same time filled with a delirious rapture. Gossip flies us from Galveston to the swamps south of Matasánchez. As it spreads, it shifts shape. The Sheriff's insult is exaggerated, embellished; written down; turned into song; translated. It kicks up more gossip, older gossip. Someone tells a tale about the return of a vengeful white Indian, John Tanner ("this gets folks' attention more than the news about Nepomuceno"). Someone whispers about the minister ("Wicked tongues say he does more than speak with boys, though it's just gossip"). Someone claims to have seen a man carrying a Talking Cross. It has been dunked in holy water and has curative powers ("which we know is not true"). When gossip alights on new characters, it is sucked into their strange and eventful histories. But it knows when to retreat. "We don't have time for them now," the narrator dismisses the novel's too-minor characters. It cannot risk losing the thread of our story.

A new world spins into our line of vision, its movement guided by gossip's great centrifugal force. The temptation is to slow it all down—like Luis, the little boy in the marketplace whose mind "loses all concept of time" and stretches a single second into an hour. One could track the characters, noting their first names, last names, old names, new names, titles, epithets, and movements. We have Sheriff Shears, Don Nepomuceno, Frank (formerly known as Pancho Lopez), Stealman (the lawyer), Sharp (the butcher), the greengrocer, Señora Luz, Mrs. Lazy, Doña Estefanía, Alitas, Frenchie, Cherem, Miss Lace, Judge Gold (who is not a real judge), Luis, Sabas, Refugio, Judge White (who is a real judge), Nat, Glevack, Mrs. Big, Olga, Minister Fear, Eleonor, Moonbeam, Lázaro, the Smiths, Caroline, Strong Water, Blue Falls, Chief Little Rib, Smiley, Roberto Cruz, Sitú, Perla, Óscar, Tim Black, Joe Lieder, Don Jacinto, Peter Hat (whom the Mexicans call "El Sombrerito"), La Plange, Snotty, Bill,

Michaela, Ranger Neals, Ranger Phil, Ranger Ralph, Ranger Bob, Urrutia, Werbenski, Lupis Martínez, Aunt Lina, Santiago, Hector, Melón, Dolores, Dimas, Tadeo, Mateo, Mr. Wheel (the cart driver), Zachary Taylor, Lucrecia, Perdido, the Flamenca sisters, Clara, Jim Smiley, Leno, Tiburcio, Captain William Boyle, Rick, Chris, Doctor Schulz, Engineer Schleiche, Prince Solms, the Prince of Nassau, Mrs. Fear, Esther, Kenedy, King, Don Jacinto, Father Rigoberto, the Archbishop of Durango, Jeremiah Galván, the Robin brothers, the Trece brothers, Nicolaso Rodríguez, Aunt Cuca, Catalino, Lucha, Amalia, Doctor Velafuente, Doctor Velafuente's patient, Aunt Cuca's godmother, Isa, Rafaela, Jones, Felipillo Holandés, the Carranzas, Laura, Don Marcelino, Petronila, Roberto, Pepe, Domingo, Lolita, Gómez, the jailkeeper of Matasánchez (no one remembers his name), Green Horn, Captain Randolph B. Marcy, Pepementia, Gutiérrez, Carvajal, Don José María, Francisco Manuel Sánchez de Tagle, Wild Horse, Juan Caballo, Lucie, Lucie's son, Gabriel Ronsard, the overseer of the Pulla cotton plantation, El Tigre, Noah Smithwick, the Born-to-Run Indians, Bruno, Pizca, Pierced Pearl, Bob Chess, Rawhide, Chief Smells Good, Sky Bullet, Peladita, Steve, Nemesio, Charlie, a guy called David, old Arnoldo, Teresa, Mifflin, Mr. Chaste (the mayor), Mr. Seed (the owner of the coffee shop), Alicia, Dry Whitman (a teetotaler), Sandy, Sandy's cousin, Esteban, Fernando, Connecticut, the Scot, Carlos the Cuban, Dimitri, Wild, Trust, One, Two, Three, Patrick, Toothless, the woman who sells fresh tortillas, Skewbald, Mrs. Stealman (Elizabeth Vert), James, Rebecca, Silda, El Iluminado, Maria Elena Carranza, Rafael, Jose, Alberto, Polca, Milco, Lucoija, Lucia, Chief Buffalo Hump, Juan Prensa, Mr. Ellis Producer, Father Vera, Fidencio, Loncha, the delirious man, Dr. Meal, Magdalena (whom Nepomuceno's men call La Desconocida), Magdalena's aunt, Magdalena's godmother, Blas, Josefina, Mr. Blast, William Walker, a crazy man ("El Loco"), Tulio, Bartolo, Doña Eduviges, Juan Pérez, Lupita, Sam Houston,

Ludovico, Fulgencio, Silvestre, Pedro, Pablo, Ismael, Patronio, Fausto, El Güero, Frau Lieder, Herr Lieder, Lopez de Agauda, Julito, Úrsulo, Chung Sun, Mayor de la Cerva y Tana, Mr. Sand, Roho (or Rojo), the Lieutenant Governor, Captain Callaghan, McBride, Pridgen, the Senator, Catherine Anne Henry, George (Jorge) Henry, George's son, Sarah Henry, Lieutenant Ware, Georgette, Georgette's husband, Georgette's son, Georgette's oldest daughter (Sarah Ferguson), José Eusebio, José Esteban, the organ-grinder, José Hernández, Frederick Cannon, Josefa Segovia, Josefa's nephew, Judge Jones ("Busy Bucks"), Shine, Señor Balli, Platita Poblana, Blade (the barber), Josh Wayne, Mr. Dice, Pepe, Gold, Pierce, Richie, Neil Emory, Gwendolyn Gwinn, Franklin Evans, Juliberto, Juliberto's father, General Cumin, his wife, Captain Rogers, Urzus, Papa Bouverie, Tonkawa Fragrance, Owl Woman, Eliza, Rita, Mr. Domingo, Doña Tere, Dan Print, Metal Belly, Captain Ruby, Marisa, Saint Agatha, Saint Lucia, Our Lady of the Holy Conception, Saint Margaret, and Saint Cecilia.

It is a stupefying list, if not an especially useful one. This is not because it is incomplete (though it very well may be), but because it cannot account for the numberless numbers of cowboys, Indians, immigrants, and slaves that fill out the novel. Gossip takes comfort in crowds. It has little use for singular men and women, those finely individuated, emotionally complex characters whose minds and memories preoccupy the writers of realist and modernist novels alike. Interiority demands patience; it takes time to plumb the depths of consciousness. But gossip's impatience, its garrulous sociability, leaves it mostly indifferent to the characters' thoughts and feelings. The glimpses we are given of them—in, for instance, the diary of Mrs. Stealman, the lawyer's wife—reveal only the most generic expressions of bigotry and fear. "Mrs. Stealman writes in peacock blue ink, as befits her personality and class," the narrator observes. What she writes about the Sheriff and Nepomuceno is almost too unoriginal to repeat: "*Good for the sheriff. He's got to start somewhere cleaning up this place . . . The drunken greaser resisted. Another Mexican came to his defense.*" Even in her diary, she does little more than gossip with herself. In quoting her, we do little more than keep the gossip moving.

Gossip's trick is to make all its characters, no matter their race or nationality, equally peripheral and essentially interchangeable. At the party that Mrs. Stealman throws that night, the guests have an impassioned debate about a scandalous novel, *Uncle Tom's Cabin*. "Negroes can't be characters in novels. That would be like having a dog as a protagonist!" one guest exclaims. "You mean they're like a piece of furniture, a wardrobe, or a chair?" another asks. Where a protagonist should be in *Texas*, there is only an empty space, with hundreds of chair-like characters arranged in concentric circles around it. When the narrator makes an exception, it is not for people, but for animals, like the cow that floats down the river, dreaming of grass:

> *I, the rotting cow, endowed with the life of these worms, dream that I am about to eat a mouthful of fresh grass. In the grass, a caterpillar watches me. It's not like any of the worms in my belly. In the caterpillar's eye, I see the moon shining at noon. In this day that I share with the moon, reflected in the caterpillar's eye, I see myself, a cow that's very much a cow: a ruminating, sweet, edible cow that gives the milk that makes sweets and cakes.*
>
> > *Doesn't feel good to be breeding worms . . .*
> > *I'm a cow, not a coffin!*
> > *I wasn't born to become a swollen, drifting balloon.*
> > *Perhaps I should calm myself: I'm the cow who used to moo. The cow who dreams, inspired by my worms' souls.*
> > *I forget about the earthworm and her eye; I take a bite*

of the (delicious) fresh grass which might not be real, but no matter.

The cow's body drifts into the novel on a strange snatch of poetry. Here is one of the few instances in the novel when gossip's first-person plural yields to the first-person singular, "I, the rotting cow," whose lyric address seems like a freakish parody of Walt Whitman's *Leaves of Grass*, a poem regularly praised for its speaker's receptivity to all forms of life. Yet the poet's imagination did not extend to Mexicans. "What has miserable, inefficient Mexico to do with the great mission of peopling the New World with a noble race?" he wrote in the *Brooklyn Eagle*. Where Whitman's democratic spirit failed, our narrator steps in to teach his admiring readers a lesson. The worm-ridden cow has a wonderous double consciousness, far superior to that of the novel's human characters. It can see itself, reflected in the caterpillar's eye, as "a cow that's very much a cow," and it can see itself as the humans see it, as "a ruminating, sweet, edible cow that gives the milk that makes sweets and cakes." Its corpse reminds us that, while the Americans are guilty of theft, this does not mean that the Mexicans are innocent. As Nepomuceno's sidekick, Óscar, worries, "no matter how you look at it, we're guilty of the same kind of hubris as the gringos; although we don't have slaves, we call ourselves owners of horses, and of land and water too." The terrible trap of conquest is that it forces men on both sides to lay claim to what is not theirs—the land, the river, the sky, and all the creatures that inhabit the earth, indifferent to man's ownership of it. Only gossip can free itself from this trap, because it is not mortal, and it is not bound by the rules of time and space, property and ownership.

Gossip which has survived its day is epic. Who, or what, is Homer but the name that modern readers have given to an ancient line of gossips? Across *Texas*, we find references to the great works of epic literature. Laguna del Diablo, from which Nepomuceno plots his attack on Bruneville, surrounded by his vaqueros and his lover, La Desconocida, recalls the burning lake that Satan is chained to in Milton's *Paradise Lost*. The itemized list of rowboats and skiffs is modeled on the catalogue of ships in Homer's *Iliad*. On the Amazons' ranch, there sits "a pale-faced blonde, Peladita, who sews like a madwoman, all night and all day, waiting for her Ulises to return (an ill-tempered Mexican who, needless to say, has no intention of coming back for her)." Epic is the genre of imperial conquest, but gossip plunders from epic to spin a comic novel, a novel of the collective. The world of *Texas* belongs in spirit, if not by law, to the slave, the drunk, the beggar, the whore, and all the other renegades and misfits who have pledged their allegiance to Nepomuceno's army. Theirs is not an epic age. Peladita may sew until her fingers bleed, but her Ulises will never return. Nepomuceno's attack on Bruneville will fail. No conquering army will be vanquished. No city will be founded on a hill. La Desconocida will flee to the U.S. with an American journalist named Dan Print, who has come to Mexico to find his big break. "Aw, chirriones, I thought crossing the border would be like crossing the Lethe," he writes in his diary, disappointed. When he submits his article on Nepomuceno to his editor, Nepomuceno "morphs from a hero into a petty thief." Is his demotion a racist lie? Or does it tell a profound truth about the impossibility of heroism in a world of landlust and bloodthirst—the world that gave rise first to the epic, then the novel?

Dan Print will transmit the story of Nepomuceno through writing. "Write? That seems awful girly to me," one character tells another, who replies, "Writing is manly, if you tell the story right." Dan Print writes in a manly style, simple and hard nosed and deliberately unmusical. But Boullosa refuses to end her writing with his byline. In a coda, five female saints play on bells, cymbals, tambourines, and a violin while they lament not Nepomuceno's fate, but La Desconocida's marriage to an American. "*What a waste*, they must have thought, *she had the makings of a queen and she chose to be a commoner."* Their song reminds us that the raucous voice of gossip does not issue from one busybody, but from a chorus of girlish creatures, chattering, laughing, crying, praying, and conjuring up a fantastical language to tell the story of un-epic deeds. It spreads over a land that belongs to no man, hero, or thief.

Merve Emre

A BUSYBODY'S BRIEF NOTE

(go ahead and skip it if you want)

LET'S STATE IT UP FRONT, so we don't get muddled: this is the year 1859.

We're on the northern and southern banks of the Río Bravo, known to some as the Rio Grande, in the cities of Bruneville and Matasánchez. Heading into the wind on horseback we could make it to the sea in half a morning.

Bruneville and Matasánchez call themselves cities, but you be the judge of whether they should be called towns.

I should tell you a few things about them: Bruneville is part of the state of Texas; Matasánchez is part of Mexico. The former (Bruneville) hasn't been around long, only since '21, when Mexico declared its independence.

That year, Mexico's Far North was sparsely populated, though there were a few ranches scattered around—like the ones owned by Doña Estefanía, which extend from the Nueces River all the way south to the Río Bravo—you'd have to ride four days to cross her lands from south to north.

Back then buffalo flourished. Mustangs ran free. Since the grasslands hadn't been sown, you didn't find cattle in herds; they grazed in twos or threes. But the Indians abounded, and they traveled in bands.

1

Indian Territory lay to the northeast, where the Apaches had lived since God created the Earth, and where a variety of northern tribes had moved, evicted from their homelands by the Americans, or fleeing from them. Since the Indians were so different (some were hunters and tanners, some farmers, some warriors), they didn't share their territory in holy peace, no matter how similar we'd like to think they were.

To protect their northern frontier from greedy Europeans and warlike Indians, the Mexican federal government invited Americans to live there. The government loaned them land or just gave it to them, sometimes even throwing in some livestock on certain conditions. To be perfectly clear: they made them sign contracts swearing to abide by the Catholic faith and pledge their allegiance to the Mexican government. However, they refused from the beginning to allow the importation of slaves, relenting only under great pressure, allowing a few in dribs and drabs.

In '35 the gringos responded to Mexico's generosity by declaring their independence. They were motivated by their own interests, especially the right to own slaves. The brand-new (slaveholding) Republic of Texas declared its southern frontier to be the Nueces River.

At that time the sowing of the grasslands had begun—the grass seeds greedily hogging everything the earth had to offer—while acacias were burned down to make way for herds of livestock, which grazed and multiplied. The buffalo were decimated by hunters. The arrows of the hunter tribes frequently flew in vain, without finding targets.

It goes without saying that this was like a slap in the face to the Mexican government and made its landowners and ranchers hopping mad.

Then, in '46, the Republic of Texas joined the United States, becoming the Lone Star State.

Immediately Texas claimed that its territories extended to the Río Bravo.

And you already know what happened after that. The Americans invaded us.

In '48, after the invasion (which they called the Mexican–American War, some nerve!), they declared that the Río Bravo was the official border. To stake their claim, the Texans founded Bruneville where previously there had been nothing but a dock built by the town of Matasánchez, "just in case." Matasánchez became a border town.

Immigrants flooded into Bruneville from all over, some respectable folks, and some American lawyers determined to enforce the new laws, which meant shifting ownership of the land to the gringos. There were all kinds of crooks, the aforementioned, well-dressed ones who robbed (Mexicans) from behind their desks, as well as the kind who tied kerchiefs over their faces. And there were those who did a little of both.

It's under these circumstances that our story takes place, at the time of the Great Theft.

PART ONE

(which begins in Bruneville, Texas, on the northern bank of the Río Bravo, one day in July of '59)

IT'S HIGH NOON IN BRUNEVILLE. Not a cloud in the sky. The sun beats down, piercing the veil of shimmering dust. Eyes droop from the heat. In the Market Square, in front of Café Ronsard, Sheriff Shears spits five words at Don Nepomuceno:

"Shut up, you dirty greaser."

He says the words in English.

At that moment, Frank is crossing the plaza, muttering to himself, ". . . and make it snappy, make it snappy," in English, which he speaks so well that people have changed his name from Pancho Lopez to Frank. He's just delivered two pounds of meat and one of bones (for stewing) to the home of Stealman, the lawyer. Frank is one of the many Mexicans in the streets of Bruneville who run errands and spread gossip, a "run-speak-go-tell," a pelado. He hears the insult, raises his eyes, sees the scene, leaps the last few feet to the market, and runs to Sharp, the butcher, to whom he blurts out the burning phrase at point-blank range: "The new sheriff said, 'Shut up, you dirty greaser!' to Señor Nepomuceno!" the syllables almost melting together, and continues immediately, in the same exhalation, to relay the message he's been rehearsing since he left the Stealmans'

7

home, "Señora Luz says that Mrs. Lazy says to send some oxtail for the soup," adding with his last bit of breath, "and make it snappy."

Sharp, standing behind his butcher's block, is so startled that he doesn't respond by saying, "How could a puffed-up carpenter dare speak that way to Don Nepomuceno, Doña Estefanía's son, the grandson and great-grandson of the owners of more than a thousand acres, including those on which Bruneville sits?!" Nor does he take the opposing stance, "Nepomuceno, that no-good, goddamned, cattle-thieving, red-headed bandit, he can rot in hell for all I care!" These two perspectives will soon be widely debated. Rather, in his eagerness to spread the news, he (somewhat melodramatically) claps his left hand to his forehead and glides (dragging his long butcher knife, which scratches a jagged line on the earthen floor) two steps to the next stall, which he rents to the chicken dealer, and shouts, "Hey, Alitas!" repeating in Spanish what Frank has just told him.

It's been three weeks since Sharp has spoken to Alitas, supposedly they had a disagreement about the rent for the market stall, but everyone knows that what's really pissed off Sharp is that Alitas has been trying to win his sister's heart.

Alitas—happy to be on speaking terms again—enthusiastically joins in broadcasting the news, shouting, "Shears told Nepomuceno, 'Shut up, you dirty greaser!'" The greengrocer, on hearing the news, repeats it to Frenchie at his seed stall, Frenchie passes it on to Cherem, the Maronite at the fabric stand, where Miss Lace, Judge Gold's housekeeper, is examining a sample of material that's recently arrived—a kind she hasn't seen before but is perfect for the parlor curtains.

Sid Cherem translates the phrase back into English and explains to Miss Lace what has happened; she asks Cherem to save the cloth for her and hurries off to share the news with her employer, leaving behind Luis, the skinny kid who's carrying her overloaded baskets. Luis, distracted from his duties by the rubber bands at a neighboring stand (one would be great for his slingshot), doesn't even realize Miss Lace has gone.

Miss Lace scurries across the Market Square and halfway down the next block, where she sees Judge Gold coming out of his office, heading to the Town Hall just across the street.

It's important to explain that Judge Gold is not a judge, despite his name; he's in the business of stuffing his wallet. His métier is money. Who knows how he got his name.

"Nepomuceno's goose is cooked," is what Judge Gold tells Miss Lace, because he's just received another report, and with both bits of news in mind he continues on his way to the Town Hall, from which Sabas and Refugio, Nepomuceno's half-brothers by Doña Estefanía's previous husband, are exiting angrily.

Sabas and Refugio are proper gentlemen from the best of the best families of the region. Wagging tongues can't understand how Doña Estefanía could produce these two jewels, and then the rough-neck Nepomuceno, who doesn't even know how to read. Others claim it's a blatant lie that Nepomuceno is illiterate and consider him the most elegant and best dressed of the three, with the manners of a prince.

Sabas and Refugio owe Judge Gold a lot of money. They've just been to testify before Judge White (who is a real judge, though not necessarily an honest one); the Mexicans in town call him "Whatshisname" instead of Judge. Nepomuceno preceded them but they waited until their messenger, Nat, told them that their half-brother had left so that they wouldn't run into him. Nat was the one who reported to Judge Gold that the legal proceedings would be delayed "until further notice"—bad news for Sabas and Refugio, who want a ruling soon so they can get the payoff promised by Stealman. It's even worse news for Nepomuceno.

A shot is heard. No one is particularly alarmed by the sound— for every five hundred head of livestock you need fifty gunmen to

9

guard them, and each of those gunmen will pass through Bruneville at some point; each of them is capable of acts of lawlessness and all sorts of violence. Shots are nothing.

Judge Gold hurls the sheriff's words at Sabas and Refugio, thinking to himself, *Now they won't be able to pay me for who knows how long, but at least I have the pleasure of delivering bad news.* But he immediately feels uncomfortable: the taunt was unnecessary, and he has nothing to gain from it. That's Judge Gold for you, callous impulses and heartfelt regrets.

Nat, overhearing this interchange, rushes off to the Market Square to check out what's happening with Nepomuceno and Shears.

Sabas and Refugio would have celebrated the humiliation of their mother's golden boy, but they can't because the news has been delivered by Judge Gold with intent to wound. So they continue on their way as if nothing of consequence has been said.

Glevack, arriving from Mrs. Big's Café, is about to approach Sabas and Refugio but stops abruptly and turns—he sees his chance to speak with Judge Gold.

A few seconds later Olga, a laundress who occasionally works for Doña Estefanía, approaches the brothers. She wants to tell them the news about Shears in hopes of patching things up with them, but they're annoyed with her because they've heard she's told Doña Estefanía they don't have her best interests at heart. Of course Olga was right, and everyone knows it (even Doña Estefanía, even Sabas and Refugio), but was it really necessary to spread such poisonous gossip?

The brothers ignore Olga and keep walking side-by-side, each wrapped in his own thoughts, each unaware the other is counting the seconds, the minutes, the hours till they can go to Stealman's house, where they'll discuss the Shears-Nepomuceno affair at length, each thinking to himself, *We have to make it clear there's a world of difference between us and that good-for-nothing,* and worrying that if they go, they run the risk of being snubbed. *Damn Nepomuceno, that troublemaker. He had to stir things up today, just when we're invited over there.* Olga tries Judge Gold. He too ignores her. Desperate for attention, she runs to tell Glevack, who is trying to catch up with Judge Gold, but Glevack forges ahead as if no one is there.

Glevack is in a bad mood, though for no good reason, since he is a primary beneficiary of the fraud against Doña Estefanía, which Nepomuceno is trying to reverse by legal means, the reason for his recent visit to the court. Indeed, it was Glevack who sweet-talked Doña Estefanía into making the deal with the gringos, knowing full well they would take advantage of her and that he would get part of the profit. Glevack would love to be the one to insult Nepomuceno in the Market Square, to call him a worthless nobody in front of everyone. He's called him worse, the man who was his friend and associate.

Once Glevack had nearly got him thrown in jail. The two of them had hired a mule driver to steal back some livestock that Stealman had rustled from them. When the mule driver turned up dead on the steps of the Town Hall, people blamed Glevack and Nepomuceno. Glevack testified he had nothing to do with the murder, that it was all Nepomuceno's doing. He gave lots of details and made up others, even saying that it was Nepomuceno who had robbed the mail.

Glevack should be relishing the insult, but it's not in his nature to enjoy anything. And his perpetual foul humor has deepened because Judge Gold won't stop and listen to him, and because he suspects that Sabas and Refugio are turning against him. He feels beset by problems.

Olga's got her own worries. She's no longer eighteen, twice that in fact. She's lost her bloom. No one, not even Glevack, looks at her like they used to. When women lose their glow they're like ghosts to men; out on the street, no one turns to admire them. Some feel liberated by this lack of interest, but others, like Olga, won't stand for it, they'll do anything for attention. So Olga crosses the main road, Elizabeth Street, walks to the intersection of Charles Street, and knocks on Minister Fear's door.

It's not yet a month since Olga helped unpack the trousseau of the minister's new wife, Eleonor.

Although Eleonor is a recent bride, she is no spring chicken either: she's past twenty. Her husband, Minister Fear, is forty-five; he had been a widower for two years when he placed an advertisement for a new wife. The ad, which appeared in papers in Tucson, California, and New York, stated in succinct English:

> Lonely widower seeks wife to accompany Methodist
> minister on the southern frontier and assist with
> his work. Please respond to Lee Fear in Bruneville,
> Texas.

Olga knocks impatiently on the Fears' door a second time, so hard that the Smiths' door pops open (their house is adjacent, on the corner of James, which runs parallel to Elizabeth), and out comes the lovely Moonbeam, an Hasinai Indian (some call them the Tejas Indians, though the gringos call them Hasinai, part of the Caddo tribe). The Smiths bought her for next to nothing a few years back, before it became fashionable to have Indians as servants. Now they would have to pay twice as much. She'd be a bargain at any price: she's beautiful and hard-working with a pleasant manner about her, though sometimes she gets distracted.

Moonbeam steps into the street. A second later, Eleonor Fear opens her door with an expression of befuddlement. Eleonor doesn't speak a word of Spanish, but Olga makes herself understood. First, she offers her services—washing, cleaning, cooking—whatever the

Fears might need. Eleonor declines amicably. Minister Fear arrives (curious to see who is at the door) as does Moonbeam (the Smiths' young slave is always interested in gossip), and Olga tells them about the incident, using gestures to make herself understood: a five-pointed star for the sheriff, a violin and a lasso for Lázaro, but Nepomuceno's name alone is enough, everyone knows who Don Nepomuceno is.

The Fears don't show the least interest (the minister is too prudent, and Eleonor is wrapped up in her own world), but Moonbeam is captivated. She knows how stupid Sheriff Shears is—he came to fix the Smiths' dining room table and left it even wobblier than before—and she thinks the world of handsome Nepomuceno (the Smiths' daughter Caroline carries a torch for him, and Moonbeam does a little too, like all the young girls in Bruneville).

When Minister Fear closes the door, Olga turns and heads back to the market. Moonbeam glances up and down Elizabeth Street, looking for a reason not to go back inside the Smiths' and finish her chores, when around the corner come Strong Water and Blue Falls, two Lipans—the Lipans are fiercer than most Indians, but friendly with the gringos—astride two handsome mounts, followed by a heavily loaded pinto mustang, a typical prairie horse (if someone offers a good price, it's for sale).

Strong Water and Blue Falls are turning onto James Street to avoid Nepomuceno's men; they haven't come to Bruneville looking for trouble.

Despite the heat, the Lipans are in long, fitted sleeves with bright, colorful stripes, and they're wearing embroidered moccasins. They have bands of colored beads tied around their foreheads and their necks; their long hair is adorned with feathers, leather strips, and rabbit tails; and they have embossed spurs.

Neither too slowly nor too quickly—she knows what she's doing, the street's her territory—Moonbeam approaches them. The

13

Lipans dismount. Moonbeam mimes what has just happened in the Market Square, using the same gestures as Olga. Then she turns and goes back inside the Smiths' house, slamming the door, which prevents her from hearing the second shot of the morning.

Strong Water and Blue Falls interpret the Shears-Nepomuceno incident in different ways. Strong Water thinks it means something has happened at the Lipan camp, and he wants to return immediately because this bodes ill for his people. Blue Falls, on the other hand, thinks it has nothing to do with the Lipans; he's certain the only thing they should worry about is selling their wares according to the orders of Chief Little Rib, and besides, the shaman, being omniscient, will already know all about the incident.

Should they head home, like Strong Water urges, or stay and sell their goods, like Blue Falls wants? Nothing they have with them is perishable—Strong Water argues that skins, nuts, and rubber sap will keep for weeks. But the trip is long and tiring, says Blue Falls, and they need munitions back at camp; the two shotguns they plan to buy are not urgent purchases, but they would come in handy on the way home; they had to take many detours to avoid danger on the road to Bruneville, and it would be better to return armed.

The Lipans defend their points of view, arguing ever more vehemently. They start fighting. Strong Water pulls his knife.

Inside the Smiths' home, lovely Moonbeam gets back to work, filling the bucket at the cistern to carry water to the kitchen.

Meanwhile, at the market, Sharp, the butcher, is roaring with laugher. "Nepomuceno! That cattle thief! Humiliated in public, in the Market Square! He had it coming!"

The label "cattle thief" requires explanation. Sharp believes the cow in question is his because he bought it, but Nepomuceno believes he is right to call it his own, because the animal was born and raised on (and bears the brand of) the ranch where he himself was born. "Sharp shouldn't be so self-righteous," he says, "because he knew perfectly well the cow was stolen, and the price he paid didn't begin to compensate the value of such a heifer, he can peddle that argument somewhere else!" When word of what Nepomuceno was saying got around Mrs. Big's Hotel, Smiley said, "Does he think Sharp's cow is his sister?!"

Sharp puts his knife on the chopping block, wipes his hands on his apron, and, without taking it off, strides over to the Plaza.

Let's leave him there, because we should travel back in time to just before the Shears-Nepomuceno incident—to, say, 11:55 AM— to fill in some details that matter to us.

Roberto Cruz, the leather merchant who everyone calls "Cruz," has been waiting some time for the Lipans, watching the main road impatiently from his stall at the edge of the market. According to Cruz, the Lipan sell the highest-quality skins, and the best embroidered moccasins (which nobody buys besides some eccentric Germans), and incomparable leather leggings, which sell like hotcakes because the women can't ride without them lest they chafe their private parts.

Two days earlier Cruz had bought a bunch of buckles and eyelets. Situ, the kid who knows how to burn designs into belts (a new look that's very popular), is waiting at home for the Lipans' leather. Since the Lipan, like all prairie Indians, follow the lunar calendar, Cruz expects them shortly. If they don't show up, Perla will start getting irritated because of Situ sitting around, doing nothing, getting on her nerves. Perla is the girl who has kept house for him since his wife died and who he is determined to marry, as soon as his daughter gets hitched. He's made up his mind though he hasn't told anyone yet, not even her.

So there was Cruz, craning his neck, trying to spot the Lipans coming down Main Street, when Óscar passed by with his basket of bread on his head.

"Psst, Óscar, I'm talking to you! Gimme a sweet roll!"

"O.K., but only one per customer. I didn't put much in the oven 'cause I thought it was going to be a slow day, and I have to hold on to enough to sell down at the docks."

"O.K., just one."

Cruz keeps craning his neck, scanning for the Lipans, while Óscar lowers his basket.

Óscar selects a crunchy bun covered with sugar (he knows what Cruz likes, it's his favorite). Cruz pays him.

"Keep the change."

"Nah, Cruz, you don't have to do that."

"Then put it toward my next bun."

Óscar lifts the breadbasket onto his head and leaves for the docks.

Tim Black comes out of Café Ronsard. He greets Cruz and gestures that he should bring over his belts. Tim Black is a wealthy Negro who, most unusually, owns land and slaves. When Texas gained its independence from Mexico in 1836 Negro landholders were disenfranchised when Texas's Congress legalized slavery and imposed racial restrictions on owning property; Tim Black was granted an exemption from these laws by the new Congress.

Cruz puts his roll on the counter and slings a bunch of belts over his shoulder; they hang by their buckles from an iron hook in his hand.

At this moment, in the middle of the square Sheriff Shears shouts at Lázaro Rueda, the old vaquero, the one who knows how to play the violin, and whacks his forehead, hard, with the butt of his pistol. After the second or third blow, Lázaro falls to the ground.

Tim Black moves to see what's happening. He doesn't understand Spanish, which leaves him clueless about much that happens on the frontier, but no language is needed to know exactly what's going on: a poor old man is being beaten senseless by the sheriff.

Nepomuceno exits Café Ronsard and he, too, encounters

the scene with Shears. He recognizes Lázaro Rueda instantly and decides to intervene.

Black watches Nepomuceno's reaction, hears his calm tone, catches the drift of his words—with the help of Joe Lieder, the German kid who repeats everything in his broken English—and hears the sharpness of Shears's insulting response: "Shut up, you dirty greaser."

The merchant ship *Margarita*'s horn sounds, announcing her imminent departure.

On the other side of the square, Óscar hears the words Shears spits at Nepomuceno and sees out of the corner of his eye what's happening, but his sense of duty is greater than his curiosity; if the *Margarita* has sounded her horn he barely has time to get down to the docks and if he doesn't speed up they won't get their bread. He hurries away.

Don Jacinto, the saddler, crosses the square toward Café Ronsard carrying his new creation, "a really fancy one." (He's from Zacatecas, and he's been married three times. Two days a week he works in Bruneville, the rest of the time he's across the river in Matasánchez. Business is good). He announces to one and all, "I want to show this one to Don Nepomuceno. No one else will appreciate its fine workmanship like him." Everyone knows that if Nepomuceno expresses his admiration it will fetch a better price. No one knows more about saddles and reins, no one handles a lasso or rides as well. It's not so much that horses obey him as they have a mutual understanding.

Don Jacinto is near-sighted and can't see more than two yards in front of him, or he would have witnessed the scene as well. But he's not deaf; he hears the blows clearly, and Nepomuceno's words, and Shears's response, which stops him in his tracks. He can't believe the carpenter would speak to Don Nepomuceno that way.

—

Peter, whom the Mexicans call "El Sombrerito," owns the hat shop. His original surname being unpronounceable, he changed it to "Hat" for the gringos: "Peter Hat, hats of felt, and also of palm, for the heat." He is hanging a new mirror on the column in the middle of his store when, in the mirror's reflection, he sees Shears pistol-whipping Lázaro Rueda, "the violinist cowboy." He also sees Nepomuceno approach, and the kid who goes around with La Plange, the one they call "Snotty," running toward them. His instincts tell him something bad's about to go down. He takes down the mirror ("Why, Mr. Hat?" asks Bill, his assistant, "It was almost straight."), stowing it safely behind the counter, and sends Bill home with a few coins ("Help me close up shop and skedaddle! And don't come back to work till I send for you!"). He lowers the blinds and locks the front doors of his establishment, crosses the threshold that separates the store from his home, double bolts the door from inside and shouts to his wife, "Michaela! Tell the kids not to go outside, not even on the patio, and lock all the windows and doors; no one sets foot outdoors until this storm blows over."

Peter Hat goes to the patio and cuts two white roses with his pocketknife and takes them to his altar to the Virgin, next to the front door. He kneels on the prayer stool and begins to pray out loud. Michaela and the children join him; she takes the roses from his hand and puts one in a delicate blue vase, the same color as the Virgin's robes, and the other in her husband's buttonhole.

Mother and children begin drowning their worries in hurried Hail Marys.

But Peter, the more he prays the more worried he gets. His soul is like a poorly woven hat, full of imperfections.

Before leaving, towheaded Bill had just stared at Peter, unable to understand what had upset him, unable to help.

Out in the street he adjusts his suspenders. He's spent every penny he's ever earned working for Peter on these expensive, trendy suspenders.

He soon catches on to what's happening down in the market, and, instead of heading home, he runs across the square to the jailhouse.

His uncle, Ranger Neals (who oversees the prison and is highly regarded), listens closely to Bill's report.

"That idiot Shears . . . insulting Nepomuceno is gonna land us all in a heap of shit."

Others arrive at the jailhouse door, fast on Bill's heels: Ranger Phil, Ranger Ralph, Ranger Bob. They're bearing the same news, and they arrive just in time to hear him say to his nephew,

"Let's sit tight, no one makes a move, got it?"

They don't stick around to hear the rest. They run to relay orders to the other Rangers.

"We don't want to start a wildfire. This is a bad business."

Urrutia is the prize prisoner in Bruneville's jail. He's one of a gang of bandits who help fugitive slaves cross the Rio Grande. The minute they set foot on Mexican soil they become free men by law. Urrutia lures them with the promise of land in Tabasco. He shows them contracts that are more fairy tale than anything else. He describes fertile land, wide canals, cocoa plants growing beneath shady mango trees, sugar cane. He's vague about the exact size and location, but that doesn't matter, given such promising prospects.

Urrutia does take them to Tabasco. The landscape is exactly as he described. But the reality is different. Urrutia has valid contracts that commit them to indentured servitude and maltreatment—it might as well be imprisonment. The lucky ones die from fever or starvation before the first whipping.

Urrutia's men have made a fortune doing this. Sometimes, when a slave has unusual value, they return him to his original owner for a ransom. They even brag about the free Negros they catch in their net, selling them at a premium because, being strong and healthy, "they make good foremen."

Urrutia is guarded by three gringos who get paid extra wages because the mayor suspects Urrutia's accomplices—numerous and well-armed—will try to rescue him (we'll get to the mayor's story later; suffice it to say that the notion he's been elected by popular vote is preposterous). The three guards, whose names can't be divulged, overhear the story of the insult without paying it much attention. They're only here for the money (which isn't always paid on time, to the chagrin of their families); if Nepomuceno offered them more money they'd work for him, despite the fact that they're gringos.

When Urrutia hears about Shears and Nepomuceno, a sudden change comes over him; he's like an autumn leaf about to fall from the tree. And for good reason.

Werbenski's pawn shop sits between the jailhouse and the hat shop. It's not a bad business, but the really profitable part takes place at the back of the store: the sale of ammunition and firearms. Werbenski doesn't go by his real name to hide the fact that he's Jewish—no one knows where he came from. Peter Hat can't stand him, Stealman takes no notice of him (but Stealman's men do business with him, same as Judge Gold and Mr. King). He's married to Lupis Martínez, a Mexican, of course—"What can I do for you, Sir?"—the sweetest wife in all Bruneville, a real gem, and a smart one, too.

Like Peter Hat, Werbenski senses there will be repercussions from the Shears-Nepomuceno affair, but he doesn't shut up shop. He tells Lupis to get to the market quickly, before things get really bad.

"But sweetie pie, we went early this morning."

"Stock up. Buy all the dry goods you can. Get bones for the soup."

"We've got rice, beans, onions, potatoes, and we've got tomatoes and peppers for salsa growing in the back. There's water in the well . . ."

"Get some bones, for the boy."

"Don't worry, sugar plum, the chicks are growing, the hen is laying eggs, we've got the two roosters, though one is old; there's the boy's rabbit, and the duck that mother gave me. The turtle is hiding somewhere, but if we get hungry I'll root it out, and if I can't find it I'll stew up the iguanas and lizards like my aunts do."

The last bit was intended to make her husband smile, but he wasn't even listening; neither of them could stand Aunt Lina's iguana stew, not because of the way it tasted but on account of skinning the animals alive. Werbenski's head is reeling, but he takes comfort in the fact that they baptized his boy. *They may do what they want with a Jew, but my wife and my son must be saved.* Lupis reads his mind.

"Don't worry, sweetie pie."

Lupis adores him. She's naturally sweet-natured, but she knows she's got the best husband in all Bruneville—the most respectful, most generous, most sensible. A Jewish husband is worth his weight in gold.

There's a pleasant breeze down at Bruneville's docks, but up at the market and in the Town Hall—why lie?—it's like being inside a Dutch oven. Short distances from the river make a big difference. Crossing it makes an even bigger difference; the Great Plains end here, bordered by the Río Bravo to the south. On the other side they also have people of all stripes—Indians, cowboys, bandits, Negros, Mexicans, gringos—as well as profitable mines and endless acres of land, but it's different. The Río Bravo divides the world in two, perhaps even three or more. No fool would say that the gringos are all on one side and the Mexicans on the other, with separate territories for the Indians, the Negros, and even for sonsofbitches. None of these categories is absolute. In the Indian Territory there are many different tribes that don't get along, they've just been shunted there by the gringos, just as there are also Negroes who speak different languages. Not all gringos are thieves, and not all Mexicans are kind-hearted; each of these groups have both good and bad.

Nevertheless, it's an indisputable fact that the Río Bravo marks a border, because on its northern bank the Great Plains begin, and on its southern bank the world becomes itself again: the Earth, abounding with variety.

When he arrives at Bruneville's dock, before taking his basket of bread off his head, Óscar announces loudly what Shears, the crappy carpenter (and even worse sheriff), has said to Nepomuceno. He's overheard by Santiago the fisherman, who has just emptied his last basketful of crabs into Hector's cart (it rained all night, which explains his unusually large catch). Santiago's three children, Melón, Dolores, and Dimas, sit on the cart's edge, their feet dangling just out of reach of the crabs. They are binding their claws and bunching them into bundles of a half-dozen each—they've spent the whole morning at the task. The cowboys Tadeo and Mateo hear Óscar, too. Their livestock is already aboard the barge heading for New Orleans once it stops across the river to load the animals' feed and some crates of ceramics from Puebla by way of Veracruz. They're ready to feed their hunger and slake their thirst, to relieve their tiredness and boredom from the isolation of the pastures.

The cart's driver, Mr. Wheel, doesn't speak Spanish; he doesn't understand a word Óscar says and neither does he care. No sooner has he gotten underway—passing through the neighborhood where the homes have roofs of reed or thatched palm, and the walls are made of mesquite or sticks, where they eat colorín flour or queso de tuna (which doesn't deserve to be called cheese)—than Santiago's kids start shouting, "Crabs! Crabs!" working the phrase "dirty greaser" into their sales pitch, all the while deftly trussing up their remaining captives. They enter the part of town where the houses are made of brick, and they continue pitching their wares and spreading gossip.

Santiago passes the story to the other fishermen, who are detangling their nets for tomorrow's early return to the water, leaving them laid out on the ground.

The fishermen carry the news along the riverbanks.

The cowboys, Tadeo and Mateo, go straight to tell Mrs. Big, the innkeeper—it's said she fell in love with Zachary Taylor in Florida and followed him to Texas, and that when he went to fight in Mexico she moved down to Bruneville, where she opened her waterfront hotel: cheap, but with pretentions to class, it has a dining room, bar, "casino," and "café." Word is that when some gossipmonger came to tell her that the Mexicans had killed her Zachary, she spat back, "You damn sonofabitch, there aren't enough Mexicans in all Mexico to kill old man Taylor." Driving the point home, she added: "I'm gonna rip open your foot and give you a new mouth down there. You understand? Let's see if you can learn to tell the truth with your new mouth and stop spreading lies with the one you've had since birth."

Mrs. Big tells the story about Nepomuceno and Shears to Lucrecia, the cook. Lucrecia tells the kitchen hand, Perdido. Perdido tells all the guests. Mrs. Big celebrates the news by offering a round on the house.

Why is she celebrating? Because she doesn't like Mexicans? Or is it vengeance, settling unpaid debts? It's a little of both, but the main reason is that Nepomuceno patronizes her rival, the Café Ronsard, her competition, her enemy, the focus of all her envy, the testament to all the mistakes she's made, the burden she bears daily. She's the best card sharp in all Bruneville, no one can beat her at blackjack.

Her view of the river is better; there's a good breeze, and she's got an old icaco tree, which gives great shade. So why doesn't she have the best café? The Ronsard doesn't have any of this, "just stinking drunks, lying around outside in the dirt." Mrs. Big even plants tulips in the spring, and her roses bloom year-round (though when it's burning up, their petals literally roast in the heat).

The two cowboys spread Shears's insult, embellishing it along the way. Tadeo steps into one of Mrs. Big's rooms and passes the news on to two whores, the Flamenca sisters, with whom he's about to begin a relationship that's almost brotherly. Mateo tells both of his girlfriends. First, his publicly recognized one, Clara, the trapper's daughter (she was waiting for him down by the dock), and then he tells his secret girlfriend, Perla, Cruz's housekeeper, whom Mateo has sweet-talked into bed. She really does it for Mateo, she has a sweet ass and boy does she know how to use it, even better than Sandy can. But let's be honest, she's no looker.

A little later, Mrs. Big tells her fellow card players about the "Shears-Nepomuceno Affair," while one of the Flamenca sisters muddles the story in the hotel bar. Tadeo remains in the room with her sister, it's taking him a while to get it up.

Three people are playing cards with Mrs. Big: Jim Smiley, a compulsive gambler (he's got a cardboard box with a toad next to him, for a while now he's been trying to train it to jump farther than any other); Hector López (who has a round, childlike face, is an incurable womanizer, and owns the cart in which the trussed-up crabs are making the rounds of Bruneville); and one other guy who never opens his mouth, Leno (he's desperate, and is only here to try to win some money).

On one side of the table, Tiburcio, the sour, wrinkled old

widower, is watching them play; he's always got some comment as bitter as his breath on the tip of his tongue.

Captain William Boyle, an Englishman, is the first of the dozen sea-men who are about to set sail on the *Margarita* to understand the insult—most of them don't speak a word of Spanish—and he trans-lates it back into the sheriff's mother tongue, though his rendering alters it somewhat: "None of your business, you damned Mexican."

The sailors celebrate the insult, "At last someone put the greasers in their place." Rick and Chris embrace and begin to dance, singing "You damn Meexican! You damn Meeexican!" in a joking tone that carries across the water. Before the day is over, people on both banks of the Rio Grande, from Bruneville to Puerto Bagdad will have heard about what the gringo sheriff said, more or less accurately.

From Puerto Bagdad the news sails out into the Gulf, on boats headed north. After passing Punta Isabel, the story runs up the Coast, working its way past one river delta after another, and it's car-ried upstream on the Nueces, the San Antonio, the Guadalupe, the Lavaca, the Colorado, the Brazos, the San Jacinto, and the Trinity.

And from a rotting dock the news travels with the mail boy to New Braunfels. The Germans are the only ones who give the mail carriers more work than the gringos.

In Galveston, no sooner has the phrase made it off the boat than it doubles back southward, finding passage on a steamboat that's just arrived from Houston and is headed to Puerto Bagdad, Mexico, almost directly across the river from Punta Isabel, Bruneville's sea-port. The majority of the passengers are Germans who've spent the better part of the trip's first leg singing songs from the old coun-try, accompanied by a violin, a horn, and a guitar. They even have a piano on board, but no one can play it because it's wrapped for shipping.

One passenger, Doctor Schulz, is one of the famous Forty, the Germans who came to the New World to build a new world. In 1847 he helped establish the colony of Bettina (named after Bettina von Arnim, the writer, composer, social activist, publisher, patron of the arts, and acolyte of Goethe—"My soul is an impassioned dancer.") In Bettina there were three rules: Friendship, Freedom, and Equality. No man was treated differently from the next; there was no such thing as private property; and they all slept together in a long house that wasn't remotely European, with a thatched roof and a tree trunk in the center. The butcher prepared wild boar for the communal table.

Each of the Forty wore beards. The youngest was seventeen and the two eldest were twenty-four, free thinkers one and all. No one knows why they lasted only one year. There are lots of stories: some say that they harvested only six ears of corn because no one wanted to do any work (it's true they spent most afternoons guzzling whiskey from barrels they had brought from Hamburg), while others say it was because of a woman, which makes no sense, because there weren't any women in the colony.

When the community disbanded, the piano itself proved a source of friction. Schulz asked to take it—it had been a present from his mother—but because "everything belongs to everyone" it was nearly chopped up into pieces. In the end, the piano, which had accompanied the doctor on his long voyage from Germany, is making its way with him to Mexico. This part of his travels has taken a good long while. Schulz plans to set up shop as a doctor in Puerto Bagdad, where the piano will once again be played.

Another German passenger, Engineer Schleiche, began the trip from Houston half-heartedly, and by the time he arrives in Gálvez, he's decided that life without his Texan girlfriend would be empty, meaningless. He decides to jump ship and wait for the next steamboat to New York, where the girl has fled, tired of waiting years for a marriage proposal that never came.

Although Schleiche finds Gálvez beautiful—and it is—he is disgusted by the loose morals of its locals. He is at his hotel, giving instructions about having meals delivered to his room (he's decided not to set foot outside until the steamboat is ready to depart "this den of iniquity"), when he hears about Shears's insult and who the sheriff is; he already knows all about Nepomuceno. Fearing the worst, he instantly shuts himself in his room, so he's not up to date on everything else that happens and arrives in New York with only the first words uttered by Shears.

Schleiche was not one of the founding Forty from Bettina; as assistant to Prince Solms, he arrived in an earlier Prussian migration from the Adelsverein, or Society of Noblemen, the aristocrats who founded the Nassau Plantation in '45 (his godfather was the Prince of Nassau). The nobles acquired land and servants (they bought twenty-five slaves), but the society broke up a few years later, for reasons different from those of the Forty.

Generally speaking, the Germans were appalled that a gringo sheriff would insult such a well-respected Mexican—you could say what you want about Nepumuceno but no Prussian would ever accuse him of stealing a cow (admittedly the Germans were clueless about cattle; they were useless when it came to livestock—"If a Kartofel lays a hand on a cow, she keels over.")

When the third-class carpenter-sheriff came out with his little insult in 1859, it was only twenty-four years since Texas had declared and won its independence from Mexico, through a series of skirmishes and battles, some of which were fought more fiercely than others, and both sides have continued to accuse each other of atrocities ever since. Say what you will, the truth is the Texans won the war by river and by sea because the Mexicans didn't have a navy to speak of;

during the entire Spanish occupation not one Mexican was trained to lead a flotilla, and they didn't have any boats anyway.

Texas declared its independence in 1835. Since the Mexicans had invited Americans to live on large tracts of their land, granting them land concessions at very favorable rates, this declaration didn't sit well with them. That's why the military confrontations, skirmishes, and battles between Mexicans and Texans didn't stop.

In '38, more than a thousand Comanches coordinated attacks south of the Río Bravo on ranches, towns, and settlements. Since the Texan rebellion, not one Mexican had been able to go out and kill Comanches and Apaches in the Indian Territory—it had become impossible to cross the Republic of Texas because the warlike tribes were running roughshod over the countryside, stirred up by the arrival of new tribes from the north and the disappearance of the buffalo.

In '39, the Texan Congress gathered in Austin, which was declared the capital of the Republic. Skirmishes continued.

In '41, two thousand Texan soldiers were taken prisoner by the Mexicans and incarcerated in Mexico City.

In '45, Texas was annexed by the United States. It went from being an independent republic to becoming one of many stars on a foreign flag. Although it seemed like a terrible idea, it wasn't bad at all, because it completely changed the balance of power with Mexico. The struggle for the Texan frontier worsened. The Texans argued that everything from the Nueces River to the Rio Grande was theirs. The Mexicans denied the claim, saying that it wasn't in their previous agreement.

And that's how it came to pass that the American army invaded Mexican territory in 1846. Shortly thereafter they declared victory and took over the disputed territory, and the land between the Nueces River and the Rio Grande was no longer Mexican.

Throughout these war-torn years, Doña Estefanía was the one

and only legitimate owner of the land called Espíritu Santo, which extended far into the territory that became American. It made no difference that she was a savvy landowner, with herds of livestock and good harvests (mostly beans, but she had different crops on her other ranches). Stealman arranged to carve off a healthy (and profitable) portion of her lands. And it was on this profitable stretch of land that he established Bruneville, selling plots at inflated prices, which was a great business.

Eleven years have passed since the town of Bruneville was founded on the banks of the Río Bravo, just a few miles upriver from the Gulf. It was named after Ciudad Bruneville, the legendary shining city to the northwest, which was razed by the Apaches. In appropriating the name, Stealman aimed to trade on the good reputation of the original.

At its founding, the following were present (without a shadow of a doubt):

   a) Stealman, the lawyer;
   b) Kenedy, who owned the cotton plantation;
   c) Judge Gold (back then he was just plain Gold, he hadn't yet earned the nickname Judge);
   d) Minster Fear, his first wife, and their daughter Esther (may the latter two rest in peace);
   f) A pioneer named King.

King had a royal name, but when he'd arrived in Mexico he hadn't a penny, he didn't own even a snake. But he had the Midas touch. When some locals lent him low-grade land to use for seven years, it took him only a few months to emerge as the legitimate owner of immense tracts on which it seemed to rain cattle from the clouds, as if they were a gift from God. But there was nothing remotely miraculous about the way King made his fortune. He was as good a trickster as any magician with a false-bottomed top hat. If King had been Catholic (as he claimed to be in the contract he signed with the Mexicans), the archdiocese could have been able to build a cathedral with what he'd have paid for his sins.

In 1848 King wasn't the only one who went looking for a fortune, convinced that "Americans" had the right to take what belonged to the northern Mexicans by whatever means necessary.

A year after it was founded, Bruneville suffered its first outbreak of cholera. The epidemic claimed the lives of one hundred citizens and almost choked the life out of the region's economy. Around that time, the rumor was that Nepomuceno robbed a train west of Rancho del Carmen and sold its cargo in Mexico. If it's true, he was only making up for the many robberies he had suffered.

That same year, to the northeast of Bruneville, Jim Smiley arrived at the camp of Boomerang Mine, which was played out, and discovered his addiction to gambling.

Just across the Rio Grande the city that Brunevillians called their twin, Matasánchez, prohibited several things:

1. fandangos;
2. firing weapons in the streets;
3. riding horseback on the sidewalks;
4. and any animals at all on the sidewalks.

The arrogant Brunevillians applauded these measures, saying, "at last they're leaving their uncivilized ways behind." Which was a bit rich, given that Brunevillians half-drowned in mud each time it rained and suffocated on dust every dry season, their city being so poorly constructed. When all was said and done they were just a handful of palefaces, struggling to cope with a sun that assaulted their senses, yet they acted like they were the center of the universe. (Matasánchez, on the other hand, was something to see.)

Bruneville was two years old when an assembly took place at which the new land-grabbers, led by King, played the Great Trick on the Mexicans—a.k.a. the Great Theft—dispossessing them of their property titles by pretending that the new state was legitimizing them. The citizens of Bruneville thought this was a good move; they believed the law was going to protect them, but they were quickly disabused of this notion.

The truth is that the gringos took advantage of several things:

1. The Mexicans didn't speak English;
2. The Mexicans were given citizenship and told they had rights; but
3. The rights meant zilch unless they could be defended in a court; and
4. The lawyers who were supposed to defend them were thieves, stealing land that had been owned, inherited, or worked by their clients for generations.

The gringos stole and proceeded to act like they were the legitimate owners of what they had stolen.

This is the truth, the whole truth, and nothing but the truth.

This was also the year of the yellow fever.

Bruneville now had a population of 519 (in Matasánchez there were seven thousand, half of what there had been before several wars and two hurricanes hit the region, before Bruneville even came into being). It's worth mentioning that most gringo Brunevillians knew nothing about the neighboring town and could not have cared less.

—

Bruneville's third year was just more of the same.

Bruneville was four years old when its population doubled. Pioneers from the north arrived by the boatload, prepared to do anything to make their fortunes. At the same time, penniless Mexicans fleeing the troubles in the south were crossing the river, looking for a way to make a living. More of these folks went north than runaway slaves went south to find their freedom. Bruneville's reputation as a den of thieves (or a land of opportunity) grew. Where there are thieves there's loot, the smell of easy money.

The Mexicans set up portable grills on street corners everywhere over which they cooked their own food and more to sell.

In the Rio Grande Valley, the theft of Mexican livestock was a daily practice, like picking herbs or berries in a forest. The branded cattle and shod horses might as well have been mustangs and mavericks, they were treated no differently; and there were plenty of animals for the taking—grabbing strays when possible, taking them at gun point if not. Armed bandits roamed the land, crossing the Rio Grande to drive livestock northward from the south.

Bruneville's fifth birthday was celebrated with the construction of a lighthouse at Punta Isabel, its seaport. A group of Brunevillians proposed naming the lighthouse Bettina, after Bettina Von Arnim, who had recently passed away: "beautiful and wise, the embodiment of the powers of nature." The Germans, the Cubans, and a pair of Anglos held a memorial service in her honor and placed a gravestone in the community gardens: "She had a remarkable amount of energy, which she radiated upon everyone around her; she was equally at home with people and with nature; she loved the damp earth and the flowers that bloomed in it." But the Texan authorities were both ignorant and reactionary—though claiming to be republican and liberal they were in fact diehard defenders of slavery—and sent them packing.

—

Bruneville was six years old when a law was passed prohibiting the employment of Mexican laborers. But the law wasn't enforced because no one was better at taming and caring for horses and keeping house too.

When Bruneville turned eight, four dozen camels arrived. Some say they were intended for the ranches, where it was thought their humps would enable them to survive both heat and drought. They were also rumored to be a cover for slave trading; a witness swore to having seen young men, women, and children arriving on the same ship.

Two camels, a male and a female, continued their travels by water, heading upriver on another boat, while the rest hoofed it to their final destinations; except one, a pregnant camel, which was bought by Don Jacinto, the saddler, though it died shortly thereafter of unknown causes, before giving birth. Minister Fear declared this a manifestation of God's wrath, though the reasons for such wrath remained unspecified. Father Rigoberto said this was absurd; he usually took care not to contradict gringos, but Fear was going too far. This was the year that Father Rigoberto chose to follow orders of the archbishop of Durango instead of those of the Gálvez diocese, which served only to leave the parish worse off than it had been before.

Before we abandon the camels, it should be noted that witnesses had still another story about how they came to be in Texas: they were imported by the army, which planned to use them against the Indians.

Bruneville was about to celebrate its ninth birthday when Jeremiah Galván's store by the river burned down. Many people suspected it was arson. There were ninety-five barrels of gunpowder on the second floor of the store. The explosion destroyed the neighboring buildings, blew out all the windows in Bruneville, and even rattled doors in Matasánchez. Soldiers, Rangers, and citizens all lent a hand dousing the building with water from the river, pumped by steamboats, in an effort to control the fire before the flames made it all the way up Elizabeth Street to the Town Hall, razing four square blocks in the process.

At the Smiths' house, a spark landed on the mosquito net in Caroline's room; it went up in flames in the blink of an eye (it was very fine netting). Some say it left Caroline a little touched in the head; but others said she hadn't been quite right since birth.

Another outbreak of yellow fever hit Bruneville on its tenth anniversary. That was the year the legend of La Llorona (The Wailing Ghost) became popular; though most gringos pooh-poohed the story, more than one swore they had seen her walking the streets, wailing, "Ay, mis hijos!" "Where are my children?"

That same year some gringos from the north, where it's hideously cold, arrived hungry and eager. They were four brothers, skinnier than mine mules, with the last name Robin; all they had in common aside from their last name was their good looks, and their being skinnier than skeletons. The eldest was a redhead. The next one had black hair. The third had hair that was curly and blond. And the fourth, the youngest, barely had any hair at all, just a little transparent peach fuzz.

The Robins gaped at the land of milk and honey, salivating as if there were sausages hanging from the trees (not that there were many trees, only mesquites and acacias, but the Robins had had enough of pines and spruces, which didn't bear fruit or provide homes for honeybees). They saw that the wealthy Mexicans on the north bank had nice ranches, fattened livestock, arable land, and people who knew to care for both land and animals. They searched out judges and mayors who could be bought—in Texas corruption was widespread—and then set about taking a piece of it all for themselves.

34

Since this was a civilized land, the Mexicans weren't prepared to deal with these professional thieves.

The brothers were tipped off about their first hit, and it wasn't just any hit, it was a mail coach full of gold and gifts the miners out west were sending back home to their mothers, uncles, children, fiancées, sisters, friends, priests, and even nuns.

This first robbery filled their wallets and allowed them to stock up on guns and ammunition. Now, armed, dangerous, and with the law in their pocket, they set to work (it must also be mentioned that though the Robins detest Indians, Negros, and Mexicans equally, they don't let such prejudices get in the way of business; nothing matters to them more than money).

Across the river lies Matasánchez, the city that Bruneville (talking out its ass) calls its twin. It isn't true. Long before the Iberians set foot on the land, Matasánchez was founded by the Cohuiltecans, after whom came the Chichimecs, and then the Olmecs, and then the Huastecs, who built their trojes (their elegant barns), and brought their markets, dances, traditional cuisine, and prayer circles. It would be more correct to say that Matasánchez is Bruneville's grandmother, or if you were to stretch the truth, Bruneville's mother, with one caveat: Bruneville and Matasánchez have nothing in common.

In 1774, the town was baptized by the Spaniards as Ciudad Refugio de San Juan de los Esteros Hermosos. A mass was celebrated, and everyone had tamales and liquor that had recently been shipped across the ocean. When the liquor ran out they began drinking sotol, tequila from the north. They spent the evening playing music and dancing; and from that night on, the city was famed for its fandangos. Its carnivals were also something to see; people of all stripes showed up: men looking for men; maricones who were happy to oblige; prostitutes a little long in the tooth; as well as ones who had recently been bought by their pimps. There were marimbas everywhere—that peculiar half piano, half drum—and street musicians who were always coming up with new ditties. Like their peers in the south, sometimes they called themselves jaraneros, other times minstrels, and on other occasions balladeers. They liked to change their name, just like they changed their ballads, their verses, letting their imaginations dance.

They built some gorgeous houses, and even palaces. The church was a sight to see, as was the central plaza, with an arched, covered walkway surrounding it.

Life in Ciudad Refugio (Matasánchez) was anything but boring. It was attacked by English, Dutch, and French corsairs and pirates. Indian warriors also left their mark. But the citizens were peaceful folk: they were into farming, harvesting, marketing, partying. So instead of fighting with the pirates they did business with them.

They tried this with the Indians, too, but it didn't work so well.

In celebration of Mexico winning its independence from Spain, the town's name was changed from Nuestra Señora del Refugio de los Esteros, to Matasánchez, in honor of the man who ended the threat posed by the Trece brothers, two arrogant pirates. But we should get back to Nepomuceno and Shears, the story of the highfalutin Trece brothers will have to wait.

When the Anglos from the north became more hostile to the Indians, pushing them into Indian Territory, the whole region bore the brunt of their fury. How could they not be furious? But there was no time to take their feelings into account; folks had to defend themselves or else all the males would have been scalped and chopped to pieces, the women raped and sold. But there weren't enough walls, moats, and other defenses to protect them. It became necessary to "Pursue them the way they pursue us; harass them the way they harass us;

threaten them the way they threaten us; attack them the way they attack us; rob them the way they rob from us; capture them the way they capture us; terrorize them the way they terrorize us."

The first challenge was being slowed down by the supplies that burdened them. The livestock they brought along to eat slowed them even more, and there was a risk that the Indians would drain the watering holes or poison them with the cadavers of their prisoners, or even their own horses, before the Mexicans reached them. That's why, in 1834, the Mexican authorities came to an arrangement with the Cherokees and other tribes, offering them land, the opportunity to trade, and even livestock. One year later, three hundred Comanches stopped in San Antonio en route to Matasánchez to sign a peace treaty with Mexico but the deal fell through. The day eventually came when the Mexicans began trading with them, and that was the end of the Indian threat, at least for a short time.

On the day that the Shears-Nepomuceno incident took place, Matasánchez celebrated its eighty-fifth anniversary as a Christian town.

Who knows how big the population was in that year of our lord 1859, no one had counted heads recently. To hazard a guess, it was around eight thousand, if not more.

Matasánchez is, and always has been, the big city of the region. Bruneville doesn't even come close. Eleven years ago, Bruneville was nothing more than a dock on the north bank of the river, used only when the city's docks were full, or for goods that were en route to a ranch to the north, unless they were headed to the Santa Fe Trail, in which case it was better to continue even further up the muddy river.

Matasánchez, on the other hand, continued to grow, blessed

with endless showers of riches. Here's one example from the era when the Spanish were still in charge: for ten years Matasánchez had the export license for all Mexican silver; the customs office earned a fortune (seven out of every ten ships that docked in New Orleans originated in Matasánchez), and despite the facts that (as previously mentioned) hurricane after hurricane battered the city and regional conflicts cut the population in half, Matasánchez continued to be the principal metropolis and beating heart of the region.

When Bruneville was founded, Matasánchez converted one of its docks, down where the Río Bravo meets the sea, into its principal port. They christened it Bagdad. Bagdad quickly became wealthy, because that's where the customs house was located, and there was a tremendous amount of traffic.

In fact, no sooner has Sheriff Shears uttered the now-infamous phrase than the dove-keeper Nicolaso Rodríguez scrawls it on a piece of paper, which he folds and slips into the ring around Favorita's foot. She's his favorite of all the messenger pigeons that fly back and forth between Bruneville and Matasánchez every day, carrying all sorts of messages: "The Frenchie dry goods vendor wants to know if they want beans." "Need strychnine urgently; please send on next ferry. Rosita's in a bad way." "From the priest to the nuns: bake some more host quickly. We ran out and soon we'll have to use bread as a substitute." (This particular message caused a commotion at the convent; one nun swore that unleavened bread attracted the devil and claimed to have "scientific proof" of this, because in San Luis Potosí the mayor's wife had become delirious after taking unleavened bread for communion when the host ran out.) "Fetch my daughter from the afternoon ferry." "Don't come, the steamboat has already left for Punta Isabel." If the message said "Rigoberto" it wasn't good news—the priest's name was used when some unhappy soul needed the Last Rites, on either side of the river; for example, "Rigoberto to Oaks" or "Rigoberto to Rita" or just "Rigoberto" when everyone knew who was at death's door.

—

Favorita has shiny eyes and tiny pupils, she's the cleverest pigeon; nothing distracts her. On Favorita's foot Shears's phrase crosses the river, over the levees, over Fort Paredes and its casemate, over the moat and the sentry boxes, all of which Matasánchez had built to try to keep the prairie Indians, the mercenaries, the pirates, and the river at bay. She arrives in the center of the town where Don Nepomuceno is so deeply and widely respected and alights on the eaves of the courtyard behind Aunt Cuca's house, where the other Rodríguez, Nicolaso's brother Catalino, keeps Matasánchez's dovecote.

Favorita is their favorite for good reason. Without entering the dovecote, she pecks on the door, which rings the bell. Catalino takes the message from her and, her work done, Favorita enters the dovecote. Catalino takes the message to the central patio.

The sun above Matasánchez is the same one that's roasting Bruneville.

In the middle of the courtyard Catalino Rodríguez reads the message aloud for all to hear, including:

1. Aunt Cuca (who is crocheting in her rocking chair on the balcony outside the living room)
2. The women in the kitchen (who are making tamales; two of them are kneading the hominy while one of them adds small pats of lard, until it makes a paste with the maize flour that they use as a base, while Lucha and Amalia cut the banana leaves that they'll roast over the fire)
3. Doctor Velafuente (who's in his office)
4. And his patient (whose name we can't reveal because he was seeing the doctor for a malady he picked up in an encounter off a noisy street in New Orleans, where he should never have set foot, but the deed is done).

Aunt Cuca sets her crocheting aside, puts on her shawl and goes to tell her godmother the news. Lucha and Amalia leave the kitchen on an urgent trip to the market: "We're just going to get another quarter-ream of banana leaves, there aren't enough for the tamales." Doctor Velafuente ends his appointment; the patient leaves quickly for the church and the Doctor heads to the arcade. Each of them will go spread the word about how the Sheriff has insulted Don Nepomuceno.

The news is like a bomb going off in Matasánchez. The city wonders, *How could a dirtbag like Shears (who was nothing more than a carpenter's apprentice, and a bad one) speak like that to Don Nepomuceno?*

But this general sentiment doesn't mean that people don't have bones to pick with Nepomuceno.

The old ladies who attend mass every day, shrouded in black, pray for Nepomuceno but wonder if the insult might be punishment "for doing things that embarrassed Doña Estefanía"; they haven't forgiven him for romancing the widow Isa sixteen years ago when he was fifteen, or for the way his marriage to his cousin Rafaela ended (he had agreed to it reluctantly, only to please his mother). When Rafaela died in childbirth they blamed him: "How could she have survived the ordeal with her broken heart?" (Some people swore that she hadn't been kissed during the entire marriage, and that Nepomuceno did it to her quickly just to get her with child. Although others said—out of maliciousness, no doubt—that she had already been with child when they wed.) Nor had they forgiven him for his subsequent marriage to his former lover, Isa, the widow who bore him his first daughter (they're still married); nor for the other dalliances people whisper about on the way out of mass.

On the other hand, everybody was full of sympathy and compassion for Lázaro, Shears's victim: an old cowboy who could no longer rope or keep up with the cattle, though he could still play the violin beautifully—they'd invited him to play at baptisms but he refused to cross the river. He'd been around forever—grew up in Matasánchez till he was taken north while just a child, violin in hand, not knowing how to rope cattle; they said that his aunt sold him to the Escandón family, ranchers who gave him to their cousins. Later, Doña Estefanía would brag about how well the boy roped cattle and how he could sing and play, too.

Jones, a runaway slave, is leaning against the (so-called) cathedral portico, frightened by the news he overheard while selling candles and soaps from his basket. He leaves his spot and goes from house to house with his soaps and the gossip, heading toward the Franciscan monastery, always adding something along the lines of, "Like it or not, that's how they are; they don't know what respect is," in his excellent, newly learned Spanish.

He knocks on the Carranzas' door to offer his wares and deliver the news, which causes quite a commotion. The boy of the house, Felipillo Holandés—whom the Carranzas adopted not knowing he's a Karankawa—is overcome by a dark melancholy that he cannot explain to anyone; it's like he's lost the ground beneath his feet.

Then Jones delivers the news to the house next door, where Nepomuceno is practically a god. "Don't let Laura hear!" But Laura, only a few months older than Felipillo Holandés, has already heard. Angry tears begin to pour from her eyes: how could someone dare insult her hero, her savior, the man who rescued her from captivity?!

Don Marcelino, who rises at dawn every day of the week, including Sundays, to search for plant specimens for his herbarium ("that crazy old plant man" as the old women and children call him) is returning to Matasánchez from a two-week expedition when he hears the news. It's only half-translated and the "Shut up" part's been run together. He immediately takes a piece of paper from his shirt pocket and writes with a sharp-tipped pencil, "shorup: used to order someone to be quiet. A scornful command." He thinks it's a Spanish word. He collects words the same way he collects plants.

Later Don Marcelino folds the paper and puts it away next to his pencil, careful to put the tip up so it doesn't become dulled. He goes inside his house. He removes his boots just past the front door and doesn't give the subject another thought.

Petronila, a cowboy's daughter—she was conceived on Rancho Petronila, hence her name—is standing on her balcony when she hears the news. She goes inside, puts on a shawl, (although it's hot outside, that's what decent women do, otherwise her neck would be exposed; at home she leaves her head uncovered) and goes out shouting to her friends, "The Robin brothers are coming!"

The legend of these handsome bandits has been passed from señorita to señorita. The brothers are the Devil incarnate: the most terrible threat, and the most hoped-for.

In the street, Jones sees his friend Roberto, one of the Negroes who escaped when Texan landowners fled to Louisiana before the battle of San Jacinto (they dropped everything and ran for their lives, absolutely terrified, shouting "The Mexicans are coming!" The slaves took advantage of the chaos, "Let's scram!" and escaped).

"Roberto, come here! I have to tell you something . . ."

No sooner does he hear what Shears said than poor Roberto breaks out into hives. The Mexicans had welcomed him with open arms. But now the gringos are getting bolder, perhaps they will cross the Río Bravo to capture fugitives? It had already happened once before, when the mayor locked some escaped slaves in the town jail to protect them, but now things aren't the same because Nepomuceno and the mayor have their differences, and no one is going to come to their rescue. Ouch, his hives! His skin is covered in tiny red bumps. He begins to scratch and can't stop.

—

At the arcades, while having his shoes shined, Doctor Velafuente tells the bootblack, Pepe; then he tells the tobacconist when he stops in to pay for his snuff; at the post office he announces the news loudly to Domingo, who seals the letter the Doctor sends to his sister Lolita every week; and on Hidalgo Street he repeats it to Gómez, the mayor's assistant, whom he runs into when he's deciding whether to follow his routine and go to the café, or go to the barber (where Goyo recently cut his hair), or even go home (but it's too early, the news is really messing up his daily routine). All he really wants to do is get on board the *Blanca Azucena* (*White Lily*, the one luxury in his life, his fishing boat), but "that would be irresponsible."

Gómez, the mayor's assistant, has no sooner heard Doctor Velafuente's news than he wants to go directly to tell his boss, but first he must hurry to deliver a "personal and confidential" message for Matasánchez's new jailkeeper.

He delivers the message and the news about Shears's phrase as well. It's received quite differently than it was in Bruneville's jail. Here there's only one prisoner, not a prize catch, like Urrutia on the other side of the river; however, in the presidio on the outskirts of Matasánchez, there are scores of prisoners, among whom there are at least a half dozen big fish.

This solitary prisoner is from the north. He's a Comanche called Green Horn. Captain Randolph B. Marcy (one of the good gringos) brought him in and accused him of torturing a Negro girl named Pepementia, who is no longer a slave under Mexican law.

Captain Marcy recognized Green Horn in Matasánchez one day, seized him on the spot, and took him directly to the authorities.

In his defense, Green Horn said in perfect Spanish (he speaks several languages): "We did it solely out of scientific interest. We wanted to see if they're as black on the inside as they are on the outside; that's why we were peeling back and scrutinizing her layers of skin and muscles."

Gutiérrez, a lawyer known for his guile and his profitable connections in the Comanche slave trade, is defending Green Horn.

It would have been impossible for Captain Marcy to bring charges in Bruneville, or any other city in American territory, but in Mexico he knew the authorities would take it to heart.

Green Horn is being kept in the jail at the center of town because the presidio—from which it's impossible to escape—is on the outskirts and vulnerable to Comanche raids.

When Green Horn hears the news of the Shears-Nepomuceno affair, he thinks that the gringos will ride into Matasánchez in reprisal and liberate him from "these disgusting meals and salsas, these flatulent greasers." He has to restrain himself from breaking into song.

The jailkeeper—who doesn't have an official title—is a friend of Carvajal, Nepomuceno's political rival; he has many reasons to rejoice:

1. At last he has something to distract him from his boredom.
2. The position he's been given by the mayor is humiliating—he's no more than a security guard, a lowly post unbecoming to a man of his lineage, but he needs the money. "If I'd bought land to the north of the river when the time was right, I'd be set for life" (which, given the gringo takeover, is not true).
3. He thinks he's finally got his shot at glory; he's always been on the sidelines when things happen, but not this time, he's in the jailhouse and something big's going to happen here.

The jailkeeper caresses the pistols in his holsters. No one remembers his name.

—

His duty done, Gómez, the mayor's assistant, returns to the office. He arrives to find his boss, Don José María, whose famous family's surname has been popularly replaced by "de la Cerva y Tana" (meaning "blow gun," a nickname that mocks his inability to open his mouth without spitting verbal bullets at people), carrying an envelope bearing the central government's seal. Upon hearing the news about Shears the mayor tears the letter open and tosses it onto his desk, unread, and begins to rant and rave as usual, while folding the envelope over and over again, as though it were the envelope's fault:

He curses Gómez for bearing the news.

He curses Bruneville.

He curses Shears: "idiot, good-for-nothing, doesn't even know how to hammer a nail."

He curses Lázaro Rueda for being drunk: "booze isn't good for him, the violin, on the other hand . . ."

He curses up and down, left and right.

When he's vented this string of insults he asks loudly, "And now what are we supposed to do? There's no doubt that Nepomuceno will retaliate, and how! Where does this leave the rest of us?"

The letter lies on his desk, still unread. It's signed by Francisco Manuel Sánchez de Tagle. It says, in large, clear letters:

I recommend that the Negro fugitives from the United States remain in the cities along our northern border, as much to provide lodging for them with dignity as befits any Mexican citizen, as to protect our country from American raids.

—

In the courtyard of Aunt Cuca's house, Catalino changes the message tied to another pigeon, Mi Morena, and sets her flying southward.

Mi Morena arrives in the camp of the Seminoles (or Mascogos, as the Mexicans call them). The message is handed immediately to

Wild Horse, the chief, and to Juan Caballo, the leader of the fugitive African slaves, an ally of Wild Horse from long before their sojourn south of the Río Bravo.

The message makes the Seminoles anxious. It reawakens their worst fear: the frontier may no longer provide protection against the gringos.

"We left everything we knew," says Wild Horse, "to escape from the White Cholera. We bade goodbye to the buffalo, the plains, the birds, and their songs. Now we risk our lives living in caves where moss grows on our clothes, beneath an unknown sky where no ducks fly, in stagnant air that reverberates with the sounds of unknown insects, on unforgiving land, just to get away from the gringos. Have we changed our world for nothing, only to suffer them again?"

The members of the camp wail and beat their chests. In a few hours they send Mi Morena back. She returns to Matasánchez without a message.

They send *their* message to Querétaro, via Parcial, Juan Caballo's pigeon, who flies off. If we were to wait for him to arrive we'd lose the thread of our story, so we'll leave it there and go back to the Valley of the Rio Grande, the prairie, Indian Territory.

Nicolaso writes out copies of the phrase and entrusts them to several pigeons. We saw the first one fly to Matasánchez with Favorita. The second travels northward on the feet of Hidalgo, the white pigeon. On the Pulla cotton plantation, a young mulatto (son of Lucie, the slave they say was mistress to Gabriel Ronsard, the café owner) receives the pigeon, scratches his crotch, and reads the message aloud. The overseer scratches his head and listens. The Negros under his supervision listen, too, scratching their chests and necks in front of a small group of Indians who have come to trade—they've brought two tame mustangs they want to exchange for bullets and cotton, which they'll take back to Indian Territory and exchange for prisoners.

The Indians don't itch themselves now—the Pulla plantation is infested with fleas—but they'll be itching later, after they bring the bug-ridden cotton home with them.

For the cautious, vindictive foreman the news is of little interest, no matter how he looks at it he can't see why it matters.

For the Negros it's downright scandalous. Nepomuceno is a living legend. According to local lore he was kidnapped by Indians as a boy, an unfounded rumor that was spread by El Tigre, the run-away slave from Guinea who was captured by the Comanches and returned to his owner for a handsome reward. A good-looking, healthy, young Negro with strong teeth who could read and write, he was clean, conscientious, and hardworking, worth his weight in gold. From the day of his arrival, he has told stories, many untrue, about Nepomuceno.

Having been kidnapped isn't the only reason Nepomuceno is a living legend. It's the stories about his riding, cattle-rustling, skirt-chasing, and fighting, along with his unparalleled roping skills and having been born into money, that make him a living legend; cowards fear him and women dream about him for good reason. There's no one like Nepomuceno—who's also a redhead, according to some.

The young mulatto puts Hidalgo in the pigeon loft and begins to pray: "Holy Mother, look after Don Nepomuceno."

A third pigeon flies the first leg of his trip alongside Hidalgo. When Hidalgo lands in Pulla, the other pigeon continues across a stretch of bare land, where there's not even one lonely huisache tree, just stone-hard earth, before landing on the adobe arch that guards the Well of the Fallen.

That's how Noah Smithwick, the Texan pioneer who leads slave-hunting parties, hears the news. These men make a fortune by returning slaves to their so-called owners for ransom. As you might imagine, Shears's insult is a joy to Noah Smithwick's ears. He detests Nepomuceno and anyone else who so much as resembles a Mexican. Mexico ruins his trade, with its nonsensical ideas about property and other crazy notions, which would drive any self-respecting businessman to rack and ruin.

"The Mexicans will never amount to anything, they're a people without wherewithal, good for nothing but cooking and looking after the horses."

Two Born-to-Run Indians carry the news northward from the Well of the Fallen.

The news quickly reaches the King Ranch, neither by pigeon nor by Born-to-Run. A godlike horseman (dressed in white, riding a white mare) delivers the news, so quickly, in fact, that it was said to have been delivered by lightning bolt.

The news travels north toward the Coal Gang with the Born-to-Run Indians.

The Coal Gang are bandits who roam both sides of the frontier; they go wherever the loot is. The majority are Mexicans. They have their preferred targets:

1. Gringos. And anyone who looks like them, with the exception of their leader, Bruno, who has the blondest beard in the region—his men say it's because of the sun, which has bleached it, but those who knew him back when he hid beneath his mother's dark skirts and the brim of his father's (very elegant) hat know that he was born with white hair, and skin so white it was almost blinding. But now Bruno is dark as ebony. A miner who made his own fortune rather than inheriting one, he had silver mines in Zacatecas and a gold mine further north. Business was

doing so well there that he decided to sell the silver mines to finance his prospecting, investing everything but the shirt on his back. But it was his bad luck that the Great Theft had begun, and they took his mine from him using the law. He had conquered the bowels of the earth, but he couldn't prevail against evil.

2. Stealman's friends. Stealman is the one who, from his office in New York, carried out the aforementioned legal proceedings.
3. The Nouveau Riche, who made their fortunes off the new frontier.
4. Priests, and especially bishops, who knows why.

His guiding principles were clear: firstly, his profit and his benefit. Secondly, his benefit and his profit. Thirdly, his profit and his benefit. Fourthly, his enjoyment—and that's where things get complicated.

The Coal Gang is like a family. Their leader, Bruno, was born on an island in the distant north. Some call him The Viking, but he doesn't look it—his father was the bastard son of the King of Sweden. The rest of the gang was born in the region, in or near the Río Bravo Valley. It's all the same to them.

Each of them has been betrayed by his nearest and dearest:

Their leader, Bruno, by his own blood. His father was the first-born—though illegitimate—and he's also the firstborn, and illegitimate too, in keeping with family tradition. Logic and justice would see him crowned king. He believes he is the true heir of Gustav, the Grace of God, King of the Swedes, Grand Prince of Finland, Duke of Pomerania, Prince of Rügen and Lord of Wismar, Duke of Norway, Schleswig-Holstein, Stormarn and Dithmarschen, Count of Oldenburg and Delmenhorst. But he's just a bandit from the heart of Mexico: the Prince of Highway Bandits, the King of Terror (it wasn't that he didn't like the idea of being king, but since he didn't like the cold he would have moved the capital of his kingdom to Africa; and King of Terror sounded pretty good to him).

His right-hand man, nicknamed Pizca, betrayed by his older brother, who stole his birthright and left him with nothing but his own two hands, against their father's wishes. Tall as Bruno, with the same Viking complexion, his skin has become black as coal.

The others have their own less well-known stories of betrayal.

Bruno the Viking and his men have just eaten. Most of them have gone back to work (brushing the horses, laying out strips of beef to dry); the boss is lying by the embers of the fire, next to a demijohn of sotol. A Mexican falcon flies overhead. Bruno takes his slingshot from his shirt pocket. He places a smooth pebble into the rubber band. He aims . . .

The shot misses, despite the fact he had plenty of time. It's the falcon's good luck that the hunter had too much to drink.

The falcon circles. Once again Bruno has him within reach, he reloads his slingshot . . . But the sun plays a trick on him and blinds him just as he's about to take his shot.

The falcon is one-in-a-million, and it escapes! This infuriates Bruno, mostly because of the sotol running in his veins, which puts him in a foul mood. He hides his face beneath the brim of his hat. And, just like that, he falls asleep.

He snores.

Pierced Pearl, his captive—the Comanches recently sold her to him, but she won't last long, he can't stand having a woman around—has watched the whole scene with the lucky, free falcon.

It pleases Pierced Pearl—bravo for the falcon! A hand's breadth from Bruno, she lays her head on the ground—there's nowhere else to lay it—and curls up to try to sleep—it was a bad night. She dreams:

That Bruno's snoring is the falcon's voice. That the falcon

approaches, flying close over her, flapping its wings noisily. It has a human torso. It's neither man nor woman. It caws:

"There. Theeere. Theeere."

The falcon develops legs, they grow till they reach the ground. It bends them. Continues flapping. It speaks:

"Leave this place. Here. You're . . . hic. You're interrupting my . . . hic . . . hic . . . hic . . . I'm . . . like a fish . . ."

The falcon stretches its legs, swaggers around, and disappears into thin air, like smoke.

Pierced Pearl, Bruno's prisoner, awakens. Yet again she is overcome by anxiety and bitterness. Knowing the falcon escaped gives her the only flicker of hope she's had in a long time. And then the falcon became meaningless in her dream.

Pierced Pearl grinds her teeth.

Just then one of the Born-to-Run arrives in a cloud of dust, like a ghostly apparition at a vigil, his eyes bulging. He pulls up short. He drinks from the goat's bladder he wears around his neck. This liquid is poison to most, but it makes him feel tireless, immortal.

Pierced Pearl forgets her worries for a moment and pays close attention to the messenger. She hears him swallow, listens to him gargle, making sounds to clear his throat.

"Bruno!" the Indian messenger shouts. Bruno awakens immediately, lifts his hat, and his pupils are still adjusting when the messenger drops the news about Nepomuceno like a hot potato.

And in the blink of an eye, the messenger, like a flying arrow, whizzes off, back to the Well of the Fallen, his blood burning with the poison that fuels him.

—

The pigeon Hidalgo has just passed over Bruneville when Bob Chess arrives to visit Ranger Neals. Bob's not a Ranger—not even close—"I'm a Texan, from this side of the river, the American side." He likes horses, women, guns, conquering Indians, and killing Mexicans. He thinks sitting in the Café Ronsard drinking and shooting the breeze is stupid. "I'm a man of action, life is about what you do, everything else is a waste of time; it's thanks to places like that, and to temples and churches, that Texas is going to hell in a handbasket."

Bob Chess wants money and absolute power to enjoy himself as he pleases. No faggotry for him—sitting around drinking, rocking a baby, doing needlepoint—and that's why he doesn't like games, music, dancing, fine food, or any other ("idiotic") aspect of domestic life. "My ten commandments for being a real man: First commandment—Sleep in the open air; Second—Eat meat roasted on an open fire; Third—Have a woman once a month; Fourth—Never get drunk; Fifth—Increase your landholdings; Sixth—Never speak to a Negro, or a Mexican; Seventh—Do not attend church or temple; Eighth—Get around on a horse, never on wheels, which are for the lazy (and are the source of all evil); Ninth—Always have a pistol on your hip; and the Tenth commandment—Love yourself as yourself."

He follows his commandments, more or less. He never sleeps in the open air—"It's just a saying, sometimes the open air's not good for you; if we were on the prairies it would be a different story"—he rents a room in Mrs. Big's Hotel, a real luxury for him since, as a boy, he never slept in his own bed. ("Who woulda thunk it!" his mama would have said, "A mattress makes you soft." And by "mattress" she meant thin cotton mat.) He likes (and how!) a good meal—which some would say is the most sedentary aspect of domestic life. He doesn't ride because the saddle and the motion of the horse are no good for his hemorrhoids. And he doesn't have a woman on a monthly basis, just whenever the opportunity arises.

He always wears a hat—despite the fact it's not one of his commandments.

The Kwahadis, invincible Comanches who refuse to have anything to do with the gringos (they prefer to trade with the Mexicans), receive another Born-to-Run on the high plains, five thousand feet above sea level, in Indian Territory (which the Mexicans call the "Apachería"), past Llano Estacado and the Caprock escarpment, a three-hundred-foot cliff that separates the high plains from the Permian basin.

The Kwahadis are renowned for their violence. They are experts at battle. No one lives to tell about a Kwahadi attack unless they're taken captive. And fighting isn't their only distinctive characteristic. They can withstand anything. If they can't find water, they drink from the stomachs of dead horses. The rest of the Comanches fear them. They're the wealthiest Indians, they have more than fifteen thousand tame horses. Their camp is deep in the Palo Duro Canyon (second in size only to the Grand Canyon), and they roam the Pease River, McClellan Creek, and Blanco Canyon.

Their battle strategy is difficult to decipher.

Rawhide (the newest Kwahadi—a few months ago he was taken captive by the Comanches, who bought him to have someone who could read, to be able to communicate—he takes care of both verbal and written correspondence at the camp) listens to the message.

Rawhide asks the messenger to wait and delivers the news to Chief Smells Good.

The Born-to-Run waits. Since he doesn't have farther to go, he doesn't drink from his jug of poison. He squats and waits.

The Kwahadi chief, Smells Good, is preparing to lead an attack. Naked to the waist, his face daubed with black war paint, he wears a long eagle-feather headdress that flies out behind him on horseback, he leans back, his headdress nearly skimming the ground, his copper earrings jingling in the air, leaving everyone speechless. Especially Rawhide.

"Speak!" Chief Smells Good says, when he sees Rawhide, the newest Kwahadi, standing before him, immobile. He understands he brings a message.

"Chief Smells Good . . ."

"Speak!"

Rawhide knows that delivering unwelcome news will imperil him, if the chief doesn't like the message he may pay with his life. He masters his fears and relays the Born-to-Run's news.

Smells Good listens. He departs without a word. He tells the shaman, Sky Bullet (who has also just finished preparing for battle, with war paint and his headdress) what he's just heard. Seconds pass. Sky Bullet pronounces: "A good sign, a good sign."

They exchange a few words.

Certain the news brings good luck, they give Rawhide orders.

They have decided to sacrifice the Born-to-Run. It's nothing out of the ordinary, and not worth us dwelling on. They keep his scalp and his magical jug. They depart camp ululating.

We'll leave them to their business, which doesn't have much to do with us.

Rawhide doesn't participate in the attack, he stays in camp with a group of elders—his guards—responsible for looking after the slowest livestock. He writes a message and ties it to the Kwahadis' only messenger pigeon, Penny.

Penny flies south across Indian Territory, to a nearby Comanche camp. The captives, who are well cared for because they will be traded (Mexicans, gringos, Germans; all young men who are treated like the finest livestock), listen to the news as it is announced by the tribe's herald. The majority don't like it, but there are a few who have unfinished business with Nepomuceno and celebrate it.

The Comanches ignore the news. They couldn't care less about Nepomuceno, some sheriff, some shitty town. They were hoping for a different message, a response to their earlier one. Now they worry that the Kwahadis have decided to attack.

★

Let's back up a little. The pigeons are on the wing, the Born-to-Run streak across the prairie, the white horseman crosses the Valley like lightning, the falcon hunts its prey, Indians rush around getting decked out for their attack, but not a soul stops at the Aunties' Ranch—no one dares call these women what they really are: Amazons.

It's something to see, the entrance to this ranch, painted with Teresita's family tree (flowers, leaves, and names all painted in bold, harmonious colors). There's no wall, just this entrance.

The inhabitants of the Aunties' Ranch are unusual on the Great Plains, some even claim their ranch doesn't exist. They live in the open air like cowboys on the trail; they use lassos; they know how to use pistols; they can't stand farming; and they hate living under a roof, with two exceptions: a pale-faced blonde, Peladita, who sews like a madwoman, all night and all day, waiting for her Ulises to return (an ill-tempered Mexican who, needless to say, has no intention of coming back for her); that's her story. The other is a different kettle of fish: she's ancient, and though she's wrinkled like a raisin, her nose grown long, she looks almost childlike. She was once kidnapped and no longer remembers anything else. You can't set foot on the Aunts' Ranch without hearing all about her kidnapping.

The other Aunts just let her be.

The Aunts chatter:

"Don't dismount here, no way. On this ranch we ride like the wind. No one falls to their knees at Aunts' Ranch, no one defers to a superior. We're all queens. And here's the thing: we ride so fast we could fly, all we need are wings."

"We tame mustangs. Twelve handy, pistol-packing women who defeat anyone who dares to take us on."

"No one sets foot here without asking our permission. Nobody even dares to take a drop of water from our well without asking first."

"The chickens roam free."

"The donkeys sleep where they want."

"We drink when we feel like it, the good stuff."

"We have sex with each other if we want, and no one takes it the wrong way or thinks they're sinning."

"You bet!"

"We dance until daybreak."

"We're amazing cooks."

"Only Doña Estefanía cooks better than us; better to admit it than get found out."

"What good is it to her, to have so much land, livestock, and money? It's better to be free."

"I was at Doña Estefanía's once. The women didn't sit at the table, they just served the men."

"Shameful."

"Absolutely."

"Know if she had any lovers?"

"Doña Estefanía, lovers? A few might have tried, if they did, they fell wide of the mark."

"Why would we women go looking for that kind of trouble?"

"Because some of us like men."

"I just use them for sex."

"Get outta here, you're gonna spend your life begging for something you'll never get. Look what happened to Peladita, you should go sit and sew with her."

"I wouldn't do it even if they tied me up, you can't tame me! I don't have hands, I have hooves! Plus I know how to run and to hunt."

"Has anyone here ever seen that guy Nepomuceno?"

"Some folks call him the Red Menace, because he's a redhead, and he's dangerous."

"He's really a redhead?"

"Depends on how the sun hits his hair."

In Bruneville Frank returns to the Stealman mansion with the oxtail for the stew wrapped in dried corn husks—finely chopped, like Señora Luz likes it. The women who work for Mrs. Lazy have already heard what happened in the Market Square, they know even more than Frank because, while he was spreading the news and haggling with Sharp over the ingredients for Señora Luz's soup, he missed out on quite a bit. A detailed report was delivered to the Stealman home by a longshoreman called Steve.

Steve is a tameme, he always has a basket of goods on his back. Today it was full of long-stemmed flowers to fill the Chinese and English vases that will decorate the salon where the best—or worst, depending on your perspective—of Bruneville society will gather.

Steve has added a flourish to the story, to get a better tip: "Nepomuceno, the cattle thief, Doña Estefanía's black sheep, got what he deserved from the sheriff!" Here he paused to laugh. "He called him a 'greaser'!" Then he told them how, after a few seconds of silence during which the sheriff stopped beating the drunkard and no one on the scene, not even Shears or Nepomuceno, blinked or drew a breath, Nepomuceno emptied his pistol into the Sheriff, "He shot him . . . I think he mighta killed him. Then he picked up the drunk guy, fired once more into the air, and took off with his men."

———

Let's dot the i's and cross the t's. Sheriff Shears had wanted to arrest Lázaro Rueda for being drunk, disturbing the peace, and urinating in the Market Square. "Since when do they arrest folks in these parts

57

for drinking themselves stupid and taking a piss?" Lázaro resisted with what little dignity he had, which wasn't much (old and worn-out, he was falling-down drunk), but it was enough resistance for Shears to give him a thrashing. He was beating him with the butt of his pistol when Nepomuceno stepped out of the Café Ronsard.

Inside the café, Nepomuceno avoided discussing what had happened in court that morning, but didn't hesitate to talk up a deal he made with a Galician from Puerto Bagdad called Nemesio—they say he has bags under his eyes from eating so much chorizo. "Yeah, I signed a contract for thirty-five hundred head of livestock with him; I hand them over and he takes them to Cuba. Business is good . . . My ranches are overflowing with cattle and horses: roan, bay, chestnut, piebald, dappled (and, I won't deny it, there are mavericks, too, though I don't go looking for them. Why would I, when my corrals are already full of animals, happy as clams? It's not my style to go looking for wild ones. If I have mavericks it's because they came to my ranch of their own free will, they like it on my land, we treat the animals well, they never lack for water, grass, or feed, or protection from the wolves)."

"So what do ya need Nemesio for? You can take care of things yourself . . ." the barkeep said.

More than a few customers nodded. Nepomuceno didn't deny it.

Charlie, a recent arrival, asked him if the boats that would be transporting the livestock were his.

"They're all Stealman's," answered a guy called David. His family makes a big deal out of their ancestry but they're poor as fleas; he thinks he's Nepomuceno's rival and likes to talk trash about him. "I said 'all,' and I mean everything that floats, except the tugboat, but as of today that's his too. He paid almost nothing for it because he was calling in unpaid debts. That's how he does business . . ."

David speaks like he's working up to go in for the kill: "Bagdad, Nepomuceno? Ha! Bagdad ain't nothing! If you'd made your contracts in Galveston back when things were going well for you, you'd be singin' a different song today! Now you're just a hungry gull peckin' at some crumbs!"

The news of Stealman's latest business acquisition turns Nepomuceno's coffee bitter. If you smelled his breath you'd back away, he's so full of bile.

Two weeks earlier old Arnoldo had asked Nepomuceno for help. "These wily gringos want my tugboat. They say I have a debt and I gotta pay it off with my boat. Listen, Nepomuceno, they invented this so-called debt, they say I owe them rent for the dock, can you believe it? And they calculated it from the date the law was passed. What kind of plague has befallen us? And how are we going to get rid of them? They want everything, you see, and I don't need to tell you, just look what they did with your mother's land, they wanna take over the whole damn world, these freeloading gringos..."

You can imagine how, for Nepomuceno, this was like rubbing salt into a wound.

He doesn't say another word. He motions for the bill. Teresa approaches the bar and for a moment he is drawn out of his own problems.

Ah, lovely Teresa.

Teresa thinks in all Bruneville and Matasánchez, in the entire Valley, there's no one as dreamy as Nepomuceno; when she sees him she smiles in such a way that, some other time, it would have made his whole week; and though right now there's no smile in the world could achieve that, it distracts him from his fury. "Teresa, pretty, Teresa," he's not defeated yet, after all, turnabout is fair play. He recalls how, ten months ago, he stole the election from under Stealman's nose when he was certain of victory...

The gringos who are invading the Rio "Grande" Valley are fortune-hunters who fall into two camps: the Blues and the Reds.

The Reds are the big business owners and ranchers, wealthy and powerful. Stealman is their leader, along with a select few: King, Mifflin, Kenedy (it would be interesting to know the details of how they agreed to divvy up south Texas, but that's not our business).

The Blues are small businessmen who struggle day-to-day to make a living, including Mr. Chaste, the mayor and pharmacist; Mr. Seed, who owns the corner coffee shop; Sharp, the butcher who owns the stalls on the east side of the market; Herr Werbenski, owner of the busy pawn shop who sells firearms and ammo on the side; and Peter Hat.

Nepomuceno supported the Blues in the mayoral election; he gathered Mexicans from across the Río Bravo and offered them a good meal (which he paid for) and a few coins (from his own pocket), then he transported them across the Río Bravo (he'd made a deal with old Arnoldo), plying them with quantities of sotol (which he had bought in bulk), and delivered them half-drunk to the polling booths to vote for his candidate, Mr. Chaste.

And that's how the Blues won the mayoral election.

Nepomuceno recalls all this in the Café Ronsard, once again savoring his victory and the joy of crushing Stealman, which boosts his spirits, but a second later they plummet; it makes no difference whether Mr. Chaste is a Blue or a Red, he's a wretched gringo (a pale-faced Anglo who pretended to be a Mexican's best friend before the elections, no sooner had he won than he called them "worthless greasers").

Teresa smiles at him again.

No matter, Nepomuceno thinks, contented; he won that battle.

Ooh, that Teresa is something else . . . but then he begins thinking about Stealman and old Arnoldo again, and he feels even worse.

His moods are unpredictable these days. He's jumpy. He goes out into the street. Four of his men wait with their mounts; the other eight or so who accompanied him into Bruneville have stayed away from the Market Square so as not to set the gringos on edge. Three are waiting at the turnoff to Rancho del Carmen, and the rest are even further ahead. These days it's safest to travel in packs.

Mexicans might think his men are simply cowboys, or shady bandits, or lively young men. To gringos they're all worthless greasers.

The fact is that cowboys are no longer what they used to be, back in Lázaro's day: they were both tender and tough with the herd, defending it from buffalo stampedes, wolves, and drought; leading the cattle to green pastures and rescuing them from gullies if necessary; fattening them up daily and always returning them to the corral.

Some say everything changed when the slaughterhouse opened in Bruneville. Others say it happened before that, when the buffalo began to be hunted to extinction, the Indians started carrying firearms, and grass began to be sown, causing the land itself to change. Grass grows fast and feeds the fast-growing herds, but it needs a lot of water—if it doesn't rain it dries out—and it's destructive: it kills trees and other plants, including grains and fruits, even sweet potatoes.

The truth is that the volume of cattle has ravaged the prairie . . . When a herd passes through it's worse than wildfire because the earth isn't cleansed for renewal, it's just trampled.

(The slaughterhouse is past the docks, near Mrs. Big's Hotel. Cattle and swine low, bellow, and bawl; they're slaughtered by the dozens, sliced in half, they're hung on hooks and shipped out on boats; there's a constant stream of blood, and a pervasive stench.

In the slaughterhouse they experiment with ice, trying to freeze the meat to prevent it from rotting . . . it's not that they have a problem with the flies and worms, but they want it to appear fresh, despite the fact it's nearly rotten—if they could find buyers, they'd even sell the worms and flies by the pound.)

But back to our story: Nepomuceno sees Shears beating the old cowboy mercilessly in the Market Square.

"What's going on here?" he asks calmly (despite the fact he's deeply fond of Lázaro Rueda), to take things down a notch.

La Plange, the photographer who claims to be French, though no one knows where he's really from—some say he's Belgian or Dutch, though these days he asks folks to pronounce his name the Anglo way and signs his prints "Leplange"—came to Bruneville to make money taking portraits of the gringos; he's already cleaned up with the rich folks across the river in Matasánchez. He leans over and takes a few steps so he can see everything. How he'd love to photograph this scene, but it's one thing to want to and another to actually do it. Eyes riveted, he motions to Snotty, the kid who helps him out (day and night, through thick and thin, even between the sheets), making signs with his left hand to bring his camera so he can capture the moment:

"Quick, Snotty!" It's La Plange's fault the kid got stuck with this nickname.

Alicia, Captain Boyle's Mexican wife—wagging tongues say she's not his only one—sets down her new earthenware pot, which is filled with berries she just bought from Joe. "Good heavens!"

A step behind Alicia, Joe, the Lieders' oldest son, nervously scratches the earth with his bare feet. With the few words he knows in Spanish and English (no one understands the Germans because they speak with such a strange accent), supplemented by gestures, he's trying to sell the harvest his mother worked so hard to gather. He's so fidgety that he's accidentally struck by the ring of belts the trapper, Cruz, has hanging from his shoulder.

Right behind Joe is Dry Whitman, a teetotaler from the Temperance Society. He's been in town for four months preaching the virtues of sobriety, persecuting drunkards, and pestering the owners of establishments that sell alcohol, threatening them with the fires of hell.

Nepomuceno repeats his question:

"What's going on here?"

Joe explains to Nepomuceno in his broken Spanish.

"Leave the poor man alone, Mister Shears." Nepomuceno is not prepared to call this imbecile "Sheriff." "I'll take care of this. Just a few words to help him see . . ."

And without waiting for an answer, Nepomuceno begins: "Lázaro, arise and walk . . ."

Laughter. The joke strikes a chord. Good old Nepo! He's so witty!

That's when Sheriff Shears spits the phrase at Nepomuceno we've already heard, "Shut up, you dirty greaser." And that's when Snotty, La Plange's apprentice, runs to get the tripod, camera, and other equipment, thereby missing the insult.

Frank hears it while he's repeating his orders to himself, *And make it snappy!*, to avoid forgetting them. He hastens his pace.

Everyone else stands stock still, it's the calm before the storm, even though a breeze from the Gulf, warm and salty, has kicked up.

A tense second passes, a long one, the kind that existed back in the days when everyone carried Colts. Three more seconds pass in the same manner.

Six seconds.

Not even the birds are moving; just the hair on Sandy's head (the town coquette), and Nepomuceno's (which looks reddish in the sun), and Joe's blond shock of hair. Their hair moves in the breeze, waving on their heads, a controlled flight of sorts, sweet and gentle.

Twelve seconds. Fifteen. Eighteen. Twenty.

A hat flies off someone's head. No one chases after it. A feather escapes from pretty Sandy's thick hair, an ornament from the previous evening.

They're frozen in a face-off: Sheriff Shears leaning forward, his fine hair stuck to his face with sweat, his face twisted with rage, the barrel of the gun (the butt of which he was using to beat Lázaro Rueda) in his gnarled hands, his cross-eyes sweeping the floor, his pants a few inches longer than his legs, his grubby shirt untucked, his five-pointed star hanging from his vest; Nepomuceno stands erect, tall, his bright eyes staring straight ahead, his fine riding pants (made from Scottish cashmere) made to measure by the best tailor in Puebla, his sharp-looking jacket (made by a tailor in New Orleans), the cuffs of his white (Dutch) shirt showing, his silk tie (French), his beard and his hair well-groomed (by a barber from Doña Estefanía's ranch), and clean boots (only the finest, made in Coahuila).

The breeze blows the seeds off a dandelion puffball, scattering them everywhere.

Shears is famous for his temper; conversely, it's impossible to tell what's going through Nepomuceno's mind. He appears to be watching everyone at once, cold and calculating, there's something commanding in his gaze, except that in the reflection of his pupils there's the memory of how Lázaro taught him how to use a lasso when he was a boy and of his violin and songs.

The breeze persists. The naked dandelion stalk sways. You won't find the feather that blew out of Sandy's hair.

The flyaway hat floats to the ground, blows around the corner and out of sight.

In Nepomuceno's memory the cowboy's lasso is dancing in the air.

Thirty seconds. The breeze hasn't stopped; but the hairs on Sheriff Shears's greasy head don't move.

Thirty-five.

Suddenly the gust of air from the gulf stops as if it turned into lead and plummeted to earth.

Nepomuceno puts his hand on the butt of his pistol at the thirty-sixth second. Copying him, Shears grabs his gun with his right hand (since he is holding the barrel of his pistol in his left)—thirty-seven, thirty-eight, all the way up to forty-four and he still hasn't got a good grip on it. You can tell from his pale hands with their scaly skin, which look like floppy fish, that he's a terrible carpenter.

Nepomuceno's eyes widen, his eyelids lifting slowly—his long lashes make him look like a wolf—now his fiery gaze lands on Shears.

The star on Shears's vest is trembling; it looks like it might fall off any second. Shears doesn't even attempt to mirror Nepomuceno's look; his eyes are two slits, no fire and no spark.

Nepomuceno's men form a semicircle behind him, ready to draw their guns. Esteban makes a sign to Fernando, the one who looks after the horses; no need to speak: if he moves his head to the left it means "watch out on your right"; if he purses his lips it means "you're about to get bitten by a snake." (Fernando's uncle is Hector, the cart-owner; they have the same round face.)

Shears, on the other hand, is alone like a stray dog, he's got no backup. They gave him this job because someone has to walk around town wearing the star.

A couple more seconds pass, it's like time has stopped. Fernando unfastens the reins tied to the Café Ronsard's hitching post and gathers them in both hands; the horses are ready.

Far away someone shouts, "Teencha! Your bread is burning!"

In a split second Nepomuceno draws his gun, he cocks it while he aims and pulls the trigger; Shears has just started to search for his gun's trigger when Nepomuceno's shot penetrates his right inner thigh, where it won't cause much bleeding but will hurt like the dickens.

With a surgeon's precision, it misses the vein. Nepomuceno could easily have shot him through the head or the heart, but prudence prevailed.

Shears and his Colt hit the floor.

The five-pointed star lies beside him, face down.

Nepomuceno prepares to save his own hide and those of his men, he knows he's got to throw caution to the wind and be bold, or he's a goner. Now it's the Rangers' turn to be cautious; some of these gringos work for Judge White ("Whatshisname") and lawyer Stealman, others make their living on the prairie, using their weapons to protect livestock from bands of cattle thieves.

These gringo gunmen are calm, they only fire their pistols for money; their hands rest on their Colts.

The Rangers have just returned from visiting Neals when they hear the shot; Ranger Phil smooths his hair; Ranger Ralph picks his teeth with a fingernail; Ranger Bob examines the heel of his boot.

More than one of them (they double as both hired guns and Rangers) has the urge to riddle this greaser with bullets, but this isn't the moment.

At the shot, some onlookers scurry away. Not that it's out of the ordinary, these things happen in Bruneville with some regularity.

Everyone else: the old folks, pretty Sandy, two madmen (Connecticut, who only says, "I'm from Connecticut," and the Scot, who says lots but in his country's strange accent it's impossible to understand, which is just as well, because his babbling is full of obscenities), two yokels, and a few others are frozen stiff.

Now's not the time for us to pause and take in Sandy's revealing neckline, but it's important to note that among those in the know she's called Eagle Zero.

Carlos, the Cuban, hears the shot when he's passing through the swinging doors of the Café Ronsard. In his role as Eagle One he was waiting for Nepomuceno to leave, and as soon as he saw him get up from his chair he slowly picked up his canvas bag and the violin he plays in the evenings—alone or with his close friends, he's no cowboy or some travelling minstrel who goes around making his violin screech tunelessly—and casually follows Nepomuceno, intending to have a few words with him when he mounts his horse (the Eagles' top secret business is handled with utmost discretion), so no one notices.

The matter is urgent, but he must exercise caution. The rules of espionage require it. That's why he doesn't follow him immediately out of the Café Ronsard; he hears the shot, looks up, and sees Nepomuceno holster his Colt. He doesn't move, stuck between the two half-doors, holding them so they don't swing. He didn't hear the insult that provoked Nepomuceno and doesn't understand what he's seeing. No matter what happened, for the good of the Eagles—Nepomuceno would agree—he should hang back. He doesn't take a step or make a sign. He raises his eyes, pretending to look at the sky, and half closes them; out of the corner of his eye he observes what's happening in the Market Square and does his best to breathe calmly.

The only person who notices Carlos stop dead in his tracks is Dimitri. He'll remember this later. But for the moment he watches Carlos and finds satisfaction in the fact that he appears to be a coward.

Inside the Café Ronsard are: Wild, the buffalo hunter recently arrived from the prairie (a shameless and violent opportunist); handsome Trust, his sidekick; and their three slaves (One, Two, and Three), all with .50-caliber Sharps rifles on their shoulders. Wild hears the shot in the Market Square but doesn't move from his chair. Teresa runs upstairs to see what's happening from the balcony of her room. She's done this before; the view from up there is excellent. The bartender begins to hide most of his bottles under the bar in case bullets start flying. Wild makes a sign to handsome Trust with his head.

Trust motions to One, Two, and Three to follow him, and they file out into the street, pushing past Carlos the Cuban. They pass through the saloon doors and leave them swinging.

Dimitri (who's from the steppe) watches them from his table and observes that Carlos appears not to notice either being pushed or the stench of Wild and his men (who all reek of blood). Dimitri takes all this in as if he sees straight through Carlos—it's because of the differences in the climates where they come from, which have forged them differently: the flat light of the tropics, and the darkness and veiled light of the north. The climate and luminosity of the tropics have made Carlos a good actor, skilled at pretending (though this is a contradiction), while the darkness of the Northern Hemisphere has made Dimitri adept at seeing things. But Carlos doesn't understand the blinding light that shines on this stage, while veiled light has taught Dimitri to observe carefully, but he can't stand bright light.

Trust walks along the north side of the Market Square without approaching the scene of the crime. He nearly bumps into Nepomuceno's servant, Fernando, the one with the round face.

By the time Trust returns with the news, Wild already knows everything. His boss rebuffs and insults him: "Thanks for nothing, slowpoke."

(Trust is like the buffalo hunter's shadow, resentment building inside him. He was so young when he began hunting some say his very bones are made of dead bison. Handsome Trust—there's something graceful, even sensual, in his melancholy and strange docility—has the same dream every night that he sodomizes a buffalo, or the buffalo sodomizes him. When he can't sleep the dream haunts him, bewildering and shameful. The pleasure he feels when he's asleep is dark and powerful, and when he recalls it upon awakening the muscles of his thighs contract, his chest and his abdomen throb; his pleasure is more intense when he penetrates the buffalo.)

After unhitching the horses and approaching Nepomuceno, Fernando the servant was the second to flee. Alicia, Captain Boyle's wife, was the first. It's not that she's jumpy, just this morning as it was getting light out the Captain urged in his broken Spanish:

"You run if pistol smokes."

"Why are you speaking to me like an Apache all of a sudden, my Captain?" She uses his title as a term of endearment.

"I not joke, things go bad ... You, run if pistol smoke." Of course the Captain is joking, but for good measure he tells Alicia a few stories to convince her that if bullets start to fly, it's best to get outta Dodge.

Today of all days she's carrying the new clay pot she just bought in the market to replace the frijolera that belonged to her mother (which was so well used that eventually it cracked and started to leak, not much, but it would eventually break completely; anyways it needed to be replaced because it constantly dripped bean broth onto the fire, stinking up the kitchen).

As she races along, Alicia glimpses Glevack out of the corner of her eye.

When she's about to turn into Charles Street in the direction of James Street and down to the dock—she's still running full speed ahead—she sees the Lipans' knife fight.

Better keep going straight.

So she continues along Elizabeth Street. But at the next corner (Fourth Street) she turns toward James Street. Before she reaches it she pauses to catch her breath, leaning against the Spears' house.

She waits for her heartbeat to recover from the shock of Nepomuceno's gunshot, her sprint, and the vision of the two savages attacking each other with knives. She breathes deep. Once. Twice. Alicia feels an unsettling sensation of pleasure similar to what handsome Trust felt when he saw the Lipans brandishing their knives at each other. But she wants to shake the feeling off, get rid of it. She turns her attention to her pot, lifting it to get a better look. Its curves are beautiful. She taps it with her knuckle.

"Goodness, it sounds awful!"

For a moment she ponders returning it to the pot merchant, but then she remembers it's full of berries, that's why it doesn't sound right.

She sticks her nose in to get a good look at the berries.

"Heavens, they're all mushy!"

Pitiful. Bruneville is no place to grow or buy such berries; it's far too hot. Alicia glances at them again:

"They look like they've turned into jelly already, they've cooked in the heat, or from being all shaken up."

They don't look like jelly, however, but something much darker and deeper. They awaken that same unsettling sensation of pleasure again. She embraces her pot once more and runs off down the street.

The Lipans have injured each other. Strong Waters has a cut across his cheek that hurts but doesn't bleed much; Blue Falls has been cut across three of his fingertips, barely a scratch but they're bleeding profusely. They embrace, contrite and ashamed. They mount their horses and head out of town at a vigorous trot, packhorse in tow.

Blue Falls's fingers drip blood on the cobblestones. After passing the Bruneville dock, it becomes more noticeable, drops of red ink on the dry earth.

By detouring to avoid Main Street on his way to the market, Nat, the messenger, almost bumps into the fighting Indians; he sees one of them drop his dagger. He doesn't take his eyes off it for a second, disregarding all else; he doesn't even see what the Lipans are doing, he only has eyes for the knife.

Nat glances around. There's not a soul in sight. He looks around nervously again. The coast is clear. He bends down, picks up the dagger, and shoves it into his waistband. He feels the knifepoint against his belly and contracts his stomach muscles, hotfooting it down to the river. He can't run at top speed with the knife where it is, but he goes as fast as he can, walking with long strides, his shoulders hunched.

Olga watches him pick up the knife and goes to tell Judge Gold, he'll pay attention to this news for sure.

———

In the Market Square, Sandy stands rooted in place for ten seconds. Then she takes flight; where she's headed is not clear. Standing on the other side of the market, Father Rigoberto would like to call her over and admonish her for her neckline—she always looks like this—but he begins to stutter and can't get his words out. It's her décolletage's fault, it does funny things to his blood. Damned woman. She comes closer and he catches a glimpse of what her dress leaves uncovered. An overwhelming desire for sleep overcomes him. There's a crate of alfalfa at his feet; he squats and lies down—that's how he's dealt with nervousness since he was a kid—he lies down and goes to sleep, he's not the type to go racing away.

Sandy keeps on running. (They didn't make her Eagle Zero for nothing; while she runs, she takes in everything she sees.) She detours inland, to go check out what's happening on the outskirts of Fort Brune.

(An aside about Fort Brune: its moment of glory is long past. Nowadays there's only half a dozen lazy soldiers that live there, and they spend more time at Mrs. Big's than standing guard. It's been so long since King and Stealman got sick and tired of requesting military reinforcements that now they each have their own gunmen. King's are the most famous—and the toughest—especially with Mexicans; people call them kiñeros or reyeros [since King in Spanish is "rey"].)

———

Fernando, the servant, runs and dives between the hides in the buffalo hunter's cart; you'd have to be desperate to put up with that stench.

No sooner has he hidden himself between the hides and the carcasses than he begins rebuking himself. "I'm a coward, I should never have buried myself here among dead buffalo." But he doesn't dare come out. "They'll kill me! They'll say I'm one of Nepomuceno's men and not even God could protect me." He repeats, "I'm a coward, a pathetic coward!"

Patrick, who sells persimmons (he arrived in Matasánchez from Ireland as a kid and has earned enough to afford his own horse and pistol), clearly hears Shears call Don Nepomuceno a "greaser." His eyes glaze over, like some of the customers tempted by the fruit he sells, he's trying to make sense of what just happened—it's not that easy for him, he's not the sharpest tool in the shed—until he announces in a loud, serious voice, "It's John Tanner, the White Indian. He's back! We're screwed!" in a tone that instills fear in all who hear him. Especially Toothless, the old beggar, because he knows what Patrick's talking about.

Luis, the boy who was looking at rubber bands for his slingshot in the market, the one who was carrying things for Miss Lace (Judge Gold's housekeeper), realizes his bosslady has left. And then he remembers that he's supposed to go pick up his sister before his aunt leaves for you-know-where. He'd better hustle down to the riverbank or else he'll get a whipping. He runs to deliver the shopping baskets, certain they won't give him a tip; his aunt will slap his neck: *You were standing around with your head in the clouds like you always do, you good-for-nothing boy.* The thought torments him as he stands before Judge Gold's door.

Luis knows he's not a good-for-nothing, it's just that sometimes he gets distracted. It's like time stops for him; what seems like half a second to Luis is an hour for normal folks. And sometimes it's the reverse: one second seems like it lasts hours to Luis. He loses all concept of time.

The door opens. "The shopping baskets?" Thump, thump. Luis sets them down and shoots off like a firework, thinking it's getting late.

The woman who sells fresh tortillas (she has them wrapped up in her shawl) sees him coming and calls, "Luis! Luis!" She's fond of him, he works so hard and he's always hungry. She puts a rolled-up, salted tortilla in each of his hands, "Here, sonny, your tacos."

Toothless, the old beggar who's more wrinkled than Methuselah, sidles over to see if there's a handout for him, too. The tortilla-seller pretends she doesn't see him—she can't stand him, she knows him from back when he used to say he was a monk and chased anything in a skirt; then word came out that he wasn't a monk at all; he had tried to become a priest, but they kicked him out of the seminary. She goes on her way.

Luis stands, chewing his warm tortillas, no longer lost in time, just savoring his food. Toothless wants to speak to him:

"John Tanner, the White Indian, is back, his ghost has arisen from the swamp . . . He's looking for his last wife, Alice, she was his only white wife. I knew her but I won't say why she left him, took their children, and got a divorce. Imagine that! Even the Law has a screw loose; whomsoever God brings together let no man put asunder! It's those gringos, they're heretics . . . John Tanner lived with the Ojibwa for thirty-one years. There's no mistaking that. Returning to the south? Seems like his stay in hell screwed up his sense of direction . . ."

The toothless beggar squats down and grabs poor Luis by the shins, continuing:

"He'd be better off going after his second wife, that floozy tried to kill 'im. As bad as she was, Alice never sank a knife into him. She even made him a little bit happy . . . Don't misunderstand me! John Tanner wasn't passionate about her, he only loved her a little, like an old man who spits on his dick and yanks it up and down to no effect. And that's all I'm gonna say because there are kids around—I'm not talking about you, you've been a midget since you were born . . . but you'll grow out of it."

Luis offers Toothless his second tortilla, which has gotten cold and broken into pieces. But Toothless doesn't let him go. He has a hold of him by the shins and keeps on talking:

"John Tanner is in these parts . . . After Alice left him, they accused him of killing Young Schoolcraft, the brother of the guy who was driving the Indians down south. They called him Old Schoolcraft and he was a bastard, he burned their teepees, stole their women and let his troops abuse them, and then returned them to the Indians after, so they could see what had become of them; he blocked their wells, he drove them into rocky territory where it never, ever rained, and of course he stole their livestock and horses, but I guess everyone does that nowadays. But money doesn't grow on trees anymore and people have started stealing everything from one another . . . Yeah, the White Indian used to fly into rages, but he's not the one who killed Young Schoolcraft. They strung him up on the gallows all the same, the crooked Law got its hands on him. You know where the Law keeps its hand, right? It fell off and got stuck up its ass."

Luis's eyes widen. Silent, so absorbed that he doesn't even swallow.

"The White Indian is a lost soul! He roams these parts . . . wreaking havoc, he's hoppin' mad . . . no one I know would dare call his spirit . . . You, shortie, cross yourself if you think he's nearby. And light candles to the Virgin if you can."

The old beggar lets Luis's shins go, and—ta-da!—disappears as fast as a soul in the devil's clutches. Thanks to the specter of the White Indian things have become much worse for Luis . . . "Boy, now I'm really late!"

Skewbald passes through the Market Square on his way to stock up on coal for the kitchen and the bathroom (his mother has fallen out with the coal merchant), whipping his donkey because he wants to get home to close the windows and sprinkle dill water on the doors. No way is John Tanner, the White Indian, going to sneak his way in.

Sandy, Eagle Zero to a select few, continues running in the same direction, along the river to the Gulf, instead of toward Mrs. Big's hotel's dock. Her neckline displays her charms as a means of distraction: it is her protection, her shield, her armor, her passport, her strength, her currency, her attraction, and her means of providing for herself in times of need.

Olga is hurrying to Judge Gold's house to tell him about the knife when she runs into Miss Lace. In faltering speech (she's out of breath) she tells the story.

Calmly, Miss Lace shares the news about the return of the White Indian, John Tanner. Olga forgets about the knife and moves on to spread the news about John Tanner.

Miss Lace goes to tell Minister Fear about Nat stealing the Lipans' knife. Miss Lace also tells him about the return of the White Indian, John Tanner, and Minister Fear rebukes her as if she has stolen the knife herself for believing in "such foolishness." Minister Fear asks Miss Lace to find Nat and bring him over; he'll speak to the boy. (Wicked tongues say he does more than speak with boys, though it's just gossip.)

The news that Steve, the longshoreman, delivers to Mrs. Stealman doesn't please her, although he had hoped it would. Mexicans aren't welcome at her parties but, at the express request of her husband, Sabas and Refugio have been invited today.

"I know I shouldn't swear, but . . . damn!"

Mrs. Stealman (née Vert, but that's a secret because her husband doesn't want word to get around—there's a rumor that France is plotting to invade Mexico which makes the gringos nervous) doesn't celebrate Shears's insult. The sheriff's shoes were too big for him to fill, he's just a lousy carpenter, and she really doesn't like the news about the gunshot. She takes the news better when she hears it from Frank, who speaks with less enthusiasm about the carpenter and more fear about Nepomuceno ("You know, Ma'am, the one they call the Red Bearded Rogue, the bandit, but he's also a respectable man"). Well done, Frank. He'll get a handsome tip, which will be entered in Elizabeth's accounts ledger under the heading *July 10, 1859*, beneath costs of the flowers, soap, ironing of the linens, meat and produce, milk, eggs, cream, and cheese. She never recorded the cost of the cart (it's her own property) or the cost of the feed for the horses that pull it. But no more expenses today, it's not payday.

Elizabeth is a Southerner, the daughter of a sugar plantation owner who became so obsessed with creating the elixir of youth that he became insufferable. So his wife moved to the northeast with her two marriageable daughters.

In Bruneville Elizabeth is called Mrs. Lazy because she never sets foot outside the house. She doesn't even let her slaves go out—these stunners were part of her dowry, but she couldn't take them with her to New York. They've become overweight from being kept indoors.

To spell it all out: the former Miss Vert forbade her slaves to set foot in the street to protect them from Mexicans, "Because I read the papers!" She had read that the locals were polygamous and walked around half-naked, satisfying their basest instincts. When Bruneville began to fill up with gringos, Germans, Frenchies, Austrians, Cubans, and even some Chinese (Chung Sun and his companions), Mrs. Lazy didn't lift her ban for the simple reason she was afraid one of them might try to escape across the river ("The help is restless!") since Bruneville is right on the border. But she's careful not to mention this around her slaves—she doesn't want to give them any ideas. She herself doesn't go out because, in her opinion, there's not much to see.

If you spent any time observing life within the Stealman mansion, you'd see that "Mrs. Lazy" isn't a good epithet because she endeavors to maintain the ostentatious standard of living to which she's accustomed, no small feat in this "isolated island," as she calls Bruneville in her diary, "an island of ever-changing indecencies."

Perhaps she uses the word "island" to describe Bruneville because she's confused: Originally they were going to move to Galveston Island, which was a tax-free zone, but when the tax-free zone was expanded (back when it was part of Mexico), and since Stealman believed that better profits could be made by owning land, he decided to try his luck further south. It was a good instinct: he leased hectares from the Mexican government and manipulated the law to make them his own, along with neighboring property and even more land along the Río Bravo.

The former Miss Vert dreamed of Galveston—her husband and his friends made it out to be a bustling metropolis—imagining a city without wild Indians, hurricanes, greedy immigrants, or, most importantly, Mexicans. For years now she has spent her time complaining instead of dreaming.

After Frank and Steve depart, Mrs. Stealman gives specific instructions to her servants and shuts herself in her room with her worries:

1. Will they find that fugitive, Nepomuceno, today? Yes or no?
2. Will his brothers come to the house to appeal for clemency on his behalf? Yes or no?
3. Will guests show up or will they think it's wiser to cancel?

She's overwhelmed, fretting: "so much expense, and it could be for nothing"; "he may be their brother but he's a red-bearded rogue";

"I hope they hang him from the nearest tree to take those Mexicans down a peg."

She opens her diary, as she always does when she needs to bare her soul to a confidante. But she never writes about her guests—that would be bad luck. As a result, her entries are somewhat opaque.

Mrs. Stealman writes in peacock-blue ink, as befits her personality and her class.

Her diary is written in the style of letters to her unmarried self. Each entry begins the same way. In cramped letters she writes the sender's name and address at the top, and in the center in even tighter script, "12 Elizabeth Street, Bruneville, Texas" (Stealman named Bruneville's main street after his wife despite opposition; he named the street running parallel after his firstborn son, James; and he named the one to the Town Hall Charles, after himself). A half-inch lower, her handwriting loosens up. Her penmanship is elegant and steady, unlike the figures in her accounts ledger, which look like they've been scribbled in a hurry to hide something:

Dear Elizabeth Vert:

What happened today in Bruneville would have made you happy. Finally, something to rejoice about in this godforsaken place. It was high time someone began to enforce law and order and that someone else got their just desserts. The sheriff—for whom you know I hold little regard—tried to arrest one of the drunken greasers who loiter around the Market Square as if it were a den of iniquity. Public decency is destroyed by the Mexicans' disgusting ways. I don't wish to offend your sensibilities by sharing tales of drunkenness, dirtiness, depravity, gambling, and loose women. But what happens in the marketplace in the broad light of day before the eyes of women and children is worse than what happens in the most sinister of places.

Good for the sheriff. He's got to start somewhere cleaning up this place.

But such labors are never carried out unopposed by evil. The drunken greaser resisted. Another Mexican came to his defense. The Sheriff cut him off. The Mexican emptied his pistol into him, but thanks to his poor aim they say the sheriff is only superficially wounded. They're taking him to Minister Fear's clinic because Dr. Meal is in Boston. The minister's new wife, Eleonor, who is a saint (and has the face of one, too), will attend to him. We all hope he's in no danger and will be better in a few days. Mexican evil should not be the demise of one of our own!

All this, as I said, is cause for rejoicing. Tomorrow I'll tell you who the Mexican who wounded the sheriff is, because it's quite upsetting and I don't want to ruin your day, although I will share one thing: do you remember the woman with long black hair that people kept telling me about—the one who follows Charles around too closely and whom I suspect he might have feelings for? Well, she was in the crowd cheering on the sheriff for arresting the drunkard. Perhaps she's so ignorant she never learned this phrase from the book of the holy word: Let he who is without sin cast the first stone. The vixen! The devious vixen. (I came up with this name for her last night when I heard that she had been following Judge White around. She's chasing a different man every other day!)

I send affectionate greetings, with a dash of hope,
Mrs. Stealman

Rebecca, Sharp's sister, is so ugly that everyone assumes she'll become an old maid, despite the fact she's wealthy. Nothing would make her happier than to marry Alitas—or anyone else—but Sharp is also single and disinclined to marry her off, least of all to a new-comer who has stolen some of his business with the crazy notion of selling dead, plucked chickens in parts—that's how he got the nickname Alitas, "Wings," in Spanish. Sharp was dumbfounded by how successful it had been. Some folks buy the heads for soup, some buy just legs or breasts or organs. "People are crazy."

The news that Shears insulted Nepomuceno makes its way to her house, along with word that Sharp has finally spoken to Alitas. But she hears nothing about the gunshot, they left that part out so as not to worry her. She couldn't care less that Shears has insulted Nepomuceno—when they were younger she had tried to attract his attention, but in vain; he had eyes only for the widow he ended up marrying (Isa) after the unfortunate episode with Rafaela and a brief, passionate fling with her friend Silda, who died of a broken heart, thanks to Nepomuceno (it would be pointless to try to change her opinion: after what happened with Rafaela, all sorts of tragedies have been pinned on him).

"He spoke to him! There's still hope!" She's not sure if she can still bear him children but at least she won't be an old maid.

Rebecca is overjoyed. In her head she sings, "Alitas, Alitas, ra-ra-ra!"

On the other side of the Río Bravo, in Matasánchez, El Iluminado thinks he must be the last to hear what everyone's talking about.

He's coming out of a trance: "The Virgin has spoken to me" (his previous vision had been of the Archangel Michael): "My most enlightened son, you were given your name for a reason; men without faith are like the sleeping Lazarus. A spear flies through the air. Follow it, it will awaken your people and they, the sinners, will be redeemed; but be careful, carry my light at the tip of the spear, and take care not to drink from Devil's Lake."

Numbers aren't his thing, but even El Iluminado can put one and two together (the spear plus Nepomuceno). Should he go join Nepomuceno? Is the Virgin's apparition a coincidence?

He retreats back into his state of grace, no longer in a delirium, just dreaming.

—

María Elena Carranza knows something's bothering her son, but she doesn't know it's the news that Jones has delivered. Anyone can see that something has come over Felipillo Holandés, but she notices the most. Felipillo is the substitute for her three grown sons, whose departure she'll never recover from.

She sees them only when they're on vacation. The eldest, Rafael, studies at Chapultepec Military Academy in the capital. The second, José, is at the state school in Puebla. The third, Alberto, is at Jesuit boarding school in Monterrey.

It was on one of these visits home, four years ago now, that they spotted an enormous black heron resting on the trunk of a kapok that had been uprooted by a hurricane and washed up on the beach during the night. The tree was ravaged yet magisterial. The tide was beginning to come in. Wedged at a right angle between two branches of the trunk was a naked boy in a hollowed-out log lined with cotton buds, like a Moses basket, crying. Maria Elena saw him first—her sons' visit had renewed her feelings of loss and lately she found her eyes following little children. José, Alberto, and Rafael got out of the car to rescue the abandoned child.

"An hour more and he would have been a goner."

"He was about to fall out of his crib."

He looked like he was about three years old. He was so blond his hair was white. He had blue eyes. When Maria Elena took him into her arms the kid stopped crying.

They named him Felipillo Holandés, because they thought he was from Holland on account of his hair and the fact they didn't understand a word he was saying; they thought he was a survivor of the recently shipwrecked *Soembing*. In actuality, it's unclear whether his mother was the Indian Polca, who was famous for searching among the battle dead for the body of her husband, Milco, or Lucoija, a beautiful warrior.

Felipillo understood Spanish though, and realized they thought he was from the shipwreck; he intuited that this misapprehension was a good thing, and he never spoke another word of Karankawa again.

To this day he understands that he must never reveal his true identity, he must masquerade as another; he has no idea that Holandés means "Dutch."

Everything and everyone frighten him, except birds, especially one called Copete; small and brown, he has a colored crest and Felipillo comes every morning to see Copete flit between the flowers in the climbing vines. Felipillo is drawn to him because he's the most nervous of the birds, so fearful he never alights on the bougainvillea where he can be seen, but only out of sight.

Felipillo would like to be like Copete, attending to his needs in seclusion.

He understands, though he can't articulate it, that for "his" new family, he is like one of the pieces of broken china he used to collect on the beach. A curiosity from far-off shores.

If they only knew the truth.

Felipillo Holandés knows Nepomuceno well: he is a heartless man who, along with his ragged band of followers, murdered Felipillo's kin.

Felipillo Holandés recognized him in Matasánchez, soon after he was rescued. He recognized his voice coming out of church one day. He heard people call him "Don Nepomuceno, a man of courage who protects us from the savages." At the time the boy wasn't beset by the melancholy that plagues him today with images of slaughter. Nepomuceno is a mirror that reflects amputated limbs, running blood, and spilled brains.

The last of the Karankawa has his ancestors etched in his memory, though they're nothing more than fragments. Folks from

Matasánchez see a beautiful little boy, but he is a walking chopping block. His Karankawa feelings run so deep that even they can be traced back through his ancestors. Felipillo Holandés is paleskinned because his grandmother came from the other side of the ocean—another piece of broken china. She was traded for a canoe full of skins and ten pounds of dried fish (she was broken, but useful; hardheaded, with her wrinkly pale skin, she became the chief's favorite wife, "not that it means much," it didn't afford her a life of "dignity." She was one of the savage's four or five wives, she spent long days cleaning, curing, and dyeing hides with foul-smelling liquids that ate through her fingernails; yet she always knew things could have turned out worse).

He especially remembers (in his bones) his mother and his older brother—a mean-spirited and unhappy boy who thought he ruled the world, but that's another story. His older brother was the son of a woman who fell out of favor with the Karankawa paterfamilias and grew into a bitter young man without talent or brains who, to avenge himself, sexually abused his younger sisters. He was an ugly and lazy good-for-nothing.

Felipillo has a recurring nightmare: he arrives at the beach where the Karankawas left him like Moses (there's nothing new under the sun). He walks away from the water. Nepomuceno and his men appear, screaming and shouting on that terrible day. He knows he's been saved by a miracle once, and that it won't happen again. He bawls, anticipating death. Then he awakens, sometimes with "mama" Maria Elena at his side, shushing him.

Today he's bursting with grief, but he doesn't show it.

Laura, his neighbor, is the one who can't stop crying and sniveling. She was captured by the Chicasaw and Nepomuceno rescued her. He's her hero, her saint: "How could they do such a thing to my savior?"

The truth is there was nothing heroic about her rescue. If you don't want to be scalped in the Far North, you need fearlessness, imagination, courage, bravery, and a little heroism, but under the circumstances none of these were necessary. It was pretty straightforward, but we should explain what the girls were doing there:

Some idiot decided to build his ranch (called El Bonito) north of old Castaño, thinking it would be a cinch. He brought along two pretty little fillies (his wife and his sister-in-law) to look after his needs night and day, as well as some servants to do the work. He thought things were going well, but in actual fact the women didn't even know how to crack an egg. But that's not the reason he was unprepared to defend them when the Indians attacked. He didn't have the faintest clue about anything out there: not that the Americans were driving the tribes into Indian Territory, not that the buffalo were dying out due to the planting of grasslands for cattle and because of all the buffalo hunters, nor that their lands had become barren. Why on earth would they let him set up house in the same place they wanted to settle?

They burnt both husband and wife to a crisp inside their home. Him for being in the way, and her for belonging to him. The servants were scalped because they worked for him. The housekeeper had her throat slit, who knows why (she had always been a little ornery, if they had taken the time to look at her, they might have thought she was his mother). They took what little livestock there was (the fool was clueless about animals, too), along with Lucia and her niece, Laura, who was just two years old.

When Nepomuceno recognized Lucia in the Chickasaw camp and offered to ransom her, she refused. She couldn't return to Matasánchez with the half-breed baby she had borne them, it would bring shame on her parents, especially her mother. And she wasn't about to leave the baby behind. She asked Nepomuceno to take her niece, but not in so many words. She simply removed the kerchief that was covering her head.

"Look, Nepomuceno."

The beautiful head of curly, fair hair that he had once admired was gone, her locks shorn. This hit Nepomuceno hard. He recalled their walks around the bandstand in Matasánchez while the band played when, boldly, he took her arm. His first wife had just died. Lucia awakened him from his reverie:

"I'm talking to you! Wake up, follow me."

She took him to Chief Buffalo Hump, her husband, and pointed openly to his long hair—her hair—matted and stinking.

When the chief saw they were looking at him, he stroked his fake hair with pride.

Then they retreated to where they were out of earshot.

"Now you've seen what he did to me. He cuts the hair of all his women and weaves it into his own. And there's more."

She told him all about the savages' sexual habits. From the herbs they smoked to help them see the world differently to how they loaned each other their women "to use them, all the males of his family, along with his friends, have used me." She had once spoken like a young lady, now she described these orgies with specific details about all kinds of penetration. "There's something else I can't tell you, Nepomuceno." What could it be, after everything she had already told him? This really did hit him hard. That's when she begged him, "Take the girl home to my mother, her name is Laura, she was born on El Bonito Ranch."

The printer, Juan Prensa, steps on the pedal of his press and pulls the lever of the ink roller. He arose before dawn, intending to finish printing the full run of posters for the circus's upcoming visit before lunch. This is his second job for Mr. Ellis Producer, and he's hoping for more.

The previous day he had set the type (large wooden letters that read TRIUMPHANT WORLD TOUR) and he had printed all the posters with the image of a red elephant, which would not be appearing in this pitiful circus. There would be other animals but no elephant; he had just finished the proof of the letters in blue ink.

Perhaps it's due to the humidity, or the paper's quality, or a rebel ink roller, or because the printing block shifted during the night, but the fact is that Juan Prensa can't run even one good copy. He is in a foul mood when Roberto, the runaway slave, delivers the news about what has happened to Nepomuceno, at which point his work for the day is done. He cleans the ink roller, leaves the wet paper to dry, and heads out.

Dr. Velafuente walks along Hidalgo Street on his way home, his shoulders a little stooped, tired and worn down by the change in routine, when he runs into El Iluminado.

"Good afternoon, Guadalupe."

El Iluminado no longer recognizes his name. He doesn't hear it. Skeleton-like, his teeth rotting and blackened, he is lost in another world.

"Say hello to your mother for me, tell her I was asking after her."

He doesn't respond because he doesn't hear. The doctor goes on his way, mumbling to himself, "Lupe, I always knew something was wrong with you, even before I set eyes on your face, when you came into the world feet first, as if being born was like going to your grave. Ay, Lupe, Guadalupe. Your poor mother couldn't sit down for months because of you. I had to stick my arm up inside her to get the cord unwound from your neck. And then you had to go wind it around yourself again, you were twisting and turning uncontrollably in there. Your feet were sticking out like a cadaver's but you were kicking. Lupe, Guadalupe. You've been crazy since before you were born. I wouldn't have expected anything else from you. And now you call yourself El Iluminado. The truth is you're mad as a hatter,

Lupe, and always have been. Who the hell was your father? What stars were shining the night you were born?"

Jones, who makes candles and soaps, tirelessly walks the streets of Matasánchez with his colorful basket, though no one ever buys any of his perfumed wares. He sees downcast Father Vera sitting at the top of the seven stairs that lead to the wooden door of the main church.

Jones never stops for Father Vera, he's not stupid and he knows that the priest dislikes him and thinks he's a heretic because he's read the whole Bible from cover to cover several times (proof to the priest that Jones is a damned Protestant). But he doesn't look threatening, sitting there in bewilderment with his cassock rolled up, and since today is a special day when everyone is talking to each other, he greets him.

"Padre," he addresses him the same way everyone else does, "have you heard about the lousy carpenter and Don Nepomuceno?"

"I already heard about it, my son, from the pigeon-keeper in Dr. Velafuente's office." He immediately regrets telling him, it's like he's confessed his unspeakable sin. He blushes. Then he raises his eyes. He immediately recognizes a slight arrogance in Jones—the well-read usually are—but he wants to take advantage of this opportunity and his evangelical instincts overcome his shame.

"Don't you want to confess, Jones?"

"What for?"

Father Vera sighs loudly.

Jones takes the sigh as an invitation. He sets his basket down on the third stair, steps on the fourth, and sits down on the fifth.

"Father Vera, you think the gringos are going to attack us?"

"Out of the question. Absolutely not."

"Why?"

"Because they won't. God's truth."

As he says this he gets to his feet and leaves.

Jones leans on his basket. He closes his eyes. He immediately falls asleep. He dreams of boats, treasure, sugar, food; a series of images that have nothing to do with one another. Boats, desert, ice, lion. A Cherokee woman. Dog. Plate. Rice. Altar. Odor. Castle. Caramel.

It all makes no sense.

While Jones sleeps on the steps of the church, Fidencio passes by with his mule, Sombra. He's wrapped up in his own world.

Back in Bruneville, the buffalo hunter Wild and his sidekick, handsome Trust, leave the Café Ronsard with One, Two, and Three. Their cart and its stinking load are on the north side of the plaza. It's better to walk in the open where they can see what's happening.

Toothless tries to tell them about John Tanner, but they pay him no mind. He asks them for money but gets none.

They get to the cart (where Fernando, Nepomuceno's servant, is still hiding; he knows he's not safe till he's well out of Bruneville without anyone laying eyes on him).

Without further delay they climb in, Wild and Trust up front, with One, Two, and Three in back atop the cargo (squashing poor Fernando, who struggles even harder to breathe), and take the road to the dock where they'll wait for the steamboat out of "this shit town" as soon as possible. Wild is cursing because they couldn't get on board the merchant ship Margarita, Captain Boyle's boat, which has just left. The Captain said there was no room, and it's not the first time he's refused them passage. They'll have to wait, and it's better to do that down at Mrs. Big's.

In all Bruneville there's only one person who hasn't heard the news. Even deaf old Loncha, who cooked for Doña Estefanía for years, the one Glevack lured away from her just to be mean (she was no longer good for anything), even she knows what's happened, thanks to Panchito—the kid everyone else calls Frank, he'll always be Panchito to her, the son of "that poor woman who they took advantage of."

"Indians?" asks Loncha, and Frank-Panchito cuts her off, "No! No!" "Who? Who are you talking about?" Panchito-Frank makes the sign of a star on his chest with one hand and pretends to saw with the other. "Oh! I get it! The sheriff! That dummy Sheas!"

There's no point in correcting her and getting her to add the "r." The realm where r's and s's matter is no longer important to Loncha. Her world is carved in stone. She can hardly see. She can't hear a thing. She doesn't move from her chair. She understands outlines, weight, and courage better than ever. "Knowing everything about everyone," says Loncha, "is boring, all that matters is whether something's interesting or not."

Her head is clearer than it's ever been, unaffected by affairs of the heart. Because Loncha had lots of those. In her day she fell in love with anyone who wore pants, especially vaqueros, who are a dime a dozen on the edge of the prairie.

Let's go back to the guy who is the only person in Bruneville that doesn't know about Shears and Nepomuceno:

In a bed in a room at the back of Minister Fear's house, which Eleonor has set up as an "infirmary," a man shivers and sweats. He is unconscious.

It could be yellow fever; less than three days ago he returned from a trip to the swamps south of Matasánchez, across the Río Bravo, looking for timber as well as laborers to fell it. He found plenty of timber, but finding labor was impossible. He tried to hire the (peaceful) local Indians but he didn't know how to deal with them and decided "they're useless." He didn't bother trying with the Mexicans, he'd heard too much about their habits and vices. So he crossed back over the river to buy Guineans or other slaves who wouldn't know that where he was taking them they would be free men by law.

But before he could make a purchase he got sick with a god-awful ache in his bones. Bruneville's doctor, Dr. Meal, is away in Boston—his daughter is getting married—and hasn't left anyone to cover for him (he watches his back: they'd just steal his patients from him). By crossing the river (or so Dr. Meal thought) the folks from Matasánchez would have access to top-quality medical care (in fact, the doctors over there are better than him: two of them got their degrees in Paris yet they charge their patients less, the only problem is that they don't speak English, only Spanish, French, and German). But this man didn't want to try his luck with *them*, he doesn't trust Mexicans. The little room in the Fears' house is the last resort for folks who might not get better—which would be the case if he has what they think he does—but it's difficult to know for certain under the circumstances.

For the moment, in his fevered delirium, he's not with us.

Eleonor, the minister's wife, attends him. At first sight it's a scene of neutral devotion, a wife fully engaged in her husband's vocation.

But there's more. Eleonor cares for the patient with a secret hope: she wants to catch the sickness of this man whose name she doesn't know.

Eleonor doesn't want to live.

Over in Matasánchez there's also only one person who doesn't know about the insult Shears dared to throw at Nepomuceno: Magdalena, a pretty young woman from Puebla.

Her story, in brief: just before her sixth birthday her mother died. Her father, the son of Spaniards, left her with her aunt and returned to the land of his ancestors, or so he said.

The aunt took in Magdalena partly out of duty to her (deceased) sister, but also for the money. In exchange for looking after and educating the girl (or providing for blah blah blah) she receives a monthly stipend, which is a godsend because she has twelve children and always needs more than her husband provides. That's how things were, and how they would have stayed until Magdalena became an old maid, if not for a lawyer named Gutierrez. He came from the north, had a lot of land, and money too, or so folks said. He was the most prominent lawyer in Matasánchez, and he came to Puebla to wrap up some business for a gringo client. Gutierrez heard about the beautiful orphan girl, her faraway father, her aunt's money problems, the girl's good breeding, and he knew without asking that she would be a virgin.

Magdalena was a sure thing for Gutierrez, an unsullied woman for him and him alone, with no mother, no attachments, no one to come asking for a handout. Since she was young he could mold her as he liked. The ideal wife. She would give him children, and he would finally settle down.

He showed up and made them an offer they couldn't refuse. He didn't ask her aunt for a dowry; in fact he offered them a lump sum payment as a gesture of good faith and promised three more payments over the course of the next ten years. He wanted it to be clear that, once his offer was accepted, Magdalena would be his to the full extent of the law. She would become his exclusive property. There would be no visits, requests, or other nuisances. No favors, no exchanges. He would invite her relations to the wedding, but after the day of the ceremony that would be it. No interference in his life. His only condition for the purchase of the girl was that they leave them in peace.

The aunt (and her family) would lose the monthly stipend from Spain, but they weren't killing the golden goose. Despite the fact the three lump sums amounted to slightly less that the total of the stipend for the same period, there would be no associated costs. Plus, what if Magdalena's father stopped sending the stipend? It had been ages since he'd written or sent a gift. What if he died and left her unprovided for? Sooner or later, the girl would become another mouth to feed. And she was useless as a maid.

"No," the aunt thought, "given such an opportunity, we should accept immediately. If nothing else, for the girl's welfare; my brother-in-law will be indebted to us. It's a good match, and we'll relieve ourselves of this burden." She didn't have to think twice. She accepted the money, signed the contract, and wrote to inform the girl's father. She wisely omitted telling him about the payment to leave the Spaniard wondering if she'd had to marry the girl off quickly for an unspeakable reason. The matter was settled once and for all, no strings attached.

So Magdalena left with this lawyer from the north, Gutierrez. But she didn't go alone. She couldn't be alone with him until they were married. Her aunt had no desire to go to Matasánchez, her world was limited to Puebla—she'd never been to Veracruz, Mexico City, or Havana, why would she go to Matasánchez?—but she accepted the lawyer's invitation to send a chaperone and sent the girl's godmother instead—a woman her own age who was also past her prime but looked years younger because she hadn't given birth twelve times or married an idiot and suffered from poverty and the misfortune of not hearing from her brother for years, despite the fact he was in Bruneville.

It had been ten years already.

Gutierrez celebrated the wedding with a party to show off his pretty bride, and the cream of Matasánchez society showed up to see her. At the end of the evening he took his new wife home in a horse-drawn cart. On the short trip he kept telling her, "Take a good look at Matasánchez, Magdalena, because you'll never see it again."

She heard these words, but she didn't get it. It took some time before she realized Gutierrez was never going to let her set foot out of the house again. "You have to lock up a woman, there's no shortage of cuckolds in the world, and there's no such thing as a female who can keep her legs closed."

The wedding night terrified the poor girl. She had no idea what men did to women or what part women were supposed to play. She wasn't old enough for what seemed to be repulsive, cruel gymnastics. But she didn't call it gymnastics—the poor girl had never even been to the circus—she had no idea what to call this bouncing exercise in which he used her as a trampoline. Gutierrez, on the other hand, who was twelve years older than her (and had gotten around), had his first lover at seventeen.

And that's how it was for four years, until the lawyer got bored and found somewhere else to wet his dick.

"Stupid girl, you're all dried up." How could he fail to realize he might have been the problem, after so many years of whoring without producing a single bastard child? Although, of course, there's Blas, but who knows whether or not he's his. "I'm not going to use you anymore, you bag of bones; you can't have children. I should never have married you. We'll see if you ever bear fruit."

Gutierrez never stopped to think that when he began to use her, she still hadn't begun to menstruate.

Due to the shock of what he did to her, Magdalena's body took longer to mature. When she got her first period four months after he had rejected her, Magdalena thought she was bleeding for two reasons: because Gutierrez had ruptured her insides by doing what he had done to her so many times, and because he had stopped doing it. She felt guilty for the second reason.

"I'm bleeding and it's my fault, my own grievous fault."

It was a while before she understood what the accusation of a barren womb meant. Josefina, the old cook, who was kind to her out of pity, explained.

Magdalena was full of resentment when she realized that's why he had begun to hit her. He began to embellish his farcical trampoline routine by hitting her afterwards. For any reason at all, or for no reason, because the table wasn't ready when he arrived ("Magdalena, lazy, lazy!"), or because he didn't like the soup, or because he'd had a problem at work, although Magdalena had nothing to do with it, or because she became more beautiful each day, or because she laughed easily and had fun with the servants, the needlework, the housekeeping, and the cooking.

She might as well have lived on the moon, yet even his blows couldn't dampen her innate joy. Who knows where it came from.

The day Shears insults Nepomuceno, Magdalena doesn't know a thing. And even if she heard the news it wouldn't matter, because she has no idea who Nepomuceno is.

(Wagging tongues say the lawyer Gutierrez had a fling with Magdalena's godmother. They say he gave her a son, which was a miracle, a barren land yielding a flower; she called him Blas, a pompous old name, which suits a bastard to a T.)

An "I-wanna-be-freebooter" gringo stops in Matasánchez, Mr. Blast. In this Shears-Nepomuceno business he smells the opportunity he has been waiting for: to invade and annex more territory for Texas. "I know how this will go down, I saw it firsthand in Nicaragua with William Walker, the original freebooter." He's confident Nepomuceno can be the springboard for his plan, and he prepares to put it into action.

All of Bruneville experiences several hours of confusion, even the one person who doesn't know what Shears has said, the adventurer who's lying in the rickety old bed in the missionaries' infirmary. His fever develops into a violent delirium, he shouts, hits, and kicks.

Eleonor considers asking for help from "that man," whom fate has made her husband, Mr. Fear. But she immediately rejects the idea. It is a physical struggle, but she manages to control her delirious patient; she gets him back into the rickety little bed and removes his shirt. She runs the palm of her hand across his damp chest. She is sweating too, from so much exertion.

She is the minister's wife, trained as a teacher, devoted to the well-being of the community, serving the needs of others, and all these facts would lead anyone observing the scene to be favorably inclined to her. But they'd have an altogether different impression if they could understand the feelings awakened by touching the sick man's chest.

To clarify: she perceives in him the shadow of death and it seduces her, stirs her emotions, draws her in and, to be completely frank, excites her.

She dips a cloth in a bucket of cold water. She rubs it across the patient's chest. She dries him with a rag. Then she touches him. She has grown fond of the hairs on his manly chest; she twists them around her fingers.

She caresses him once more. His delirium has abated. He's breathing normally.

Then he becomes agitated again, as if something in his dreams is disturbing his peace. He's sweating buckets. Eleonor quickly wets the cloth again and rubs it across his chest.

The patient calms down. Eleonor puts her hand on his chest, runs it up to his chin and back. She winds the curly little hairs on his manly chest around her fingers again. His breathing is calm. But hers is not.

Let's return to the confusion in Bruneville:

In the market, Sharp proclaims his opinion (he hates Nepomuceno because he stole one of his cows, which didn't give much milk but would have given him a calf), and Alitas gives *his* opinion. Sharp and Alitas come to blows. The greengrocer jumps in.

Then the Frenchie seed vendor joins the fight and thumps Sharp. Sid Cherem, the cloth merchant, begins to shout because he doesn't want to take sides. A crazy man, "El Loco," who sleeps beneath the eaves of the main entrance to the market—we haven't met him yet because he's usually out of sight—looks for something to set alight, he feels the urge to start a fire. Tadeo, the cowboy, can't get an erection with Flamenca. Clara, the daughter of the trapper, Cruz, learns from her father's seamstress that her boyfriend, Mateo, who is also a cowboy, was getting it on with Perla, her maid. Much to his regret and contrary to expectations, the womanizer Hector loses a card game to Jim Smiley, who doesn't celebrate, because his jumping frog (the one he's been training to win bets for him) is croaking in its box, "What's wrong, my little pretty?" Leno, seeing he has lost—he needs the money much more than Hector—resorts to a humiliating tactic: he begins to cry and beg for loans. Tiburcio the widower, desperately lonely as always—it's been eighteen years since he was widowed by the saintly woman who (he's never dared confess this to anyone) died a virgin because she had asked him to be patient, and he was so patient that Saint Peter opened the doors of heaven to her before she opened her legs to him—sits frozen in his chair, confused. Sabas and Refugio, Judge Gold, the traitor Glevack, and Olga the washerwoman become embroiled in a stupid argument that really doesn't have anything to do with them—a cart loaded with bundles of cotton knocks one of the flowerpots off Doña Julia's balcony, Olga hears the noise and calls for help; Glevack, the brothers, and Judge Gold come running, under the impression it's an emergency—the five of them circle around the pieces of broken flowerpot, not understanding why Olga raised the alarm, grinding the pieces of broken flowerpot into dust.

The maid who cleans rooms in the hotel where the photographer La Plange is staying—she's cousin to Sandy, aka Eagle Zero, the one with the revealing neckline (and who shares a room with her in the annex of Mrs. Big's hotel, much to her shame, since it's also a brothel)—is horrified by the photographs she finds in the window: Snotty, the kid who follows La Plange around like a shadow, is naked in positions that make her feel sick.

Miss Lace remembers she's left her baskets at the market; she doesn't know Luis delivered them. She stops looking for Nat and walks to Judge Gold's house.

The wealthy Negro, Tim Black, is in a quandary. Ten years ago, when he arrived in Indian Territory from New Orleans with a fur trader (via the Mississippi to the Arkansas River, and by land to Santa Fe), he was welcomed with open arms and made a fortune, allowing him to buy a white woman from Texas and her two-year-old daughter from the Waco Indians. In the middle of the crowd of people in the Market Square he has just seen a man who ("I swear on my mother's name.") is identical to his wife and daughter. The spitting image. A more distinctive face you won't find. It must be her brother, or worse, her husband, come to take her away—or so he thinks—*This'll be the end of me, the end, they'll ruin me . . .* He's so consumed by his worries he doesn't realize they're completely unfounded.

Eleonor is still wetting the cloth in the bucket of water and rubbing it on her patient's chest, devoted to her work—and fascinated, too—when they bring her the bloody carpenter (or sheriff) Shears. Four or five of them are carrying him. They have already stopped to see Mr. Chaste (the pharmacist and mayor), who cut Shears's pant leg away from the wound to get a better look at it. Mr. Chaste said he wouldn't touch it because the bullet is lodged in Shears's muscle. Eleonor had better steel herself because the poor devil won't make it to Matasánchez bleeding like this—"It would kill him to try to make it to Matasánchez."

She leaves the damp cloth spread across her patient's chest.

She asks them to lay Shears on the table. She lifts her patient's bucket of water from the floor and empties it onto Shears's leg to get a better look. Immediately Eleonor inserts the infirmary's tweezers into the wound—they're meant for removing splinters and the like, but they might do the trick; they penetrate his muscle, "Ow, ow," Eleonor can feel them scrape the bullet, "ow," she shoves the tweezers deeper, "ow"—each "ow" weaker than the last—the tweezers pinch the bullet, "ow," they slip off the metal, "ow," she keeps digging, "ow, ow" (you can barely hear him any longer). "Be brave." Eleonor keeps digging with the tweezers, "Ow." "Be quiet." They stumble upon the bullet again, and voila, who knows how, the bullet appears between the bloody, flat ends of the tweezers.

Eleonor's face lights up, she is pleased. She leaves Shears, grabs the damp, warm cloth off her other patient's chest, wrings it out, wraps it around Shears's wounded thigh and ties it tight, knotting it with all her might, which is considerable.

"No one touches the sheriff, he stays right here."

Shears is pale, mute.

The minister is on the patio, his stomach is upset at the sight of so much blood so near. He too is pale and mute.

Eleonor leaves the room to fill her bucket. She walks past her husband without even noticing he is there.

She passes him again on her return, the full bucket in her left hand and the oil lamp in her right. This time she does notice him.

"I'm going to cauterize the vein. I'll try to melt the bullet so that a drop falls on the wound to close it. If that doesn't work, I don't know…"

Melt? Cauterize? Minister Fear is afraid of this woman, his wife. He thinks, "I married some kind of pirate, she loves blood." His stomach does a somersault and cramps ignite like sparks, all of a sudden he urgently needs to use the chamber pot.

—

Minister Fear squats over the chamber pot. The lightning and the sparks in his gut have disappeared in the darkness. But this darkness is suspicious; he knows that if he leaves the chamber pot he'll just have to hurry back. A storm is approaching in his gut. Meanwhile, all is calm and he thinks about Nepomuceno.

Years ago, when Nepomuceno first learned about Glevack's betrayal, he left the Town Hall and turned onto Charles Street, where he stopped in front of Minister Fear's front door and exploded: "Me, a cattle thief! How dare they accuse me, Nepomuceno, of stealing livestock! How many head have these newcomers stolen from *me*, folks who think they're important because they "created" the Independent Republic of Texas! They're outrageous! Who cares whether they made some republic! What else would you expect from people whose number one priority is to defend slavery?! Texans! And after they annexed our land, the Yankees showed up, thinking there were easy pickings here—stealing our land, our livestock, our mines— they took over everything from the Nueces River to the Río Bravo!

Because let's call a spade a spade: they didn't buy it, they didn't fight for it. When all is said and done it was theft, pure and simple. And I'm the very last person who could be accused of such a thing. You'd have to be shameless to do that. Their hands are full but they keep taking more. They don't even do the dirty work, they hire Indians or low-lifes who know what they're doing and pay them per head of cattle captured. You see, it's one thing to hustle the animals that get separated from the herd, help the animals that wander off, they're obviously surplus, because you always leave stragglers behind, that's just the way it is, it's only natural. It's the plains that feed the animals and the animals belong to the plains, and if you're handy with a lasso then it's your right to take them and breed them because you know you're gonna leave some others behind. That's how things were before these gringos arrived and laid down their newfangled laws. They're animals. I've done a lot for the breeding of herds and sowing of grass. And they try to accuse *me* of being a *cattle thief*? Me?! They're the thieves, every last one of them! You, Glevack, you dog! That's how you repay my family's generosity, you double-crossing snake?!"

And that's how Nepomuceno harangued the minister's front door.

Seated on the chamber pot, Fear thinks of him, then tries to make sense of what his wife is doing with the bullet that Nepomuceno fired into Shears's leg. That's what he's thinking when the lighting in his gut returns, and a fetid stream fills the chamber pot.

Peter Hat, having closed up his house in anticipation of all hell breaking loose, erupts into a fury as soon as he finishes praying. He directs his anger at Michaela, his wife, as if she were the one responsible for what's happening in Bruneville. Any reason will do: Michaela had planned to meet Joe, the Lieders' oldest son, in the Market Square to pick up some bread. They hate the white bread that's popular in Bruneville due to the bad influence of the French: small individual rolls, some of which are decorated with sugar; they have no heft, no weight, no seeds. At his orders she didn't go to the market and now there's no bread in the house. Peter Hat is livid. "You can't have a meal without bread, that's absurd! Who knows how many days we're going to be shut in! You're such an idiot!"

("White bread doesn't nourish you," Joe's mother says. "Give your child white bread and you'll end up with a Dry or a Minister Fear, pigheaded folk. You have to leave seeds in the bread. The dough should rise, but not like foam. It's bread, not air! You want a stupid son or a useless daughter? Just feed them French bread.")

Trapper Cruz walks through his front door and finds his daughter going crazy, screaming and tearing her clothes. "What's wrong with you?" He goes out to the patio; at the far side his maid Perla's door is open and he sees what has upset Clara: the woman he thought was his faithful servant has hitched up her skirts for a cowboy, that pathetic Mateo.

Carlos the Cuban is trying to circulate a message to The Eagles. But there's a missing link. Eagle Zero is not at her post—she's usually there, but today of all days she's missing. He suspects someone is following him, but not Dimitri the Russian. He fears this is the end of the Eagles; he thinks the dispute between Shears and Nepomuceno, the girl's absence, and the coming storm are part of a conspiracy to eliminate them. He knows the whereabouts of the money that Nepomuceno gave them after selling the cotton, but he doesn't dare go get it. He doesn't know what to do. He paces up and down the steps of Bruneville's Town Hall, thinking that he won't arouse suspicion in such a public place. Two steps up, two steps down . . .

Everything is in chaos but it's not noisy everywhere: in the room at the back of Minister Fear's house the sick man rests peacefully. Next to him, her eyes wide and fixed on him, sits Eleonor.

Behind her, "It hurts!"

Crybaby carpenter!

"It hurts, it hurts . . ."

So many "it hurts" that Eleonor finally gets up, much to her irritation. She looks at the sheriff's wound, left open to prevent infection. Less than a palm's length up his leg, the cloth remains tightly tied, preventing further bleeding.

She applies mesquite honey from an earthen jar to the wound, it comes from Matasánchez.

The sheriff stops his "it hurts."

"I'm thirsty."

Eleonor fills a cup with water from the bucket.

In the jailhouse, Urrutia and Ranger Neals sit motionless and silent despite their agitation. They look like two statues. The heat is unbearable; drops of sweat drip slowly, slowly down.

On the other side of the Río Bravo, in Matasánchez, things aren't calm either. Shortly after running into Dr. Velafuente, El Iluminado comes to his senses. He hears a voice calling him. It's not the Virgin. It's different, a man's voice, not unlike his own but more high-pitched.

"Psst, Iluminado!"

El Iluminado thinks the voice is coming from the ruined fence around the land next to Laura's house, the girl who was kidnapped by the Indians.

If he had come to his senses a few seconds earlier, he would have heard Laura crying.

"I'm going to help you. Make me your cross and I will speak the Word to all."

The voice is sharp and childish, no one would believe it's coming from this old piece of wood.

Without asking anyone's permission, El Iluminado yanks up the talking board. One strong pull and it detaches from the fence.

"That's right! Well done! Now nail me to the board next to me, crosswise."

El Iluminado puts his hand on the adjacent plank.

"This one?"

He doesn't receive a reply. He takes the silence as a yes.

He breaks it off with his foot, he has only one free hand.

"Well done, Iluminado! Now nail it to my waist."

"What nails should I use?"

"We're going to get some at the store."

"I don't have any money, and Señor Bartolo doesn't give credit."

"I'll talk to him. Let's go!"

El Iluminado carries the two boards, ruined and rotted by fluctuating temperatures and humidity. He carries them in front of him, side by side, his arms extended and his eyes looking heavenward, praying.

"Now what is Lupe up to?" thinks Tulio, the ice cream man, pushing his wooden cart, which keeps the two barrels (lemon and chocolate) cold, packed in salt. The two of them shared a desk in school, he knows Lupe from before his transformation, "though he has always had a screw loose." Back in school, people said Tulio was the crazy one, always making things up.

When he gets to the store, El Iluminado lowers his eyes. The board begins to speak, giving him orders:

"Put me in front of Bartolo."

El Iluminado obeys and goes a step further: he thrusts both boards in Bartolo's face.

Bartolo is just finishing serving Doña Eduviges. Taken aback, the shopkeeper looks at the deranged man who has shoved the boards in his face, so close they're practically touching his eyelashes.

He hears the high-pitched voice clearly as El Iluminado lowers the first board onto the counter and lays the second board perpendicular to it.

"Donate four nails to put me together, so that these two boards can become a cross."

Señor Bartolo is relieved that El Iluminado has lowered the threatening boards, although "they're going to make a mess of the countertop . . ." He turns to get the box of medium-sized nails down with the stepladder. He picks up the hammer. He hits the first nail on the head.

"Ay!" the voice says.

A second blow, another "ay!" (which Bartolo finds amusing), a third, "ay!" and a fourth, "ay!"

The two boards are now a cross. El Iluminado picks it up off the counter, looks at it, says a few incomprehensible and incoherent words, and takes it away without so much as a "thank you."

"Poor Guadalupe gets crazier by the day. What were you saying to me, Doña Eduviges, what were we in the middle of?"

"Say what you want about El Iluminado, Señor Bartolo. I heard that cross, loud and clear. Holy Mother of God!"

Doña Eduviges leaves the store, crossing herself several times. She's barely out of sight before Bartolo starts grumbling:

"What a dimwit! Guadalupe fakes a voice and keeps his lips from moving, and she thinks it's a Talking Cross?"

María Elena Carranza, who is facing him, says thoughtfully:

"Pardon me for saying so, Don Bartolo, but she's right: that cross spoke."

Doña Eduviges goes off to spread the word to all the old church ladies that El Iluminado has a Talking Cross.

North of the Río Bravo, Eleonor is still devotedly wiping the sick man's chest with a damp cloth, completely engrossed in her work. Behind her she hears a weak complaint: "It hurts." It's Shears, the crappy carpenter and crappier sheriff. "It hurts."

South of the Río Bravo, El Iluminado enters the church and stops in front of the font of holy water, whether of his own accord or at the Cross's bidding is unclear.

When El Iluminado is about to dip the (filthy) cross into the holy water, Father Vera (who might also be acting on orders of a holy voice) dashes out of the confessional.

"Hey! Lupe! That's holy water!"

The Talking Cross responds in a frigid tone of voice: "Crucified under Pontius Pilate, he suffered, died, and was buried," and the group of old church ladies following El Iluminado murmur, "Praise the Lord." "Holy be." And other such blessings.

Father Vera takes water from the font and blesses the cross with a long prayer. The church ladies, reeling off strings of "pray for us sinners," keep a short distance; the Talking Cross fills them with fear.

Immediately word gets around that the Talking Cross has been dunked in holy water (which we know is not true), and folks start to believe it has curative powers.

Dr. Velafuente sits down to drink his coffee, though it's earlier than usual. Given the hour, he might upset either his stomach or his bowels. If it's the former, a soda water would put him right; he buys it in bottles imported from London. If it's the latter, he'll take some Atacadizo syrup—Aunt Cuca makes it, she's the only one who knows the recipe—and soon feel better. It's nothing to write home about. *It's the only benefit of not being born a savage . . . not being subject to the vulnerabilities of the flesh. Civilization has remedies, cures, and even surgery if necessary. In all other respects the savages are better off: three or four wives, lives of leisure—when they want to eat they just stretch out a hand and grab a mango or a banana. They have everything they need for soup—turtles and herbs—right at their feet . . . while we just work our fingers to the bone . . .* (He was thinking about savages from the south; for Dr. Velafuente the north was something else altogether: the source of all evil.)

The Café Central in Matasánchez is on one side of the city's Central Plaza, facing the cathedral. The trees' thick foliage obscures the renovations being done on the church—the 1832 hurricane damaged its bell tower. The tables are beneath the arcade, which runs along the storefronts up to the façade of the Hotel Ángeles del Río Bravo, the finest in the region. It's very elegant. In Matasánchez they say that it lacks nothing compared to the best hotels in the world, and it's true. Over the years, Nepomuceno's relatives, as well as his business and political associates, have all stayed there since the very first night it opened. Wagging tongues claim it's yet another of Doña Estefanía's businesses, but that's definitely not true.

At the Café Central there's a little of everything. In the evenings, musicians play late into the night. By day street vendors mill about, civilized Indians from the south who bring exquisite handicrafts, vanilla from Papaloapan, woven crafts from Bajío, embroidery from the southwest, chocolate from Oaxaca, tamales from Istmo, and mole from Puebla. It's quite a sight. Yet there's even greater variety in the clientele sitting at the tables, from folks who can afford the prices, which are not inconsiderable, to folks who while away the hours by stirring a teaspoon in a complimentary glass of water. And the clientele changes by the hour. On weekday mornings, men sit and read the papers or discuss them; after the lunch hour, before siesta, they hang around for a drink or a coffee. Tuesdays at five, when the menfolk have finished their siestas and returned to work, the women gather to drink chocolate and trade gossip, such as news of recent engagements, upcoming baptisms, or their health—it runs the gamut. Travelers also frequent the establishment, the majority of whom are men who have come to buy or sell merchandise, but occasionally they bring their wives and daughters (if they're from the region or if they're en route to the steamboats bound for Havana or New Orleans). When night falls, the folks who are trouble come out. More and more, gunslingers and fortune hunters from north of the Río Bravo can be found at the Café Central's tables. They're the ones primarily responsible for corrupting the establishment, because they come to satisfy appetites for things they wouldn't think of even trying in the north.

Juan Pérez, the wealthy, unscrupulous Indian trader from Mexico, who would sell his own sister if it would profit him, sits two tables over from Dr. Velafuente's usual table. He's no spring chicken, and his sister is the only living relation he has left. His mother died nearly ten years ago, advanced in years and ruined by money and regrets. His brothers were all low-ranking members of the army and became cannon fodder in a variety of battles. He never knew his father. He doesn't have a Christian wife; they say he has married several Indians, but he doesn't recognize any children as his own, and if he ever did have women, he's forgotten them all, even their names (that is, if he ever knew them). To him women are a pair of spread legs, or several pairs, to be exact.

But let's not discuss his sexual appetite and his pelvis-thrusting, which was as legendary as his greed, and how easily he became bored, and his quest for fleeting, intoxicating pleasure. For that you need a young body, two tits (preferably bare), hips, and legs. Once he slept with a woman who had one leg. It wasn't bad. In fact it was somewhat liberating—until he ejaculated, and then he found her repulsive. For a while afterwards he had a recurring nightmare about her until it was replaced by other nightmares, which aren't part of our story.

Juan Pérez, the Indian trader, whose complexion is white as chalk (but if he had a child it might turn out quite dark, you can see the Mexican in him), is drinking rum. He's wearing the finest clothes you can buy in Matasánchez, they're brand-new. He arrived on the barge with plenty of goods to sell, he sold everything successfully, and now he needs to buy goods to take back with him for sale, but before that he's going to enjoy himself a little. The money he's spending is not the money he's just earned. His sister, Lupita, who is dim-witted (on top of everything else), gives him money once in a while, especially when he returns from his expeditions all dirty and skinny. She's an idiot. She thinks it's because he's poor, and she wants to help him. He loses weight from so much riding and eating lean meat, but that's life on the range. She never married, mostly because she's so dark-skinned.

Juan Pérez, the Indian trader, hears the gossip about Shears and Nepomuceno. He knows them both, he's got their numbers. For the time being he thinks, *What do I care.*

At another table at Café Central folks are talking about "their Texas, the Texans' Texas":

"What do you expect from them, their first president . . ."

"Sam Houston . . ."

"Yeah, him. Houston is Apache. Texans are savages, of course."

"The governor?"

"Houston is Scottish."

"No, he's Irish."

"He may be born Scottish or Irish or whatever, but he spent his life with the Indians, and he is one, but not because he was captured; he joined the Cheyenne because he wanted to. He left home at sixteen, he hated working at his brother's store, he learned their ways and the chief adopted him . . . He has a Cherokee wife, maybe several . . . and when his first wife left him he returned to live with them."

"I don't believe you."

"Ask the Indian trader."

"Hey, you, Indian trader! Juan Pérez, I'm talking to you! Isn't it true Sam Houston is Apache?"

"Cherokee, yep."

"But is he really an Indian? Have you seen him with your own eyes?"

"Dressed like an Indian, yep."

"Didn't I tell you? Our lands were taken by the savages."

"Sam Houston," says the Indian trader, "is, besides the Indians, the only good thing north of the Río Bravo, Mexicans included. And that's because of the Cherokee in him."

They ignore his comment and continue their conversation:

"I'm positive he lived in Coahuila, that's where he started fighting to take the North away from us."

"They're such barbarians that they took an Indian name for themselves: Texas!"

"Well, the name Coahuila is also Indian, and that doesn't make us barbarians or savages . . ."

The line that beggars and believers have formed to bless themselves with the holy water where the (miraculous) Talking Cross was dunked snakes all the way to the Town Hall.

In Bruneville, Olga is going around saying that John Tanner, the White Indian, has returned for revenge. This gets folks' attention more than the news about Nepomuceno. Because she didn't move fast enough, folks have already heard that news before she delivers it. By contrast, the way she describes the supposed appearances of John Tanner captivates her listeners in different ways.

She tried to tell Glevack. He thought: *What you need is someone to feel you up, but I'm not about to.* She told the kids who were selling crabs from Hector's cart (Melón, Dolores, and Dimas), and they bought her story hook, line, and sinker. She wanted to tell Eleonor Fear, but no matter how long she banged on her door, there was no answer. Eleonor was in the room out back, attending to her patient, surrounded by a symphony of Sheriff Shears's "it hurts." And the minister is still on the chamber pot with cramps.

At Mrs. Big's card table—gossips say she drinks like a Cossack because she's still in love with Zachary Taylor—someone brings up the story about what she said when she heard the rumor that he had been killed in Mexico. The hostess interrupts in her husky, imposing voice to finish the story herself:

"I told that runt of a man who had the nerve to speak such crap,

'You damn sonofabitch, listen up good to what Mrs. Big's gonna tell you: there ain't enough Mexicans in all Mexico to take down old man Taylor.'"

Everyone knows this story by heart, but they listen all the same, it's still amusing.

Why is she called Mrs. Big? Is it just because she's large, or is it because she was named after the biggest ocean liner of her day? She weighs over two hundred pounds, she's six foot two, her feet are larger than a man's, yet she's perfectly proportioned with a tiny waist, healthy breasts and hips, and large eyes. She's a giant version of a gorgeous woman. Her lips are big like her name, and her tongue is too. Those who can afford the steep price can see for themselves. She's changed husbands several times. She learned early how to make a living off unfortunate women, and she's still at it.

Mrs. Stealman (née Vert) is biting her nails, wondering who will come to her gathering and who won't. She gives contradictory orders to her slaves. She fears the worst. Today could be the day she becomes a laughingstock, and she's not sure if she will be able to maintain control over the situation and, worse still, she has no idea what the hell to expect. How many people will show up? Who? And on top of all this, Mr. Stealman is nowhere to be found. "Where on earth could he be?" The hour is fast approaching and she still doesn't know. Perhaps people have sent regrets via his office.

What is she, a sack of potatoes? Why this total lack of consideration? *Damn, damn,* she thinks in silence while she shouts at her slaves for any old reason.

Rebecca, butcher Sharp's unmarried sister, has made lunch herself; they don't have a maid, why would they need one? It's a home without children, just the two of them, in a city where they've lived only nine years (no cousins, no relatives, not even a dog to bark at them). Sharp doesn't show up. Rebecca worries he has been killed on his way home. Her fear is an expression of her most intimate desire, and it makes her lungs feel as if they're about to explode. She calms herself. She breathes deeply. With what clarity of mind she has, she dares to wish it's true, which makes her more anxious. She needs to breathe, her chest feels heavy, it's like a cold hand is pressing her eye sockets, squeezing her eyeballs up against her brain. Her throat burns, her tongue feels heavy. It's like she has entered a war zone. Colors are brighter. She feels an uncontrollable desire to scream. But she doesn't.

Glevack, who always puts his own interests first, gloats that Nepomuceno has received his comeuppance and will soon be brought to justice, but he doesn't know how to begin celebrating. He's incapable of seeing the bigger picture. He can only think of things in terms of the benefit to himself and doesn't realize things are about to go up in smoke.

Bruneville's army—a motley crew which is always changing depending on who is paying them and how regularly—and its volunteers, who are equal or greater in number, are on tenterhooks. No one has yet hired the ones who work for pay, and the volunteers are worried about defending themselves, but against whom? While they wait, on the verge of exploding with anticipation, Mexicans are shot dead in the streets from time to time, but no one sets the law after them.

Reds and Blues band together. They don't even recall who's what. They all feel exactly the same, they're Texans to the bone.

And Nepomuceno? Faster than his own speeding bullet, he scoops drunken Lázaro Rueda off the ground, tosses him over his shoulder, and mounts his horse, seating Lázaro in front of him in the saddle.

From his saddle he lassos Sheriff Shears's firearm, the Colt the mayor's office provided—the one Shears couldn't fire, it fell to the ground when he was clumsily trying to find the trigger—and picks it up; he pulls the horse's reins to spur his horse forward. He shortens the lasso as he advances.

He heads for the highway. Four of his men follow.

Without pausing he holsters Shears's Colt with his left hand, then passes the reins to his left, grabs Shears's Colt with his right hand, fires into the air, and holsters it again.

On James Street, just before Charles, a small group of his men are chewing the fat, gathered around Doña Estefanía's shopping: sacks of unripe oranges, onions, and garlic, tied to the back of a mule.

Ludovico—a gunman and an excellent cowboy—has stopped in this spot next to the window where the smiling face of Moonbeam, the pretty Asinai Indian, sometimes appears. She's so pretty. If the Smiths would sell her, he'd buy her in a heartbeat. And if they won't sell her, he might just steal her from them, or else he's not a man. He eyes the window, searching for Moonbeam's face.

From her bedroom balcony, hidden behind lace curtains, Caroline, the youngest Smith, spies on them, hoping to catch a glimpse of Nepomuceno, whom she's completely infatuated with.

Ludovico is daydreaming, blinking at the window; Fulgencio and Silvestre are busting a gut laughing at him, who knows why; they don't spot their men until they're right in front of them. They toss the sacks of oranges across their saddles, mount their horses, and hurry after them.

In their haste, one of the sacks of oranges turns upside down. No sooner have they passed the corner of Charles and James than— wouldn't you know it!—the fruit begins to fall out, bouncing on the cobblestones.

The pack heads toward Elizabeth Street, Nepomuceno in the lead. The mule carrying the onions and garlic follows fast on their tails out of sheer instinct—who knows where it gets the energy from—its short legs look like they're flying.

On the outskirts of Bruneville, further inland, another small band of Nepomuceno's men waits. When they see where the group is headed, they mount their horses and follow.

They're creating one big cloud of dust. They take the turnoff to the dock, and as the earth becomes damper the telltale cloud of dust settles down. They arrive at the muddy riverbank.

They stop several feet from the barge, which is already loaded with livestock.

Pedro and Pablo, who help old Arnoldo on the boat and have been well-trained (both boys are barefoot; and since their combined age is sixteen their nickname is "Two Eights"), have just loaded the last of the herd onto the boat and are about to close the gate. The barge is balanced. When Nepomuceno and his men appear, the boys are just closing the gates, walking along the edge of the deck. The coal has been moved to the tugboat to keep the barge balanced, the motor is running hot, they're about to release the moorings, two thick chains which keep the barge moored to the dock at its bow and its stern. They both have rope wrapped around their torsos, they'll tighten it if the barge begins to list. Pedro will travel on deck with his German shepherd; Pablo will sit with old Arnoldo at the tugboat's stern, in the cabin.

Old Arnoldo, who is deaf as a doorknob, is already at the tug's tiller. He doesn't like transporting livestock one bit; in addition to the whims of the river, you have to contend with the whims of the herd. He's got the bullhorn at his feet, in case he needs it.

The livestock aren't restless, but they rock the boat and roll the tug. Pablo and Pedro work with steady hands. One mistake could set the barge off-balance and tip them over. If the animals panic, there's not much they'll be able to do. The herd is traveling unattended; the wranglers are depending on the barge's rails and the animals' fear of water. They wait on the opposite riverbank. On the dock, without saying a word, Nepomuceno motions his orders. Ismael, a cowboy, leaps off his horse and jumps across the gap between the dock and the barge. All aboard!

Patronio takes the reins of Ismael's horse.

Pablo and Pedro watch and weigh up the situation. Pablo thinks, *Nepomuceno is crazy,* but there's nothing he can do against fourteen men, or thirteen, if we don't count drunken Lázaro. Plus, who in their right mind would take on Don Nepomuceno?

Ismael opens the barge's main gate; the herd senses this immediately; Ismael keeps them back with his riding whip, cracking it and shouting "Back!" in a stern voice.

Pablo's dog barks at Ismael, baring his teeth. From land, Fausto throws a stone to scare him off, and the dog retreats between the legs of the cattle, who also shy away.

Patronio passes the reins of Ismael's horse to Fausto. He pulls his horse back, causing it to whinny, and takes a running jump onto the barge—landing so softly (as if he's polishing a gem) there's hardly a sound; the animals shy away from the impact of his landing, rushing against the railings of the barge. After Patronio, Fausto follows immediately, shadowed by Ismael's horse and the others.

Once aboard the barge, Ludovico, Fulgencio, Silvestre (who's no longer laughing), Patronio, Ismael, and Fausto (all good cowboys) attend to the Herculean task of controlling the animals. Once the cattle are subdued, they must ensure they don't bunch together on one side of the barge, which would capsize it. Nepomuceno's remaining horsemen board one by one.

What horses! They're like one with their riders; full of vigor, they are momentum incarnate, and handsome devils. The same can't be said of the cattle—focused on the unpredictable waters, who knows how they can be controlled? But they respond to the whip, shoves, and the dog nipping at their ankles (Two Eights' dog understands who's in charge now and joins in to help Nepomuceno's men). In short, the herd fears the cowboys and obeys them out of fright, not because they understand.

As soon as the herd is under control, El Güero jumps aboard, followed by their riderless, fresh horses (six in total, one horse for each rider). Then Nepomuceno, with Lázaro Rueda, who has passed out. It's the last jump and the most graceful, a beautiful arc, the highest of all; their bodies trace a miraculous triangle through the air (the three points of the triangle are their three heads: Nepomuceno's, Lázaro's, and Pinta's).

(You might ask, why did he go last? Isn't he the one they're protecting? But if you think about it, the answer is clear: they don't want to take any unnecessary risks and he might have capsized the boat, plus on land there's not a soul who could catch him.)

The mule with the sack of garlic and onions stays behind on land. She ran after the horses through the streets of Bruneville, following them like a faithful dog, but jumping such a wide gap over the water, old and heavily loaded as she is, that's out of the question. She's an ass but she's not an idiot.

With the assistance of Two Eights, who understand who's calling the shots, Ismael closes the gate he opened to let Nepomuceno and his men aboard.

The repositioning of the herd continues, the very picture of wrangling skill.

Now the barge is really full. To ensure they aren't crushed by the cattle, they must keep the herd calm.

Nepomuceno doesn't need to speak his orders. Fausto points at Pedro and Pablo, "Go tell old Arnoldo that we're ready to go, now! Release the moorings!"

Pedro asks, "Where are you in such a hurry to get to?"

"Where were you headed?"

"To Matasánchez, to pick up some feed and some pots; from there we're headed to Bagdad."

Fausto and Nepomuceno exchange looks and make a few signs; Fausto understands and shouts the orders at the top of his lungs, "To Matasánchez, to the Old Dock, the herd disembarks with us. Let's move it!"

Pablo heads to the tugboat's cabin, working his way along the side of the barge, outside the railings; with swift agility he places his bare feet on the ropes and chains that moor it to the barge. He's already aboard the tug when he feels a jerk: Pedro has just released the first mooring, and the motor is pushing the vessel, though it hasn't started forward yet.

"Let's go, Don Arnoldo!" he shouts in the old man's ear. "To the Old Dock in Matasánchez!"

"The Old Dock? But no one uses it anymore! Did you say the Old Dock? And what the hell was all that rocking? What was going on back there?"

"I'm telling you, Don Arnoldo, the old one! The Old Dock! Old like you are! Let's go!" Pablo tells him.

"Off we go to the Old Dock," the old man says, as merrily as he can, "old like me!"

"And make it snappy!"

"I can step it up . . . if you want us to capsize, you wacky kid! I can waltz but I can't fly!"

He feels another jerk, stronger than the first: Pedro has just released the second and final mooring.

Moonbeam, the pretty Asinai Indian, has appeared on one of the Smiths' balconies (not on account of the Lipans' quarrel—which she didn't see—or because of the sound of the shot—which she didn't hear because she was in the patio fetching water—or because of Nat; it's because of Nepomuceno's horsemen galloping past, although she arrives too late to see who was in such a hurry); she saw the oranges rolling around, opened the balcony windows and jumped down into the street to pick them up. On another balcony, Caroline Smith—she knows whose fruit it is because she's been standing at attention by the window—opens her windows too, but Moonbeam doesn't hear, absorbed as she is in gathering the oranges into her skirt.

Mrs. Smith is wondering why her daughter is shouting. When she sees her hanging out the window into the street shouting nonsense, culminating in "I love you, Nepomuceno!" and sees Moonbeam, "that exasperating Indian girl, picking up oranges" off the cobblestones "with her legs fully exposed," she faints, unable to bear either of these indignities.

Santiago watched Nepomuceno and his men board the barge. Most of the fishermen, who were mending their nets, had left to investigate the ruckus in the Market Square and hadn't returned. Several of them got lost. Santiago, on the other hand, knows what has happened as if he has seen it with his own eyes, the same ones that witnessed Nepomuceno's escape.

"Now that's a real man!" he says aloud. "That's what you call balls, big ones!"

As soon as they have finished tying up the last crab, Melón, Dolores, and Dimas get down off Hector's cart; Mr. Wheel will only transport what's for sale. Without talking it over, they all run to Mesnur, halfway between the center of Bruneville and the place where the fishermen mend their nets. Mesnur is where the children always gather at the end of the afternoon, and sometimes when their work is interrupted. Most of the kids work, and most of them are Mexicans or immigrants. They fly kites, sail toy boats they build themselves, catch dragonflies and tie them up on leashes, play ball (if there's one around), jump rope, and share secrets. Sometimes they're mean to each other, but mostly they share the treats that might have come their way.

Melón, Dolores and Dimas want to share the news about John Tanner, the White Indian, and about the sheriff and Don Nepomuceno.

Luis arrives at the same time holding his little sister's hand and with empty pockets; he's worried about that, it won't go down well at home. Along comes Steven—hanging his head because he hasn't made any money either—and Nat, with his hidden treasure.

But Melón, Dolores, and Dimas don't talk about John Tanner, and no one stops to discuss what happened with Shears and Nepomuceno, no one even thinks about swimming or playing freeze tag, because Nat removes the Lipan's knife, the one he picked up on Charles Street, from his pants. They all agree they should hide it.

It takes the gringos a little while to mount their horses and begin pursuing the "banditos." Their horses are in the stables, on the city's outskirts, and the minutes drag by as they wait for their servants to bring their horses (on the way they were distracted by the oranges Ludovico carelessly dropped—the Asinai had gathered what she could, but many remained—and after they gathered what was left of the oranges it took a while to hide them in Judge Gold's stables).

Once mounted on their horses, the gringos lose more time stopping at each intersection and corner to ask everyone in the vicinity if they've seen the fugitives and where they went. "They headed inland." "I think they went thataway." Folks' directions are no quicker than their explanations. There's no one on the road to the river to tell them whether "the fugitives" went toward the river or inland; the kids who usually gather to play there are nowhere to be found (they've already gone to hide the knife). Just in case, Ranger Phil, Ranger Ralph, and Ranger Bob head down to the dock. The rest of them head inland, continuing to question folks along the way.

Near Mrs. Big's Hotel, Ranger Phil, Ranger Ralph, and Ranger Bob catch sight of the barge loaded with cattle, floating slowly down the river (no matter how much the boy hassles him, old Arnoldo wisely maintains a snail's pace, he takes good care of his cargo), and they hear the herd lowing at a distance. The vessel rocks a wobbly dance. There's no way it could be brought back to dock.

"That's a lotta rocking!"

"It looks like there's a ruckus on board, there must be an angry bull."

"Nah! He's not angry, he's in heat!" As usual, Ranger Ralph has a one-track mind (you can hardly call what his brain does "thinking").

"A bull in heat, you say? Ain't no bull, it's a steer like you!" Ranger Bob says in bad Spanish, which Ranger Phil understands, but not Ranger Ralph.

All three laugh, two because they get the joke, the other because he's so stupid.

Watching the barge float along like it's fighting the waves is both humorous and soothing, like watching sheep being rounded up into one big flock with mastery and skill; they don't know the real reason for the boat's swaying.

The barge turns upriver toward the Old Dock.

"I thought from here they went downriver to Punta Isabel and then to New Orleans to sell cattle, but it looks like they're heading upriver," says Ranger Bob.

"They'll be picking up feed, no doubt, they don't want to deliver 'em hungry," says Ranger Phil.

"Or maybe they're trying to catch the current," says Ranger Bob.

"Don't make no sense to me," says Ranger Ralph.

They turn their backs and enter the swinging doors of Mrs. Big's Hotel.

Inside, it's business as usual: a few whores are waiting for customers, folks are drinking liquor, four musicians begin to torture their instruments, competing for attention, and at her table Mrs. Big presides over her never-ending card game. To one side of the swinging doors—which don't cover his face or the lower half of his legs—Santiago the fisherman hangs back, barefoot, by the entrance.

Jim Smiley is the only one who gets up when the Rangers come in. But not to shake hands or show respect. Smiley bends over to pick up the cardboard box where he keeps his frog, and says clearly for all to hear, as if he's rehearsed it, "I betcha two bucks my frog can jump farther than any other."

"And where am I gonna find a frog to bet you with? I don't ride around with a frog in my pocket!" Ranger Phil says.

"What else you got in your pockets? What's more important than a frog?" Smiley smiles.

Ranger Phil holds up his revolver. He smiles too, showing his gold teeth.

"You wanna take my bet or not?" Smiley dares him, still smiling.

"I'm askin' you where am I gonna get a frog?"

Santiago the fisherman mutters, "Down by the riverbank, I'll bring you one, Ranger. Wait here."

Santiago is itching to get out of the saloon.

Ranger Phil turns and looks at him with admiration. If this backwater fisherman dares to speak to a gunslinger like him, there must be good reason. Santiago heads outside, the doors swing behind him.

A few seconds later, Ranger Phil follows Santiago, and the two other Rangers follow reluctantly—they wanted to grab a drink. Irritatingly, they can still hear the music, which makes them even thirstier. But when they see the fisherman looking so helpless, jumping around like a child, they turn around and head back into Mrs. Big's.

Santiago continues leaping around on the muddy riverbank, without realizing the Ranger is nearby. He catches sight of a frog at the edge of the river. He follows it, leaps to the right, and then to the left. He squats to capture his prey.

Ranger Phil follows him stealthily, so as not to scare the frog—now he understands what Santiago is up to—until he arrives at the edge of the dock. He stops and watches the fisherman. Then he notices the hoofprints in the mud.

Santiago captures the frog.

By this time the barge appears to be fading away and you can no longer hear the cattle lowing.

Pointing to the horseshoe prints in the mud, Ranger Phil asks Santiago, "What's this?"

Santiago, who has the frog in his hand, doesn't say a word for a few long seconds.

You can still hear the music of the four fools in the saloon (each of them wandering around with own their instrument, gathering only to look for handouts), scratching strings, their music lacking all melody.

What happens next takes place in the blink of an eye. Santiago, who is a good man and doesn't know how to lie, realizes what trouble he's in and begins to cry in Spanish, "I don't know anything, I saw them jump on the barge but didn't understand what was going on." He drops the frog he caught.

Unfortunately, Ranger Phil understands Spanish.

In Mrs. Big's Hotel the musicians' torturous song ends. Ranger Phil whistles to his men; they appear through Mrs. Big's swinging doors.

The musicians start a new song. Ranger Phil grabs Santiago by the arm and drags him over to his partners, the fisherman bawling like an animal on the way to slaughter. Ranger Phil translates the fisherman's confession for his partners, pointing to where he found the prints in the mud.

From the barge, Fulgencio (who has an eagle's eye) observes the three gunmen approaching Mrs. Big's Hotel. He whistles to Nepomuceno (softly, not to disturb the herd), who dismounts and hides behind his horse. His men copy him, using the horses as shields to keep them from sight of anyone on the riverbank, in case they have a spyglass, despite the fact this leaves them exposed to the herd.

The herd reacts to their movements. They nearly capsize with the commotion. Old Arnoldo curses the herd and steers the tug, yanking its tiller. Fulgencio cracks his whip. Just the sound of it is enough; the herd recognizes his authority—luckily all Nepomuceno's men are cowboys—and settles back down.

Nepomuceno wants to go to Matasánchez. He would have preferred to go to his own ranch, but he knows the gringos' vengeful nature; it's better to hide out somewhere that doesn't endanger his own people. For the time being he knows he can't go near the place, or any of his mother's ranches either (where the food is much better than anywhere else, there's no contest). He must cross the border and prepare to face the Rangers there. If not, they'll crush him. Once again, it occurs to Nepomuceno, as it has on many occasions, *We should have allied ourselves with the warrior tribes; it's a shame it didn't work out, but they're like wasps' nests, even among themselves. Together,* Nepomuceno thinks, *Indians and Mexicans would fry the gringos up with a little chipotle, some garlic, and a pinch of* . . . You can tell he's the son of Doña Estefanía, the best cook in the whole region. Her desserts are without compare, as are her marinades and her stews. You're fortunate to dine at her table.

Chipotle, frying, garlic: this is no way to talk about gringos, who don't even know how to hold a frying pan. Even the Karankawa were more civilized, may they rest in peace.

While all this is passing through his head, Nepomuceno has an idea. Traveling with the herd puts him in good spirits, there's a lot of cowboy in him . . . Since they're hiding behind their horses, they don't see what's happening on the dock in Bruneville.

—

Those awful musicians have begun yet another tune back at Mrs. Big's. One of them squeezes an accordion. Santiago the fisherman is on his knees, crying silently like a child, clasping his hands and begging for mercy. Ranger Ralph takes out his pistol. He points it at Santiago. The shot hits him in the forehead.

(The bullet that has come to rest in Santiago's head comes to life. It knows it wasn't meant to end up there. The fisherman's noble, sweet brains, washed with the sea air and the silence of high tide, soothe it. His brains pour out in luminous silence, the bullet has rendered them insensate. No fear, no fatigue, no longing, no children, no wife, no nets, no Nepomuceno; not even the river remains.)

The Rangers stick a fishhook into Santiago's ass—one that might have belonged to him. Then they tie a rope around his neck and hang him from the icaco tree, "Mrs. Big's stick."

"Leave him there to teach 'em a lesson."

The three Rangers mount their horses. The animals seem oblivious to them. It's not that they don't obey them, it's like they don't recognize them.

Before yanking the reins, Ranger Bob notices a frog leaping in the mud. He dismounts and follows it; his boots get muddy; he traps the frog without chasing it, as if the frog has surrendered.

"I'll catch up with you," he says to his partners. "I'll see you in the Market Square, or at the Town Hall, somewhere around there!"

Ranger Phil and Ranger Ralph pull their reins and gallop back to the center of Bruneville, straight to the Town Hall to share their discovery.

The mayor-pharmacist gives instructions: send a telegram to Austin asking for reinforcements. (On Stealman's orders: "If they return without the outlaw, send a telegram to Austin for reinforcements, things could get ugly.") Then Ranger Neals, the warden, arrives at the Town Hall; he whispers to the mayor to send some men down to Mrs. Big's, someone needs to keep watch over the dock. What if Nepomuceno and his men return to attack tonight? They might even be returning on the next barge ...

The order is given: there will be no vessels arriving or departing from the Bruneville dock, or any other dock for that matter.

"But the afternoon steamboat, the *Elizabeth*, is about to arrive, it's running late."

"Well, it won't stop in Bruneville."

Wild, who has an unusual constitution (he hears stampedes approach without twitching, kills thousands of buffalo without blinking, smells the rivers of their blood as if they were magnolias), goes berserk when he hears that the steamboat won't be stopping because it has been forbidden to dock. Goddamn it! The last thing on earth he wants is to be stuck in this shithole!

On the outskirts on the other side of Bruneville, down toward the coast, where the heat is even more unbearable and the humidity is inconceivable, where bugs and vermin cohabit with ghosts and specters, live the Lieders, poor German immigrants from Bavaria. They learned from their ancestors how to deal with cold, but this heat is crippling them. The Lieders built their house from sticks, stones, blood, sweat, and tears along the impassable road to Punta Isabel, where land is still cheap because no one wants it. This is where Frau Lieder grows blackberries and makes dense rye bread (nothing like the white clouds Óscar produces in his oven), and where Herr Lieder battles the swamp to sow and sell grain—he's built something that resembles a dock where he does business (Lieder doesn't have a boat, he hasn't even tried tying some logs together to make a raft, because the water scares him).

The paterfamilias dreams of building a mill.

Joe, his son, returns with the news and some of the goods he was unable to sell. When he hears it, Herr Lieder sheds tears of rage. Frau Lieder's heart shrinks with worry, but she puts on a brave face and sets a beautiful table, calling the whole family to eat. It's her way of resisting, her strategy. It's like a feast day with everything she's taken out of the larder. She wants to raise her husband's spirits, as well as Joe's, and her own. But part of her, like Herr Lieder, thinks they're done for. Might as well enjoy the cheese and the preserves before the end of the world arrives any minute now, for the world is certainly coming to an end! There will be pandemonium, the river will run red with blood! No more gold-and-silver dawns. No more blackberries. No more flour or dough or ovens baking bread . . .

But her strategy works. The table set, her soul is more at ease. Herr Lieder forgets his sorrows. Seated at the table, he recites quotes from Bettina, "In my crib, someone sang that I would fall in love with a distant star, that would lead me to dream of my fate, I must listen to the end of my days."

Joe stops worrying and begins to daydream; in silence he repeats to himself what he's said a thousand times, ". . . And may I go and live with the Indians."

Inland, on Indian Territory, captive Lucia—the aunt of Laura, who lives next door to Felipillo Holandés—the mother of a Chickasaw and one of Chief Buffalo Hump's seven current wives (and former infatuation of Nepomuceno), senses danger approaching, though she doesn't know why. Her hands are burning—it's her job to tan hides twelve or thirteen hours a day, and if there aren't any she must collect popinac seeds and grind them up to make something like flour. There are no days off. Being the Chief's wife is not like being queen or having lots of servants, though there are slaves in the household (other prisoners). Life on the prairie is hard and gets harder every day. The noble buffalo is gone, horses are disappearing too, they need to eat and stock up on firearms to protect themselves (that's what the skins are for, they trade them). Her nostrils burn too (tanning hides damages the mucous membranes as well as the skin).

She hurts all over. Especially her ears, which are like two withered flames, because the sun is pitiless and, like a good Indian wife, her hair is shorn—Chief Buffalo Hump cut it himself. She closes her eyes and dreams: Nepomuceno comes to the camp, she accepts the offer he made her years ago, and she returns home, crying because she is leaving her son, who will soon be a man. But that's where her dream stops. It's too terrible to continue.

She has a different fantasy that she'll never return to her home in Bruneville, but her parents come out to meet her. Her father has long since passed away, it was a terrible tragedy (an Indian trader, a Mexican who has family in Bruneville and Matasánchez, told her), but in her dream they are both alive. But her dream becomes a nightmare: her mother is tanning hides, her father dances and smokes like an Apache. She shakes her head to get rid of the image. She feels her short hair brushing her cheeks: it's grown brittle like a mare's. She fantasizes about something else: the day is over. She is leaving the store in their makeshift camp. There's no moon. There's not a cloud in the sky. She has become a mare, she whinnies with pleasure; she wakes up.

She has dream after dream, she awakens when each comes to an end, when they become unbearable. Her fingernails have been eaten away by the stuff she uses to tan hides; the burning is unbearable, especially on her fingertips.

(She does not dream of the idiot who brought her out to the prairie in the first place with his dreams of glory, thinking wild cattle were there for the taking, and that danger was a figment of fearful imaginations.)

Back at Mrs. Big's, surrounded by the music of the so-called musicians, the race between Ranger Bob's frog and Smiley's frog is over.

Smiley's frog won. Angry, Ranger Bob leaves the agent of his defeat on the floor—if he were French he'd cut off its legs and eat them, despite the fact they're not near as meaty as a cow's.

He heads for the door. On his way out, he turns:

"Oh yeah, we left the fisherman for you in the icaco tree. Traitors beware, he won't be the last!"

He leaves without explaining whom he's talking about.

At the kitchen window Perdido, the ragamuffin, screams; he's seen Santiago swinging from the icaco tree.

It's easy to get what's going through Smiley's frog's head. The frog has no interest whatsoever in leaping. Smiley has subjected it to torture (not intentionally, he's not cruel), but it wants to learn to do something interesting. Not leaping, which comes naturally. Practicing that is a stupid waste of time, the frog thinks, especially considering how short life is. "Frogs' legs invariably end up in the frying pan. But if I were able to . . . for instance, sew . . . or cough . . . or sing instead of croak . . . not even real singing, just a little ditty with some well-pronounced words, comprehensible and rhythmical . . .

"Or if not, I'd love to be a frog with hair, a head of long and luxurious hair . . .

"Or else a floating frog, not a flying one, because those exist. It would have to be something really special . . ."

Eight of Nepomuceno's men are waiting at the turnoff to Rancho del Carmen, brushing their horses, chewing tobacco, and killing time.

One of the groups of gringos that left Bruneville in pursuit of Nepomuceno, heading toward the Valley, approaches at a trot. They stop in front of them without dismounting and ask if they've seen anyone pass by.

"What're you looking for?"

They tell them how Nepomuceno shot Shears and fled, they're searching for him far and wide. They're unaware that they're delivering news.

"Well no, we haven't seen him."

The gringos take off at a trot.

Nepomuceno's men know he must have gone in a different direction.

"You think they crossed the river?"

"Definitely."

"Or did they take the back roads?"

And they head toward Bruneville.

On paths leading to the river they look for hoofprints to see if their horses have passed by. Nothing.

One of the cowboys has a spyglass. They move slowly, searching the riverbank. Nothing.

They continue toward Bruneville's dock. From a distance they can see that it's protected by armed guards.

They see a man hanging from Mrs. Big's icaco tree.

"Who do you think it is?"

"Santiago, the fisherman. An innocent bystander."

"Those gringo bastards."

They ride northeast. They don't stop until their horses can't take it anymore. They scan the horizon and consider camping; not too far off they spot the smoke from a campfire.

They remount their tired horses but no longer gallop. They arrive at the source of the smoke; there are only corpses around the campfire.

They were, rather, they had been some of Doña Estefanía's Mexican cowboys. What happened?

They had just finished herding the cattle into the corrals and completed the chores of caring for the animals.

They were roasting meat on the fire and sotol was flowing

from jugs; they were making large flour tortillas, a forearm's length in diameter, tossing them until they were so thin they were nearly translucent—and putting the first ones on the griddle.

One of them was playing the violin. And that's how a group of Rangers found them. They invited the Rangers to eat something. The Rangers asked about Nepomuceno.

"We haven't seen anyone pass this way, brothers."

The one with the violin continued playing, and the other Mexicans gathered around the campfire again. The Rangers weren't sure whether they should stop and eat with them or go on their way. But they knew they shouldn't. They were arguing among themselves when one of the cowboys began singing. He had a good voice. They listened to him sing:

Vendo quesos de tuna,
Dulces y colorados,
Pregón de aquel paisa honrado
Cuando cambia el sol por luna.

Ni quién te lo va a comprar,
Los hacemos sin pagar
Cuando hay sol que no con luna,
Le porfía un entendedor.

Dice el gringo que los ve,
Sin sabe qué pitos tocan:
Carajos de mexicanos!
Ordeñan a los nopales.

The gringos are in such a foul mood that when they hear the lyrics to the song they fire two, three, four shots into the Mexicans' backs, killing the vaqueros in cold blood just because of their music.

Then they take the cattle and head over to King's ranch—they've given up the search for Nepomuceno—but a half mile away they stop to celebrate their victory.

That's what the Rangers were doing, celebrating and drinking the sotol they grabbed from the Mexicans and eating the roasted meat they had stuffed in their rucksacks (it was still warm) when Nepomuceno's men spotted them with their spyglasses.

They sneak up on the Rangers. No shots are exchanged—the gringos don't even have time to grab their weapons. Most of them are shot in the back of the neck, a few of them in the forehead because they had time to turn around, but it was the end for every last one of them.

Nepomuceno's men look at what they've done; they don't want to hang around a bunch of dead men, and they certainly aren't going to bother burying them. They round up the cattle and take the road to one of Doña Estefanía's ranches, there's just enough daylight left.

(These poor cows! In one day they've changed hands three times. Some might think they didn't even notice. But they're exhausted, thirsty, tired of being herded here and there, and to top it all off one of them is about to birth a bull calf . . .)

In Bruneville many folks are still all tied up in knots.

The rich Negro, Tim Black, was born a slave—just because his parents were slaves, which makes no legal sense, it's like inheriting a crime, though there are those who would argue that if you can inherit a fortune you ought to inherit misfortune, too. His surname is an expression of the notary's sense of humor. He learned how to earn money from cattle, not because he's clever but because he's calculating and cautious. These have been his greatest virtues; how else can you explain his owning so much livestock and land when he could have been treated like an animal himself once Texas declared its independence?

He doesn't worry, as he often does, about the "Mexican threat," so real and so near. He's consumed by fear after seeing his wife's features in the face of that young man.

He should overcome his fear, or else all will be lost, he thinks, and he's right. But he doesn't know how. He sits in his room, staring at the wall, staring and staring, not stirring a bit.

High noon and the hours that follow are when the river is calmest, seemingly in deference to the sun (which presides over everything).

But today the Bravo pays no heed, it's temperamental and rebellious. It's choppy, with eddies at its deepest points. The truth is it's always treacherous, its waters dark and muddy. Right now it looks like the nighttime river, the one that follows the moon's dictates and hides cottonmouths. A highway for bats. The hunger of a she-wolf about to give birth. A blind man following a hungry dog. It's the darkness that the crazy man fears and the sane man is oblivious to.

The metallic luster of its surface is deceptive. It appears to be one solid body.

When Captain Boyle's steamboat embarked, the current was cooperative, like a child on its way to school. But that's an illusion.

Cautiously, the tug delivers the barge to the Old Dock in Matasánchez.

Years ago the city council and the port captain agreed to build the New Dock at a more convenient location for marine traffic and for business, in the city itself, right by the town center. They no longer fear pirates and they haven't yet learned to fear gringos.

To break the longstanding habits of sailors, the Old Dock was suddenly abandoned, and traffic moved further south, closer to the town. Luckily the Two Eights, Pedro and Pablo, have a few boards they keep handy for disembarking; they tie up the moorings and make a bridge to the dock.

They boys look to the center of the barge, to see if Nepomuceno's men have further orders. Nothing. Nepomuceno and his men are laying low, hiding behind the bodies of their horses, still using them as shields. In one horse's saddle there's a body hanging like a blanket, that's Lázaro Rueda. They've tied him to the horse while he sobers up and recovers from his beating.

Two Eights understand, they look left and right, then shout, "The coast is clear!"

Nepomuceno's men appear and climb into their saddles, one of them motions to open the loading gates.

The cattle push out, lowing.

"In a hurry to piss?" jokes Ludovico.

"They want to go to communion, they're old church ladies!" Because most of the cattle are black, everyone starts to laugh.

"Pay attention!" begs Fausto, wary of the difficult wrangling ahead.

The animals, hungry and nervous, have let themselves be rounded up.

The plains provide no natural cattle chute, no creek bed to corral the animals that stray from the herd like drops of water; and left to their own devices they are bound to wander.

A cowboy must be resourceful on the plains. He must exert himself to keep the herd together, using his horse's body, his own, and his voice, with the assistance of his dogs (which they have none of today), his lasso, and his whip. He must take advantage of the herd's momentum without letting it override the herd's welfare, which involves staying together.

One of the vaqueros is momentarily distracted from his titanic labors, and, yeehaw!, he snatches Pablo. "Now what?" Someone else nabs the other half of the Two Eights, Pedro. They sweep the boys right off the ground before they can put up a fight, lassoing them, and they fly several feet through the air before the vaqueros place them in their saddles like Apaches. Someone else lassos Pablo's dog by the tail like an unruly calf, and they drag him along so he understands who's boss; there's not a dog in the world who won't obey his master, but soon enough they stop and release him. The dog understands now, and follows along nursing his wounds.

"Who's going to untie the barge for Don Arnoldo?" Ismael thinks, so he shouts it aloud.

Ludovico backs up his horse. He draws close to the moorings, takes out his quietest pistol (to minimize upsetting the herd) and shoots through them both twice; they're thin ropes and don't break clean through, they're still held fast by a few smoking threads which soon begin to burn. Quickly, he catches up with the others.

The lowing, the sound of the hooves and the horseshoes, the giddyups of the vaqueros, and the cracking of the whip grow farther and farther away from the banks of the Río Bravo. There's no river breeze, but a prairie wind blows along the riverbank, refreshing; it extinguishes the flames on the mooring ropes.

Old Arnoldo doesn't understand a thing. Like clockwork, he falls asleep as soon as he takes his hand off the tiller. It's his age, he inevitably needs to take a siesta on each trip; it's like a reflex—as soon as they make land he begins "my shuteye." There's wisdom in the rhythm of his siestas, at the end of each trip from Bruneville to Matasánchez, or vice versa, he takes a short nap. His boys always come and wake him up when they've tied up the moorings. On this occasion, he awakens by himself, confused, because he has had more than his usual "shuteye." "Why didn't you wake me up already?"

He struggles to free himself from Morpheus's embrace.

The tug's motors are still running.

"They left me here like an idiot . . ."

Where are those boys? He picks up the bullhorn and shouts, "Pablo! Pedro! Twoooo Eeeeeiiights!?"

Nothing.

"You goddam kids! Get back here right now or I'll tan your hides!"

Still nothing. Nothing at all.

What should he do? With great difficulty—it's not easy for him alone, he always leans on Pablo's or Pedro's arm—he leaves the cabin for the stern to take a look around. Without his bullhorn (he can't risk moving from the tug to the barge without both hands free), he shouts two or three times.

"Pedro! Pablo!"

He sees, but he doesn't believe his eyes; he blinks. Without a doubt the barge is empty, the three sets of gates are wide open, and there's no trace of the boys.

"Damn it all to hell! How could they do this to me?"

What's going on? For crying out loud! Did they steal his cargo? Have they run away? He can't believe it.

He returns to the tug with a little more agility. Surprise and worry have taken years off him. He retreats to the tiller. He picks up the horn again and shouts, "Pedro! Pablo!"

He feels a jerk. He knows the feeling. The moorings have just come undone. A rotting post on the Old Dock has bent, freeing the rope that wasn't burnt through by the gunshot. The second rope the boys tied couldn't hold the weight of the vessel and snapped. One snapped and one twisted; the barge is free. The river's current takes over.

The old boards that the boys threw across to the Old Dock fall into the river.

Old Arnoldo sits down behind the tiller. No point in staying angry. What if they didn't steal the cargo? What if . . . No, there's no other explanation.

"I don't believe it, I just can't . . . I must be dreaming . . ."

He steers the boat back to Bruneville. He thinks, *They're good boys, I know that. They wouldn't steal from me . . . so what happened? What lightning struck them?*

At the inn known as Mrs. Big's Hotel, furious Wild, the Buffalo Hunter, rants and raves. There's no boat to Punta Isabel today?! What will happen to his cargo? He insults his slaves, One, Two, and Three, curses and throws a glass at his sidekick, handsome Trust.

He kicks them out of the bar. "Get outta here! Scram! Out!"

Outside, Trust leans against the log wall of Mrs. Big's, one boot on the wall, the other on the ground; he takes a piece of straw from his shirt pocket and begins to pick his teeth, talking to himself loud enough that One, Two, and Three—all barefoot and dressed in rags—can hear.

"That's it. I can't take it no more. I'm gonna go prospect for gold in Nevada, or silver in Virginia. I can't stay with him another day."

One, Two, and Three are taken aback. They won't be able to put up with Wild without Trust around. They repeat the arguments handsome Trust has used on them before, when the topic of prospecting for gold comes up.

"You gonna spend years in darkness, scratching away at stones with a shovel in your hands? That life's for the dogs!"

"You gonna shut off your sight for good, without waiting for your life to end? Better die an early death!"

"You gonna bury yourself where nothing grows, where there's no women, not even a slave, and eat stone soup every day? Dying of hunger to earn something that they'll rob you for when you try to sell it?"

"You ain't never gonna ride a horse again!"

"You ain't gonna have no one but a mule for company."

"Good grief! Damn! Holy Mary, Mother of God! Hell!"

They're alluding to a cartoon that appeared in the Corpus Christi papers a few days ago. It depicted three miners trying to lead their heavily laden mules out of a deep, swampy canyon. Handsome Trust showed it to them, saying, "Here's One, Two, and Three, enslaved by the gold they dug up. They're worse off than you because they chose to do this!"

"You gonna die of blood poisoning . . ."

This last line was one of Three's ideas, not something he's heard handsome Trust say. It snaps Trust out of it. He throws the straw he was picking his teeth with to the ground.

"I'd rather lose my legs than put up with Wild one second longer. Goddamn buffalo killer! Fucking buffalo hunter . . . he's a sonofabitch . . . But don't worry, I'll take you across the river today no matter what, I won't leave you here for that idiot to abuse you. Come with me. As for myself, just so you know, I got no choice, even if there's only shit in the Virginia hills."

They begin to walk along the riverbank, leaving Bruneville behind them. They don't carry a thing: each of them has his hands clasped behind his back.

Nepomuceno, his men, and the refreshed herd charge after Fausto, who knows these parts like the back of his hand. Soon they'll arrive at a watering hole where there's grass for the cattle. It's a horseshoe bend in the Río Bravo that has been cut off by the accumulated sediment the river carries, creating a ring of water called Laguna del Diablo, not to be confused with others by the same name. That's how it got its name, it doesn't belong to anyone, it's just a ring of water that used to be part of the river but is long since cut off. And that's why it's not deep. Under skilled hands, the cattle can cross here. The water here flows gently, it couldn't sweep away the youngest calf, though a newborn might not be able to touch bottom and keep its head above water, but there are no newborns in this herd Nepomuceno's men are leading.

In the middle of Laguna del Diablo there's an ideal pasture that resembles the shape of an "o." The water will serve as a pen. It's the perfect place to camp. The herd will stay in the middle, the men will stay between the ring and the river, protected and with an open escape route to the south, in case they need one.

At the New Dock in Matasánchez, the port captain, Lopez de Aguada, watches the barge's irregular and unpredictable movements through his spyglass. Under such circumstances others might be suspected of carrying illegal cargo, but not Arnoldo, it's more likely his compass is acting up. He can't see that the herd disembarked at the Old Dock because it's out of his line of sight, but clearly the barge is empty . . . What's going on? What's wrong with Arnoldo?

He watches the barge and the tugboat heading back to Bruneville.

"He's not coming? He's not going to Bagdad? What's happening? He's gonna leave me here with these boxes of fragile crockery no one's going to want to store? And the feed they asked us to get? What on earth? What's he thinking about?"

It was a lot of work to wrap the dishes to protect them from the rocking of the barge. They even put them into a basket to carry them in the tug's cabin. Now all they can do is wait. Shoot!

He gives an order. "Have the *Inspector* go check out the Old Dock, that's where Arnoldo went. If there's trouble, we better deal with it before night falls."

And he adds, "Arnoldo's getting too old . . ."

He knows that forcing him to retire would be condemning him to die. Maybe what he should do is give him a partner who has more experience than those boys. But that won't be easy either. Anyhow, for the moment he's got to figure out what's going on. And find somewhere to store the baskets of fragile crockery. It's fine porcelain, called "china," destined for the new hotel in Bagdad, called, fittingly, The Bagdad. He can't leave the baskets out where anyone can knock them over.

Julito runs to deliver Lopez de Aguada's orders to Úrsulo, who just awoke (he worked all night and is just getting up now: he slept on the boards of the dock, like an Indian). Úrsulo jumps into his canoe, happy to get back into the water.

The buffalo hunter, Wild, leaves Mrs. Big's Hotel to take a piss and get some fresh air. Santiago's body is hanging heavily from the icaco tree, without swinging, like a mangrove root searching for the earth. A black bird lands like a stone on his shoulder. The Rangers sent by the pharmacist at Neals' suggestion have arrived. The cart laden with the buffalo hunter's foul-smelling, grim cargo, or "harvest," stands out against the river. That's all.

"Where are those idiots?"

He goes back inside to ask Mrs. Big if she knows where Trust and his slaves are. Behind her, Sandy's cousin answers, "They left a while ago."

The buffalo hunter Wild pays the bill and makes a deal with Mrs. Big to leave his cart there. "If you wanna leave it here, that's your choice." Who'll look after the animals? "We'll take care of them for you; it'll cost . . ." They come to an agreement (which humiliates Mrs. Big, "That's what things have come to, I'm just a barn-keeper now"). He mounts a horse; that's the last they'll see of him for a long time.

The *Inspector* is a canoe that belongs to the port authority in Matasánchez. It handles all conditions equally well: wind, high tide, calm waters. Úrsulo paddles; he prefers to take to the water alone, but he can carry up to four passengers. Úrsulo has long, straight hair decorated with various ribbons, and he's wearing a leather shirt, moccasins, and tailored pants. Young men in Matasánchez imitate the way he dresses, but no one dares to copy his hairstyle.

—

The Río Bravo is being rough with the empty barge, playing with both it and the tug as if they were shells. It has changed. "Even Miss Bravo is angry at those boys! Settle down, girl, what have I done?" Arnoldo says aloud to the river.

It feels like something's about to happen. Is there a hurricane coming?! That's the last thing he needs!

Now he can see the dock in Bruneville. There's no other vessel docked there. He sees the steamboat *Elizabeth* anchored at a distance from the dock. How strange. Plus, now is the time when fishermen should be preparing their nets for their next sailing on the open sea, but there's no sign of them. All he sees is a group of uniformed men.

"Goddamn town of gunslingers. It's their fault my boys are gone. Such good boys. I raised them. I fed them for all those years. They were like sons. More than sons."

He sees something unidentifiable swinging from Mrs. Big's tree. His eyes aren't what they used to be. Those two boys were indispensable. He's suddenly quite melancholy—the impotence of old age, the betrayal of the boys.

He just can't come to terms with what they've done to him, and even less with the burden of his age. "They've gone and run away from me, and took everything?"

Now that the Bruneville dock is right in front of him, he regrets coming here. He should have gone to Matasánchez, the Captain would have helped him find the kids, but the way the moorings came undone took him by surprise . . . What is he going to do, all alone with the barge and the tug? He should have gone to the New Dock, there he would have found Julito or someone else to help him. But that's it. It's too late.

"I'm an idiot, an idiot. I'm good for nothing these days. It'd be better if the Grim Reaper came for me now. The older I get the more worthless I am . . ."

He curses because he just can't believe that his boys, who were so good, his kids ... it's his own fault ... some unknown misfortune must have befallen them.

On land, the uniformed men crowd together, discussing how to receive him.

"Now what? What are they up to?"

The barge approaches the dock.

"At least there are enough of them that they can give me a hand. There's so many of them!"

Putting his self-criticisms aside, Arnoldo tosses the rope he keeps tied to the tiller for emergencies. How long has it been since he used it? By way of an answer, he recalls a woman's sweet, bitter scent, she was wearing a flowered dress. Her armpits tasted like pineapple, what a delight!

The uniformed men on the dock tie up the rope, fastening the barge to land. They don't even greet Arnoldo or wait for him to leave the cabin.

One of them cocks his pistol.

He points it at his forehead and fires between his brows, right between the old man's eyes.

They hang him from another branch of Mrs. Big's leafy icaco, stringing him up high next to Santiago "So those outlaw Mexicans learn their lesson."

Úrsulo's canoe arrives at the Old Dock in a hop, skip, and a jump, like he and his canoe are one body. He takes the *Inspector* out of the water and leaves it where he always does (in the fork of a giant kapok tree that keeps it out of sight—he doesn't know how long it'll be before he returns).

It wouldn't take an expert at tracking like Úrsulo to figure out dozens of cattle have been here. And at least twelve horses. One of them is carrying two men: the shoe prints are deep. He recognizes them: the shoes of Don Nepomuceno's mare, Pinta. Úrsulo was there when she was shod.

"What's he up to now?"

And it wouldn't take Úrsulo to figure out they headed to Laguna del Diablo. He returns to the *Inspector*, he should deliver the news to Matasánchez. He tosses the canoe into the water and boards it skillfully, like an expert rider mounting his horse. He finds the current and uses the oar to avoid a tree trunk the Bravo uprooted, a victim of its moods.

(Úrsulo knows how to hear the tree's laments, tears that are made of unblossomed flowers, unripened fruit, fallen leaves that will rot; the lament the fallen tree murmurs as it bobs along makes Úrsulo pensive.)

It's like Úrsulo is one with the *Inspector*.

The current carries the *Inspector* straight to the New Dock in Matasánchez.

Úrsulo delivers the news (which is like a cannon ball landing at the port captain's feet, though he hasn't lit the fuse: he doesn't mention the fact he recognized Nepomuceno's mare's shoe prints). In turn, Lopez de Aguada tells him everything that's happened in Bruneville in three swift strokes: about Sheriff Shears; Nepomuceno's gunshot; and that he fled.

"You heard it here first, Úrsulo . . . this means trouble. You can't just shoot an American with impunity. It must be Nepomuceno and his men . . . on the lam . . ."

"It's true," is all Úrsulo says. "A white horse ain't a horse."

"God's truth: a white horse is not a horse," answers Lopez de Aguada, without fully understanding why Úrsulo has chosen to quote something he'd heard from the Chinese visitor, Chung Sun.

Lopez de Aguada departs to deliver the news to Mayor de la Cerva y Tana himself.

Úrsulo regrets having made his report. "If I'd known about Shears and Nepomuceno, I would have kept my trap shut. A white horse ain't white, it's a horse . . . or however it goes!"

—

Úrsulo heard that quote from Chung Sun, the only Chinese man in Bruneville, who arrived three years ago with an Englishman who long since set sail; whether he wanted to leave Bruneville or the Chinese man, no one knows (it depends on who's telling the story). It's not clear what the nature of their relationship was. They dressed very differently but with the same panache; they both kept servants; they treated each other like colleagues or brothers, sitting together at meals and holding lengthy, philosophical discussions. They didn't seem to know they were repeating the argument of Gongsun Long, and their conversations were difficult to follow:

"I believe a white horse isn't a horse."

"A white horse is not a horse?"

"A white horse is not a horse."

"Its color isn't its shape, its shape isn't its color. If you ask for a white horse at a stable and there isn't one, but there is a black horse, we can't say we have a white horse."

"If we can't say we have a white horse, then the horse we are looking for isn't there."

"Because it's not there, what it comes down to is that the white horse isn't a horse."

Their conversations were of little interest to Bruneville's "intellectuals," but on the other side of the river these conversations were often quoted by folks in Matasánchez, circulating around the plaza's arcades and debated at length around tables in the Café Central. Only Dr. Velafuente made light of them, changing their meaning a bit. Their discussions really came to life in these jokes, capturing folks' imaginations, and became oft-quoted snippets of wisdom.

The Englishman, Mr. Sand, and the Chinese man, Chung Sun, had traveled the world together. No one knows their story, not even their slave (Roho, or, in Spanish, Rojo), because they bought him shortly before arriving in Texas, when they disembarked in New Orleans. It was impossible to get information from their servants, who were all Chinese and spoke only their mother tongues; they had a hard time even understanding each other.

Once when the Englishman, Mr. Sand, became suddenly ill—he passed out cold, completely losing consciousness—Chung produced a bundle of powder from his pockets and a felt case with long needles from his sleeve. He requested a glass of water, mixed in the powder, and made Sand drink it while he punctured his prone body with the needles in various places.

When Sand came to, he looked like Saint Sebastian (the needles were long, almost like arrows), and he was horrified. Chung removed them and apologized. He was never seen to employ them again, but the chambermaid at Mrs. Big's Hotel (Sandy's cousin), where the men stayed for some time, swore she had seen him in the mornings when he was alone, using them on himself "on his shoulders and his feet."

As far as the powder was concerned, no one ever saw it again either.

(Word is that the Chinese Chung is over a hundred years old, some say even older than that, but in all honesty it's impossible to tell how old he is.)

Four of King's gunslingers go to the fisherman Santiago's house. They think two greasers hanging from Mrs. Big's tree aren't enough to teach them a lesson, so they're going after the fisherman's family. The three kids still aren't home.

"I saw them on Hector's cart."

"But that was a while ago, right?"

"Yeah, but they're not here, whaddaya wanna do about it?"

His wife, who sells empanadas in the market, is still working.

They set fire to the thatched roof.

Then they go after his wife. It's better we don't follow them.

Charles Stealman returns home just when the party is supposed to start. He asks loudly, "Elizabeth?" The slaves answer in unison, "In her room." Without pausing, he climbs the stairs two at a time, strides along the hallway and opens the door, shuts it, and leans back against it.

"Elizabeth?"

Elizabeth jumps up from her desk (she's fully dressed to receive their visitors and hearing him say her name aloud startled her), a drop of ink trembling on her penholder.

Charles's muddy boots dirty the rug. Elizabeth averts her eyes, exclaiming "Charles!" in a disapproving tone.

"Don't say my name like I'm one of your dogs!"

Your humor seems to have gone to the dogs, and my nerves are shattered, Elizabeth thinks, she'd like to write that in her diary.

"Go change! You're filthy! Has anyone cancelled?"

The lawyer is silent.

"Tell me, have you received any cancellations? Is anyone coming?"

Heavier silence.

The drop of ink falls from the penholder, but they don't notice.

"I'm asking you if you've had any cancellations."

Still, silence.

Lawyer Stealman's hearing isn't very good. He can't always trust his ears. He's becoming deaf, though his wife doesn't want to acknowledge it because of a silly cliché: a man's hearing is indicative of his sexual potency, which is why deafness is seldom discussed, practically taboo; there's no prejudice against deaf women, they just disappear: they're a nuisance, that's all; but men on the other hand, are another story . . . hearing and hard-ons go hand in hand, so they say (which is a stupid saying, because homo erectus wasn't called that because of his dick, plus it's not easy to get an erection by listening).

In any case, today's no day for clichés. Lawyer Stealman won't let her disturb his composure. He goes over to the washstand, its ceramic jug is filled with water, and half-heartedly washes his face, straightens his slightly dirty tie, and tries his best to ignore his strident, screaming wife. The former Miss Vert is really furious.

When his mental calculations are complete, Charles finally turns, and, still hard of hearing, begins his report in a calm, low voice:

"The Lieutenant Governor is coming. Captain Callaghan is coming. McBride, Pridgen, and the Senator . . . you don't know him, he took poor Pinckney Henderson's seat, just call him 'Senator.'"

His words couldn't possibly have a worse effect on Elizabeth. She explodes.

"Matthias Ward? Senator Matthias Ward is coming to my house? He's a Mason!"

Charles says, loud and clear, "Mason?"

"Mason! Where do you get your information? Who do you talk to? Even my slaves know that!"

Stealman is about to lose his cool, but he draws upon his phlegmatic reserves.

"You want to know who's coming to the party or not? The Mexicans aren't coming. They had a problem . . . with one of their relatives. That highfalutin Nepomuceno who fought against Zachary Taylor. So much the better. Callahan wouldn't have liked seeing them here."

"Didn't I tell you that myself? But you didn't listen to me! And now you quote me my own arguments, today of all days? My arguments! Mine! And now you're going to tell me about that Mason, Ward, because . . ."

There's a knock at the door, the timid voice of one of her slaves.

"Ma'am . . . you have visitors. A woman and a young lady, we don't know them."

The slave slides her calling card under the door. Charles picks it up and reads aloud:

"Catherine Anne Henry."

Before leaving the Stealmans' conversation—if you can call it that—there are three important digressions we need to make. The first is about Senator Matthias Ward. The second about Stealman. The third about Callahan:

1. Senator Matthias Ward replaced former Senator James Pinckney Henderson, whom Elizabeth likes to think of as an old friend simply because she signed a petition, along with approximately 499 other Texans, "The protection of slaves as property," in which they requested "a plan to ensure the protection of slaves in Texas"—the petition's first stipulation was "the need for an extradition treaty between the U.S. and Mexico in order to require the return of criminals guilty of capital offenses, if necessary," above all to protect the constitutional rights (and human rights, sovereign rights) of property owners; in other words, the right to recover fugitive slaves. Its goal, "despite the lying, fanatical dogs in Congress," was to defend the rights laid out in the Constitution, "Liberty, Justice, and the Pursuit of Happiness." The document referred to Santa Ana as the "bloodthirsty Mexican tyrant, that black murderer of children and Americans." It held that defending the right to own property (i.e., slaves) was at the heart of American institutions and that persecutory northerners had lost their minds over the issue of slavery, "threatening and attempting to destroy the vital tenets of

our Constitution—that 'chart and chain' which has united us since the days of Washington." Et cetera. Out of irrational and cantankerous loyalty to her supposed "friend," Elizabeth despises the man who now occupies his Senate seat—that's why she called him a "Mason," which is the worst possible insult she can think of.

2. Second digression: Stealman arrived home with a swollen ego for several reasons. It had been a busy day. He had assumed ownership of the barge and the tugboat as well as two other vessels without paying a cent. Then that thing with the damn-fool sheriff and Nepomuceno happened. True, Texas was a land of great opportunity, but it had one major problem: the Mexicans.

Perhaps "big-headed" isn't the right word to describe a man like Stealman. He'd made a respectable fortune from three silver mines in Zacatecas—they didn't belong to him but, as they say, "finders keepers," that is, if the finder is a gringo (the Mexican view is different: the ones who get to keep fortunes are the ones who deserve them, not by virtue of hard work, but by virtue of birth and family ties, etcetera). The truth of the matter is that the money he made was not from hitting the motherlode, it was his management of the mines—with extremely low wages and long hours for the miners, while the impure silver they produced was sold as if it were the very highest quality.

He was canny, that Stealman. He laid the foundations for Bruneville with minimal investment; he got money from the State to build the two main roads; through the sale of plots of land a miraculous transformation took place, and this forgotten end of the earth became a bustling city. With all his connections (not to discount those of his wife's family), politicians considered Bruneville an important outpost and offered it military protection, which brought the economic benefits of an army base.

Everything Stealman has he created from nothing (just like Gold and many other recent arrivals); in other words, from his own initiative and enterprising nature, despite the obstacles presented by the Mexicans, who had a legal case pending to reclaim the land on which he founded Bruneville. In his defense, Stealman presented a piece of paper signed by the widowed plaintiff, Doña Estefanía, in which she agreed to the use of the land "for the improvement of the region." To shut her up, Stealman paid her two elder sons one peso per hectare (no joke: one miserable peso, when he had received much more than that for each plot of land, but he thought it was fair because it had been his idea to begin with and he had done all the work). "Same as always," Stealman said to himself. "Those lazy Mexicans" wanted to make money off what he had in spades and what they lacked: "ingenuity, hard work, and dedication. Just like women."

In his argument, Stealman omitted a few details. To wit: he rented the mines in Zacatecas from a Mexican who had already mined all the high-quality silver out of them; what Stealman managed to dig out of them was of the poorest quality. He knew very well that he had taken advantage of the widow Estefanía, that she had never intended to establish a city there because, in her own words, "The land between the Río Nueces and the Río Bravo is meant for raising cattle." She was right, plus it must be emphasized that Estefanía never sold her land to Stealman—he made her sign a piece of paper retaining his services to legalize her ownership of it under the new Texas government; they agreed that he would help her put the land to good use under the new government—and she had good reason: she was worried they would tax her out of owning it. Lastly, the dispute between the brothers (those from her earlier marriage and Nepomuceno) created the opportunity to pretend he was sorting things out legally when the fact is that the only thing he planned on doing was mollifying them, he'd find a way to shut them up sooner or later.

And that's not the only shady business he's engaged in. Charles Stealman has a box full of "squatter titles," "labor titles," and more; but now that the party at his house is starting, we don't have time to get into that. Still, there's no need to be quite so merciless about him: he really is quite enterprising and organized. He knows everything, and he follows the law to the letter when he's doing business with Anglo-Saxons, unless he has a good reason not to, of course.

3. The third and final digression: It's more than a month since Captain Callahan—who Stealman said is coming to the party—and some of his men ran into a band of horse thieves in the York Ravine. They killed three or four of them and the rest escaped into the prickly bushes that grow in those parts—their small, sweet-smelling yellow flowers blossom only once a year; bees love them and make well-known honey from them.

The next morning, his men decided to follow the tracks of one of the bandits who had been wounded in the leg: easy prey. They found him in the blink of an eye; without his horse he'd had to drag himself along the ground like the snake he was.

When he saw them approach, he made signs that he would surrender. Captain Callahan approached on his horse without dismounting.

"What, greaser? You wanna go to Seguin?"

"Yes, sir. I need a doctor, I'm bleeding to death."

"Okay. Get up in the saddle behind me."

The Mexican took a large silk handkerchief from his pocket and tied it tightly around his leg—the keepsake was dear to him, he always carried it folded away in his pocket, probably a love token, and now that he had a ray of hope he used it. The Mexican struggled to his feet and hobbled over to Captain Callaghan with a mighty effort. When he was an arm's length away, the Captain took out his pistol and shot him in the forehead.

When Chung Sun, the Chinese man, heard this story, he said what he usually said about gringos: "Properly styled barbarians," the only comprehensible English phrase he knew—his white horses and all his other maxims and epigrams make no sense in any language.

We'll have to digress again to introduce the women who've just arrived at the Stealmans' home, but we've got time; Elizabeth is slow to leave her room because she must give specific instructions to her slaves on how to dress Charles (he can't show up looking like a beggar), plus it takes her time to descend the stairs because her shoes are too tight.

The first writers in the Henry family were two sisters who authored two books of poetry written by "The Sisters from the West." Some of the poems allude to reincarnation, as if they had lived before. What is certain is that they were born under the shadow of a crooked forebear. Their grandfather, George, claimed he was descended from the house of Henry, when in reality he was an infantryman who fled the misery of England to seek his fortune, leaving a wife and two children behind. He crossed the ocean. In the new world he enlisted in the Spanish army, changed his name to Jorge, married, and was widowed. In recognition of his service, the Spanish granted him land along the Mississippi River. Then the territory changed hands to the Anglo-Saxons. Jorge changed his name back to George Henry and got remarried to a young Anglo-Saxon heiress. They had children.

One morning George's son from his first (legitimate) marriage, the one he had abandoned in England, showed up on his doorstep. He had come to claim damages for his abandonment (he was orphaned early in childhood after watching his mother die in poverty). When George kicked him out he settled down further upriver to plot his revenge. He had his plans. He had carefully studied George's way of doing business from afar, through the lens of bitterness and envy while living in poverty. He knew how to manipulate land, and people.

Father and son became rivals. Their competition helped to turn that stretch of the river into the world's foremost source of cotton.

The Henrys' fortunes grew atop a pile of bodies, buried and forgotten: slaves who were the secret to their success; as well as the local Indians, whose hunting land they stole and whom they hired mercenaries to murder for them.

But that shady character, the eldest of the Henrys, paid his price. George-Jorge was struck by deep depression, a depression so deep it proved impossible to conquer. His soul went into free fall until he reached the very nadir of desperation and lost his mind. In 1794, suffering from a hellish depression that knows no name, George-Jorge Henry tied an iron cauldron around his neck and jumped into a branch of the Mississippi, the Buffalo, whose waters were dark and deep, and which goes by his name to this day: Henry. His youngest daughter, Sarah, was ten.

The cauldron is an important detail for some, because they say it's the only possession he brought with him across the ocean, and that he used it to earn a living his first few weeks here, selling tasty punch. But that's a tall tale, an obscure myth that has no roots in reality. How could he have carried such a large, heavy cauldron on his voyage? And the story (and the damage done by gossips) doesn't end there. Some folks claimed he had crossed the ocean *inside* the cauldron—captain, sailor, and passenger of his own vessel; now that really takes the cake. A man crossing the ocean in a cauldron? Not even in a fairy tale!

In time Sarah married, twice. The first marriage was rather unfortunate, and better forgotten. She was lucky to be widowed early. When she received the news of her husband's death she burst into tears. She ran to her room and shut the door. Alone, she stopped crying and began to rejoice. "I'm free! I'm free!" No matter how much she said "free," it didn't help her, though. Because she got married again, to a peculiar man, one Lieutenant Ware, who was a well-read, mustachioed widower given to grandiloquence and outlandishness thanks to his travels and adventures—he had explored North Africa, supposedly looking for mines, when in fact he was trying to establish connections for the slave trade; he failed because the Portuguese beat him to it. However, he returned full of tales of his exploits, this unsuccessful slave trader.

Lieutenant Ware's penchant for storytelling was legendary. Some even attributed the story of the seagoing cauldron to him, but those of us who are familiar with his tales know that's impossible, without the shadow of a doubt. He was a raconteur and a liar, but he wasn't an imbecile.

Lieutenant Ware and Sarah had two daughters, the future authors—the first of their line—the so-called Sisters from the West.

Catherine Anne was the firstborn. It was four more years before Sarah conceived her next child because Lieutenant Ware was away. When he returned he said he had been in Zacatecas "looking for mines," but we shouldn't believe a word of what he said, because in Mexico there were no cheap slaves for sale, which he could resell at a higher price, and that was always his business. We'd do better to believe that he went into alcoholic seclusion during those years.

At the age of thirty-nine Sarah gave birth to her second daughter, Georgette, and promptly fell into a deep depression, nearly losing her mind, the ground beneath her, the roof, the walls, heaven and hell, she even lost herself. There's not a soul who attributes the story of the cauldron to her, though she did try to drown herself in the river. Lieutenant Ware sent her off to a mental institution.

Once she was locked up, Sarah Henry Ware spent her days pining for her husband and lamenting her abandonment. When Lieutenant Ware visited Sarah didn't recognize him. Sarah also pined for her daughters, especially baby Georgette, and would cry out for her eldest, Catherine Anne. When the girls came to visit, she didn't recognize them either, and she was repelled by their desire for affection.

Sarah kept her looks and her beautiful, thick hair. Lieutenant Ware moved her to the home of one of his children from his first marriage, and they locked her away on the top floor like Rapunzel.

By the time the two sisters, Catherine Anne and Georgette, published their first book of poems, Sarah had passed away. We don't know how she perished. There was no cauldron to jump into the river with, despite the fact some claimed she jumped into the Henry with a cauldron around her neck . . . but let's leave it there, because it's all too absurd. The fact is, she died.

Georgette married a man who doesn't matter to our story; he said he had plantations in Virginia but that was probably a lie. Outwardly she appeared to be happy. They had a son who nearly died at birth from an infection of the umbilicus, and about whom she became so anxious that her milk dried up; her husband had to hire a Negro wet nurse. Then she had two girls, though some folks say the girls were nieces who went to live with them, turning her girls into nieces before their time (when she died they went to live with their aunt). The eldest was named Sarah, after her grandmother. When the second was born she had a huge falling-out with her sister, Catherine

Anne, and fell into the same deep depression that had claimed her grandfather and her mother; then she caught yellow fever and died. Of course there are idiots who say she ended her life in the river with a cauldron around her neck, and others who say she filled the pockets of her dress with stones, but she never had the chance.

But let's get back to our story. En route to New York, Catherine Anne has stopped in Bruneville; the new steamboat to New York embarks from Punta Isabel instead of New Orleans (one of Stealman's little machinations: he was planning to sell tracts of land in Punta Isabel and needed to inject some life into the region). Catherine Anne is on her way to sign the contract for publication of her novel, and, at the request of her editor, she will stay in New York until the novel comes out, to promote it. She wrote it as "A Southern Lady." She's traveling with her two nieces. The eldest is quite a character.

Neals, the Ranger who runs the jailhouse in the center of Bruneville, has not been invited to the Stealmans' party. He knows all about the party and the other gatherings they've had; people always ask him, "You going to the Stealmans', Neals?" He thinks it's downright shameful they never remember to include him.

Neals is one of the few folks on the town payroll, most of the Rangers are free agents. He was given this "honor" in recognition of his service to his country, that's his reward for being one of the "Texan Devils."

Overheard at Mrs. Big's: "'Texan Devils' is what those greasy Mexicans shouted at us when we rode victorious through the streets of their capital. A motley crew, some of us on mules, others on mustangs, and others on thoroughbreds; some of us standing in the saddle, some of us looking backwards, some riding sidesaddle like the ladies, others with their arms around their mounts' necks, others lying back on their animals like they were dodging bullets. Everyone wore hats, caps, and berets made from the hides of dogs, cats, raccoons, wildcats, and even Comanches. The Mexicans said we were only a half-civilized species, part human and part demon, with a touch of lion, devil, and snapping turtle (the huge ones from Florida that live in the mud) mixed in. They were more afraid of us than the devil himself. When we returned to Port Lavaca, Texas, we were received like heroes, because we had conquered a country that had repressed freedom, deprived the rights of men, and for the past twenty years interfered with our manifest destiny to rule these shores."

The three Henry women have no idea what happened in Bruneville today. Though three of them are in town, only two have come to Elizabeth's house. The one who hasn't come is strikingly beautiful, her name is Sarah Ferguson (the daughter of Georgette Henry); she and her sister have lived with their aunt since their mother died in '49, and from their aunt they've learned to enjoy riding, betting, card games, reading, and writing.

Sarah made an appointment with Jim Smiley weeks ago. They agreed to meet on the banks of the Rio Grande, in Mrs. Big's "Casino." "It'll be a great night!" Sarah wants to play at least one hand against the most famous card sharp in the land; it's a stroke of luck they'll both be in Bruneville at the same time, she can't pass up such an opportunity.

She's known as Doña Estefanía throughout the land: in the ranches, hamlets, and cities of the Valley and the plains, in the river-ports and seaports, in both Indian and cowboy camps. She owns half the world, or at least this world we're in. And she's Nepomuceno's mother.

She's an important woman. Some folks talk about her famous bad humor, others talk about her incredible acts of generosity, and still others talk about her miserliness. There's not an Indian or a Mexican who doesn't consider her the owner of everything she lays her eyes on. And there's not a gringo who wouldn't like to steal what she has, many of them think she's an incompetent who has not served the region well (and that's how they justify their theft, saying it's "in the region's best interests"). The Negroes think she has magical powers. The Mexicans think she has the Midas touch. The Indians despise her, she's responsible for the obliteration of entire settlements, they think she's a force of evil. For Father Vera, the parish priest in Matasánchez (who occasionally gets confused and calls it "Matagómez" or "Matamóros" because "mata" means "kill" in Spanish), Doña Estefanía is a saint, an angel, or a cherub, depending on how much she puts into the collection plate. She doesn't give a penny to the (pathetic) Catholic church in Bruneville, so Father Rigoberto thinks she's a witch and a heretic.

Who's right and who's wrong?

People examine the clothes she wears down to their last stitch, the horses in her stables, the size of her herd (which has grown, thanks in part to Nepomuceno's lasso), everything she owns, even her chapels—which look more like churches—her silos and feedstores, her furniture, her various carriages, her jewels, and of course everyone talks about her cooking. "She has the hands of an angel." "It puts you under a spell, eating from her kitchen."

She, however, thinks of herself differently, and we should let her speak for herself. But Doña Estefanía doesn't exactly *think* of herself. She thinks in terms of the domain of the Holy Spirit, about rain, livestock, her vaqueros' skill, and the transport, payment, and treatment of the animals in the slaughterhouse. We'll soon come to see her point of view and how she views herself.

Doña Estefanía doesn't see herself as an important woman. She doesn't even see herself as a "Doña." She refers to herself by her nickname, "Nania." Nania is what her father called her. Nania had a white pony, "Pretty and little like you, and her name is Tela" (which means "web" in Spanish). Her father had a cabriolet made for her; he called it her "spider." "Let's see my Nania with her Tela and her spider!" She learned how to drive it all by herself in a heartbeat, her face protected from the sun by a veil (she couldn't hold both her parasol and the reins at the same time). White gloves on her hands, of course.

But she preferred to ride her pony, despite the fact "that's not for Nania, young ladies shouldn't ride." Sometimes it occurs to her that she has three children and has been "blessed" with two more—usually only at Christmastime, when she can't avoid them—because her daughters-in-law and her sons' quarrels irritate her.

Up at Rancho del Carmen, Nepomuceno's two stepbrothers, José Eusebio and José Esteban, are near the headwaters of the Río de la Mentira, which some inaccurately refer to as Río del Carmen. They have stayed behind at Rancho del Carmen to protect Doña Estefanía, and all three of them anxiously await the Bruneville judge's decision on the lawsuit over her land.

But the brothers don't stand around awaiting the news because they're both men of action. At the crack of dawn, they went after more than a hundred head of cattle that had been stolen by King's men the previous day. The tracks were still fresh, that's why they were in a hurry; it wasn't the rainy season and the wind wasn't blowing. They were lucky, the cattle thieves were just a stone's throw away. But they didn't want to confront them; they preferred to play their own trick on them, take back the livestock and return to the corral before they had a chance to rebrand them. Here's how it went down: while the cattle rustlers were sleeping, the brothers shot them so they wouldn't have a chance to resist, and took back Doña Estefanía's cattle, returning in time for breakfast: delicious huevos rancheros made with soft tortillas, tomato salsa, and runny yolks.

Some folks say her stepsons stayed at the ranch with Doña Estefanía because they don't want to get involved in the dispute— they know that suing gringos is playing with fire—but the truth is that deep in their hearts they do care about the outcome of the lawsuit. Despite the fact it's not their property, they cherish the hope that if they remain on good terms with their father's widow they'll get a piece of it, especially now that Glevack is gone, they always knew he was a bad egg, but they were clever enough not to confront him directly, they just called him a freeloader and a scumbag behind his back—when all is said and done, though, they were deeply loyal to her and were willing to risk their hides for her.

There's also no doubt that Nepomuceno's not afraid to tangle with the Texans, he's taken them on before, he couldn't just stand idly by and let them steal his mother's land by manipulating the law in order to create Bruneville, selling what wasn't theirs to begin with.

The news arrives, without the oranges, garlic, or onions Doña Estefanía had ordered. Two of her cowboys deliver the details of what has transpired. They carelessly left the mule at the dock—who knows what the Rangers are going to do with it, by now they're probably screwing it from behind. Let's not worry about the oranges, they all eventually got picked up; but the onions and garlic were left behind, and that was just careless.

It goes without saying that Doña Estefanía and the two brothers aren't pleased by the news.

It's true Glevack was bad news, but compared to the Texans he seemed as harmless as a dead, plucked chicken whose beak had been chopped off.

Those damn Texans, they accepted land from the Spanish and then the Mexicans, signing documents swearing they were Catholics and would be loyal to their government, but at the first opportunity they claimed that the Mexicans were oppressing them (what!?), that the Catholics were intolerant (seriously!? compared to the Protestants?!), that they weren't free, and so on and so forth. They had already profited from the land that had been given to them, selling it off in parcels—in violation of the aforementioned contracts—at exorbitant prices, and they had already grabbed huge swaths of land, claiming they were exercising their legal rights. But owning slaves is the real issue: Mexico forbids it on principle, while Texans deem it a God-given right.

Before we return to the Stealmans', let's take a gander around Bruneville.

In the Market Square, the gringo with a monkey is playing a hurdy-gurdy. The monkey dances, the hurdy-gurdy wheezes, but no one pays any attention to them, there's almost no one around, and those who are, hurry past in fear. The organ-grinder is tired of playing to an empty crowd, he's an artist! He closes his hurdy-gurdy, calls to the monkey, clips a leash to its collar, and heads to the Café Ronsard with the leash in one hand and the hurdy-gurdy pressed against his body. He's afraid, too. He enters the café. He leaves his instrument by the door (he knows he's not allowed to play inside, they've told him before, and he won't drink with it at his side, that would look ridiculous—he's still angry they won't let him play, but today's not the day to renew that argument; he brushes his anger off like a fly). He orders a drink at the bar.

"Tell that gringo to take his monkey outside. Last time it kicked up a ruckus." Ronsard says this but no one makes a move.

The barkeep repeats himself to the organ grinder in his broken English. The gringo thinks it over for a moment. His loves his monkey, but he only has one life, and out on the street things are looking bad. He takes the leash, goes outside, ties the monkey to the hitching post at the Café Ronsard's front door, the one that Gabriel put up—two poles and a crossbeam, some folks call it "The H," it's meant for horses—and he goes back inside, not because he really wants to (they don't treat him right) but because (as we said) he's afraid.

The Eagles are meeting at the Café Ronsard. But no one who sees them there would know. That's why they're meeting in public, to avoid suspicion. The Rangers, hired guns, have thrown themselves headlong into taking revenge upon Nepomuceno, for years now they've been scaring Mexicans every chance they get. Today the Rangers are going from house to house, searching for what is taking place in plain sight. Meeting in secret would be tantamount to a confession of guilt.

Besides, Gabriel Ronsard usually takes part in card games and chats with his friends, he's the owner and the host.

It doesn't look like they're confabulating.

At Ronsard's table: Carlos the (insurgent) Cuban; Don Jacinto the saddler; and the foreigner, José Hernández—who calls the café "la pulpería." Half a dozen Eagles wander around, some sit at the bar and adjacent tables, alert: Sandy, who has returned from her reconnaissance; Hector, the round-faced cart owner; Cherem the cloth merchant; Frenchie the seed merchant; and Alitas, the chicken farmer.

Don Jacinto to José Hernández:

"Where's your singsongy accent from?"

"The plains down south."

"I've been down south. What plains? Say what you want, Don José, there ain't no prairies down there, not even brushwood or flat valleys; it's all ravines and giant trees that are big enough to hang long strings of . . ."—he was about to say "Texans" but just in time he says—"Indians."

"Don't you try to tell me, gaucho, there's much more down south than what you've seen . . ."

Carlos the Cuban shuffles the deck—there's not a trace of clumsiness in his movements, the cards fly through his hands, he's right at home. He deals and they quietly begin to speak of crimes. Since the Café Ronsard has begun to fill up, he sets the tone: they won't talk about anything new, and they won't go into details. It makes it nearly impossible for anyone to follow their conversation.

Carlos names the first atrocity.

"Josefa Segovia."

Ronsard immediately responds.

"1851."

"Frederick Canon." That's Hector sitting in his chair, four feet away.

Laughing with barred teeth. That's how they let off steam.

(What are they talking about? Not a soul can figure it out! In Penville that year, the gringo Frederick Canon raped a Mexican, Josefa Segovia, who reported his crime to the authorities along with conclusive proof: she was accompanied by her doctor who presented a written report, and her nephew who was a witness— Frederick broke into her house, beat up Josefa's nephew (who was barely ten years old), tied him to a chair, and forced himself on the young woman before the boy's eyes. They also presented something rather scandalous: photographs of a reenactment of the crime, in which the victims—the girl who had been raped and her nephew— acted out the scene with Josefa's oldest cousin playing the part of the criminal, Frederick Canon. Among the photographs were pictures considered indecent, close-ups of the boy's injuries and the bruises Frederick left on Josefa's body.)

(Two days later, Frederick Canon's body was found in the dirty stream that carried away Penville's sewage and trash; it looked as though he had fallen into the stream in a drunken stupor. The authorities accused Josefa Segovia of murdering him, and, despite the fact there was no evidence to support their accusation, they took her into custody. The following Saturday, at sunset, the townspeople stormed the jailhouse with the sheriff's cooperation. A group of men took Josefa from her jail cell, groped her and showed her off to the crowd, drenched her, and tore her dress off, leaving her nearly naked. The townspeople witnessed her beating and how they dragged her through the streets and doused what was left of the lovely young woman with turpentine. They threw a rope around the lowest branch of an ancient pepper tree and hanged Josefa. Her rags made a stark contrast to the clothes of the people celebrating her lynching: women dressed in their finest, men in clean clothes—shirtsleeves (because of the unbearable heat) and hats—as if they were going to church. Musicians played. People began to dance at the feet of the dead woman, celebrating the death of the "greaser," and some set Josefa's corpse on fire.)

How the Eagles laugh. They smile in bitter revenge, as if saying these names has repaired these offenses, as if it has given them pleasure.

"And what about the guy who kept his herd 333 miles north of Rancho del Carmen?"

Silence. The number 333 makes their blood boil. In one swift stroke, like a general's, King's men had taken every last head of cattle from this Mexican in a skillful coup by the lawyers. Judge Jones (who people called Busy Bucks) accepted the evidence—all as counterfeit as twelve-dollar bills—presented by King's legal representatives (Judge Jones was the predecessor of Judge White, old Whatshisname).

"It's apples, the . . ."

Another pause. "Apples" is a code word for one of their slogans: "The Anglos' violence is a strategy to intimidate us, its obvious goal to take away our rights and our property. What they call laws and dress up like laws are nothing more than an ongoing battle for our property, our privileges, and our basic rights. No matter what a Mexican does to get his property back, even if it's as honest as growing apples, they call larceny, robbery, or theft."

They each recite this in silence; it looks like they're just sitting there, mouths shut. Jacinto the saddler snorts. Carlos imitates Shine, the customs agent, wrinkling his nose like something smells bad.

"And what about those seven lemons?"

They're referring to Mexicans who had been maltreated by the lawless gringos when the Mexicans came to visit Bruneville. Customs agent Shine was the only American who dared speak out about it, which earned him a beating on the way home from work one night. The next morning Shine found a message painted on his house: "Death to pro-greasers." The work of the Secret Circle, who didn't sign it but most everyone knows it was them.

Carlos's expression provokes more laughter, but he quickly changes it, pretending to speak with an accent:

"Be right back, gonna get some tobaccy."

He acts cross-eyed, his eyes either side of his nose, caricaturing Shears.

"Wait! Let's go visit those guys at Espantosa!"

"Yeah! Let's go join them!"

It's because King killed seven Mexicans near Laguna Espantosa, in Dimita County, for delivering stolen cattle. On previous occasions he paid for them, even paid well, and was happy. Folks suspect he had unfinished business with them.

They sit there making allusions and obscure, cruel jokes aloud, yet no one understands them, they're speaking in code. Once in a while they lower their voices to keep folks from hearing what they're saying because it's obvious what they're referring to.

"Say, are the cart-drivers from the south winning the Cart War?"

Anyone watching them would think they were crazier than hungry loons. They quickly raise their voices to avoid arousing suspicion:

"Yeah! Who wouldn't want to meet their maker on one of Barreta's wheels!"

A certain Señor Balli went to visit his property, Rancho Barreta, north of the Colorado Creek. A band of gringos waylaid him on the road and tied him to one of the wheels of his wagon, then flogged him and left him to die, laying siege to Rancho Barreta until he had breathed his last. Then they set upon his widow like horseflies, without even giving her a moment to dry her tears, and made her an offer she couldn't refuse—three Mexican pesos for all of Rancho Barreta—threatening that unless she agreed her male children would meet the same fate as her husband and her two adolescent daughters would be assaulted.

In a very soft voice Don Jacinto added, "goddamn larrabers" (he means "land grabbers" but they know what he means).

"What do you hear about Platita Poblana?"

That was their nickname for a silver smuggler from Puebla. Like others in his line of work, he was murdered by the Texans who hired him. Of course they had the goods safe and sound before they did away with him.

Platita Poblana had had drinks with some of the Eagles on more than one occasion. No one has the stomach to laugh at this one. Plus the mood has become sour, despite their forced, rebellious laughter—their attempts to deny the reality of the Texans' reign. Triggered by this walk down memory lane, other offences come to mind: King ordered a bridge to be built, and any Mexican who dared cross it was shot; in Nueces County any Mexican who rides with a new saddle will meet the same fate; cadavers swing from the trees, and they're not gringos; La Raza (the Mexicans who had accepted American citizenship) are leaving their ranches and abandoning their property, crossing the Río Bravo in search of safety, and even then some aren't even safe because the Texans couldn't care less about the border (since they had moved it from the Nueces to the Bravo on a whim).

Two tables away, a drunken gringo—it's been a long day— thinks he's having a conversation with someone, when in fact he's sitting alone: "Here's what I know: if they're wearing fringed leather, they're Injuns; if they're wearing hats, they're Mexicans; if you see either one, just take a shot and start running. Mexicans are cruel by nature, and Injuns are downright wild."

Mrs. Big is all alone—even her employees have gone home, the musicians have hit the road too; only Sandy's cousin is still there, at the back of the kitchen—and she's furious. The Tigress of the East was supposed to sing tonight.

Sarah Ferguson enters the Café Ronsard. At the last minute, when she was about to head down to the Bruneville dock (dressed as a man) to keep her appointment at Mrs. Big's Hotel, she received a message from Smiley.

We moved the game to the Café Ronsard in the Market Square.

We already know why.

It's not a bad disguise, she spent a lot of time on it—how could she not: she's an attractive coquette—but who would believe she's a man with that angelic face?

In one hand she carries a walking stick with a golden handle carved with a horse's head. She orders a coffee "with brandy, please," without altering her voice.

"Who's this faggot?" Carlos says quietly to Ronsard.

"Shh. Such a delicate flower probably has ears of . . ."

"Gold, like his walking stick, right?" says Don Jacinto.

After Sarah, Jim Smiley appears through the swinging doors, he has his frog in a cardboard box in one hand. He orders a drink at the bar without noticing Sarah; he pays the barkeep a deposit (in advance, according to house rules) for the deck of cards.

Smiley sits down at a table with Blade, the barber.

"Hi, Smiley! Remember the Alamo?"

It's Blade's catch phrase, his signature, and he greets everyone with it.

At the bar, Sarah asks for Smiley. The barkeep points to the table where he just sat down, and says loudly, "Smiley! Someone here wants to speak with you!"

Smiley and Blade look at Sarah in surprise. *Him? Him?* thinks Smiley. *He's the one I've been writing to, challenging him to a game? Life is full of surprises!* Blade just repeats *"Remember the Alamo"* to himself; this fancy young man makes him nervous.

Here comes Wayne, he motions to the barkeep (who knows what to serve him, the usual) and sits down at the table next to Smiley. The foursome is complete: Blade, Sarah, Wayne, and Smiley.

"Good evening. Nice to meet you," he says to Sarah. "My name is Wayne. Josh Wayne. I don't know what I was looking for when I came to Texas. I made some money. I got some land. But that wasn't enough. I wanted to feel useful."

"Yeah yeah yeah, we already know ... I'm Smiley and I don't like small talk. Shuffle those cards, let's play."

"Remember the Alamo."

"I'm Soro," says Sarah.

Trapper Cruz enters the Café Ronsard with some riding pants under his arm, underclothes the Lipans make for women (who haven't been brought up properly), which he's bringing to one of the girls who works the room.

Trapper Cruz is desperate to marry off his daughter Clara. Partly out of prudence (*Who knows how much longer I'll be around, better leave her in good hands because what would happen if I died, I'm the only family she's got.*), and partly because he can't get along with her (*I can't take it anymore, you're exactly like your mother!*), and partly because he wants to be free to marry, though that desire has diminished; his heart, which beat for Perla, must find another.

Who else is going to find her a husband if not her father? *My sweet girl.* Although today is an exceptional day, although he feels betrayed by unworthy Perla (*It don't matter to me, she's just a maid.*), and although he's relieved because that cowboy Mateo wasn't good enough for his progeny, he heads to the Café Ronsard. The day was a loss anyways, he'd already heard about the Lipans' showdown and how they skedaddled. But he's not afraid like Peter Hat and the organ-grinder and so many others. He just feels fragile. "Today I'm gonna find a husband for my daughter." He talks to himself as he crosses the Plaza, saying "What if I die? What if I die?" in a way that sounds like he almost wants to.

As soon as he passes through the swinging doors, the brutish trapper's eyes settle on Soro-Sarah. *Him! I'll marry my daughter to that guy!* And he decides not to let him leave without having a few words. *I'll be direct, he won't get away, he looks polite, educated, and even better, he's a gringo! The way things are going a gringo would be best.*

Cruz doesn't understand why it's silent at Smiley's table and he takes advantage of the moment to approach Soro-Sarah.

"Are you married, sir?"

All four of them understand the question is directed at Soro, and that it's absurd. Married? Impossible! He wouldn't make the cut, even for the priesthood!

"Me?" Sarah asks in complete surprise.

"Yeah, you, who else?"

"No!"

He's a faggot, Wayne thinks, *that trapper is such an idiot!*

"Why not?"

"Can't you see he's awful young?" Smiley says wryly, he's not so much embarrassed by this inappropriate advance as he is eager to put an end to the discussion.

Wayne gets the joke and wants to keep it going. But he can see from Smiley's expression that if he keeps it going, there won't be a game.

"Enough chitchat. Let's play."

"Remember the Alamo," Blade says, by way of agreement. "Just never, ever, forget the Alamo."

Cruz gets the hint and lets them play. But he shouts back over his shoulder.

"I'm leaving for big bad Mexico . . . I'm headed south, you assholes, see you around . . ."

Wayne looks up and stares right through him.

Cruz goes to the bar. He won't let them make him feel like he has to leave.

The organ-grinder is sitting quietly at his side. Taking his time to finish his drink. He doesn't want to set foot outside either.

Elizabeth thinks it's fortunate the Henrys are the first to arrive at the party; both aunt and niece live in their own world. Her guests are oblivious to her last-minute adjustments. The vases aren't where they should be, the carpets are a bit out of place, the napkins aren't laid out properly, the spittoons are in the way, the benches are too, the musicians have set down their instruments where the ladies could trip over them. "What's everyone thinking about?" It's as though this is the first party she's ever hosted, everyone's head is somewhere else today.

The Henrys talk incessantly; one opines, the other comments, or vice versa. They talk to be heard, or more precisely, to hear themselves. They've never been this far south. They've both traveled through Europe, seen Boston and New York, but they've never been here. "This is Mexico?" They've repeated the question all along their journey, and now in Elizabeth's salon.

"Texas is *not* Mexico," Elizabeth breaks in, while she snaps her fingers at one of her slaves to move the carpet, which the laundresses returned this morning.

The other guests are beginning to arrive. Glevack shows up despite the fact they thought he wouldn't come since he's Sabas and Refugio's friend. That's why, seconds before he enters, the gossips are huddled, talking about how he and Nepomuceno went their separate ways because Glevack made a move on Lucia, the prettiest of Nepomuceno's girlfriends. Wicked lies—Lucia disappeared from Bruneville before the Austrian arrived. What is true is that the theft other gossips pinned on Nepomuceno was actually perpetrated by Glevack: the two of them got involved in bringing stolen cattle across the river and things turned out badly, or perhaps the Austrian made them turn out badly so he'd have a reason to part ways with Nepomuceno, since he was already planning to dispossess Doña Estefanía.

On the other side of the ocean, he was known as Glavecke. When he arrived in Mexico he changed the vowels in his name around, taking advantage of the illegibility of his Austrian passport: Glevack. He'll never open his Austrian passport again; when he arrived the Mexican authorities granted him the title of "rancher" along with three head of cattle, well-suited to the region, and a plot of land which he could use as he pleased in return for paying taxes.

He's disappointed when he sees his "land." It's small and bone-dry, like a block of stone. He wanted to be like the men who owned property as far as the eye could see, like the ones he read about in a Bavarian newspaper, "We rode for five days to reach land that didn't belong to our host." Plus, there's nothing appealing about it: there are no trees that will shed their leaves come winter only to bud again in the spring; there's no running water; he doesn't like dry grass. To sum it up, for him it's like the sea: a solid, charmless, and luckless thing that is completely oblivious to mankind.

He likes riding, but he'd prefer a wagon drawn by oxen or something faster; it's not the animal that appeals to him, just the movement, the travel, the adventure.

Glevack's adventure becomes interesting when, one day, he sees the Comanches passing by with twelve captives whom they will ransom or sell. He offers the Comanches water—true, there was a well, but it didn't make any difference to him, "There might as well not be any water"—just to start a conversation with them because he was curious about their business. He made friends with them and accompanied them to meet some bandits who hunted Mexicans along the highway—stealing everything they carried, torturing them to learn what property they owned, and killing them (they were quite meticulous, according to their story: with the information they obtained they took possession of the land belonging to the women they had recently widowed, it was a booming business).

Then he met Nepomuceno.

Every time he meets someone new, they make him an offer.

Among the captives there is a young woman who speaks a little German, she begs him to pay her ransom and free her from her captors, promising that her family will pay him double and "you'll free me from the humiliation of living with these savages another day."

After he sees the way Glevack treats her, the head of the bandits thinks he's got potential. Plus, Glevack claims he's a doctor, and a doctor is worth his weight in gold.

Nepomuceno, who's his neighbor (he's everyone's neighbor, because he owns so much land you could ride for three weeks without stopping and still be on his land), proposes to manage his land and the few head of cattle he received (for a percentage of the profits) so Glevack can return to Matasánchez and enjoy city life.

Of the three offers, Nepomuceno's is most interesting, but Glevack doesn't decline any of them. As for the captive girl, "I used her"—riding has awakened his desire for a woman. To "use her" he gives one of the savages a few coins, asks the girl to mount his horse, rides about fifty yards, asks the girl to dismount on the pretext that he has lost his pocket watch and needs help looking for it; no sooner is she on the ground than he accosts her, pushing her up against a prickly mesquite tree, grabbing her by the shoulders and pushing her skirts up, he takes her standing up without hardly lowering his pants. He leaves her there, for the Indians to come and find her—after all, she was their property.

He tells the bandits that he's going to give their offer some serious thought, that he likes the idea, and it's the truth, because he senses he'd make money with them. And the idea of spending his days full of adventure, assaulting and seducing, appeals to him.

He doesn't need to think twice about Nepomuceno's offer. He likes the kid. He can smell the money on him, it runs in the family, and he can tell he's enterprising. On the other hand, he could accept his offer *and* join the bandits too, there's no reason not to.

The passport that Glevack will never open again said that he was a "medical student at the University of Frankfurt." Why did he abandon his studies? It couldn't have been financial problems. He arrived in a first-class cabin, well-dressed and carrying money; sure, it wasn't a lot, but he didn't arrive with holes in his clothes.

But that's neither here nor there, it's in the past. We're interested in the present: Glevack curries Nepomuceno's favor. Then he gets cozy with the whole family. He marries Doña Estefanía's favorite niece. Faking his loyalty, he pushes Doña Estefanía into her own undoing. Stealman was able to become Bruneville's developer all thanks to Glevack, who's a downright traitor.

Which takes us back to his escape from university. He left because of another betrayal. That story will come later, if we can sneak it in, now we don't have time, the party at the Stealmans' house is underway.

Snippets of the men's conversation in Mrs. Stealman's salon:

"I heard there's a decent piece of land for sale, it has a pond and a ravine to the north that protects it from Indian raids. Anyone interested?"

"Are they selling by the hectare?"

"Depends on who's buying."

"To my mind, the best time for buying land has passed."

"It'll still increase in value. Land is Texas's gold."

Minister Fear is speaking quietly with a strange-looking man, it would be impossible to guess his trade or his provenance by his looks.

"It's a big favor I'm asking you, Mr. Dice."

He lowers his voice even further. It's impossible to hear him, especially since he's drowned out by a colonel who has recently arrived at Fort Brune.

"Things are even worse than I expected. Just three miles from here Indian raids never stop; they don't attack but they steal cattle. The Mexicans pass by the fort smugly, parading their Indian prisoners past us before crossing the border. What can we do? Our hands are tied. But what shocks me even more is the state our troops are in. My immediate subordinate, the one who's been assigned as my assistant—you all know him—announced to me yesterday afternoon that he's going to sell alcohol to our men. *Of course* it goes without saying that's prohibited! He asked for authorization to waive the rules and before I even had time to respond he announced that he'll do it in the commissary. When I told him absolutely not, he said he's been doing it for a while now and he's not willing to stop. Everything around here is backwards."

The women's topics of conversation aren't much different:

"We arrived in the Wild West with the intent to conquer the forests, beasts, and the natives. We brought culture and salvation."

"What matters most is to Americanize Texas, and the first priority should be race. I understand that there are slave owners in these parts who are opposed to letting all the Negros leave, let them escape to the south and take their people with them, all the dark-skinned people, the loafers, in other words, the inferior ones. Let them cross the Rio Grande and leave us pure . . ."

Catherine Anne gets up from her seat, stands and straightens her skirt with her hands, and, in a voice louder than all the other ladies she's speaking with, she says with aplomb, "That's Richard W. Walker's opinion: it's best if the Negroes escape from Texas to Latin America, crossing the border and mixing with the Mexicans . . . He believes it's a 'natural migration' for the Negroes to go to Mexico and Ecuador. In the south, the Negroes will find their place among the colored peoples of Mexico."

Here Charles Stealman interrupts: he crosses the circle of men and walks toward the group of women.

"Excuse me, but I disagree, ma'am. That opinion lacks all common sense. The slaves are our property. How would Walker feel if his houses got up and walked across the border, or his furniture, or his investments . . ."

Laughter.

But Elizabeth, who's especially interested in this topic, doesn't laugh. How long has it been since she hasn't felt jealous? Well, she's so jealous she can't think straight. She's bursting with jealousy. She doesn't like these women, and she really doesn't like the way Charles is talking to them . . .

A cold wind blows through Bruneville, but it's still hot as hell. The wind makes some folks' teeth chatter. And other folks' teeth chatter too, in fear.

Blown by the wind, the hanging corpses swing in front of Mrs. Big's Hotel: young Santiago and old Arnoldo. She's never been heavier than she is now, she's become fat and unattractive, sitting on a log some stranger left on the riverbank as a makeshift bench, watching the wind.

Well, I'll be damned! What a shitstorm, she thinks furiously, but her thoughts are incoherent. She doesn't understand. She's ruined. She's in the business of giving folks a good time and having a good time herself. Now all she has left is a graveyard hanging in the wind, her tree has become a gallows, her home a window onto death. "Stop dancing... And you, stop dancing too!" she says to the cadavers. Her face feels strangely cold, her privates feel frozen and dried up, her teeth feel as heavy as if they were made of metal.

Then she speaks to the river. "It's like you're trying to kill me."

Pretty Sandy's cousin looks out the kitchen window, where she's washing glasses, and sees Mrs. Big talking to herself; she says, "I never realized she's getting old."

Mrs. Big is not crying, but she feels an uncontrollable urge to burst into tears. "I'll jump in the river," she keeps saying, "Should I jump in the river? I'll jump in the river!" She tosses back one glass of liquor and another. Some might want to dwell on how drunk she's getting, but we'll ignore it, suffice it to say it's disgusting and of little interest.

At Peter the Austrian's house, enough of prayers, his irrational bouts of fury have passed, now he's got cabin fever (and it's only been a few hours). His curiosity is killing him—"What's going on out there in this goddamn town?"—it's eating him alive, so he gets up to no good.

Peter does the unspeakable, he goes to his daughter.

Next to his grill out in the street, Pepe, the corn-on-the-cob vendor, cooks and drinks some liquor made from who-knows-what from who-knows-where; it smells like cinnamon and pepper.

The liquor gives him a vision of a burning candelabra, red as hot coals. He rubs his eyes. When he opens them he feels the cold wind on his face. Then a respite, as though the wind has carried the unpleasant candelabra far away.

The cold wind in Bruneville blows uninvited through an open window at the Stealmans' party; the draperies, carpets, flowers and vases, coiffed hair, skirts and jackets all warm it up.

In the circle of men (to which Charles has returned) there's King, Gold, Kenedy, Pierce (who owns the most successful cotton plantation in the region), and Smith, among other prominent Reds. Unusually, they have invited two Blues—the pharmacist, Mr. Chaste (because he's the so-called mayor, under Stealman's control, although the reason he's there today is to keep him out of trouble, "Don't let him make any more screwups, we've had enough of those today thanks to Shears"); and Mr. Seed—which irritates Elizabeth because neither of them meets her standards ("The man from the general store!"). At least he didn't bring his wife. Stealman wants to broaden his party's field of action, some say he's trying to ally himself with the Blues for the forthcoming elections, but the truth is he's trying to break his rivals' unity by corrupting them with the promise of improved social standing, for instance inviting them to this party to split them up; he'll shatter them to pieces with kid gloves.

King says, "When I opened the slaughterhouse south of the Rio Grande I spent some time in Matasánchez. I went to some fandangos. Even the priest went without giving it a second thought. They're obscene . . ."

"I don't doubt it, only lowborn folk could engage in such devious dancing," Pierce adds.

"They all go."

"Mexicans are downright disgusting, they've got the worst qualities of both races, the Spanish and the Indians," says Pierce.

More than a dozen of Pierce's slaves have escaped across the border, that's why he's got a bone to pick with Mexico. Gold interrupts. To tell his story he pitches his voice, first as a girl, then as a woman. It's hilarious.

"A girl says to her mother, 'Mexican children are almost white, right, Mama?' And her mama answers, 'Their blood is as pure as yours and mine.'"

Laughter.

"That's wrong, she's lying to her daughter," Pierce says.

"I know," Gold continues, "it just goes to show how ignorant folks are. On my last visit to the refinery, I read a piece in the *Brooklyn Eagle* by a fellow called Walt Whitman"—he pitches his voice again, lowering it like a preacher in the pulpit—"What has miserable, inefficient Mexico to do with the great mission of peopling the New World with a noble race?" Then he returns to his normal voice without getting a single laugh.

"Anglo-Saxon blood can never again be dominated by anyone who claims to be from Mexico," says Pierce, quoting President Polk.

"The White Republic should prevent white Texans from becoming slaves to the mongrel Mexicans," says Kenedy. We'll use the word "mongrel" on this occasion because the Texans use it to refer to Mexicans. The correct word is "mestizo," which doesn't have the negative connotations of "mongrel."

"Justice and God's benevolence will prevent Texas from falling once more into the hands of savages from the wilderness, ruled by the Mexican government's ignorance, superstition, anarchy, and robbery. The colonists have brought their language, their customs, and an innate love of freedom that has always defined them and their forefathers," Stealman says.

"At the slightest provocation they'll take us back to the awful times when men of true Saxon blood were humiliated and enslaved like Negroes, Indians, or mongrels," says Gold.

King: "The Mexicans are different from the Indians, who are a lost cause. Mexicans can be hired to work on a ranch, they make decent servants, but that's it. A Mexican could never (don't even consider it!) be a foreman. No question, it's their race. Some dreamers, like my friend Lastanai, think that with friendship, impartiality, and good faith we can achieve peace and even live alongside the wild Indians, turning the savages into good people—no doubt about it, they're brave, but Mexicans aren't. Yet there's no one who doesn't see the error in that argument. All Indians are irrational beings, born to pillage and fight.

"Except the Comanches. Their sugar and cotton plantations are proof, and the way they treat their slaves . . ."

"It's because they're mixed race. Think about it. The offspring they have with white women captives has domesticated them a little. And not because of the captives' customs, which they've been forced to abandon, living the unspeakable lifestyle of their captors."

"They'll drink the contents of a dead horse's stomach! And that's one of the few examples fit for discussion in this house."

"That don't matter," King says, ignoring the interruption, "the key issue is their blood, and what their blood dictates. The more white captives bear them children, the better off they'll be."

"Then the solution would be a total mixture . . ."

"Not at all! Look at the mongrels. The Mexicans are living proof," it's King again, "like I was saying . . ."

"Greasers!" Pierce spits scornfully.

They speak freely because Nepomuceno's brothers haven't shown up.

"It's a race condemned to robbery, laziness, stupidity, and dishonesty. And they have no comprehension of the future, like animals."

"They're more like dogs than men."

"Don't insult my dog; he's loyal, clean, obedient, and good-looking!"

"He's blond, your dog. What's his name?"

"Dog. What else?"

"Mexicans are lecherous. That seems to be their primary characteristic. All they care about is immediate gratification. They don't know what ambition is."

"I agree, it's because they're mixed blood," Stealman takes up the reins of the conversation once more. "In the olden days Mexicans weren't so incompetent. When you think about it, they did manage to build an empire."

"Didn't we just agree that mixing races is the only way to save them?"

"Only for Comanches, because you can't be anything worse than a savage . . ."

Pierce: "Calling it an 'empire' was an exaggeration by the Spanish, to make themselves look better; they were savages."

Kenedy: "They've always been violent."

King: "I don't doubt it. You can't question their obvious inferiority, or their unsuitability for hard labor. But they're alright at brushing down horses and, like children, they have a way with animals."

"Not mine. My Richie, my firstborn (and my only son, out of eleven children, such bad luck!) always torments our foals; he damaged the ear of his pony real bad."

"Because he's real smart."

It's hard for Mr. Chaste, the pharmacist (and mayor, though to look at him now you wouldn't know it), to keep his mouth shut. Up to this point in the conversation he hasn't thought about whether he agrees or disagrees with the views being expressed, he's too worried about this problem with Nepomuceno and Shears, plus he's well aware they've made an exception to include him, and he doesn't want to rock the boat. But the topic of Richie is something else entirely. Mr. Chaste knows all too well that intelligence is not what motivates that monster of a boy, because they brought Pierce's cook's daughter to him with burns on her legs and lacerations on her abdomen after Richie had been playing with her. They didn't want to take her to Dr. Meal—he can't keep a secret and the Pierces didn't want a scandal— so they left her with the pharmacist to give her something to alleviate her pain. Mr. Chaste had suggested they cross the river to take her to

Dr. Velafuente, but they didn't listen to him. The girl died. They said she caught yellow fever. But it was Richie's cruelty.

"Well, they know how to throw a good party," King says, "they can cook, dance . . . and some say their women are the best in the sack."

This comment is not well received by Minister Fear (who arrived without his wife, she's attending to the sick and the wounded, when he arrived he apologized to Elizabeth. "I understand, I understand," she said with genuine sympathy), who hears it despite the fact he's not in their circle; he walks over to them and interrupts.

"Gentlemen, gentlemen, this is a decent home, I don't see why you have to bring up the subject of . . ."

Chaste is still dwelling on the previous topic. *Once I saw Richie playing with a messenger pigeon. He tortured it until it was completely featherless and then he gouged out its eyes. He said he wouldn't let it go till he found its teeth. No matter how hard he looked, he never found them.*

In the Café Ronsard, Sarah-Soro holds her cards. The other three players study her face and pick their cards off the table. Sarah-Soro puts hers face down. The others study their cards, Sarah studies their faces.

"How many cards you want?" asks Josh Wayne. "Just remember the Alamo." He's trying to tease Blade, stealing his line.

Blade: "Don't mess with me, man!"

"Two for Smiley, yep, yep, mine."

"Three for me," says Blade.

"You, Soro? How many you want?"

"None."

He's bluffing, Smiley thinks. He watches him. Soro's expression is sweet, peaceful, serene, beautiful. He begins to whistle "Oh! Susanna": "I have come from Alabama with a banjo on my knee . . ." Smiley is certain. *No doubt about it, he's bluffing.*

The players exchange glances, they're ready to bet. Without saying a word, Smiley puts good money in the middle of the table.

Wayne puts his cards on the table, face down.

"I'm folding."

"Oh no! Remember the Alamo!"

Soro slides some coins next to Smiley's, and decorously adds a few more.

"I see you," Smiley says, while he puts in two more coins, "and I'll raise you. But first things first, I wanna know what makes you tick, Soro. What are you after?"

"What am I after?" Soro answers. "Four aces."

"I'm not askin' about the game," Smiley says, laughing as he speaks. "In life, what do you want outta life?" and in a serious tone he adds, "As for the game, I'm calling."

Smiley puts one more coin on the table, he really does want to see what Soro's got, he's curious.

With a flip of her wrist, Soro-Sarah shows her cards: four aces and a joker. She has five of a kind. And she answers Smiley's question without altering her girlish voice one bit.

"I want to act. On the stage of the Theatre de L'Odeon"—she pronounces the theater's name in perfect French. "As a Kickapoo Indian in a romantic comedy, lithe and pretty, dancing bare-legged. A Kickapoo or a Hasinai or a Tejas Indian, a very pretty one."

She throws her head back in laughter, with a woman's grace. No one joins her. She gets up from her chair and moves her arms strangely. This breaks the ice, the men break into laughter, everyone except Smiley. *Goddamn fucking faggot! I wasn't born to lose a card game to a faggot—who wants to be an actor! As a Kickapoo! Who the hell am I playing cards with! I was told he was . . . argh!* Saying these things to himself will have to suffice. He can't let this faggot beat him at cards *and* make him act like a fool, so he hides his anger. *So the young man wants to be an Indian girl? You think you'll shock me with that? Go be a Kickapoo, or two Kickapoos, for all I care!*

"Kickapoo Indian," he scoffs, throwing her a look that's like he's spitting at her with his eyes. "How bizarre!"

"It's not a bad idea," Sarah-Soro says. "Who wouldn't adore me if I were a beautiful Kickapoo in love?"

She says this loud and clear. Along with the three card players, the rest of the Café Ronsard turns to look at her, curious about something which, at this point, there's little doubt: is this young man a woman?

"Next question," continues Smiley; every inch the card-sharp, he sees through her ruse. "What's your favorite story?"

"*Cliquot.* Someday I'll write it."

"Write? That seems awful girly to me," Blade says, voicing the thought on everyone's mind, not just Smiley's.

"I disagree," says Smiley. "Writing is manly, if you tell the story right. I'm not familiar with the one you mention," he changes his tone, he was about to start laughing, his curiosity has lifted his spirits. Now he's genuinely interested in this person. Nothing interests him more (not even cards) than a good story. "*Cliquot?*"

"I'll tell it to you, because I like you, sir," Sarah-Soro says, looking into his eyes. She gets up from the table, goes to the bar, gestures for a drink and points to what she wants.

"The same?"

Sarah nods. The barkeep fills a glass and comes over to her, as close as he can. Cruz walks over and stops right next to Soro.

"Shh. Listen up!"

Even the Eagles stop talking. All eyes in the Café Ronsard are on Sarah-Soro.

She turns a little, without turning her back completely on the barkeep. She begins:

"The story of Cliquot. Told by its author, before writing it. Once upon a time there was a racehorse called Cliquot. Cliquot ended up belonging to a young mustachioed man . . ."

A man interrupts. "Like you."

Silence. Sarah lets her expression do the talking. *Me? All y'all here know I'm a woman. I just dressed this way to sit with Smiley and play cards, I never thought I'd fool anyone; don't tell me you're that stupid.*

"A real man. *Not* like me."

"I'm not familiar with this story," Smiley says, admiring the faggot's nerve. A smile lights up his face. "Cliquot?" he asks again.

"I don't want to be interrupted, gentlemen. Telling a story is like staging a play. Now listen up.

"The story of Cliquot, as told by its author before writing it. Cliquot was a horse famous for his speed. His new owner, a handsome fellow, let's call him Neil Emory, hired a famous jockey. But the jockey couldn't ride Cliquot, the horse was too spirited. He had everything it took to be the best, to win every race, but . . . who could ride him? The owner tried another jockey, who failed, and another, who failed, and another . . . whom Cliquot killed. Or maybe not, let's say he just wounded him badly because killing him makes Cliquot look bad, but he really did kill him. Cliquot had a strong, unpredictable spirit.

"Then, Neil Emory, Cliquot's owner, suffered a reversal of fortune. He was going to have to sell Cliquot. To a guy who was a real bastard. You heard me right: a bas-tard.

"Then a tiny jockey showed up with his manager. This tiny jockey never opened his mouth. The manager told Cliquot's heavyhearted owner that this jockey wanted to race Cliquot, and that there was no doubt he'd succeed. His fee? A small percentage of the winnings. That was the deal, no trials. If he accepted the offer, great. If not, forget it.

"Neil Emory, broke as he was, accepted, despite not knowing what he was getting himself into. He needed the money. There was no risk to him, just to his handsome Cliquot, but under the circumstances he didn't have an option.

"So they announced that Cliquot was going to race. Everyone bet against him. 'And they're off!' Cliquot was slow off the start. Three seconds later he hit his stride, he was gaining. Two seconds, he was neck and neck with the leader. The crowd went wild. Cliquot looked like he was flying. Neil Emory, his owner, was afraid it was the jockey who would go flying any second. Cliquot stayed focused. He continued racing, concentrating on the course and the finish line, with composure he'd never seen before. He pulled ahead and won the race by two lengths.

"Neil Emory got out of debt. More victories followed. He made a small fortune lickety-split, even larger than the one he had before.

"The winning jockey, after several incidents I can't tell you about because I haven't invented them yet, won Cliquot's owner's heart. The jockey was really a woman named Gwendolyn Gwinn. They began a passionate love affair. This isn't an important part of the story, and it won't take up much space, it's a concession to female readers; the horse races are what's important, because Cliquot has to keep winning them . . . I prefer cards and horse races to affairs of the heart, which bore me to tears. They're all the same. Have you seen the size of a human heart? It's about the same as a fist. How can that compare with the whole wide world?" She spreads her arms.

"We'll discover (you'll see how) that Gwendolyn was Cliquot's previous owner and had been forced to sell him because of her own financial difficulties. I need to work on the details, I mean I haven't made them all up yet. There needs to be some conflict with the fellow who pretends to be her manager, I can't leave that loose end. There should be something about his role in her financial ruin, he's a real evil guy. And the guy who wants to buy Cliquot is the one responsible for Gwendolyn's financial ruin, he's her father's lawyer and wanted to marry her for her money. She refused, and he fucked her over . . . Hear that? Fucked her over.

"So Neil Emory's real wife shows up (I still haven't made up her name), returning from a trip to Paris where she was spending what little money her husband had left. She's back because she heard fortune is smiling on Neil Emory again and she doesn't want to lose it (you see, it's the fortune she cares about, not Emory), and certainly not to a woman who came into his life dressed as a jockey.

"That's it, for now that's all I've got . . ."

Silence. If what Soro said is true, that telling a story is like staging a play, then it's time to clap. But it doesn't seem right.

The barkeep moves away from Sarah, turning to look at the doors, which are swinging; someone is pushing them from the outside. They swing again, announcing an imminent visit.

"Well, look who the cat dragged in," he says, "it's Dry."

In walks a man as skinny as a hitching post—a hitching post that's been hastily whittled by a lazy carpenter with a bad piece of wood (with neither grain nor color), looking like he doesn't weigh a thing. It's Dry. A man who goes from town to town, city to city, ranch to ranch, preaching the benefits of abstinence and the evils of alcohol. His real name is Franklin Evans.

"El Seco!"

Children say he floats, that the soles of his feet are soft and clean like a baby's. But they're rough because he goes around barefoot, they're full of corns and calluses from walking long distances; his feet are forever sore. He is misery and severity incarnate. He preaches the evils of liquor fanatically. His chosen pulpits are cafés, cantinas, and bars, as well as distilleries.

Despite the fact he'd like to turn everyone teetotal, the man always looks like he's drunk. He's crazed in his fanaticism.

Franklin Evans was born in a Long Island village. He left the country life and moved to New York, where he got a good job, drank like a fish, got married, lost his job and got a worse one; then his wife died so he got remarried to a freed slave, had a daughter with her, started sleeping with a white woman whom his second wife murdered before she took her own life; then he lost his job and couldn't get a new one, kept drinking, began begging, fell into abject poverty; and then when his daughter died he finally he gave up drinking and became a teetotaler, preaching sobriety. Anyone who'd lived this life—like a bad sensationalist novel written in three days powered by gin to earn a few dollars by promoting temperance—couldn't help but turn into a Mr. Dry.

He has nightmares night after night. Terrifying, colorless dreams in which he cannot scream, burdened with grief; they make no sense but they're powerful because he wakes up paralyzed with fear. They have no beginning or end. One example: Dry goes to the barber, who is a drunk greaser; he complains about something, it's not clear to whom, there's only the one barber there. He hears laughter. The barber picks up his razor, and Dry sits down in his chair.

He doesn't run. Nothing happens. Dry thinks he has woken up. He goes to the bathroom. His pants fall down. Once again he thinks he's awoken. Again his pants fall down, but they can't because he's still lying asleep on a board, wrapped up in his dream. Distressed, he stiffens, he can't move, he awakens, this time for real, he's so stiff, his arms crossed on his chest, immobile. Now he's fully awake. He tries to move, he can't, he tries again, and finally he can move.

What was the dream about? Why doesn't it have an arc or some specific source of grief? All his dreams are like that. Like the crazy things Dry eats: boiled fish without salt . . . and that's the least disgusting. He cooks flavorless scraps on the fire. He eats just to fill his stomach. Whatever's around.

His pinky toe always hurts, it's always peeling, blistered, with ingrown hairs and warts. All his ailments seem to manifest in his toe. It's as though this part of his body is the voice of his soul.

He despises alcohol because it gives pleasure, but his arguments don't make sense.

Sarah looks at Dry with curiosity. Forgetting about her disguise—and her story and her card game—she moves to arrange her skirts; Carlos the Cuban notices.

Since she's not wearing her skirts, she smooths her palms along her riding pants in a rather absurd gesture.

Carlos gets up from his chair and moves toward Sarah, who asks him, "And this guy?" She asks in perfect Spanish, pointing to Dry.

"A lunatic who goes around saying alcohol is the devil incarnate. Nice to meet you, I'm Carlos, Cuban . . . and," he lowers his voice, "I like your style." He extends his hand and Sarah-Soro takes it with more tenderness than elegance. Carlos lowers his voice further and moves closer to Soro-Sarah, he can smell her orange-blossom scent. "Dry hates Mexicans. They say he belongs to the Secret Circle."

"Sounds like a lunatic to me," Sarah mumbles in English as she backs away from her interlocutor (it's not because of the way he looks, Carlos is blond and light-skinned; it's his bad breath); then she looks him straight in the eye (to keep her distance). "What's the Secret Circle?"

"Shh!" Carlos says very softly, trying not to lose his composure; he's got no doubt now she's a woman, but it's not her orange-blossom scent that renders him helpless, it's her response to his comment about hating Mexicans. What if she's a member of the Secret Circle? But she doesn't seem like one, so he says, "Circle, it's a circle." He immediately regrets opening his mouth. "It's not safe to talk about it."

The prohibition proselytizer stares down anyone who dares speak in his presence. He's like the Grim Reaper. Wherever he goes, he brings silence, immobility, tears, and terror, and if folks wear black (like he does, in this heat!), so much the better.

Sarah walks over to her table and Carlos returns to the Eagles' where he asks, as he usually does, "What's wrong with that guy? Why's he so mad about sotol? What devil possessed him?"

"T'warnt no demon, buddy; it was an angel, and she was black."
Hector shouts over to the musicians, "Play 'The Little Drunk Girl'!"
The musicians have been sitting in silence. All three are dejected.
They know Nepomuceno and his mother well, and they know the
disputed territory by heart—but then, who doesn't, Bruneville is
built on it . . . They have played at weddings, baptisms, birthdays,
funerals, and even bullfights. Juliberto's father was a cowboy who
learned to play the violin by watching and listening to Lázaro for
many years before Lázaro himself taught him the art with his hands
like wrinkled wads of paper, deformed by decades of wielding the
lasso and the whip. The musicians have already decided not to play:
"No singing in here." "Not unless someone with a lotta dough shows
up." "Not even then!" "Depends how much money they have, Sila
asked me for money this morning and I told her I'd bring some
home." "That's what you get for getting hitched." "For getting hitched
to a poor woman!" "Women are supposed to support you, otherwise
they're useless." The musicians don't forget for one second the grief
that has stopped them playing, but they can't resist the temptation to
rile up El Seco (that's what they call Mr. Dry). They strike up a tune,
breaking into song with the second beat:

Es bueno beber torito,
Pa'l que está muy agüitado,
Es bueno el torito.

They turn to face Dry; he hasn't caught on. They stop short and
begin a different tune.

El domingo fue de gusto
Porque me diste tu amor,
Y por eso me emborracho
Con un señor sotol.

El lunes por la mañana
Bastante malo me vi.
Fui a curarme al de Ronsard,
Se me pasó y la seguí.

Out on the prairie at Rancho del Carmen, Nepomuceno's step-brothers, José Esteban and José Eusebio, are trying hard to keep their cool. They're absorbing the news about what has happened to Nepomuceno. They must protect Doña Estefanía, her land, her livestock, her men . . . They'll form a posse, that's what they need to do.

In the kitchen at Rancho del Carmen things are same as ever, no matter what happens there are perfectly balanced sauces, meat and vegetables wrapped in scented leaves, cooked in beautiful pots, and extraordinary dishes are served in the dining room. Everything here is prepared with care, attention to detail, and skill. If we were to judge by our noses, it would appear that Doña Estefanía (she's the one who gives all the instructions on how to prepare the food, and she tastes it all before it's served) has not noticed war is about to break out, and that her son is the one who has started it.

Snippets of conversation overheard at the Stealmans' home:
"A group of settlers decided to rid Texas of what's left of the Indian tribes. Three hundred Caddos escaped to Oklahoma. They killed the traitor who tipped them off."
And these from Elizabeth's slaves—less coherent because they're running back and forth:
"How are the pastries?"
"Taste them, don't ask."
. . .
"Which one is the mayor?"
"Why do you want to know?"

"I just do."

. . .

"Did you empty the master's spittoon?"

"Are you crazy? Guests are still here."

"Empty it anyway."

. . .

"Did you see the woman in the pink dress asking for the chamber pot?"

. . .

"What's wrong with you, why are you crying?"

"The man with the blue handkerchief followed me into the hall and stuck his hand up my skirt . . ."

"Okay, okay, okay . . . I thought something had happened to you . . . Cheer up."

"Easy for you to say, I won't even tell you what he did because it would make you sick to your stomach."

"Tell me."

"He stuck his finger inside me."

"Where did he stick his finger?"

"Where's he gonna stick it!" the other slave interrupts. "Go wipe your face, straighten your apron, and pass the tray again, girl."

. . .

In a loud voice one of the guests is reciting from memory, "Justice and God's benevolence will prevent Texas from falling once more into wilderness, inhabited by savages, ruled by the ignorance, superstition, and anarchy of the Mexican government. The colonists have brought their language, their customs, and an innate love of freedom that has always defined them and their forefathers."

"Who are you quoting?" guests ask.

"I couldn't tell you, someone quoted it to me but didn't know the author."

—

In Matasánchez, the Negress Pepementia has left the city center for the riverbank where the fish market is, but it's closed now and the streets are empty. She wanders around, lost in thought. It's not the kind of neighborhood for proper women, and Pepementia is one.

The news about Nepomuceno has got her thinking, but it's not until she arrives here that she formulates a plan of action: *Ever since I arrived in this country I have been treated only with kindness. On the other side of the Río Bravo, they nearly made mincemeat of me. Here they have imprisoned the man who did that to me, and they treat me as their equal. But what have I done in return? I have to go and offer to help at Nepomuceno's camp. If I'm going to make good. I only know how to make beans, but there must be something for me to do. I don't know what, but something.*

She retraces her steps. She's back in the plaza. The church ladies are just leaving Mass. They don't speak to her, but she doesn't care. She doesn't want to speak, she just wants to be near other people. She's heard they're in Laguna del Diablo; who can tell her how to get there?

North of the river, Fernando, Nepomuceno's servant, hidden in buffalo hunter Wild's cart, a few feet from Mrs. Big's Hotel, has overheard everything: that the steamboat won't leave today; that Nepomuceno escaped on the barge; that they killed Santiago the fisherman; that they killed Old Arnoldo too; that Wild has left; that the Rangers are on guard. Night is falling. He gets up the nerve to glance around. He confirms no one can see him. As soon as he is certain, he jumps off the cart. He runs along the riverbank toward the outskirts of Bruneville.

Nightfall begins to unfold its blanket of darkness. It's the witching hour and visibility is poor, especially on the river, where mist is beginning to form. The barge's tug, which wasn't moored to the

Bruneville dock (they thought it was part of the barge, which they did tie up securely), breaks free and begins to drift.

You might say it's remaining faithful to Old Arnoldo. That it can't stand the sight of his hanged body. He was a proper fellow, Arnoldo. He will never realize that trip with the empty barge was destined to be his last. His fate was sealed before the barge trip, in the papers Stealman signed earlier that day making him the owner of the tug and the barge, as well as three steamboats that travel the Rio Grande and the Colorado—from Bruneville to Galvez and Houston, the consolidation of his shipping business. Stealman would doubtless have fired the old man; he didn't believe there were secrets hidden in those roiling waters. To Stealman, there is nothing besides punctuality, efficiency, and cleanliness. Arnoldo was toothless, old, and deaf; Stealman would never have kept him on.

There was nothing heroic in the barge's comings and goings, but that was the old man's life, crossing the river, back and forth, never heading out to sea or upriver to where the river widens. But for Arnoldo that was enough. He was finished with women, but he could still ride the river.

Night yawns and tucks itself in, languid and leisurely. It reaches the south bank of the Río Bravo. With it, volunteers begin to arrive at Nepomuceno's makeshift camp: Roberto, the runaway slave who escaped southward when the Texans fled to Louisiana; Jones, still carrying his candles (but not his soaps); Julito from the dock, the young man whom Arnoldo thought he should have gone to, just before he died. They want to join the rebel's ranks "against the blue-eyed menace."

Three bottles of sotol later, they begin to shout.

"Death to the gringos!"

"Viva Nepomuceno!"

"Viva México!"

—

Night is well underway when the mail from the Eagles in Bruneville arrives. Úrsulo has delivered it from the other side of the Río Bravo, from a prearranged meeting point where there's a makeshift dock that very few know about—the request to pick it up was delivered by one of the Rodriguez brothers' pigeons; Úrsulo went to Aunt Cuca's house to see if there was a message and Catalino gave it to him—closer to Bruneville than Rancho del Carmen, but away from the Americans, because the main dock is still being held by the Rangers.

The "mail" delivers the following news: the gringos have requested help from the federal government, they received a telegram that the army is coming, a regiment is en route (commanded by General Cumin) and it's not far off, it will arrive at the fort in two days' time. More importantly: there are details about the Rangers and the ranchers' gunmen. This mailman spent the day walking around, scouring the riverbank, listening to people in the Market Square, talking to Hector and Carlos and even Sandy Eagle Zero—he almost didn't catch her—she saw up close what was going on at the Fort on the other side of Bruneville, she spoke to a couple of soldier friends who think she's just a naïve woman. He delivers Nepomuceno a complete portrait of what he's just left behind. He goes into detail describing Santiago and Old Arnoldo, and the fisherman's house.

We already know this mailman; it's Óscar, the baker. He's not alone. He arrives with Trust, One, Two, Three, and Fernando.

Trust, One, Two, and Three, who all wanted to go to Mexico but had no way to get there, were sitting on the deserted riverbank when Óscar came across them, his breadbasket on his head (just a precaution, he didn't have any bread). He was coming from Bruneville.

"What are you doing here?" Óscar asked in Spanish, his face bathed in sweat from running.

"I ran outta patience," handsome Trust said. "I don't know why it didn't happen sooner. Enough. We're going to Mexico."

Three translated into Spanish. Óscar always liked Trust. And the bottom line was that One, Two, and Three were slaves on this side of the river, but they'd be free men in Mexico.

"Come with me. I'll take you across. I have to make a delivery. Follow me."

Óscar was sad. He thought, *What about the bread?* Tomorrow his customers in Bruneville wouldn't have any. But he can't neglect his duty as an Eagle . . . And he knows that if they don't defend themselves, soon there'll be no dough, no oven, and no bread baking either. He's the Eagles' messenger when they need one because he doesn't arouse suspicion. The information he collected today is detailed and complicated. He should deliver the news in person.

He hid all four of them in some scrub brush. He had just left them when he heard someone nearby.

"I'm an idiot, an idiot."

Óscar followed the voice. It was Fernando, Nepomuceno's servant, talking to himself.

"Psst, psst!" said Óscar.

Fernando's eyes widened.

"Here, over here!"

Óscar knew he had to save the servant too. He showed Fernando where to hide, in the same scrub brush where One, Two, Three, and Trust were waiting for him, and went on his way with his basket.

Hidden in the thick brush, they kept silent.

Óscar returned a few hours later. He didn't get them out of the brush until Úrsulo arrived aboard the *Inspector*. Everyone boarded quickly, squeezing in to fit.

Fernando had been bitten by a tick in the brush, perhaps even earlier. He wanted to get rid of it but since they had been crowded together it was impossible to take off his boot, he had to wait.

—

On the Rio Grande, folks' spirits aren't at ease either. Rick and Chris, the sailors who set sail on the merchant ship *Margarita*, the ones who made up that little ditty—"You damn Mexican!"—and danced, such good friends, are in unknown territory. Rick has fallen in love with Chris, who feels the same way. Chris is afraid that if he confesses his attraction to Rick, they'll fall into unpardonable shame. Rick thinks that if Chris forgets about it, no one will ever know, least of all his father, who would skin him alive; to him there's nothing worse than a faggot.

On board the *Elizabeth*, the passenger ship that runs Bruneville —Matasánchez—Bagdad—Punta Isabel—Galvez—New Orleans, Captain Rogers wants to send a telegram from Bruneville to advise Punta Isabel of their delay. He's impatient because he knows he's got passengers waiting in Bagdad. He's obsessive about punctuality— that's how the *Elizabeth* got its good reputation, that and its amenities. But Captain Rogers isn't finding it easy: first, because he can't dock in Bruneville; second, because, thanks to Shears, the telegraphist is busy sending and receiving messages, questions, and instructions, so busy that even with his wife and children helping he can't keep up. So the *Elizabeth* won't arrive? So what! There are more important things, the messages from the federal government to the mayor's office, their instructions; official business takes priority.

In Matasánchez, a candle illuminates Don Marcelino, the crazy plant man, in his study, sitting at his spotless desk—it's nothing special but it's immaculately organized, even the samples he has brought back from his expedition are laid out in an orderly fashion.

He takes the piece of paper where he noted Shears's phrase several hours earlier out of his jacket pocket. He unfolds it and makes a note in the book where he keeps notes for a dictionary of frontier language, under the letter *S*.

"SHORUP (imperative expression): *used to indicate...*"
He doesn't stumble on the spelling. He doesn't think about Nepomuceno or Lázaro (whom he knows, he made notes on his songs long ago; he went camping with the vaqueros specifically to hear him sing), even less of Shears; he doesn't have the least interest in him because he doesn't speak Spanish.

Old Arnoldo's tug has drifted down to the mouth of the Río Bravo. The stevedores on the Bagdad dock watch it float past, they're unloading the cotton delivery from upriver, after stops at Punta Isabel, the Lieder's dock (for preserves), and the slaughterhouse in Matasánchez.
Chris and Rick see it too.
"Has the old man lost his mind? He's left the barge behind..."
"And he's headed out to sea..."

We don't know exactly what Elizabeth Stealman thinks about the Henrys because she doesn't mention them in her diary entry for the day. She lists all the other guests but not them. This omission is telling: the woman who clearly loves the art of writing and dedicates her time to penning letters to herself uses what literary power she has to *erase them.* She does not place these important Texans in her own pantheon. She makes them nonexistent.
In her diary she does not relate that when Catherine Anne was asked what her book was about (the one that's by "A Southern Lady") she said, "It's a novel."
"Is it set in the South?"
"Yes, in the South."
"Who's the main character?"
"A young woman who has been orphaned; she arrives from England to live with her grandmother and discovers that her grandfather, Erastus, whom no one remembers, is shut away on the top

floor of the house. He's relentlessly searching for the secret of eternal youth, with homemade anesthesia and electrotherapy, he tries to mix the virgin blood of the main character with gold . . ."

"Is there a love story?"

"There's no such thing as a novel without a love story. Of course there is."

"It is long?"

"Two fairly long volumes . . . yes, it's long. It explores the protagonist's emotions. An investigation of the heart. I wrote it when mine was broken: my sister Lily, who was like my other half, as you know, died. It was thanks to my niece, Sarah, whom you see here, that I began to write again, encouraged and inspired by her."

"Aunt," her niece interrupts, "I'm not Sarah, she isn't here."

"Ah, yes, right? You . . . you . . . you?"

Clearly the aunt cannot remember the name of her more faithful niece (who's so dim-witted, she doesn't realize everyone is watching and that she's the only one who can save her aunt by saying her name). One of the ladies lends a hand, asking, "What's your name?"

The niece doesn't have time to answer the question because her aunt jumps in with the name of her book.

"*The Household of Bouverie.*"

"Is there a corrupt or heartless character?"

"There is . . ."

"Are there Negroes?"

Everyone understands this is an allusion to *Uncle Tom's Cabin*, the bestseller.

"My protagonist is an innocent soul. In contrast, Urzus, who's in the slave trade and has the good fortune to own land, wants to own her. He's determined to have her. While we explore their hearts, which are trapped in their own labyrinth, Papa Bouverie stays shut away on the top floor of the house, without entry or exit . . ."

"Are there Negroes?" a guest asks again. Everyone wants to know what the Henrys think of *Uncle Tom's Cabin*, but no one dares to ask the question.

"There's not one single Negro! For obvious reasons. Negroes can't be characters in novels. That would be like having a dog as protagonist!" Derisive laughter all around. "A horse, on the other hand . . . A horse has character and soul."

"Mexicans know how to handle horses so well because they're similar, they're equals. It's remarkable how they understand one another."

"There's an obvious explanation: Mexicans' souls are identical to horses.'"

"But not Negroes."

"Not at all. I would never use them as characters because all Negroes are cut from the same cloth, it's completely different, anyone can see that. There's no difference between one Negro and another. That's why they can't handle horses, they're not simpatico. Horses are all feeling . . . Negroes have absolutely no *personality*," she emphasizes this last word.

"You mean they're like a piece of furniture, a wardrobe, or a chair?"

"My chairs have personality."

"But we're agreed that Mexicans don't have personality either."

"Definitely not!" the author says. "A horse, maybe. Because it's beautiful. But a Mexican . . . Every character must be beautiful in their own way, even if it's evil."

"I've tried to get rid of my servants' odor," this is Miss Sharp, Rebecca. She's jumped into the conversation to make her position clear. What if they knew she had been thinking of marrying a Mexican? But her interjection is so inappropriate everyone ignores her. It's not good breeding to mention human odors at such an elegant gathering.

"I agree, it's impossible to have a novel with beasts, animals, or things as the main characters."

"Then how do you explain that so many people adore *Uncle Tom's Cabin*?"

"The criteria for judging a book can't be taken from the masses. They can't make literary judgments. That would be absurd! The book called *Uncle Tom's Cabin* isn't a novel, it's an abolitionist treatise, a piece of propaganda, vulgar and depraved. I haven't read it but . . ."

"If it weren't for the English no one would have even taken notice of it. Have they lost their literary sense? They just supported it to hurt this country. It's unpatriotic to like *Uncle Tom's Cabin* . . ."

"Of course!"

"It would make more sense to write a book with inanimate objects as characters. Humans leave the marks of their souls on objects. Because, when it comes down to it, we've created them."

"Let's toast to your success, esteemed Catherine," the hostess breaks in, to change the topic. There's not a whit of abolitionist in her.

General Cumin, who leads the Seventh Cavalry Regiment, had been sent south of the Nueces River several months earlier to dismantle illegal operations and get rid of some Mexican bandits in those parts (he wasn't instructed to get rid of the gringo bandits, though those were the only ones he came across, despite . . . well, we'll get to that). He was born for military campaigning; life in the saddle on the open plains fills him with joy: his reins in one hand, his Colt in the other, and if he can shoot an Indian, even better!

General Cumin wears a red bandana. He's always accompanied by his guide (or scout), a Tonkawa (Cumin boasts, "The Tonkawas are cannibals . . . sometimes!") who rides a pony black as night and fast as lightning. They call the Tonkawa Fragrance.

Fragrance is a giant who wears black face paint (his war paint) and copper loops in his pierced ears. Despite General Cumin's objections, he removes his shirt at the drop of a hat. Sometimes he even sings:

We walk, we walk
To where the lights shine bright;
we danced, we danced.

If he's asked, he says he comes from the Turtle family, who knows what he means, his mother was called Owl Woman, and she was a captive, supposedly French.

They make a good pair, Cumin and Fragrance.

General Cumin has another companion in life, his wife, who's not like him, and even less like Fragrance. She likes the quiet life, not a life on the move. Luckily, her slave, Eliza, accompanied her, and she trusts her and confides in her. It's three years since they've been living among the savages.

Whenever General Cumin receives a new assignment, he celebrates at home, breaking chairs out of joy ("Chairs don't grow on trees in these parts, Gen'l," Eliza would say, true to her mistress), while his wife sat downcast on the floor, deep in thought, watching her home destroyed in a fit of jubilation.

Out on the endless grasslands, where white men get lost and die of thirst, General Cumin feels like he's being born, out there where there's no stone, no tree, no brush, no hillock, nothing to orient him.

Let's get back to the present. At nightfall a message arrives for General Cumin.

"I'm in no mood to read, tell me what it says."

The messenger knows what it says, without having to open it.

"Make haste to Bruneville, some bandit called Nepomuceno has started a rebellion. He already fled to the other side."

The celebrations in General Cumin's house begin even before

the messenger leaves. But they don't last long. They'll depart at dawn with their carts for the fort, which is a stone's throw from Bruneville, with their livestock and their horses. It's a brief celebration, but Cumin and Fragrance have had enough time to pretend they've drunk more than their fair share. At General Cumin's house the chairs are all in splinters.

A conversation overheard in Nepomuceno's new camp: "Stealman may have stolen the barge, but it's going to be a filthy pigsty without those two boys to clean it—all those cow pies and horse shit and whatever else people leave behind—being a gringo it'll never occur to him to get a bucket and a mop . . . Who'd want to travel in that dump!?"

On the other side of the Río Bravo, at Mrs. Big's, Sandy's niece is mopping the kitchen floor because she can't sleep. The night breeze, which rocks the two strangled men, and the guffaws of the armed gringos, who have built a campfire a few paces from the tree, make her feel ill.

"They'll burn the leaves of the icaco tree, and it won't be able to bear fruit this year."

In the Stealmans' mansion, when the last living being has fallen asleep, worn out from exertion—the last will be the first there, too—one slave will open her eyes as soon as dawn breaks, she couldn't sleep for fear of John Tanner, the White Indian, she saw him getting into the bed she shares with four others. Elizabeth dreams that someone is knocking on the door of her room. In her dream, she gets out of bed, wondering why none of her slaves are answering, and she opens the door half asleep. It's her father. He's not old anymore. A potion he spent years concocting has given him eternal life. Elizabeth wakes up with a start. She turns over in her bed and falls back asleep.

—

South of Matasánchez, Juan Caballo and Wild Horse are talking, oblivious to the fact the sun set six hours ago. Time has lost its meaning for the Mascogo and the Seminole since the messenger pigeon arrived. They speak in Gullah, the language they brought with them from the Sea Islands, full of words like "bambara," "fulane," "mandinga," "kongo," "kimbundu."

To witness the conversation between the two chiefs (Indian and Negro), the Mascogo have all remained awake and alert, children and elders gathered round. When one of them shuts their eyes, they all sing to wake them up: "Kumbaya, kumbaya," that's how they call them back from sleep, *"Don't go, we're all in this together..."*

"Dem yent yeddy wuh oonuh say."

They should just make the decision they know they must. Although it's nearly settled, they won't announce it until dawn, after a nightlong vigil discussing the matter in darkness, to the hooting of owls, the dreaming of foxes, the nighttime wiggling of fish.

In Bruneville, at the Smiths' house, their daughter Caroline listens closely and anxiously to what's happening in the Fears' house. In the room at the back, fever has sunk its claws into the sick adventurer's neck. He raves while Shears bleats in pain (and terror, afraid Nepomuceno will come back to finish him off).

Their nursemaid, Eleonor, doesn't relent in her battle against the fever. She fills the pail with fresh water, wetting the rag that used to be part of her blue camisole. She wrings it out and listens to the drops falling in the pail.

Caroline, her ears straining, hears that the fever and delirium have changed the adventurer's heartbeat, it sounds like a savage's, following a singsong beat.

Angry and lying sleepless in bed, she begins to hear things. With perfect clarity, she hears El Loco shaking the branches of ivy on the wall at the south side of the market. Later—the sound drifts away—she hears a dove. Then she clearly hears the cat they have put in the market to eat the rats swallowing a fat one, which has just given birth to a half dozen babies.

The Lipans arrive in their settlement. They had to stop on the road three times to rest their horses and let them recover. One of them has barely survived the trip—it's hobbling, and its left rear shank is swollen: when they see this, they realize they should put it out of its misery. The sooner the better. The keeper of the horses—an important role in the community—takes his rifle. Bang! The bullet whistles, as if it laments its task for the fraction of a second it takes to fly its course.

In Matasánchez, Dr. Velafuente gets up to pee. He could use the chamber pot beneath his bed, but he feels the need to go outdoors and breathe fresh air. He passes the bed of his wife, Aunt Cuca, who's snoring lightly, "Like a hummingbird, Cuquita, just like when I met you, I went to spy on you from your balcony, and your hummingbird snoring drove me wild." The Doctor feels an uncontrollable urge to cry. "I'm just an old sissy, crying at a memory."

He tries to repress his faint sobs, which sound like mourning doves: u-u, u-u.

A cat scampers by, black as night, jumping along the wall toward the neighbors' rooftop.

Back at the Lipans' settlement, the horse, shattered by its journey at a pace it couldn't keep, falls, mortally wounded, its muscles spent.

Its final thought: *They never gave me a name, even though the Lipans stole me from a runaway slave.*

(One day the local poet will pass by that spot, singing the horse's final thoughts:

No one ever named me.
I was a crazy horse,
A slave beyond compare.
I could have been called Cinnamon,
Or Hack, maybe—I would have liked that dull name.)

At Mrs. Big's Hotel darkness is nearly complete.

Mrs. Big and Sandy are asleep.

Sandy's niece's eyes are still wide open, watching the weakening shadows from the Rangers' smoldering campfire beneath the icaco tree. Their macho enthusiasm has faded.

Suddenly, Sandy's niece falls asleep, so quickly that her eyes remain open. Her eyelids close slowly.

The Rangers justify their actions to each other. They no longer guffaw. They murmur secrets among themselves. They're oblivious to everything else. A golden whale could come floating past the riverbank like an angel from on high, right past their noses, and they wouldn't notice it.

The cadavers sway beneath the icaco tree. Toads croak at their feet. Frogs jump, startled.

The most remarkable thing in this scene is what's happening in Mrs. Big's bed.

In Mrs. Big's belly there's a hurricane force wind, if we take into account the relative proportion of Mrs. Big's innards to the gas therein. The gas is dark, like its surroundings. It's impatient, and in a foul mood. It's not exactly mute—the sounds it emits are not words but sinister rumblings, equal to lightning in their intensity and electric nature. Mrs. Big's lower gut endures the pangs of this attack, putting up with them as she dreams she's in an elegant salon, watching Zachary approach her surrounded by fair-haired men.

The gas struggles to escape. There's not enough room for it in this box of muscle and bone, even though we're talking about Mrs. Big here. It makes like it's in the bowels of a gigantic volcano. It fights to erupt. Despite its tenacity, she neither burps nor farts. Its entrapment prolongs Mrs. Big's discomfort, and the gas's, too.

A war is underway inside Mrs. Big, but no one is aware. Pain is futile because it elicits no response. Cramps, though intense, are equally ineffective. The blood takes control; it joins the battle.

Mrs. Big's cheeks burn. She's helpless. Her dream changes direction. The storm changes direction, too. "Zachary! Zachary!" Zachary looks up disdainfully at the sound of his name. He fixes his attention on another young lady. He ignores Mrs. Big.

She feels like she's going to explode.

The gas inside her strengthens. Without fully understanding its own will, except this urgency to escape—the only thing fate is denying it—the gas inside Mrs. Big pushes against blood, guts, muscle, her soul, everything that stands in its way.

Mrs. Big's mood blackens further: as far as she's concerned both Shears and Nepomuceno and their tempest in a teapot can go to hell...

In Nepomuceno's camp, Lázaro comes to. He gets up to pee. He takes a gourd of water. He listens to what folks are saying around him—a couple of men are awake, keeping watch.

Lázaro thinks things over.

He speaks:

Do I need to excuse myself for what I did, for being drunk? Well, I'll tell you how it happened. I was out of work, because of something that happened with Doña Estefanía, or her two older sons, to be specific, who don't care for me one bit, and with each passing day I was losing hope that things would look up. One of those days, when I was waiting to go meet her boy Nepo in the Plaza del Mercado—he's the son, the grandson, and the great-grandson of my bosses, the only ones I've had ever since I arrived in these parts—to see if I could join for one of his jobs—no sure thing, because for cattle drives they always want gunslingers, and it's not that I don't know how to fire a gun, I do, but I'm better with a lasso than a Colt, I don't carry a gun, I'm an old fella, I've been around (that's what I was going to say to Nepomuceno to get him to hire me)—besides, I was prepared to do anything due to the stroke of bad luck that had left me penniless . . .

(Just quickly I'll tell you that Nepo was coming from Rita's tobacco shop, what a woman—good enough to eat—he went to get some, and I don't mean just tobacco! I waited near the Café Ronsard, though I could have gone to find him at Rita's, I used to look after her foals but she doesn't have any left, she sold them all . . .)

(Since Rita is widowed, gossips might say Nepomuceno likes widows, but that's hogwash: what he likes are women with flesh on their bones. I knew the woman who was his true love, and I'm telling you she was something special, she woulda knocked the breath out of you.)

In the cantina at the back of the market one of King's cowboys challenged me.

"Su no hombre."

"Su what?" I asked him, because, really, I couldn't understand what he was trying to say.

"Su! Su! Su, su no hombre!"

His gestures clarified his meaning; he meant "tu" as in "you." As in, "You're not a man."

"Of course I'm a man! I'm not a . . . bird!" I wanted to say "eagle," but I am one, and I can't tell a lie. I've been a loyal Eagle for a long time.

"Hombre saber beber. Su ni pico."

What the hell was the guy trying to say? Did he mean that he could drink and I couldn't? I asked him, gesturing, and that cleared things up.

"Listen, you dumbass gringo, go ahead and challenge me, I'll take you down."

So because I don't like to fight we sat down to drink, but not in the cantina. People had started to crowd around us, so we stayed in the plaza, one glass after another, to see who was more of a man.

The gringo cowboy seemed like good people, but it turned out he was nothing more than a shameless lush. We emptied our glasses, but you have to understand it was like he hadn't even had one drop. I, on the other hand, was a goner, and sooner than I would have liked.

It was humiliating; I'm so old I ended up like a sack of potatoes. And what's even worse is that once I was good and drunk they took the money from my pockets to pay for the drinks. My last pennies, the only money I had. When I felt them frisk me and take the money, I began screaming and screeching like a macaw.

"Gringo thief!"

Shears, that darned thug who wears a star on his chest just because no one else would take the job, that useless, good for nothing, idiot . . . He saw me drunk and furious, and he announced, like Augustus, that he was going to lock me up.

What was I supposed to say? Hell no! Lock me up on account of a few drinks?

"What planet are you on?"

Folks broke out laughing when I said "what planet," so Shears began to beat me.

That's when that boy, Nepomuceno, appeared, and who knows what happened next; he threw me over his shoulder and we got outta there like bats outta hell.

And the worst thing of all is that the era of the cowboy is over,

sitting by the campfire and grilling meat, scraping the strings, shooting the breeze, and reminiscing . . . these gringos have eaten our pigs,
our cows. They've even eaten our memories.

PART TWO

(six weeks later . . .)

PART TWO

THE DARK, MOONLESS NIGHT IS approaching its end. The sawing of the cicadas quickens, almost deafening.

In Matasánchez, in the courtyard of Aunt Cuca's house, by the light of a candle in a hurricane lantern, Catalino approaches Sombra, Fidencio's mule.

Sombra spent the night tied to the kitchen porch with a short rope "to keep her from eating the geraniums." The mule pulled relentlessly at the cord, breaking thread after thread, until it wore long and thin. There are no geraniums left, Sombra nibbled them all, one by one.

"What to do with you, Sombra?!"

The previous afternoon, the kitchen girls, Lucha and Amalia, helped Catalino load the dovecote onto the cart, covering it with sacks of oats and a tarpaulin to disguise the cargo.

It was Lucha's idea to protect the flowers by tethering Sombra with the short rope, but it would have been better to move the flowerpots.

Carefully—"Don't get all worked up, my pretties"—Catalino loads onto Sombra's back the cage made of reeds containing

211

Favorita, the brothers' favorite; Hidalgo, their best bird; and Pajarita, who always returns to Bruneville, no matter where she goes on land or water. "You're prettier when you're quiet, my little feather-balls." Catalino always wakes up on the right side of the bed—he's chatty this morning. But by the time the sun rises he'll be silent—he'll open his mouth only to read the messages from his pigeons.

"When that boy speaks he sounds like a little pigeon," says Amalia.

He loads a flat sack of straw onto Sombra's back, laying an old blanket—more holes than wool—on top of that, and he adjusts the harness to the cart. He unfastens the cart from the traces and, taking care not to tilt the dovecote too much, places the yoke onto Sombra's harness and secures it.

Sombra is a faithful creature—gluttonous, but faithful—accustomed to following whoever is in front of her. There's no need to tug at her or lead her by a rope. "That's how you got your name, wherever I go, my little shadow, you're right there behind me."

Sombra is Fidencio's pride and joy; the cart, rough and poorly made, is his shame.

Catalino opens the doorway to the street. He passes through with Sombra and "his pretties" behind him. He doesn't turn to close it.

He's taken only a few steps when he hears the cock crow. The pigeons reply with half-swallowed warbles, *ooos* that are more sad than songful. Catalino whistles a melody so no one will hear them and hurries along.

The horizon appears as a delicate blue line that turns pink in a matter of seconds.

Noontime yesterday instructions arrived: "Stay on their heels and keep us informed." Hidalgo delivered the message.

The messenger pigeons have been dispatched from Bruneville to Matasánchez one by one, so as not to attract attention—an unnecessary precaution, as the gringos are all het up preparing for battle, they won't notice birds. The place is brimming with amateur and professional gunmen armed to the hilt, itching to hunt Mexicans. Especially Bob Chess, who thinks of only one thing: laying a Mexican woman on the floor, yanking up her skirts by force, and nailing her, better yet if he tears her, feels her break. He imagines her body in detail. He thinks he'll cut her braids, keep them as a trophy, long, heavy, shining plaits of hair, but he won't keep any of her clothing, that might make his wife mad.

Catalino is moving all the pigeons to Nepomuceno's camp. That's why he hurries along anxiously through the center of town where the lamplighter is extinguishing the gas jets. As soon as he reaches the outskirts, he stops whistling in order to move more quickly. He arrives at the Old Dock just when sunlight begins to illuminate the colors of the flowers, fruits, and grasses; the birds awaken little by little, and it's in these moments that the landscape has the most flavor: there's such an abundance south of the Bravo that it's overwhelming.

Úrsulo, the river-watcher, awaits Catalino impatiently aboard his canoe, the *Inspector*, because he needs to make his nightly report to the Port Chief of Matasánchez before the morning gets into full swing; it's his job to watch the river while Matasánchez sleeps and report back after breakfast.

With Úrsulo in charge, the Eagles and Nepomuceno's men come and go as they please. His eyes are like tombs: he sees everything but guards their secrets jealously; in his reports, the Río Bravo's also a tomb: not a soul stirs on its banks or in its waters.

Without speaking or even nodding to each other Catalino and Úrsulo remove the tarpaulin from the cart and spread it in the belly of the canoe, securing the cages atop it with the same leather straps.

Catalino cracks the whip on the ground, which is enough to get the mule's attention; she's like her name, skittish, she'll return to Fidencio pulling the empty cart. That's why Catalino brought the whip. Úrsulo will return it via Doctor Velafuente.

Before boarding the *Inspector*, they set Pajarita free, a message from the previous afternoon tied to her leg: "From the Old Dock"—just to let them know that the pigeons are traveling the right route.

Favorita will deliver it to Nicolaso in Bruneville.

These two brothers, separated by the river, are united by their pigeons' secrets; what else do they keep hidden? It would be interesting to know, but we don't have time for them now.

Catalino moves his pigeons in order to send messages to Bruneville and Matasánchez from Laguna del Diablo. Some are sitting on their eggs, soon there will be little chicks who will learn where home is: near Nepomuceno's headquarters. In a few weeks they'll already be learning to fly. He, Úrsulo, Alitas, or one of the many kids will deliver them in cages so that they can return bearing news.

Dawn finds the Río Bravo in a mood contrary to Catalino's: unruly, ill-humored, agitated, roiling unpredictably. It doesn't matter to Úrsulo, he watches the surface and knows how to find his way.

A dead cow floats by, swollen and rotting, half split open. Úrsulo hardly notices, he's busy aboard the *Inspector*, navigating with care; what does death matter?

(The floating cow dreams:
"I, the rotting cow, endowed with the life of these worms, dream that I am about to eat a mouthful of fresh grass. In the grass, a caterpillar watches me. It's not like any of the worms in my belly. In the caterpillar's eye, I see the moon shining at noon. In this day that I share with the moon, reflected in the caterpillar's eye, I see myself, a cow that's very much a cow: a ruminating, sweet, edible cow that gives the milk that makes sweets and cakes.

Doesn't feel good to be breeding worms . . .

I'm a cow, not a coffin!

I wasn't born to become a swollen, drifting balloon.

Perhaps I should calm myself: I'm the cow who used to moo. The cow who dreams, inspired by my worms' souls.

I forget about the earthworm and her eye; I take a bite of the (delicious) fresh grass which might not be real, but no matter.")

If Catalino or Úrsulo had paid attention to the rotting cow, they would have noticed something curious: Smiley's frog is traveling perched in the cow's split belly.

There are those who might say the frog is laughing, though it's impossible to be sure.

Catalino and Úrsulo are engaged in their usual repartee.

"So you call it the Rio Grande?"

"Don't insult me Catalino, and don't get started again. It's the Río Bravo."

"I heard you say Grande."

"Well, yeah, because it's big, it sure ain't small. Let's see, could you pour it all in a drinking glass? Nope, right? It ain't small, and that's why it's grande . . ."

"That's what I'm saying! You sound like a gringo! You're calling the river Grande!"

"Catalino! You're gonna drive me outta my mind! Don't do this again . . . I'm saying it's the Río Bravo."

"Didn't you just call it Grande?"

"Because it *is* big . . . That's what I'm saying . . ."

At the first light of dawn a centaur becomes visible on the horizon: it's Nepomuceno riding Pinta.

Joy and vitality break across the open fields.

Horse and rider topple what remains of the tree of night, they are the saw's teeth.

At a full gallop, they are the teeth of the blade cutting away at what's left of the night.

Anyone who happened to see them would swear that they were one body, but that would be incorrect: Pinta and Nepomuceno are two. Neither one belongs to the other.

The river doesn't shroud them the way it envelops Úrsulo and the *Inspector* in bad weather. The air doesn't shroud them either because they're not flying.

Against the backdrop of the sky, anyone can see that they are two independent beings with their own wills—Nepomuceno and Pinta—becoming something greater together—this centaur—with their separate feelings and thoughts.

They jump a ditch, dodge a fallen tree.

It could be said that Nepomuceno is the more animal of the pair. The mare looks ahead, elegant; her movement is an artful dance; Nepomuceno, nervous, looks left and right like a jaguar preparing to pounce greedily on its prey.

After jumping to avoid a rough patch, Nepomuceno becomes more human, smiling and stroking Pinta's ears, "Beautiful, Pinta, good girl!" For a second the caress turns Pinta into a coquette; then the mare shakes her head and becomes herself again: astute and quick, muscle and brain.

They descend a slope, their nerves singing, they climb a hill. Nepomuceno spots the silhouette of a creature, moving fast, darting through the brush. Nepomuceno takes his lasso, swings it above his head, lets it fly, ropes the two hind legs, yanks on the lasso, lifts his prey aloft.

The fawn soars toward Pinta's hindquarters. Nepomuceno binds its four thin legs with the lasso and fastens it to the front of his saddle.

They return to camp at a trot.

They arrive bathed in sweat, swift, contented, like two lovers. Pinta's hooves dance, while Nepomuceno's distracted hands rest

inert on his catch. The frightened fawn—all bare, thumping heart—
is piteous.

A few steps from the fire where water is boiling for the morning's
chocolate, atole, and coffee—all three are available and there's even
a fourth choice, for those who need it, medicinal tea (a bitter infu-
sion that loosens the bowels)—Lázaro picks up his violin. It's no
nighttime tune he plays; its rough vibrations stir the world, make the
morning cough, clear its throat. The fiddle's chords echo in the cups
that are waiting to be filled.

When the cups are full, the melody turns sweet, seeming to
travel directly via mouths, not ears.

Everyone talks softly to each other, murmuring the day's greetings as they take their first sips: "Good morning." "Good day." "Thank
God for another sunrise."

Nepomuceno approaches the fire with his centaur's bearing, full
of authority and energy, and the music and muttering stops. Voices
become more vigorous and words flow more quickly, the violin's
sweet strains cease as they become possessed by the melodies of
battle.

In Lázaro's slightly trembling hand his coffee sloshes back and
forth, as if the steam rising from it were tap-dancing.

The previous afternoon heavy rains fell inland (precious rains—they
fall frequently on the coast but seldom inland). North along the Río
Bravo, the Banda del Carbón (a.k.a. the Coal Gang), led by Bruno, met
with Nepomuceno's brothers to come to an agreement on things. It's
no easy business. The market for stolen horses is growing, as is the
competition to supply them. They don't want to step on each other's
toes. On this and other issues the rules are clear and have been since
way back; long ago they agreed human trafficking is forbidden, as is
doing business with gringos. Nepomuceno's brothers respect the rules

down to the last letter. As for Bruno's gang, they don't buy people, but they do occasionally accept captives as payment for merchandise or favors, and they trade them for other things; but no one ever mentions it, and Nepomuceno's men turn a blind eye.

As the rains baptize them, they discuss new tactics. They're no longer satisfied just stealing horses. They intend to draw a line in the sand against the gringos.

"We have to push them back, don't you agree?"

Bruno, the Viking, all fire and fury and revenge, and Doña Estefanía's stepsons, who are acting on her behalf, men of a practical nature, concoct a plan. There's not a horse or cow belonging to a gringo that will be safe. And there's something else.

They like their plan so much that they begin to laugh. Lightning strikes nearby; the brothers think it's a good omen.

"I don't believe in omens," says Bruno, "we don't need 'em."

Nepomuceno had heard about this meeting between his brothers and the Coal Gang the previous afternoon.

This morning, while Úrsulo navigates quickly downstream thanks to the favorable current, farther along the river in the Mascogo camp (that's Seminole to the Americans) they're singing:

De moon done rise en' de win' fetch de smell ob de maa'sh
F'um de haa'buh ob de lan' wuh uh lub'.

Sandy fixes her hair in front of the mirror in her room at Mrs. Big's Hotel. She says what she always says, that she doesn't like living here, despite the fact it's a strategic location, "You can put up with it, Sandy, for the cause." Her duties as an Eagle, one of Nepomuceno's spies, take precedence over her own desires.

She checks her face in the mirror. She sees it as if it were new, as if she's never seen it before. She doesn't understand.

"I look like a fish," she says, looking at herself.

But Sandy doesn't look at all like a fish. She's pretty, her hair done up gracefully. Eagle Zero is a beautiful woman.

She smiles.

"Maybe not so much like a fish . . . because fish don't laugh, do they."

In what seems like the blink of an eye, Úrsulo arrives at the New Dock in Matasánchez. He meets the Port Chief, López de Aguada, who has just arrived, his hat still in hand, the scent of coffee still on his breath—the Chief doesn't drink chocolate, atole, or herbal tea in the morning. Úrsulo gives his report: "Nothing," he says, "nothing happening:

"There weren't even bumblebees last night."

"Úrsulo, bees don't fly at night."

"That's what I'm saying."

Úrsulo jiggles the whip nervously in his hand. The Chief notices. He pays more attention to the gesture, and the strange sight of this object in the sailor's hands (the whip is not an oar, a fishing rod, or a net), than he does to his informant's words: trouble's brewing on the river, and soon it'll spill over onto land. Just as he's thinking this, he sees Sombra trotting alone, pulling the empty cart. Do the whip in Úrsulo's hand and Fidencio's unaccompanied donkey have something to do with each other? "Yes, yes," he says to himself. "I do believe Úrsulo is up to something."

He leaves Úrsulo before his sentence is finished. He puts his hat on and goes to the Town Hall.

Before going to rest—he has until the afternoon to catch up on his sleep—Úrsulo stops at Doctor Velafuente's house. He finds him in his nightclothes, he's come straight from the bedroom. Doctor Velafuente directs him to his office, where they speak behind closed

doors. Aunt Cuca orders water for the chocolate. The Doctor and
Úrsulo are finished in no more than three minutes. Cuca herself cuts
a generous slice of (delicious) bread pudding and serves it on the
new plate—only one survived the trip this time, her sister's pack-
ages are more and more carelessly wrapped. And then: scandal in
the kitchen (it happens every time he visits). She sits down at the
table with Úrsulo while he drinks the chocolate in silence and eats
the pudding in small bites. Cuca doesn't speak either.

In the kitchen, Lucha and Amalia are more agitated than the
water boiling in the pot, leeching the flavor from a bone for broth:

"All he needs is a feather in his hair, that Apache."

"He looks to me like the kind who'd scalp you if you weren't
careful..."

"You took the words right out of my mouth! And the Señora is
sitting with him... Úrsulo! What a name!"

"Incredible!"

The bone in the pot moves as the water bubbles, as if in
agreement.

The mayor of Matasánchez, Don José María de la Cerva y Tana,
gives specific instructions to Gómez, his personal assistant: "Don't
let anyone bother me, especially not those people from yesterday,"
and shuts himself in his office.

He's been wretched ever since Nepomuceno installed himself
up in Laguna del Diablo. In the beginning he let himself believe the
problem would go away, or head north along the Río Bravo. (He
knows Nepomuceno—he's a bundle of energy, a lightning bolt—he
can change his disposition that fast.) That delusion didn't last long.
Don José is not the sharpest tool in the box, but he's sharp enough to
realize that Nepomuceno's cause—"That stupid crap about La Raza
that he pulled out of his hat along with a bunch of other bullshit"—
appeals to many locals, especially the ones on the other side of the

river, though even "the great unwashed from these parts will follow that red-beard."

So he shuts himself in his office. His heart is full of fear on account of the news that López de Aguada, the Port Chief, delivered. "He didn't even explain it clearly!"—it served only to fill him with pointless worries, which are bucking about like angry goats. He's in a worse mood than the geranium-less flowerpots on Aunt Cuca's porch.

During the morning, the folks he has summoned come to his office. First, Doctor Velafuente—inscrutable, he doesn't say a word, but listens to the mayor carry on for nearly an hour, ranting and shaken. He prescribes: 1) valerian to help him sleep; 2) tea for his indigestion (which the mayor hasn't complained of, but the doctor can smell it on his breath); 3) walking, to ease his ill humor, at which the mayor bursts out furiously, "Don't tell me to go take a walk, don't give me that country doctor crap, don't you realize we're going to hell in a handbasket? Walking! What the hell are you thinking?!" Then Mr. Domingo arrives, the guy who works the window at the post office (the mayor has given him specific instructions to set aside "any package or envelope that looks suspicious"), and Pepe, the bootblack, who shines the mayor's shoes as he listens.

De la Cerva y Tana, shut in his office at the Town Hall, even eats lunch. They bring him some excellent food: pan-fried quesadillas, chile poblano and onion, beef jerky seasoned with brown sugar, and fish, all of which Doña Tere, the woman with the grill on the corner, makes specially for him. Her homemade food is always delicious: her salsa is better than anyone's. She usually works the streets in Bruneville but "it's better to work over here for now, the gringos have become too ornery."

Fidencio ties the lead of his mule, Sombra, to the bars on the little window that awkwardly faces the street as if it's winking among

the vines at the back of lawyer Gutierrez's house. Fidencio whistles
to his grandmother, Josefina, the old lady who runs the kitchen (no
one remembers her name, everyone just calls her "señora," except
Fidencio, who calls her "granny").

Old Josefina is a little deaf, but she hears the whistle of her favorite grandson. She rises and gestures to him to slip through the gate
(the chain is on, but it's loose) and into the kitchen. In the half-light
of the kitchen, she hugs him and sits him down at the table, then
starts bustling around to fix him some (delicious) chilaquiles while
she tells him things of no consequence, to which he listens respect-
fully until she passes him the fragrant, brimming plate.

"Mmmm, granny!"

"Eat it fast."

"Granny, I have lots to tell you ... Nepomuceno ..."

"You can tell me later. Eat."

Fidencio eats and talks quickly—his words are as flavorful as
the food that perfumes them—all about the Shears-Nepomuceno
business (whether or not Bruneville has a new sheriff; all about
Nepomuceno's camp; if this or that guy has joined forces with
him; who knows how many Mexican gringos have arrived from the
North; whether thieves are among them, fleeing the gallows)—
when Magdalena enters to ask "the señora" for something.

"Señora," she says softly in her sweet voice.

Josefina doesn't hear, but she takes advantage of her grandson's
pause to say:

"Hurry, Fidencio. The master will be down soon, and I don't
want him to find you here in the kitchen."

Fidencio doesn't eat or speak: he is mesmerized by the girl.
Seeing him like that, his grandmother realizes that Magdalena has
entered the room.

"Shoot! What are you doing in here, girl?!"

"I wanted to ask you to sew the hook on my dress because ..."

"Sew! Magdalena! If the master finds you in my nephew's presence, I'll be the one he'd send to the gallows, not Don Nepomuceno! Psht, Psht!" She shoos her away like an animal. "Out, Magdalena! And you, hurry up, Fidencio!"

"Who is Nepomuceno?" Magdalena asks, hesitating to leave.

"You get out of here if you don't want them to send me packing. Scoot!"

Magdalena leaves, the last thing she wants is for "the señora" to get the sack. She waits a prudent moment or two in her room. Her feet return her to the kitchen with no intent other than asking questions. Josefina is alone again. Magdalena bombards her ("Who is Nepomuceno? What's this about a camp?") and doesn't stop till she understands everything.

Dan Print writes in his notebook—words very different from those Elizabeth Stealman has been writing:

> *The Rancher*—the local paper in Bruneville, city on the southern frontier—has been publishing stories, peppered with local flavor and adventures, about some guy named Nepomuceno. The bandit caught my boss's attention, surprisingly, because although he has a reporter's instincts, as a good New Yorker born and bred in Boston, he has no interest whatsoever in anything south of the Hudson. To say *no* interest isn't, strictly speaking, correct, because he does flip through *The Rancher* to keep a finger on the pulse of the frontier, but mostly to have a good laugh at the Texans. The fact is he senses there's a good story in the bandit, which might or might not be of interest to me, because he called me into his office "urgently."
>
> "This one is made for you, Dan," he said. "Go cross the Rio Grande and interview him for me. I want a story on

this bandit, Neepomoo-whatever. Put it together however you need to, with different points of view. I don't want his autobiography and I don't want your opinion (I can already hear it!). Show us how his people see him, what his enemies think of him, his family, see if he has a wife and if you can get her to talk (there's nothing like a wife to tear down a hero). Don't stand there looking at me like that! Scram! Get outta here! You got lead in your shoes?"

I left his office dragging my tail between my legs, like some devilish eagle had shat on me. Finally, an interesting assignment . . . but . . . it ain't a piece of cake! I read in *The Rancher* that the bandit's in hiding. American law enforcement is after him, the Mexicans are too (although *The Rancher* conjectures that they're covering for him, but they could be making that up). It's clear that it's not the best idea to take a boat to Bruneville or Matasánchez and start asking around for him.

I overcame my low spirits and remembered what the Mexicans say (that if a bird shits on you it's good luck) and set out to visit my "contacts"—not that I have many, I've only been at the paper six months, and I've only covered stories about city life.

Four appointments and six drinks later, I found myself at a guesthouse where a Mr. Blast, a freebooter by occupation, was staying. I found him through a stroke of luck, it was like I won the lottery—or another eagle shat on me. Two hours later I set sail with him, aboard the *Elizabeth III*, bound for Galveston. The opening for my article couldn't be better.

We're spending the trip drinking and talking, or talking and drinking. To tell the truth, he's given me more than enough raw material for an article, what with his stubborn conviction that Texas is still an independent republic, his expansionist fanaticism that took him to Nicaragua with Walker a few years ago, then to Cuba in some failed enterprise I didn't completely understand, and then to Mexico during the war—he kept calling it "the conquest"—and now setting out to forge an alliance with Nepomuceno. Blast is convinced Nepomuceno will whet his appetite for adventure. The truth is I can't make heads or tails of it, neither his ideology nor his interest in Nepomuceno. "I've had a clear vision for a long time now: the Republic of Texas should stretch from Bogota to the Nueces River, there's no other way."

"But, excuse me for saying so, Mr. Blast, what does it matter to you? You're not Texan."

"No, I'm not, I'm telling you it's not for my own good, I'm not thinking of myself; it's just the only answer for the region. What they call Mexico is a failed endeavor, all it's good for is producing lazy servants. I could say the same about Nicaragua and Colombia, they're failed endeavors too, and I could go on. Only we, our country, America, can give them direction, a reason for existence. Alone, separate from the United States, they're bedbugs without a mattress."

"I don't understand. Nepomuceno is fighting because they took away his land, that much is clear to me, but why do you, Mr. Blast, feel the compulsion to make an alliance with Nepomuceno and join his banditry? It seems to me you're like oil and water . . ."

To every dog his bone: I'm going for my interview. In any case, the quote about bedbugs and mattresses strikes me as a good headline for the article—though I don't know if my editor will agree.

—

The Bruneville administration has done this a number of times in the past, loading all the penniless and crazy folks in town—"homeless greasers"—onto the barge with the livestock (which is the origin of the song, "The Madmen's Journey," one of many tunes attributed to Lázaro:

Si falta tornillo al coco,
Tablón, te faltan tres clavos
Querreque ...
Cornados los lleva el río!)

Three days after the incident between Shears and Nepomuceno, the first voyage of the barge that now belonged to Stealman is made for precisely this purpose: deporting as many crazies and poor folks as possible from the streets of Bruneville to Mexico, and not just Mexicans and poor folks—as a bonus they throw in a few outlaws, too.

This is, in part, to clean up Bruneville and get rid of problems, and in part to benefit Stealman: The Town Hall paid him to transport these passengers, and the contract enabled him to replace the tug that some idiot had allowed to float away, "So many men guarding the dock and not one of them noticed it drifting away, that's idiots for you."

All the crazies were dumped at the New Dock. They dispersed as best they could. The majority ended up in the center of Matasánchez. Since they had made friends on previous deportations they hung around the market, like the rats and other creatures that live off what others throw out. The luckiest found work as day laborers, struggling to get by, but they weren't reliable jobs—the cattle drives and the arrival of the livestock in town weren't what they used to be—so they had to settle for eating one day but not the next, and sometimes not at all.

When they went without work for long stretches, they slept with their buddies beneath the arches of the Plaza del Mercado or in the streets adjacent to the Town Hall, if you could call it sleep. They got their hands on cheap booze that had the same effect as gunpowder, making them behave explosively, they were shattered during the day but at night they didn't stop, coursing through the streets like the madmen they were, and when dawn arrived, and folks began to come out of their homes into the streets, they fell like sacks of sand on the cobblestones. The hardhearted kicked them or spat on them as they passed. Women looked away—they often got erections while sleeping, "Which no lady should have to see." Kids peed on them, sometimes accidentally, because they blended into the ground, all filthy and ragged.

Outlaws, on the other hand, always figure out a way to get by. They can settle anywhere.

On that first trip on the barge under Stealman's ownership, Connecticut and El Loco (the one who slept beneath the eaves of the market's main entrance in Bruneville) headed straight to the encampment in Laguna del Diablo, though we don't know exactly how they found it—did Connecticut know how to track carts and animals? We'll leave them be for the moment.

Another, The Scot, wandered off down the road on his own, through villages and hamlets, sleeping out in the open by himself, insisting upon speaking English; he seemed to think he had returned to his homeland. The only thing he said over and over in Spanish: "When the bloody greasers got their hands on us, it was like they jammed bullets up our arses" in a strange accent, seething with anger and fury.

Most folks dislike him. Those who don't, take pity on him and give him nicknames. He survives thanks to the charity of these souls.

More and more, day laborers who can't find work are joining the ranks of the crazies. The streets in Matasánchez begin to look like a nightmare, full of spirits and ghosts.

One Sunday, after mass—where they had gone to beg—one of them heard the story of "Good Old Nepo." It's like a match to a haystack; the news spreads throughout their ranks.

They understand without him putting out a call. Tuesday morning, without saying a word, they began to march—no horses, no firearms, just the clothes on their backs—like a disciplined army—to Laguna del Diablo.

In Bruneville, Elizabeth writes to herself:

> Dear Elizabeth,
> You know that in my letters I'm not given to telling you about my fears for the future. What we have is, for me, sharing the passage of time: life's most significant moments, my appraisal of events, and the sorrows and joys of daily life. Well, today I find myself tempted to make an exception. I won't talk about what has happened, just the nature of my fears.
> But first, the facts.
> As you know, when the heat season approaches—when the humidity becomes unbearable in this godforsaken backwater—Charles takes us back to New York. There, despite the heat, things are completely different. You don't have to keep the windows shut because it's not a swamp, the ocean is right there, the air circulates through open windows and doors, and there aren't Mexicans and alligators waiting with open jaws on every corner. It's not Boston or Paris, but New York's not Bruneville either.
> I have never objected to our periodic returns to the City because, as you well know, I'm always hoping for the day when we can leave this backwater of savages I so detest. We escape from the heat, from the suffocation of

the season, and the nature of these people. I visit my dear
mother. I meet with my friends. Charles spends afternoons
at the Club. We both surround ourselves with people one
can talk to, sharing interests, opinions, and worries. Now
that's what I call civilization—there, the coarsest man in
the room is my husband, though he's not the only one, but
his lack of refinement begins to disappear among all those
refined New Yorkers.[1] On the other hand, though Charles
is unrefined, he is certainly no greaser.

So, that's the problem: our departure approaches and
I . . . have not the least desire to leave! Why? Let me return
to what I said at the beginning: my fear. My reasons are
clear: I'm afraid if we leave, we'll lose everything. The savages will take the opportunity to destroy my home. To
plunder it. Burn it to the ground.

When I told Charles this he said, "All the more reason
to leave, I don't want you to be in any danger. If they torch
our home, I'll build you another."

Another! What is he thinking? He thinks it's easy!
Can't that man see that almost everything here is irreplace-
able? Does he really think the Louis XVI table we have
in the hall is no different from the ones that the savages
around here make with twisted legs; that the lace is made
by magical bees; that the bed and table linens from Bel-
gium are the same as those the Indians here in the south
make; that the china in our home could be from Puebla
(horrors!); that the blacksmith (that imbecile) can make
our silverware; that the portraits of my family printed by

---

1. Refined? New Yorkers? We couldn't disagree more. We're quoting from
her diary verbatim, and this proves our faithfulness to her text. Refined! By
whose standards?

Mr. Pencil are worthless; that our furniture made by European carpenters has been varnished with lard?! Has he no eyes, no feeling, no sense of smell?! He's just like a Comanche! Or worse. I know a Comanche, Governor Houston, and compared with my Charles he's a true gentleman, beautifully refined.

So since Charles doesn't understand, I have stalled as best I could. My strategy was to delay him.

I'll never be ready, I'll run into complications at every corner; my slaves and I will never finish; what one of us does, the other will undo. In truth, we're having fun, so much so that I even forgot my fears of the Stealman mansion being enveloped in flames and burnt to dust.

Yes, I know what you're thinking: if that came to pass it would be my liberation. We would finally leave Bruneville. That should make me happy. But it doesn't. Can you explain that to me? My fear fills me with anxiety. The only good thing in all of this is that I'm no longer playing at something that was initially a bluff: in the state I'm in, paralyzed by fear of what will happen, I'm literally good for nothing. My state of mind has affected my slaves. Though there's another reason for that, as you know: slaves follow their masters. All their will is in their master. A slave is just a shadow. They can't be anything more. That's why the fortitude of their masters is so critical. It's the source of their progress, triumph, peace, and much more. I'll explain it again just to be clear: these irrational Negroes don't share my fear because they're not capable of imagining a future. I have seen proof of that many times, but this isn't the time to go into detail.

Yesterday Charles flew into a rage. I tried to explain to him about "my things" (as he calls them): he's the one maintaining order in the town, he's their spiritual guide, their pillar, their light. If he leaves, the likelihood that Bruneville will go up in flames is much higher.

But he's beyond reason. He has disregarded my desires. He gave specific orders to the servants to prepare our departure as swiftly as possible. Like shadows, my slaves have followed their master's decision-making, and our departure is imminent.

My fears grow with each passing second.

Let it be clear, my dear, that there's something completely absurd about my fear: I detest Bruneville, why would I want to prevent its obliteration? I cannot stand this isle of savages, but my home is here, my garden, my things. I wouldn't say my memories are here, though. I have nothing of value from this pitiful, wretched corner of the globe.

I'll write to you next on board the *Elizabeth*, or in Galveston if we decide to spend the night there.

I don't need to remind you of our tradition: once in New York, I'll break off our correspondence. There, you and I *will become one again*. You won't hear from me, *or you'll hear from me forevermore*. I'll return to our correspondence when I come back, that is if we do come back to Bruneville. Will I be writing from another shabby town, beside a clearer river, perhaps, if I have a little luck?

Is some of the fear that engulfs me also due to the fact that if we leave, I will lose this intimate friendship we began here, on this island of savages, where we have been kept far apart, separated from part of our life? Shall I add that to my worries? But shouldn't this also give me joy? It's more difficult to answer that here because I don't want to lose you, but the idea of making you mine again (of making you mine and me yours) both excites me and breaks my heart. I'll lose my best friend; we'll each lose our best friend, *but we will become her.*

And I, dear Elizabeth, I am my own enemy. I am my own battlefield. You, friend, are the truce.

I'm calm now. Know that I will write to you again wherever Charles may take me. He can't survive in New York or in any other respectable place. He needs an environment like this unearthly place. That's my lot. The alternative is inconceivable: separation from my husband.

Before anything happens, I need to make sure that Gold and Silver, my two terriers, are bathed, brushed, and dressed. My two children. I must leave you to attend to them.

I'll keep the portrait of myself with Gold and Silver on my lap—the one Laplange took a few days ago—here between these pages of this journal. It's for you. You are its recipient. The armchair where I sat for the photo is here, facing me. Look after it, too, like something precious.

Fondly,

Elizabeth

Things are back to normal at Mrs. Big's Hotel. Even its owner no longer remembers the bodies hanging from the icaco—these things happen along the border with those crazy Mexicans. If the memory haunts her—and it occasionally does—she puts it out of her mind; she no longer has the strength to pick up and start again somewhere else; she'll manage where she is.

Tonight the Tigress of the East will sing in her café, she was scheduled to sing the night that the troubles started.

Smiley left Bruneville at the first light of dawn the day after losing at cards to Sarah-Soro Ferguson. He headed to Punta Isabel through the swamp because traffic on the river was suspended (it resumed a few days later). It's a difficult journey, but we know he made it to a steamboat that took him up the Mississippi.

Mrs. Big doesn't miss Smiley; all the law enforcement officers and Rangers posted at the dock keep Mrs. Big's Hotel bustling. And the tuneless musicians who sang and played for tips have returned. Something about them has changed, though their music is as bad as ever; they're louder because they've agreed to crow in unison, singing verses they practice for weeks on end. What's more, they're not just practicing, they're listening to other bands and copying them. They even sing one of Lázaro Rueda's tunes, the one about a cowboy and his violin, but in English, and it loses almost everything in translation.

A few days later, after ten in the evening, the whole sky fills with colors, orange streaks that seem to be painted onto a glowing red backdrop. The telegraph is out of order for hours. In Bruneville a piece of paper on the telegraphist's desk catches fire. In Matasánchez, El Iluminado walks the streets, surrounded by church ladies, like flies on a piece of rotting meat.

Three days after that, at five in the morning, the aurora borealis lights up the better part of the hemisphere, from the North Pole all the way to Venezuela. The telegraph is working. In Matasánchez, the priest says Mass early. El Iluminado doesn't appear; he's in a mystical delirium, deep in conversation with the Virgin.

A day later, the aurora borealis appears again, though not as extensively.

People call this phenomenon the "Sun Storm," or the "Carrington Event." El Iluminado pays no mind to these scientific names; he refers to it as "The Calling." He climbs the belltower of the church and rings the bells wildly. Then he goes downstairs to collect his cross—which he left soaking in the baptismal font (without anyone objecting)—and in front of the church proclaims loudly, "Let's join Nepomuceno! Long live the Virgin of Guadalupe! Death to the gringos!"

Felipillo Holandés wets his pants. Laura, his neighbor, in ecstasy, convinces her grandmother to come outside and see what's happening. "The bells are tolling, granny!"

That same day, the procession led by El Iluminado leaves for Laguna del Diablo, singing and carrying banners of the Virgin. There are more than a hundred of them. Some don't seem to fit in with this motley crew. You might suspect, if you looked carefully, that they're using El Iluminado and his church ladies as a cover. What is Blas, Urrutia's man, and friend of Bruneville's crappy mayor, doing there? The Indian trader is there too (what's he up to?) as well as others who are well-known bandits, but they're Mexicans one and all. You might say that the rascals looking to make a quick buck have "found their calling." Father Vera brings up the rear (he doesn't want to be left out).

They're in no hurry. Periodically they stop to pray, sing, and who knows what else (the outlaws are the busiest, plundering without prejudice); there are so many old and helpless in their ranks that they tire frequently—Laura's grandmother is among them, her granddaughter has dragged her along to this "ridiculousness." And then there are the voices that speak to El Iluminado. When they begin the procession must halt. The procession walks a few minutes, and then they rest for a while.

One day before the first aurora borealis, in Laguna del Diablo, Nepomuceno and Jones take advantage of the fact the sun has not yet risen and most of the camp is still asleep. They're reviewing the draft of their proclamation: "Our object, as you have seen, has been to chastise the villainy of our enemies, which heretofore has gone unpunished. These individuals have connived with each other, and form, so to speak, a perfidious inquisitorial lodge to persecute and rob us, without any cause, and for no other crime on our part than that of being of Mexican origin, considering us, doubtless, destitute of those gifts that they themselves do not possess." They're not sure how to date it, "What should we put?"

Óscar comes in with two mugs of chocolate and bread fresh from the oven—which he built of clay—soft, fragrant, aniseed bread.

Óscar listens to the draft proclamation.

"It seems to me, Don Nepomuceno . . ."

"No 'Dons' here, Óscar, in this new world we're all equals, and we're just the arrowhead tip of the arrowhead of this New World . . . For the hundred millionth time, don't call me 'Don.'"

"It seems to me, Nepomuceno, if you'll forgive me, that's not right, we must be more aggressive. We ought to invade the territory that's ours and take it back once and for all."

"That's not what this is about."

"It certainly is."

"Who'd have thought you'd talk like this, a simple baker?"

"There's no alternative with the gringos. If we give them a foot, they take a mile. We have to take Bruneville back from them; after all, it was ours to begin with . . . it's your mother's property, Nepomuceno! You hold the legal title! Aim high, Nepomuceno, aim high! They built it right where you had that beautiful stable . . . Or else we'll just stand by while they finish us off!"

"Of course. But that's not what this is about. We're drawing a line in the sand. They're already ensconced there, part of the land; La Raza just has to teach them to show us respect."

"No, no, no. And I'm not just being contrary. No!"

"Why are you so adamant? Please explain yourself, Óscar." That's Jones speaking.

"If we don't get rid of them, before we know it they'll pass a law preventing us from working on the other side of the Río Bravo, not just poor folks, but all Mexicans. As for property . . . you've seen how they respect it, the gringos all have silver tongues. We ain't seen nothing yet, the worst is still to come. They'll put up a fence or build a wall so we can't cross over to 'their' Texas . . . as if it were theirs! . . . and then, you'll see, listen closely, they'll take the water from our river, they'll divert it for their own purposes, who knows how they'll do it . . . but you'll see! They'll take everything we have . . . there won't be a single mustang or a plot of land they don't claim as theirs. South of the Río Bravo will become violent. Mexicans will begin to treat each other with the same contempt . . . . Our women will be raped and butchered and buried in pieces in the desert."

"Go and drink your chocolate, Óscar, you're talking nonsense."

Óscar (his face shining, his eyes wide) walks back to the kitchen, toward the oven he built with his own hands, the hands of a baker. His head is full of images, of black horses, one of a kind, extraordinary to behold, like pearls. He says to himself, "no matter how you look at it, we're guilty of the same kind of hubris as the gringos; although we don't have slaves, we call ourselves owners of horses, and of land and water, too . . ." He takes a deep breath. He regards his oven, its round dome rising to his full height. He thinks, "It's true, I must be losing my mind . . ."

That same morning Sombra, the donkey, arrives in Laguna del Diablo. Her load is making noise, shouting. To clarify: Sombra is being pulled along by a filthy old man, carrying a woman wrapped from head to foot in a heavy blanket. She needs help to get off the donkey because she's tied to it like a sack of rice, not a creature with her own two legs. The old man who guided the donkey is half-blind, he can't untie the knots or help the lady himself. "The animal saved me," she says as soon as she's untied, "I don't know how to ride." The filthy old man has neither speech nor memory, his tongue has been tied by old age.

The woman, whose face is covered by a veil, repeats the same phrase, "I don't know how to ride," without anyone understanding what she's talking about (she wants to tell them how, in Matasánchez, her elderly servants tied her to the donkey and entrusted her to this old mule-driver).

Her stupefaction doesn't last long. Soon she composes herself, "I need to see Don Nepomuceno, I'm bringing him something he needs." Since she's a woman, and since, judging by her bearing, her hair, and the voice beneath her veil she seems to be an attractive, young woman of twenty-two or twenty-three, they take her to him. From that moment she was known among Nepomuceno's men as La Desconocida: "The Stranger."

"My husband nearly killed me with his last beating, but now I'm here." She removes her veil. She places a bag of gold coins in Nepomuceno's hand, taking care not to touch him. "Make me a colonel or a cook, whatever you need—but I'm warning you, I don't know how to cook—and I'll help you fight for respect; I have more money, my savings are buried deep in the earth at home."

"What do you want in return?"

"For you to help me get to the other side of the Bravo, and have someone guide me through Indian Territory, to where the husband I had the bad fortune to marry won't be able to lay a finger on me."

What Nepomuceno likes most is her looks, plus the fact that she's direct and looks him straight in the eye. Moreover, he thinks, *This woman seems like a virgin. She will be mine.* How foolish men are, foolish men . . . because she too, has her desires, though they're entirely different.

Nepomuceno gives orders that La Desconocida should be well looked after. To treat her like a queen. He also begins calling her by her nickname, it fits her, "La Desconocida." It doesn't occur to him to ask her real name. It's Magdalena, the lovely girl from Puebla, the one Gutierrez bought to be his wife.

Nepomuceno gives orders to install La Desconocida in one of the lean-tos they've erected with fresh, scented wooden poles.

As soon as she walks away—what a view!—Nepomuceno dons his spurs. His servant who breaks the horses is in charge of the corral. Nepomuceno takes the lasso. He reins in the filly. He saddles her up and mounts her.

The herd stirs.

Lázaro sings:

Gasta el pobre la vida
En juir de la autoridá

But he doesn't like something about this song, he sets his violin down. "I'm just a useless old man," he says aloud when he sees Nepomuceno trot past on lovely Pinta.

"Enough!" Nepomuceno shouts to Lázaro. "There's nothing useless about you, your only problem is that you're like a colt who's lost its mother..."

Nicolaso receives a message via pigeon: "You can't trust 'em as far as you can throw 'em."

Pedro and Pablo—Two Eights—come and go along the riverbank, in camp they're called the "mermen." Their job in camp is to help build and maintain the tents—they're skilled with sticks and cloth—their life on the barge trained them well for this.

Other boys and children have joined them. The young folk organize themselves well.

The cowboys do what they know best—caring for the herd—and a few other things, too: they get their hands on arms and munitions. There's Ludovico (who thinks of Moonbeam daily), Silvestre, Patronio, Ismael, Fausto, El Güero, and others.

In Bruneville the Eagles have become even more secretive. They don't even meet in the Café Ronsard to play cards.

You might say they're underground or underwater Eagles. Or that they're crazy. Because when they meet in the course of their daily routines, selling beans or cattle or bundles of cotton or cloth, instead of their usual conversations they list crimes to one another, adding to the litany we overheard at the Café Ronsard—Josefa Segovia and Frederick Canon, 333 and Busy Bucks, the apples and the seven lemons, the infamous wheel at Rancho Barreta, Platita Poblana, and others—injustices racking up faster than a greyhound's laps on the racetrack. The Eagles repeat these names in broad daylight, as if they were discussing prices or delivery dates.

The quality of the milk from a certain cow, a horse's teeth, the origin of imported cloth, how fresh or good the seed is—they don't talk about any of this, not even "How's your mama doing?" or "Has the kid been born yet?" No small talk. They're compiling a long list of abuses down in the Rio Grande Valley.

They pass messages along quickly. They utter phrases to balconies that appear to be empty. In the confessionals, they confess sins that aren't sins, and their confessors aren't priests. The barber repeats them in the middle of conversations, like non sequiturs. Lovers say things that aren't at all loving. Whores open their mouths more than their legs when Nepomuceno's men are around. The children continue to gather in their favorite spot, Mesnur, and messengers give them phrases they don't understand to pass along—they memorize them and deliver them home. Farewell kites, farewell dragonflies in flight.

Another messenger pigeon: "Three tons of beans . . . the stampede is on its way . . ."

Nepomuceno sends a message to Don Jacinto, the saddler: "Make me a saddle for a woman who doesn't know how to ride, so that she looks like a queen; I need it as soon as possible."

Jacinto thinks it over. He's just invented one that, to this day, is called the Mexican Saddle. It's like a raised throne, there's no way you can fall off a horse sitting in it.

To make it as fast as possible, he gets help from Situ, the artisan who decorates belts and other leather goods. This infuriates Trapper Cruz. "Too bad," Jacinto says, "he'll have to get over it; this is for Nepomuceno, it has to be the best."

There's a death in El Iluminado's procession: the grandmother of Laura, the girl who was kidnapped by the Indians. The old woman didn't even receive Holy Unction. The burial on the open plains is like a party, with singing and swearing and Nepomuceno's supporters shouting slogans. They lose a day and a half to this. The inches they advance take hours and hours. Even turtles would have arrived sooner.

On one of these delays the beans a cook is carrying begin to sprout in their sack.

Mr. Blast and Dan Print disembark at Punta Isabel and find a crossing to Bagdad (a matter of simply paying a boatman) to follow Nepomuceno's trail on Mexican soil.

Dan Print makes a short entry in his diary:

"Aw, chirriones, I thought crossing the border would be like crossing the Lethe."

At Laguna del Diablo, Robert, the escaped slave, is learning how to grill meat on the open fire from the cowboys. He tells stories, that's his seasoning.

Ludovico peppers anyone who will listen with questions, he wants to know everything about the Hasinai. "One of these days I'm going back for that pretty Moonbeam and taking her with me; and if I find a priest, I'll marry her."

"What makes you think you can marry a Texas Indian? You can't marry them . . ."

Ludovico nearly comes to blows with the guy who makes this offensive statement, but Robert stops him.

"We don't fight here, it's beneath us. Listen, why are you saying they can't tie the knot?"

"It's obvious."

"What do you mean?" says Robert. "Are you like the gringos, against La Raza? If that's how it is, you don't belong here."

There's a lot of discussion and debate, but it's good humored; folks are eager and happy, the camp is filled with their laughter.

The youngsters have made up their own rules—rather strict—and take them very seriously. "We're the Kids' Brigade."

Lázaro composes a few verses just for them.

Nepomuceno and Jones give them assignments, each more difficult than the last, and each kid gives it their all. They learn how to tie knots, handle a boat in the water, as well as how to pull the trigger and hit targets.

When someone new arrives, lost and looking for adventure (or dying of hunger), they quickly convert him into one of their own, teaching him Nepomuceno's beliefs and stirring up his hatred of the gringos so they're ready for battle or anything else that may be necessary.

Among them is Fernando, the servant. He looks like more of a man despite the fact he's thinner than he used to be, which makes him look both slighter and smaller, and he always looks frightened, his eyes wide until it's time for sleep. But he's more in command of himself, more at home in the world. No longer a mosquito who flies away at the first swipe.

The cattle yard has to keep killing rustled cattle to fill so many bellies. "Just cattle thieves with their own slaughterhouse," a young cowboy who misses the cattle drives pronounces bitterly.

Pretty Sandy, Eagle Zero—a blonde treasure, but Mexican to the core—learns by heart what she and all of her compadres have agreed upon, to wit: "We are one with Nepomuceno and those that have gathered around him of late . . . an organized body . . . We belong to the branch from the State of Texas, we recognize Nepomuceno as our only leader, despite his absence . . . and this same public opinion should be considered as the best judge, which, with coolness and impartiality, does not fail to recognize some principle as the cause for the existence of open force and immutable firmness, which impart the noble desire of cooperating with true philanthropy to remedy the state of despair of he who, in his turn, becomes the victim of ambition, satisfied at the cost of justice,"—it rambles on and on—"we're ready to shed our blood and suffer the death of martyrs . . ."

Along the northern bank of the Río Bravo, or more to the northeast, the Coal Gang, led by Bruno the Viking, with the ever-present Pizca at his side, has been drawing closer to Bruneville. His contacts are the same as always: Nepomuceno's half-brothers, José Esteban and

José Eusebio, the sons of Nepomuceno's father before he married Doña Estefanía. They have made a point of not meeting at the ranch because they don't want to cause problems, on the contrary. Doña Estefanía's sons have agreed to meet them at dawn. They make a mistake: they both leave Rancho del Carmen.

They're under close watch. Taking advantage of their absence, King's men attack, but not directly, they sneak in like cowardly thieves, more for the loot than to send a warning. (Their aim: to invade Mexico, "land of the greasers." But King won't let them: he doesn't want to waste his forces, confronting Nepomuceno would be a mistake and could bring trouble to Texas. The reyeros or kiñeros obey, but eventually their urges get the better of them and they make a long journey and set fire to another ranch that night. That's all, and they return to King's land, looking like they haven't done a thing, to wait for the moment when they can crush Nepomuceno, defender of greasers.)

Neither Doña Estefanía nor anyone else on her ranch notices King's men make off with three mares and a good cow, which gives delicious milk.

But the three mares and the cow serve a purpose: King's men don't find out about the meeting with Bruno the Viking. They have no idea the Coal Gang is in the region, and that they're allied with Nepomuceno, up to no good.

The Eagles are trying to recruit, but it's not easy. Hector, who owns the cart, stops Pepe, the corn-on-the-cob vendor, and tells him a story:

"The Eagles were born overnight, thanks to Nepomuceno, let me tell you about him. First, when he was five years old the Apaches attacked Doña Estefanía's ranch, which she had inherited from her father. But that little detail didn't matter to them, in their eyes the land belonged to no one; land titles dating to seventeenhundredthirtysomething made no difference to them . . . they entered the ranch hollering, "Death to the Christians, spear them all" . . . and that's how they ended up kidnapping him; they taught him how to use a lasso before he could walk. Then the family got him back and began to turn him into a vaquero, but by then he was like a wild Indian, that's how he learned how to track, and why he has both friends and enemies in Indian Territory. And that's how it happened. Because then the Germans and the Cubans arrived, then the gringos, all ready to fight. And that's how the Eagles came into being, to look out for your soul, not just your pocketbook. So, are you in?"

Pepe the corn-on-the-cob vendor had almost fallen asleep listening to such a long explanation—he'd risen long before dawn and hadn't slept well because his calf had been sick during the night. It was only the sound of Hector's voice rising with his final question that snapped him awake again.

"Are there ladies?"

."Women? There're tons, and they're gorgeous. With bosoms that spill out of their bodices."

Mr. Blast and Mr. Print arrive in Matasánchez. They ask for a room at the Hotel Ángeles del Río Bravo, the finest in the region, but since no one knows them they can't get one. Then Mr. Print explains that he's here to interview Nepomuceno for such and such American newspaper in New York, a very important one, to show Nepomuceno in the best possible light, just as he is, because *The Rancher* has undertaken to tarnish his reputation, which is obviously disgraceful, and suddenly Room 221 "appears" ("It was just vacated, sir."), it'll be ready in a jiffy, so now they have somewhere to spend the night and, what's more, if they want they can spend the whole week . . .

Amalia pours in the corn flour, stirs the pot with a spoon, Lucha seasons it with cinnamon, Amalia sweetens it with powdered brown sugar. It's their daily ritual, preparing atole for the Señora. Aunt Cuca takes her water and chocolate early in the morning. Then she has atole, not tea, not coffee, not herbal tea—it's atole that calms her stomach.

"A small cupful every now and then, and I can eat what I want . . . thanks to the corn flour."

Even if they tied her down she wouldn't take her own medicine, that Atacadizo syrup she makes, half of Matasánchez takes it, but not her.

Doña Estefanía can't get to sleep. Her youngest son, her favorite, an outlaw! Her ranch raided by reyeros!

She can't think straight. Her son surrounded by an army, her people have described this all to her and it makes her feel awful. None of this should be happening: the gringos' designs on her property (even the wild Indians hadn't been able to take an inch from her), their not looking her straight in the eye, their claiming she was no longer in Mexico, even the papers they sent her stating that she was now "American"—which is to say, gringa—and worst of all her Benjamin, her favorite, mixed up in this.

Nepomuceno's men need horses and arms, but they don't want to buy them at market because they don't want anyone to know that they need them or that they've gotten their hands on them.

So they cross the Bravo, but not all of them, just some of the cowboys. A little later they find some cattle that have strayed from the herd, but that's not what they're looking for—they need mustangs. It will take time to tame them, but they don't have bad habits—they haven't been exposed to the angry violence of the gringos, who train horses by beating them.

In the Bruneville market Sharp claims, "It made no difference to Nepomuceno whether they called him Mexican or American, he signed documents both ways, depending on which benefitted him more. I saw it with my own eyes. Don't come tell me now that he's the defender of Mexicans; and this crap about 'La Raza' is even worse."

Luis wanders nearby, looking for someone whose shopping he can carry, but he finds no one. He's not catching flies or getting lost in his own world. At home they're desperate for money. But there isn't any to be had.

Something has happened on the river. Úrsulo arrives with a report:

"Nepomuceno, something has happened to the river, it's impossible to cross the rapids, the cowboys who are crossing to get horses have gotten trapped."

"Then let them stay on the islet."

"They can't, what if the tide rises?"

"If it rises, let the fools drown."

Nepomuceno doesn't even glance at him. Úrsulo mumbles to himself, "I'm telling you it's the river, Nepomuceno; it's no one else's doing."

Úrsulo sleeps less each day, he's like the gears in a clock, he never stops. He hears Nepomuceno's words and commits them to memory. He departs in the *Inspector* to deliver the news to the old port.

Right before his eyes the river settles down, but he still delivers the message. Nepomuceno's men all learn to fear their leader. You have to be sharp.

Juan Prensa, the printer, works tirelessly. The circus canceled its engagement—they were coming from north of the river, and now the gringos are afraid of the "wild south"—(leaving him with the type set and the samples printed, although none of them were great quality, truth be told); there are no weddings coming up, no fancy baptisms or funerals (of late it seems only the poor are being born and dying); he doesn't have a single job, not even a small one, like a banquet with the traditional poems written for the occasion—he usually edits them and folks are grateful to him for it, they think it's part of his job.

But Robert, who's his buddy, has given him work for Nepomuceno. It's not the first time it's happened, but he doesn't understand this job. He prints—"lickety-split"—flyers with the following words:

> *It is my duty as the highest officer of this Republic to inform you, in plain language and with utmost sincerity, that the Cherokees will never have permission to remain here permanently, not even in the autonomous jurisdiction of the area governed by their peoples: their simple political claims, which they have attempted to validate in the territory they occupy, can never be validated, and that if for the time being they are permitted to remain where they are, it is only because the Government is waiting for the opportune moment to resolve this situation by expelling them peacefully. Whether this is achieved by friendly negotiations or by violence depends entirely upon the Cherokees themselves.*
> *May 26, 1839*
> *Mirabeau Lamar*

Robert arrives to collect the ream of printed pages—Prensa has trimmed them so they can easily be passed from hand to hand, as requested, "There will be as many of these in Texas as playing cards."

"Here you go."

"How much is it?"

The question is just a formality. They both know the answer before it's asked.

"No one charges Nepomuceno. But I'd like something in exchange, if you don't mind. It's just curiosity but I'd like to know . . . what are these leaflets I printed for?"

"Nepomuceno has a plan."

"So I imagine. What is it?"

"Here's what Nepomuceno wants: to have at least one represen-
tative from each of the five tribal nations on his side: a Cherokee,
a Chickasaw, a Choctaw, a Creek (or Muscogee or Muskoke), and
a Seminole. And better yet if he can get a Caddo—a wild one—
plus one of the Hasinais that used to live scattered across eastern
Texas, a Kadohadacho (the ones from Oklahoma and Arkansas), or
a Nacogdoche from Louisiana. But he's only counting on the first
five I mentioned because the Chickasaw severed relations with the
Caddos, and the Hasinais are scattered to the four winds, sold off as
slaves. That's why."

"Yeah? I still don't get it."

"It's for the Cherokees."

"It won't be easy, they're staunch supporters of the gringos."

"Yes and no. That's what the leaflets are for. We're gonna give
them to Pérez, the Indian trader, today. He's heading there tomorrow
at dawn. If we circulate them throughout Indian Territory we'll convert the Cherokees into our allies, that's what Nepomuceno thinks."

"What business do you have with the Indian trader. He's not
good people."

"This is the time for making alliances, Prensa. Not for finding
problems."

El Iluminado arrives in Laguna del Diablo with the Talking Cross,
surrounded by his court of believers: church ladies, delinquents,
hangers-on, and opportunists, some of whom believe they're
there to wage religious war against the Protestants and savages. It's
been so long since he heard about Shears's insult that he no longer
remembers it—he believes the Virgin herself compelled him to follow Nepomuceno; yet despite the fact he no longer remembers,
his determination to join Nepomuceno remains intact (although

he's become wrapped up in his "own" cause: the Talking Cross, the Virgin, the Archangels, and even a little devil all give him advice and instructions).

A bunch of foreigners have been arriving at Laguna del Diablo too, some Europeans and a half dozen Cuban rebels (trying to win support for the independence of their country or fleeing from political persecution on the island). The news really has spread like wildfire.

Mr. Blast, the freebooter, arrives in Laguna del Diablo with Dan Print, the very young journalist.

Dan Print expected anything but this: colorful tents held up by freshly hewn poles, sotol, women, prayers, people of all stripes, and the food, plentiful enough for everyone, with the best meat he's tasted in his life.

In the region of the great Valley, from the banks of the Nueces River to the mountains in the north and the deserts to the south, there are still a few folks who haven't heard about the hurricane unleashed by Nepomuceno: the Aunts, on their ranch.

They all go about their business, except two of them who are going against the grain.

One of these is the eldest of them all, wizened and wrinkled as a raisin—no one recalls when she first arrived because she arrived before the rest of them; she's not a true Aunt, she thinks differently from the others; that is, if she thinks. She mostly ponders one memory:

"Rafa, my brother, and I were up on the roof of our house. It was my idea. Ciudad Castaño looked huge from up there, bright and shiny, like a dream. Up on the roof I wanted to belong to the city, and at the same time I felt I didn't belong. Since I liked to go up there and I had done it so many times, and the folks at home thought it was dangerous, Doña Llaca, the cook, was instructed not to let me go up there. The stairs were right behind the kitchen, and she was always just a stone's throw away, shelling peas, picking over the beans, kneading the dough for tamales, cracking the nuts for the pastries, roasting coffee, stripping corn, or grinding up some grain or other. Rafa and I took advantage of the fact that on the patio they had stored half a dozen tall ladders that were going to be taken to the store and sold, and we climbed one.

"My Aunt Pilarcita caught us. She saw us when she came into the patio, Rafa's foot was on the top rung of the ladder, and I was helping him over the parapet of the roof terrace. Typical of Pilarcita, she always was a snoop. She got mad at us—which was also typical of her—and ordered the ladder we had used to climb up there to be removed, to leave us on the roof as a punishment. She yelled that she wasn't going to give us our lunch—'So you learn once and for all not to do that! One day you'll bust your noggins!'—but I didn't believe what she said about not feeding us, I knew she always overreacted, plus she was easily distracted, but most of all she was fanatical about us taking our meals on a schedule, eating enough so that we could grow. She must have once dreamed that we'd grow up to be giants, or else why all that bother. Most importantly, if she wanted to punish us, it made no difference to me not to eat lunch, what I hated was having to eat all the food on my plate.

"This was early in the morning. Rafa and I had practically forgotten we were punished. Beneath the burning sun we were bored, there was nothing else for us to do, trapped up there. Then thirst joined boredom, and boy, was I thirsty. That's when the Comanches showed up. It happened in the blink of an eye, and it filled me with violent emotion, I began to clap with excitement.

"The Comanches galloped steadily past, sowing the earth with arrows, without slowing, leaving cross stitches, chain stitches, garter stitches in their wake, but not as skillfully as seamstresses, their stitches were hurried and uneven, they were howling and laughing hysterically—they looked drunk.

"But my surprise and the excitement were followed by fear. Rafa and I threw ourselves down on the rooftop so they wouldn't see us, we knew all about the Comanches—who *didn't* know about them? I raised my head to watch them. Rafa didn't. He had clasped his hands over the back of his neck as if he were handcuffed, like the racoon we kept chained in the back garden. I realized Rafa wet himself because his pee trickled over and wet my skirt. I didn't dare lift it out of the way or move over.

"Before covering my face I got a good look at them: the Comanches were naked from the waist up, covered with black paint, moccasins on their feet and legs covered in tight, flesh-colored, fringed leather pants. They had nice saddles. The chiefs wore large feather headdresses, crests that cascaded down to their horses' hooves.

"The federales had left town to hunt them down, leaving behind a small detachment which was still sleeping. Someone had given them bad information, maybe a spy bribed by the savages. But that wasn't really necessary, the guards were confident that there was no danger. At the store I had overheard things that weren't appropriate for girls or 'señoritas,' but I have the ears of an Aunt, I knew that the federales were the brothels' and saloons' best customers, though they only ever paid on credit—their pay was so slow to arrive that, when it finally did, they had already spent it all, so they always charged against their future wages without a care. But when their captain was in town they packed the church, in front of him they acted like little saints, or should I say big ones.

"Some Comanches had put flaming rags dipped in oil on their arrows. They followed these with arrows carrying bladders filled with turpentine. Some houses caught fire. I didn't see it, but some say they threw pouches of gunpowder too, though from up there I could see all the way to the Town Hall, the back of the marketplace, and the jailhouse. It was like I had ten eyes.

"The only noise was the sound of their ululating war cries, and the sound of their spurs. Otherwise the town had turned silent as death, as if all the Castañans had had their tongues torn out.

"Rafa began to cry when the bullets started flying. The Comanches ducked behind their horses without slowing down but they stopped howling. They had made it all the way to the church and the Town Hall and were galloping up and down the main street. They reached for their guns and began firing at those of us who were trying to defend ourselves from windows and doors. Bodies were falling left and right, some into the street. Without dismounting, a Comanche slit the throat of Don Isaias, the store owner. It was as though they each had six hands, shooting arrows with two, cocking and aiming their Remingtons or Colts (I don't know what kind of pistols they were, but they sure fired a lot of shots) with two more, and slitting throats, scalping people, and hacking out tongues with the last two.

"One Comanche jumped from his horse's saddle to the ground, grabbing the body of some poor soul who had just been wounded by one of his arrows in midair—Don Cesar, from the pharmacy—castrating him and stuffing what he'd just hacked off into the poor guy's mouth. Even, then, riddled with arrows, Don Cesar was stirring. The Comanche bound his feet with a rope, remounted his horse, and galloped up and down the street, dragging him behind and whooping all the while, as the other Comanches began to dismount.

"They broke into the homes that weren't on fire. Folks say they committed all kinds of atrocities against the residents: raping women, even old ladies, mutilating the men and scalping them for trophies, which they tied to the tails of their horses. They killed only those who put up a fight or resisted.

"From where I lay, in the silence broken occasionally by the cries of one of our own or the ululations of the Comanches, I could see the air filled with feathers from our mattresses. Some Castañans fled their homes only to be riddled with arrows, out of the fire into the frying pan.

"All the while the Comanches were ululating and roaring with laughter.

"That's when one of the Comanches, whose face I couldn't see, grabbed my sister Lucita and put her on his horse. He wore a long, white feather headdress, and had very long black hair. That was something new, because they had used to shave their heads; they must have been filthy, the Comanches, they even ate lice, they never used soap, yet they removed all the hair from their bodies. Now the fashion had changed, and long hair was their thing, but they continued to remove the hair from their bodies.

"What I already knew, along with Lucita and Rafa and all the children in Ciudad Castaño, is that the Comanches kidnapped boys and girls, taking the ones that looked the best and adopting them. They took the smartest ones from the ranches to look after their horses. I never understood how they selected adult women, because they made no distinction based on looks, they kidnapped ugly and pretty women alike. They married their captives without concern for the fact that they had already raped them, and they continued to treat them cruelly, like their own women. They enjoyed that. Folks didn't talk about it, but we all knew. One woman who returned from captivity because her people paid a ransom to an Indian trader—this was before the Texan Indians made a business of it—took it upon herself to recount her misfortunes in horrifying detail on nights when the moon was full, it was as though she lost her senses. She ran through the streets screaming, banging on doors to make sure we all heard her. Folks say she did this naked, but I never saw her; no matter how many times I peeked out on the balcony I laid eyes on her only once: she was filthy, like a savage, and she was violently shaking the ivy the Pérez family had grown over the screen that hid their milk cow; she shook the ivy branches, and her madness was quite a sight; who knows, maybe she did take her clothes off when she told her story, she was already exposing herself with her voice. But I never saw it.

"When the Comanches grabbed Lucita I heard Papa yell. He had hidden because if they found him that would be his death sentence, but death's one thing and losing your daughter is another, that's why he yelled, giving himself away, and let fly a hail of bullets which riddled the horse and its rider, the savage who had grabbed Lucita falling to the ground. If Papa had let him get away with his prize, that's where things would have ended, the savages would have gone their merry way, but no. They gathered around the front door of our house. Another savage grabbed Lucita, shouting at the top of his lungs. Rafa stood up in his wet pants and he began jumping up and down and screaming like a lunatic. An Indian stood up on his horse's back and in one leap, an incredible feat, he landed next to us as if he had flown. He didn't have a headdress, his long hair was matted and gathered up like a nest on his head. He picked Rafa up by the shoulders and tossed him down into the street, where one of his accomplices grabbed him and put him on his horse, then he jumped down and landed on his horse's back and they galloped away at full speed. The one who held Lucita let her go, who knows why, he didn't like her or he got distracted.

"They continued pillaging, taking all of the goods from the store and heaven knows what they did to Doña Llaca. I can't tell you what happened to my Aunt Pilarcita. She claimed she was hidden under the table during the whole attack and didn't see a thing, they didn't touch her.

"The Comanches departed, leaving two dozen homes in flames. They emptied the army's arsenal, taking all the arms and ammunition, and they emptied the storerooms of all the shops, too. They didn't leave a single *federal* alive. From the church they stole the

chalice and the priest's robes embroidered with gold, which had just
arrived from Italy, via Havana.

"It's best not to mention what happened to Rafa. Our house
was never the same again. Aunt Pilarcita stopped paying attention to
us, like she had lost her hearing and her sight, along with her desire
to work. Mama stopped working in the store. Papa spent the days
receiving letters and writing responses at night, he couldn't sleep for
trying to rescue his only son. Doña Llaca stopped picking the grit
out of the beans, she forgot to cook the peas, her tamales lost their
texture, as if they had been made in beef broth, all gelatinous.

"Years later, Nepomuceno, Mama's nephew, murdered all the
Karankawas to avenge Rafa's kidnapping and everything else they
had done. But it wasn't the Karankawas, it was the Comanches.
There's not a doubt in my mind. I had seen the Karankawas before,
they were fishermen, we used to see them with their nets near the
Río Bravo Falls when we went to visit Aunt Maria Elena's ranch.

"It's not true the Indian attack caused the end of Ciudad Castaño.
It had been dying slowly, like a candle flickering out. Now there's
nothing left. Most of us moved to Matasánchez, others moved away,
and years later many folks moved to the new town, Bruneville."

Eleonor enters the room at the back of Minister Fear's house. She
has changed. She's wearing black, like on the day of her wedding—a
modest black dress to signify her departure from her own family,
as was customary—but there's something about her face and her
carriage that has changed dramatically. We last saw her on the day
Nepomuceno took Shears's bait and shot him (it would have been
better if he had just walked away, Miss Lace said to Eleonor, "Like he
did with that poorly made saddle, because this was no different, in
fact it was worse"); we saw her in that room, determined to die, not

bothering to pretend that it was compassion motivating her to tend to the sick man. Unrepulsed, indeed, even *attracted* to the illness the sick man might give her, Eleonor tended to him with exemplary dedication. And either the trouble she undertook made a difference, or she had good luck. Because he has overcome his illness and is recovering in leaps and bounds—he's become talkative and flirtatious, his natural disposition. He's almost ready to get out of bed; he feels the urge to jump up and down but doesn't have quite enough energy yet. He doesn't feel the least bit sick, but rather like he's run six leagues without a drop to drink.

Eleonor's face is radiant. She's wearing her black dress because her cousin back home told her that it suits her, and she wants to believe her, she wants to look her best, although she knows she ought not to; and there's another reason to wear black: she associates it with the thing she detests most on Earth, Minister Fear.

Because Fear really repulses her. Have no doubt, the Minister saved her from shame and humiliation—he saved her life—but he immediately shut her up in this living tomb. He's a hateful creature, a heartless man without feeling, without joy in life, as well as a hypocrite who, despite being a minister, delights in . . . perverse . . . unspeakable things.

Eleonor despises him, and for good reason; or even without reason—he was her savior, etc, etc—but she does have good reason: "He's no man, he's an animal."

His name says it all: Fear. Fear of oranges, the sun, ants, the sea breeze, open windows, soap, the joy of breathing. Of dying. Living. Waking. Sleeping. A secret fear that festers and suffocates. The only pleasure he knows is despicable, heightened by his fear, demonstrated in monstrous acts. But what do Fear and his problems matter—we were talking about Eleonor. In comparison to her, Fear simply fades away for us, like a handful of sand thrown in your face that's blown away in the wind's laughter. Eleonor is radiant.

The messenger pigeons fly back and forth—set free and returned by the messenger Indians with reed baskets on their backs, or by Úrsulo via the river—the correspondence with the Eagles is constant and intense, they work both sides of the river as one body. No point in going into detail. Nepomuceno wants to attack with as little violence as possible, using cunning instead. That's why he welcomed El Iluminado, his Talking Cross, and the church ladies, "Older, uglier, and slower than . . ." The thing that really lifted his spirits was the arrival of La Desconocida.

North of the Río Bravo, Tim Black, the free Negro, has lost his mind. Totally.

His wife is plotting how to leave him—it's impossible to live with his jealousy and his irritating behavior.

It's better we don't see what's going on in his head. Sometimes he's convinced she's already left him—that her brother has arrived to rescue her as she claimed he would years ago—and he's overcome by sadness. Other times he's blinded by fury. Either way he's unbearable.

"It's not as bad for me as it is for the children . . . I don't know what came over him! Such a good man! The truth is that over time I grew fond of him . . . but now . . ."

"Please, spare me," Nepomuceno says when he hears Sandy's recitation. "Why do we have to sound like raving tyrants, as if the only things we speak about are glory, pomp and circumstance. It's so boring, I'm speechless . . ."

"We stand ready," the Eagles continue, "to spill our blood and suffer the deaths of martyrs to achieve it, La Raza . . ." and so on and so on. "The Mexicans in Texas put their faith in the capable hands of the governor-elect of the State, General Houston, and trust that his rise to power will see the introduction of legal protection insofar as he is able."

Nepomuceno wants to add, "Unintentionally separated from our brothers on the north bank of the river, without renouncing our rights as American citizens..."

Jones doesn't agree on this point. "We can't call ourselves Americans, Nepomuceno. Don't you see? For me that would mean accepting slavery, my own and that of my brothers. Nope. I'm Mexican, from this here side of the river. It's the only protection I have."

"That's your business, Jones, but if I say that, those bastards will take all my property."

"But you said you'd defend the Mexicans, Nepomuceno."

"Yeah, I said that, but let me be clear: I'm defending La Raza. Plus, just between us—and this is for your ears only, don't repeat it—this land is mine and I *am* this land. And now it's the gringos'? They've screwed me, and if that's the way it has to be, fine, I'll be a gringo, see? I am this land, this land is me."

"Of course I get it, Nepomuceno. You're the one who doesn't get it. So you get screwed by them and accept becoming a gringo, but if you stay on their land you'll be no better than a Negro, there's no alternative. They'll use you to make themselves rich. Their dollars are white, and like sea spray they need a dark body to sustain them."

"My friend Jones, such a philosopher. Enough. I need to ride for a while, I'm going stir-crazy."

The real philosopher is Nepomuceno's wife. She's never seen with him. They have a daughter who's nearly twenty. Nepomuceno had barely started shaving when the widow Isa began chasing him, though there are some folks who disagree, claiming that the life he led out on the plains, among horses and cowboys, awakened his interest in women and taught him about the birds and the bees long before he met the widow Isa, and that she, on the contrary, was quite demure! To this day Doña Estefanía can't stand the sight of her. But from the moment he shot Shears, he hasn't given one thought to his mother or his wife or his daughter. Nepomuceno's eyes wander from one woman to another, recently he only has eyes for La Desconocida, but he doesn't let on.

Dan Print does let on that he likes her, a lot. He's fallen in love with her. He knows Nepomuceno's also interested—male intuition—so he keeps it to himself and acts friendly.

He asks her what her name is. "I'm Magdalena Gutierrez, at your service." Where was she born, who were her parents, what's her story? "You married?" He hadn't heard the gossip about her husband beating her, as she told Nepomuceno. "Married, but I would never go back to that wretch, even if they tied me up."

Married? he thought. *She might as well be divorced already, what does it matter to me?*

Mr. Blast, the freebooter, can't get Nepomuceno to agree to anything. Nepomuceno, on the other hand, gets all kinds of information out of him about the U.S. troops: where specific regiments are stationed; the central government's intentions; and its positions regarding the frontier/border.

Dan Print sticks around after Blast leaves—but not to have long conversations with La Desconocida; instead of returning to New York, he shuts himself in the Ángeles del Río Bravo in Matasánchez (in Room 221, it's his base), planning to write his article on Nepomuceno. First he makes a trip to Doña Estefanía's ranch—she won't meet him, she's too upset about her son, but he speaks with both half-brothers—then he goes to another ranch to see Nepomuceno's wife and daughter, where he speaks with them both (it was a poor suggestion by his editor, Nepomuceno has no bigger fans than these two women), and he also asks around in

Bruneville. The other two brothers, the ones who are Nepo's enemies and rivals, refuse to speak to him. La Plange shows him photos of Nepomuceno from back when he was a great cowboy and rich
landowner, before he became what he is now, the leader and hero of
"La Raza." There are photos of Nepomuceno twirling his lasso in elegant circles, mounting a horse, leaving Mass (dressed all fancy), and
some taken in La Plange's studio.

Later, Dan Print returns to the Ángeles del Río Bravo, finally (he
thinks) ready to write his piece on Nepomuceno. Now he's thinking it will be a book. But he's distracted, coming and going between
Laguna del Diablo and Matasánchez. He makes these trips just to
see La Desconocida. Then he shuts himself in his room to write, but
he spends the time yearning for her.

One night he can't sleep for worrying: what will his mother
think of this woman, a Mexican divorcée with no money (by the time
he introduces her she'll be divorced)? "She has to speak English, at
least," he says to himself, and on his next visit to Laguna del Diablo,
he begins teaching her the language.

Nicolaso's dovecote is empty, his heart restless. He's tormented by
the sensation that he's imprisoned. The pigeons are his windows, his
doors, his bridges, his air, his freedom. It's not just any old day: when
Nicolaso hears the bell of the dovecote ring, signaling the arrival of
a pigeon, he runs to see what the message is. The message puts him
to rights.

He goes out, walking the few steps to the Café Ronsard. No
one's there yet. He orders a coffee. Teresa comes down from upstairs,
beautiful as ever. She's sad.

"Well, what's wrong with you?"

The beauty smiles and begins to talk, but Carlos enters the café
and duty calls. Nicolaso can't wait, he excuses himself and goes over
to Carlos to give him the message: *We'll strike in two days.*

Carlos doesn't say a word. He acts like he hasn't even heard Nicolaso. Nicolaso goes back to Teresa. She's smiling now and can't even remember why she was sad when she came down—seeing her friends cheers her up.

Carlos takes the drink the barkeep has made him and sits down at a table. He waits for the five Eagles to arrive and gather round, spitting.

"On the full moon," says Carlos.

"We put the plan into action."

"And follow it to a T."

At dusk, they take advantage of the tide to cross the river, not from the Bruneville dock but further upriver, at a makeshift dock hidden among the reeds, the one Úrsulo has used for a long time now.

Although Doña Estefanía can't stand the "widow" Isa, Nepomuceno's wife, and avoids her at all costs, she sends her a letter asking her to speak with "my son," to talk some sense into him and get him to give up his plans. She explains that it's not worth it to her to risk her son's life just to recover the land "where the gringos built Bruneville;" it would all be meaningless if she lost Nepomuceno, she must make him understand that you can't take on Samson without a barber. She must find him and convince him of this.

The letter comes as a blow to Isa—the feeling is mutual, she despises her mother in law—but it gets her thinking.

"Something must be done," she reflects.

She knows him well, she thinks. If she visits him at his camp, he'll be irritated and annoyed with her.

She must find a way to make it seem like she's encountered him by chance.

"The time will come," she thinks.

Magdalena, whom Nepomuceno's men call La Desconocida, is practically a stranger to herself. Without her room—which was kept in strict order by her maids ever since she was married—and without the threat of Gutierrez, she is caught up in the collective fervor of the Nepomucenistas. She learns the meaning of the looks she has been catching handsome Nepomuceno giving her when she receives them from Dan Print and compares the two. Dan Print has his charms, despite the fact he doesn't know how to ride or give orders. But Nepomuceno has won her. She's devoted to him. Still, there's an abyss between her devotion and her actually initiating something with him. He's a married man, and though he rules Magdalena's heart, for the time being she is content to serve his cause.

Her hair's her biggest problem. How to keep it from looking messy. But she's figuring it out. Everyone can see she's glowing, growing more beautiful by the day. Nepomuceno has bought her riding boots, but she won't wear pants like the Negress Pepementia and other women in the camp.

Fragrance, General Cumin's scout, requests permission to depart.

"Since when do you need my permission, Fragrance, to leave my presence?"

"No, my General, I mean I'm leaving camp."

"Where are you going?"

"To end my stay in this place, I don't like it one bit. I have nothing to do here. Bruneville is a city (an ugly one), not the prairie, there's no air, it's like being locked up. My General, I just need to get some fresh air and then I'll be back."

"Get some air?"

"But if you're staying here I won't return."

Dimitri, the Russian, is also leaving because he's had enough. The Americans ignore the reports he makes at the fort to the military authorities, three different ones with details about the Eagles' activities in Bruneville. They filed them away without even reading them, and they still haven't paid him either, despite their agreement. General Cumin doesn't trust him because he's a foreigner; and because of the General's prejudice against him the rest of the gringos don't trust him either, they suspect he's one of Nepomuceno's men, despite the fact it couldn't be further from the truth.

General Cumin doesn't have it easy. His men are getting soft, no matter how much he insists upon discipline. It must be the climate, Cumin thinks, or the goddamn Mexican women—he's convinced his men are visiting the brothels when they have a day off.

The fact is his soldiers are suffering from low morale because they can't cross the Rio Grande; he himself is itching to go, too. And now Fragrance has abandoned him. Cumin loses his composure. He's taken a seemingly wise young man as his personal assistant—one who used all sorts of underhanded chicanery and brown-nosing to secure his position—yet he doesn't have a shred of loyalty and poisons the troops with yearnings for violence. He was sent by Noah Smithwick, the Texan pioneer who leads hunts for escaped slaves, delivering half a dozen guns (three good rifles and three Colts) sent as "unbiased" support, "So the citizens of Bruneville can arm and protect themselves from Mexican bandits." It should be added that the guns originally belonged to the U.S. army but were stolen by the Comanches, who traded them for escaped slaves, the most valuable commodity on the frontier . . .

South of the Río Bravo, in Laguna del Diablo, Nepomuceno is briefing his men. He explains who will take part in the first charge. He gets some pushback. The volunteers want to fight the gringos and deal them a mortal blow, pushing them back north of the Nueces River, at the very least returning the Mexican border to where it ought to be. Nepomuceno explains, "We won't commit any more violence than is necessary to get them to respect La Raza. Everyone who doesn't participate in the invasion and remains in camp will still be supporting the invasion of Bruneville. We'll proceed carefully to ensure we will act fairly. We'll strike against those directly responsible, the ones who have wronged us. Three strikes: I'll lead the first, for the moment let's forget the trap we'll set for them, we don't have to worry about that; the second, Lieutenant Jones; the third, Juan Caballo, the Mascogo chief (that's Seminole to the Americans, he's blacker than three moonless nights). These are my orders, and you better follow them to the letter: capture the ones who are directly responsible: Glevack (first and foremost); that carpenter and so-called sheriff, Shears; Judge Gold (who's corrupt); and Mr. Chaste, the mayor and pharmacist (because he's a traitor). Just those four.

"What about Judge Whatshisname, ain't he corrupt too?" That's Pepementia, who has overheard all sorts of people say so. "Ain't he just a shameless carpetbagger?"

"What Pepementia says is true," Nepomuceno says. "We'll go after Judge Gold as well as that other judge who makes a mockery of his profession, the one they call White or Whatshisname. Just do exactly as I say."

Don Marcelino, the crazy plant collector, hasn't been out on one of his expeditions to collect specimens for two weeks now. He spends the days in Matasánchez—in the marketplace, the portico of the church, in the vicinity of the Café Central, on the main thoroughfare—just walking around. He doesn't miss the way he feels walking through the mountains, listening to the chattering birds, looking at the plants. The way things have changed, he's completely absorbed in taking notes on unfamiliar words: the language people are speaking seems to have reached a boiling point. "So many folks from the north, speaking a different Spanish . . . There's no time to waste, it won't last long, sooner or later folks will choose English or Spanish, things can't go on like this . . ." He's overcome by euphoria, as though he has just witnessed the evolution of man from monkey: "Folks are speaking Fishfowl, a language which is neither fish nor fowl, and I want to know exactly what it is."

In Bagdad, Dr. Schulz closes his piano. He checks his office is locked. He can no longer sit around: it's time to meet up with Nepomuceno. He's not eighteen anymore, like when The Forty founded Bettina, he no longer wears a beard, but at thirty he still has room in his head for utopian dreams. "Yes, yes." Without another word, his medical case in hand, he mounts the mare he bought to get to Bagdad, spurs her on, and heads for Laguna del Diablo.

In Matasánchez, Juan Prensa is glued to the pedal of his press. He's printing pages to distribute in Bruneville: Nepomuceno's Proclamation. It will also be included in newspapers throughout the region. He prints two versions: one in Spanish and one in English, a literal translation—both versions incorporate language from Sandy's speech, the one Nepo didn't like at first.

NEPOMUCENO'S PROCLAMATION

Article One. An organization in the State of Texas dedicated tirelessly to the philanthropic work of improving the circumstances of Mexican residents, and to killing their oppressors, to which end its members are prepared to spill their own blood and suffer the death of martyrs.

Article Two. The Mexicans in Texas put their fate in the capable hands of the governor-elect of the State, General Houston, and trust that his rise to power will see the introduction of legal protection insofar as he is able . . .

The proclamation continues with further articles that we'll omit here to skip directly to its:

PERSONAL NOTE
Though we're isolated from our neighbors in the city by
virtue of living outside it, we do not renounce our rights as
American citizens.

Up in Laguna del Diablo, it's Laura, the girl who was an Indian captive, who's isolated. Spoiled by her grandmother, who never let her
leave the house, she's useless; she doesn't know how to cook or fight,
she can hardly walk without complaining that her shoes are getting
dirty. She cries at the drop of a hat. At night she cries for her poor,
dead grandmother, for her mother, for her aunt who's still held captive by "those savages." No one pays any attention to her.

The day, the Great Day for the attack on Bruneville, arrives.
    The sky is clear, cloudless. The moon is impudent, naked,
round, the mouth of a cave, its light cold as death. It's an eye without a pupil. It's the anus of a mischievous angel. Heaven knows what
else, it makes your teeth chatter. It pulls at the reins of your heart. It
forces you to imagine things.
    The attack begins with five Yamparik Indians on the eastern
edge of Bruneville, where the road is poor (there's heavy traffic with
Punta Isabel, but only on the water); they're slowed by the swamp
with its clouds of mosquitos (which carry awful tropical diseases)
and assorted varmints. That's why this side of Bruneville is unprotected, no one has given a thought to it. Even if the snakes and the
gators were to take sides with Nepomuceno (they wouldn't dare, the
gringos would come and get them sooner or later), the landscape's
inhospitable conditions provide a natural defense.
    Joe, the Lieders' eldest son, has gone out to wander, as he does
whenever he can, to escape from his parents and siblings, trying to
go somewhere he can be alone for a while to masturbate: "I gotta

feed my worm." ("Ich muss meinen Wurm futtern.") He tells his parents: "I'm gonna go see if the hen has laid an egg."

The corral is far behind him, at his back, when he sticks his hand down his pants. He gets hard immediately. Joe rubs and rubs with plenty of saliva. His eyes roll back in ecstasy, only their whites are visible.

Two Yampariks appear out of nowhere and grab Joe by the wrists, making fun of him in their language. Joe resists.

Joe shouts. Two more Yampariks, hiding in position nearby, begin to ululate, running back and forth to make it seem like there are many of them. The fifth Yamparik rides his splendid horse back and forth (like an idiot, or perhaps he's clever and he's just acting), not far from the farm, on the only piece of land where his horse's hooves won't get stuck in the mud and caught in the weeds—though if he's not careful the tarantulas will crawl up its legs.

The boy's family are screaming their heads off: "They're kidnapping Joe! They're kidnapping Joe!" His youngest brother runs off to Bruneville to get help, thinking he's going to rescue him.

The news spreads like wildfire across the brushland: the Apaches are attacking. "What if they're in cahoots with the Mexicans?!" The question flies from mouth to mouth.

Joe's brother has unwittingly aided the attackers. He's done their work for them. Foolish simpleton.

All the armed men from the Bruneville fort head due east, to cover the unprotected side of the city.

This truly is a special day. The Mexicans have all left Bruneville for a fandango, which promises to be a really good party, in Matasánchez. They gathered on the dock to cross the river, boarding the barge—which Stealman has rechristened the *Elizabeth IV*—for Matasánchez.

"They should call it *Chabelita* now!"

"Don't you think they should have called it *Mrs. Lazy* in her honor? It's so slow and it's always late . . ." Folks have been making this joke ever since the barge started crossing the river again.

Others take their own dinghies and rowboats to Matasánchez— it's a national holiday. When the armed gringo soldiers—both the hired guns and the U.S. troops led by General Cumin—left to defend one side of the city, they did so because Bruneville was empty of greasers, who were all at the fandango on the other side.

On the other side of the Río Bravo the Independence Day fireworks have begun to light up the sky in three colors: green, white, and red. Folks have begun shouting, "Viva México!"

Dr. Velafuente is playing his part in the attack, getting Matasánchez's mayor, De la Cerva y Tana (not near as despicable a mayor as Bruneville's Mr. Chaste), good and drunk; he has to keep him nice and busy in case (as is likely) the gringos arrive to request reinforcements.

The shouts of Nepomuceno's men (the majority of whom are not Indians) join with the ululations of the five Yampariks; they've found good hideouts and have taken up positions, taking advantage of the natural hidden dangers in the swamp.

The sea breeze blows in a huge cloud that seems endless. Goodbye moon. Now no one can see a thing.

The gringo troops lose a good horse when it stumbles into a hole in the ground and breaks a leg, and another has gotten bogged down in a quagmire; three men fall into another hole, a "typical Comanche trap"—or so they think, but there's nothing Comanche about it— the Two Eights made the camouflage for it in Laguna del Diablo— and there are ten more traps like it waiting with open jaws to swallow whomever they may.

The landscape is strewn with traps that the Mexicans and their allies have taken their time to carefully prepare—how many will they capture?—while the "000, 000, 000" of the Yampariks and the other Nepomucenistas continues in the distance, faking an attack. They're just pulling the gringos' legs.

Meanwhile, Joe, held tight by one of the savages, sees the world fall into darkness, which covers everything. He wants to cry. "This is what I get for wanting to live with the Apaches, what was I thinking!"

Before midnight, the second and third waves of Nepomuceno's advance on Bruneville arrive.

Jones and Juan Caballo, one of the two Seminole-Mascogo chiefs, are their leaders, under Nepomuceno's command.

Most of Nepomuceno's followers arrive among the Mexicans from Bruneville who are returning from the party: some take the barge, others take the rowboats or skiffs of folks who aren't returning tonight because they're staying the night in Matasánchez, or who lend them their boats just because.

The barge and its tug are under the command of the so-called mermen, despite the fact they now belong to Stealman. The Two Eights know how to maneuver them well.

(The Two Eights are overjoyed to see the barge where old Arnoldo trained and raised them . . .)

They all arrive at the dock next to Mrs. Big's Hotel in Bruneville; they being:

1. The Mexicans who are returning from the fandango, and who have had a great time. They're in no state to shoot or to fight; the ones who still have energy just want to make love and continue drinking. They're good people. And they're good cover for Nepomuceno's men.
2. Nepomuceno himself, with Óscar, Juan Prensa the printer, Jones, and Juan Caballo at his side, along with a few others.

3. El Iluminado with his Talking Cross and some of his followers, almost all of them armed men—including a few outlaws. Next to him, Padre Vera, who didn't want to be left out. One, Two, and Three are with Robert, the escaped slave.

4. Well-armed Mascogos, Negroes, and Indians, ready to fight.

5. La Desconocida.

6. Sandy, who's returning after a two-week absence.

7. The Negress Pepementia.

8. One of the dreaded Robins, along with a bunch of thugs from the Coal Gang.

9. Connecticut and El Loco.

10. Pepe the bootblack (with his shoeshine box) and Goyo the barber (with his knives, hidden in the bootblack's box).

11. Dr. Schulz, his medicine case in hand. Nepomuceno gave him a black mask that covers his face without obscuring his vision, to protect his identity.

12. Some young, frenzied Mexicans who have been furious ever since the American invasion (Nepomuceno tried to keep them from joining up, but despite being barred from the camp they took advantage of being in Matasánchez to sneak in and join forces).

13. The Kids' Brigade, all well-organized.

14. A variety of Indians, all from north of the Río Bravo, the majority of whom have been forced south of the Nueces River by the gringos (but not one Comanche, despite best efforts).

15. Various others whom we don't know . . .

The folks who aren't there, to avoid arousing suspicion, are:

1. The pigeon keepers and anyone who's been helping them out on the sly, such as Sid Cherem and Alitas, Carlos,

Hector, pretty Teresa—only Sandy has joined the invasion—so as not to imperil their fragile network.

2. Nepomuceno's two half-brothers (Doña Estefanía's stepsons), who don't come either. Despite deep involvement
in planning this day, they stay behind to look out for Doña
Estefanía (there'll always be bigmouths who claim they're
cowards, but that's just cheap talk).

They take over Mrs. Big's Hotel and tie her up, just in case. They
lock up her employees, but not all of them, depending on whether
or not the Eagles and Nepomuceno's men know them. They abduct
La Plange.

Nepomuceno orders him to take photos and gives him helpers
to carry his camera and lamps—Snotty can't carry all the equipment
by himself.

They head toward the center of Bruneville in silence.

The Brunevillians go first, a smiling army of unarmed volunteers,
happy to help. They're followed by the Lady Colonels on horseback:
Pepementia, La Desconocida (in the Mexican saddle Don Jacinto
made specially for her), and Sandy. The religious brigade goes by
foot—El Iluminado and Padre Vera—as well as the brains behind
the operation, Jones and Óscar—guarded by the "savages." (That's
what Jones calls the "criminals who tarnish our movement." "When
a gunfight erupts, who's going to shoot?" "We don't want a gunfight."
"Yeah, I know we don't want one, but I guarantee that neither my
lasso nor yours will be enough to defend us against the Rangers and
the U.S. troops.") Then come the Mascogos and the other Indians.

They split up into three groups to get to the Market Square.
All that matters to Nepomuceno is that the delinquents aren't left
alone. "Tonight everyone behaves as if we're going to communion
at 7:00 AM Mass for the baptism of a child."

———

When folks return from their fandangos in Matasánchez, they're usually lively: laughing, chatting, even shouting, doors opening and closing. But not this time. Everyone moves silently, forging ahead, even folks who don't understand what's going on (a number of the Brunevillians aren't privy to the plot, they're just following the crowd, their people). Silence. A few steps from the square, next to Peter Hat's store, Nepomuceno knocks on the door of Werbenski's house—not his pawnshop. Three loud knocks. Four. Five. He keeps pounding without pause, each stronger than the last. All the men and women who form Nepomuceno's army are gathering in the square. They're confused by what Nepomuceno's doing, they don't understand.

Lupis opens up, Werbenski's wife, that sweet Mexican woman, looking incredibly frightened. Her husband is right behind her, half asleep, awakening with each step. When the door creaks open he says, "No, Lupis! What on earth are you doing? Let me open it . . ."

They find a dozen of Nepomuceno's men standing at the door, hats covering their faces, their guns holstered, wearing their good boots and their fancy shirts and jackets.

Lupis is so frightened she begins to cry.

"There'll be no Mexican tears tonight," Nepomuceno says loud enough so everyone can hear.

But he speaks gently, as if he's singing to her.

There are others who tell it differently: one guy knocks on Werbenski's door, then another and another, until a bunch of them are banging on it incessantly.

Señora Lupis jumps out of bed. She covers her nightclothes with the large shawl her mother brought her from San Luis Potosí, the one she keeps at the foot of her bed. The white shawl barely covers her. It's very pretty, made of silk.

Where Lupis goes, Werbenski, who adores her, follows.

"Where are you going?" he asks, half asleep.

"Someone's at the door."

"Don't answer, Lupis."

"What if it's an emergency?"

What kind of emergency could it be? Werbenski's not a doctor! But they're hardly awake, just reacting to events. Werbenski follows Lupis to the door. "No Lupis, let me open it!" But she doesn't listen, she unbars it and turns the deadbolt.

Some twenty men stand facing the house, most of them armed to the teeth (not figuratively, but literally), and they barge into the patio brusquely, as if they've been running and can't slow down. Among them, Bruno (the ever-present Pizca at his side) and his men, as well as the youngest of the Robins, notorious outlaws in Matasánchez. (That really takes the cake! The youngest Robin has joined up with what he'd normally call "a bunch of goddamn greasers" because he's convinced there's big profit in their game.)

Lupis begins to cry at the sight of so many outlaws in close proximity, and because she's been separated from her faithful Werbenski, whom they've shoved back to the other side of the courtyard.

Nepomuceno goes up to Lupis; loudly he says, first in English— so her husband will understand—and then in Spanish, just for her, "There'll be no Mexican tears tonight, dry your face, Lupita, it's not becoming for such a lovely woman to ruin her good looks. God made good-looking women to be happy, not to cry."

He orders them to bring Werbenski to him. He explains what kinds of firearms he needs, what kind of ammunition, he asks how much it'll be, and pays "Adam" (he's the only one, Lupis included, who calls Werbenski by his first name) right down to the last penny—Werbenski gave him a good deal.

There's a new wind blowing in from the sea, and it's stronger than usual. It's cold and unruly; those who recognize it think, *El Norte is coming.* Powerful winds, rain, and high seas. *Is it a tropical storm?*

The U.S. troops' few lamps that remain lit blow out. Most of them have been out for hours and they haven't fired a single shot; they make no response at all to the howls of the Yampariks that still ring out from time to time; they wait beside the Lieders' house while their commanders, led by General Cumin, remain inside the house until the light of day, when they'll be able to mount an attack, or at least respond to the attack they're certain is imminent.

In the darkness, Corporal Ruby (that's his nickname, he's a redhead) is telling a story about the Apaches, how they pillaged his town, taking the women and killing every last man, and scalping them to boot. Fear blows in on the wind and gives them all goosebumps.

Perhaps because the wind has stopped and their hair's standing on end the mosquitos suddenly intensify their attacks, as though a whole cloud of them has just descended, engulfing the U.S. troops.

Carrying their weapons, Nepomuceno's men take over the Town Hall—there's no one there to defend it—and take up positions outside the jailhouse—which they completely surround since there are armed men inside—and they take over the churches, the pharmacy, and the streets. They haven't fired a single shot and they've already captured Bruneville.

Their guns help to persuade folks. Because around here folks don't just roll over, it's not the Valley of Mexico, where they've put up with aggressive foreigners and abusive conquerors for centuries. Here, where everyone is a recent arrival, no one is docile like that.

But folks such as Peter Hat need no persuading—they're so frightened they could piss themselves.

They've taken some residents from their homes, to use them as hostages, but not the Mexicans, they wouldn't be of any use in that regard. Half-asleep, they stumble out of doors wrapped in shawls or quilts, covering their nightclothes as best they can to protect themselves from the night chill.

At the door of the Town Hall, in front of a makeshift squadron, they have placed Minister Fear's wife, Eleonor, who's accompanied by a man no one recognizes. The squadron is made up of Connecticut and a few scruffy Mexicans, light-skinned ones, all unarmed.

Óscar the baker's job is to make sure all the alarm bells are ringing— at the church, the Town Hall, and the one the judge had installed in the center of the Market Square, after the fire at Jeremiah Galvan's store.

You might think that it's a bad strategy: it'd be better to leave everyone sleeping and the U.S. troops where they are. But the problem is that they think some of the men they're seeking are with the soldiers; and they wouldn't attack folks who are sleeping, just the ones who sleep with one eye open, ready for anything. The bells are intended to draw their enemies to them.

Nat awakens at the first peals. He calls to Santiago's orphans (Melón, Dolores, and Dimas), who have been staying with him since they lost (literally) the roof over their heads. They go out into the street. They see what's happening. They run to get the Lipans' dagger, which remains well-hidden.

All four shout, "Viva Nepomuceno! Viva La Raza!" Though Nat is a gringo, he has caught the fever.

Father Rigoberto awakens, thinking the bells are ringing in his head. "The end of the world has come," he thinks. He puts his head under the sheets and falls back into a deep sleep.

Rebecca, Sharp's sister, hears the bells and listens to Sharp jumping out of bed, throwing his clothes on and running out of the house. Then she doesn't hear anything else: she has one of her episodes;

it seems like the night is brilliant, shining like the world is made of a huge sheet of thick, dark metal that undulates and shivers as though it's about to break because a giant fist is pounding it somewhere far away.

The U.S. troops are alarmed by the sound of the bells. "What's going on?" They realize they've been fooled, all gathered at the Lieders', obeying General Cumin's orders listlessly. They begin their retreat. A handful of men stay behind to guard the Lieders' home; the family is grieving for Joe, whom they think they've lost.

Everyone is scratching from head to toe, eaten alive by mosquitoes.

It's bad luck that Fragrance, General Cumin's scout, isn't with them. Things would have gone differently. Tracking, smelling the air—they would have understood what was going on.

The bells awaken Miss Lace, but she doesn't understand what has roused her and she feels startled and agitated by "a presence."

She jumps out of bed in a panic. She's certain that John Tanner, the White Indian, has arisen from the grave and has come to get her.

Joe Lieder hasn't slept a wink. There's only one Yamparik restraining him now—Metal Belly—who holds him firmly while he continues to ululate periodically to frighten the soldiers. As the hours have passed, their two bodies stuck together, Metal Belly has gotten a hard-on. At the same time, the one Joe had when he left the house returns.

Both erections are unwanted, but they level the playing field.

The U.S. troops and the makeshift group of volunteers (Rangers, citizens, gunslingers) enter Bruneville from the poor side of town. At the first corner they're met with a blast of gunpowder from which they recoil. Next, a ream of Nepomuceno's pamphlets rains down on them from a nearby rooftop, who knows who's throwing them, you can't see a thing, the sky is still overcast. They struggle to light the lamps the wind has extinguished.

In the center of the Market Square with the bullhorn (a new one, Stealman's) from the barge in his hand, Nepomuceno begins to read the proclamation while the Kids' Brigade goes from house to house distributing it.

All the town's inhabitants have gathered thanks to the alarm bells, some carry buckets of water, ready to put out the (nonexistent) fire, others are wrapped in their shawls and quilts to ward off the cold as best they can.

Everyone has a copy of the proclamation in their hands, some in English, others in Spanish.

(One confused gringo asks, "Is it the Blues versus the Reds?" A girl next to him answers in her sweet voice, "No, it's the stinkin' greasers!")

Halfway through his proclamation the U.S. troops enter the square firing into the air—they don't want to harm any civilians, "Watch out for the townspeople!"—by which they mean "the gringos," not realizing that most of the Mexicans gathered here are Americans too.

No one returns fire, there's not even a skirmish. The only shots are the ones La Plange takes—with his camera, his lamps, and the help of Snotty he's doing his best to capture the moment.

The Carbon Gang and the youngest Robin attack the U.S. troops from behind, starting a messy brawl, most of the soldiers are trapped between the townsfolk and the bandits, though a few manage to escape.

They lay down their weapons.

—

Frank, the Mexican run-speak-go-tell, is wandering around lost, wondering what's going on—it's unpleasant to wake up like this. "What's going on? What's happening?"

Metal Belly, the Yamparik who's still holding Joe, is wondering the same thing, right before he ejaculates—he's disgusted, he feels sick with himself. As soon as he does he heads toward Bruneville—someone else can look after the blond kid, let him rot!

In La Plange's photo Nepomuceno is standing on the bandstand the gringos have started building in the town square, holding the proclamation in front of him, not bothering to pretend he's reading because he knows it by heart (which is why the gringos claim that he's illiterate).

The photo is taken in profile. He's surrounded by Brunevillians, all wrapped in their blankets, with their frightened faces, and Mexicans, still high-spirited from their celebration. Later, Lázaro will sing:

> Oh the poor gringos' teeth
> how they chattered,
> the cowards paralyzed by their fear.
> I won't mention Rigoberto,
> the lily-livered priest.
> He'd heard so much about hellfires
> he hid 'tween the sheets.

Next Nepomuceno's men go after the men on his list.

But first they have to find them.

Olga (even at a time like this she can't resist running around spreading gossip) lets Nepomuceno's men know: Shears is at the Smiths' house, his wound still hasn't healed.

They knock politely on the Smiths' door, but as soon as the

pretty Hasinai, Moonbeam, opens the door they barge rudely past her into the house while she struggles to keep them out.

They subdue her. Moonbeam smiles at them, which disarms Ludovico. He reaches toward her, "Moonbeam! My little sunbeam!"

Moonbeam is put out that "one of them" (today they're ruffians) is talking to her this way. She pushes him away and runs into another room. Ludovico follows her, more playful than anything else. They run from room to room—back and forth across the patio—ending up in the room where a pallid Shears is resting; no sooner does he see shadows approaching than he shoots.

Moonbeam drops to the ground.

Shears drops his weapon. He shouts, "The greaser killed the Comaaaaanche!"

Ludovico falls to his knees and covers his face. He stays like that, frozen.

Dr. Schulz—medical case in hand—arrives immediately to attend to her.

"It's too late. She's dead. It was a crack shot."

He glares furiously at Shears. There's no question he's the murderer.

Ludovico rises and leaves.

The sheriff points at him, shouting, "It was him!" He obviously doesn't want to take the blame.

When she hears this, Caroline, the Smiths' daughter—the one we know is in love with Nepomuceno—steps out of the wardrobe in the adjacent room, where her parents forced her to hide. She's holding the cocked pistol they gave her to defend herself. She behaves like the madwoman she is. She runs over to Moonbeam's body, waving the gun as if it were a fan—she's out of control—then puts the gun to her temple and pulls the trigger.

There's no question it's a suicide, it couldn't possibly be anything else. Dr. Schulz himself was a witness.

She too is dead on the spot.

Shears shouts, "It was him!" pointing to Fulgencio, the cowboy, who can't take it anymore—he knows full well the gun smoking on the floor isn't Ludovico's—and he shoots Shears.

In Caroline's head the bullet has created more havoc than ever. It would have been interesting to stay in her mind for a while: her infatuation with Nepomuceno; the death of her pretty slave, Moonbeam (her companion, who tethered her to reality); her consequent incomprehension. We already know she's incapable of organizing her thoughts—her head and her heart are like the swamp near the Lieders' homestead where the U.S. troops got bogged down (like flies in honey); she was setting her own traps (just as Nepomuceno's men did): clingy weeds, varmints, ignorance, darkness. And add to that the evil moon, stagnating behind a cloud, its cold light ruling the night.

(Some say there is a God. And some of us believe it's the moon, mutable, sometimes brutal, which calls the shots. It severs the threads of life without hesitation; it takes the good and the young, yet leaves old men who want to die living, shriveling up.)

Shears, meanwhile, moans, "It hurts, it hurts." For weeks now his vocabulary has been limited to these two syllables—not that he had a wide vocabulary to begin with.

Fulgencio's bullet lodged right next to his heart, without killing him, and Shears is still breathing. The bullet is like a babe in its cradle—it's a homecoming.

One of the U.S. soldiers (Captain Ruby) goes berserk a block behind the Market Square, he was already on edge, nervous, the truth is that fear is getting to everybody—not Minister Fear's kind of fear, but the fear of animals who find themselves cornered by a hunter.

Too bad: one of the gunslingers who arrived with Nepomuceno—it's not clear who—silences him in one shot.

His death is bad for Nepomuceno's men, and even worse because Corporal Ruby is (was) the son of Mexicans.

It would appear that, unawares and unintentionally, Nepomuceno is shooting himself in the foot.

The lovely Hasinai, Moonbeam, dreams she's on stage, half-dressed in tulle, gauze, and a leather belt, barefoot, singing: "I'm a lovely Hasinai, who so many folks dream of." The theater is packed, applause.

What happens next in her dream is that Moonbeam collapses, she's in her death throes, wearing a tight black dress, her face that of the card sharp Sarah-Soro Ferguson, the one who dreamed she was Moonbeam on the stage.

Some veins burst in Moonbeam's head, her brain becomes a few milligrams lighter. She hears lightning crash.

But her dream continues, and lovely Sarah rises, composes herself, and begins to sing again, dressed as a Hasinai. The audience goes wild, she's causing a commotion, they love her more than ever.

Moonbeam's bowels tighten; her sphincters relax, she urinates, she soils herself too.

The dream goes on, but it's impossible for us to follow, it's as though it's been cobbled together into a series of unrecognizable images; there's no point in lingering here.

"One of Nepomuceno's men killed Moonbeam!"

"And another shot Caroline, the Smiths' daughter!"

"The greasers are raping women!"

To contain the damage and put an end to this debacle, Nepomuceno gives another string of orders to his most trusted men, he wants the larger group to stay close to him. "Lázaro, get over to the jailhouse and bring me Ranger Neals; Juan Prensa, go get Minister Fear; the cowhands are going to go round up all the gunslingers they can find in Bruneville, we need to teach them a lesson; you, Sandy, fetch me the Judge, you know him. You, boy, you! Two Eights! Go find someone to help you get Chaste, that treacherous piece of shit . . . The rest of you stay here . . . I want you beside me, Óscar; you, too, Jones; if we need to negotiate with the gringos, between the three of us we'll sort this mess out."

He takes Shears for dead.

Ever since they arrived in Matasánchez, all Óscar has really wanted to do is visit his oven and bake some bread, "That's what I was born to do, I'm a baker."

"Are you nuts?" Nepomuceno replies to him when the baker says, "Be right back . . . I want to go check on my oven."

"Forget about baking, just forget it! What's happened to you, Óscar? Have you lost your mind, too?"

It's Tim Black who's lost his mind, the wealthy Negro; he runs naked from his house down to the bank of the Río Bravo. When he gets to the edge, he ties his ankles together with his belt and jumps in. Beneath the water, he embraces himself.

He doesn't last long. Having run all the way from his house, he doesn't have much air left in his lungs.

Don Jacinto is trying not to show his pleasure at seeing Nepomuceno.
Cruz his displeasure.
Their attempts don't last long.

Inside Óscar's oven—the one his parents built fifteen years ago, where he learned the business of baking bread—Glevack crouches, laughing: "That dumbass Nepomuceno, that rich little shit, what is he thinking, invading Bruneville? The gringos'll make mincemeat of him, what an idiot. And what's all this crap about 'La Raza'? He's lost his marbles, or he's got mush for brains. They'll never find me here! Fools, losers, just wait! Just wait! I'll get my revenge! And I won't stop until he's hanging from Mrs. Big's icaco and his eyes have been gouged out . . ."

Chaste is hiding in the Stealmans' latrine; they've gone to New York. One of the slaves lets him in—the chain they put around her ankle reaches just to the front door, she can't take a step outside.

Nepomuceno's men pass right by, they've heard that the house (or, rather, the mansion, the finest in Bruneville) is empty.

Lázaro Rueda heads down to the jailhouse, pistol at his side. He's never been prouder, it's like he was born for this moment. Nothing compares, not lassoing his first colt, not riding his first woman, not having children.

He walks in and asks, "Is . . .?"

They don't even let him finish his sentence. Three Rangers jump him, take his Colt, and throw him behind bars.

Urrutia handcuffs one of his wrists to the bars of the cell, leaving the other hand free.

Everyone's roaring with laughter except Lázaro, who's stunned.

Urrutia shows him the key, "Here's the key that locked you up, sucker cowboy . . ." and throws it through the cell's tiny window into the street. "Give it to him, fellas, and don't pull any punches!"

Blows rain down upon Lázaro. After this he'll be fit for the boneyard; if he survives in one piece it'll be a miracle.

At this point a cart drawn by two extraordinary horses, one fair as a ray of light, the other red as fire, pulls into Bruneville.

The cart carries two passengers: Isa and Marisa, Nepomuceno's wife and daughter, and no one else—they are alone. Someone told them that Nepomuceno's men were going to capture Bruneville, an opportunity they couldn't pass up—it's the "widow" Isa's chance to have a word with him. They left the ranch at dusk, fearless, and here they are, dressed in their finest, dusty from the road, but lovely and smiling.

Two U.S. soldiers—both blockheads, but not so stupid as to miss this opportunity—take them hostage as soon as they learn who the two beauties are (the women have given themselves away, asking around for Nepomuceno, whom they presume is the victor. "We're his wife and his daughter.")

"Who's gonna go tell the greaser that we got our hands on his women? Tell him if they leave right now we'll let the women go. If not, we'll shoot them full of holes." There's no lack of volunteers, despite the possibility they'll get a thrashing.

What do you know? No one gets a beating.

But Nepomuceno's jaw trembles, and how.

He doesn't give it a second thought. It's no time for waffling, decisiveness is called for.

His orders: "We're leaving this moment. We're already on our way."

No one disobeys Nepomuceno. His voice is so powerful that even the Mexicans who live in Bruneville begin packing their bags. But the fever passes before they close them. Only folks who don't live in Bruneville board the barge, though there are some Bruneville residents who leave, fearing the vengeance that will fall on the town's Mexicans.

Melón, Dolores, and Dimas (the orphans of Santiago, the fisherman) get on board.

Nat doesn't, he stays in his room with the Lipans' dagger.

The return to Laguna del Diablo isn't easy. When they're crossing the river they see Tim Black's cadaver floating. It rose to the surface almost immediately, as if he were full of hot air.

Jones says, "He was a bastard, Tim Black, but this is a bad omen."

Everyone's heavyhearted.

Suddenly, the night seems brief. When Nepomuceno decided to leave Bruneville, he was moved by his love for his wife—the widow Isa—something bigger than himself (though you might not believe it since she's so long in the tooth by now).

Isa is spirited, full of life, and Nepomuceno has never enjoyed himself more with another woman; there's no one who makes him feel so good, he doesn't sleep or shoot the breeze with anyone else like he can with her. It's a shame she can't cook like his mother, not that she's a bad cook. Her problem is that she's too straightforward, she doesn't like complications, her salsas are fresh and smell good but there's no secret ingredient. They're like she is: honest, direct, frank, without mystery.

Nepomuceno wants to bring them back to his camp. Even his daughter Marisa (because she's with his wife).

"No, Nepito, I'm not doing that. If you want, take Marisa with you, she's your daughter. But I'm spending the night in Matasánchez, at the hotel."

No one can talk her out of it: Isa is a strong-willed woman. Marisa, poor thing, doesn't matter to him, but she knows what she wants, and that's to be with her father.

On both sides of the river the full moon is making cooks yearn for the perfection of browned onions and the drumbeat of the knife dicing them, for the sighs of bread, the fresh innards of tomatoes, the cautious flames, and sneezes caused by chiles and peppers. They dream in unison, attuned to one another.

—

Magdalena, La Desconocida, dreams of her mother. She's a girl, back in her mother's arms. She falls into an even deeper sleep. Now the arms around her are Nepomuceno's. A pleasure she has never experienced runs through her, electrifying; she wakes up.

The moon gives Felipillo Holandés his recurrent nightmare—he gets out of the Moses basket and walks along the wet sand, Nepomuceno and his men arrive, he cries out—but this time he doesn't wake up. He dies in his dream. Then he awakens.

Laura, the girl who was once kidnapped, is lying next to El Iluminado. For days she's followed him around like a shadow, except that she didn't accompany him to Bruneville. They sleep like two spoons, nestled together.

A moonbeam lands on the girl's eyelids. Laura opens her eyes. She thinks she hears the Talking Cross. She closes her eyes, afraid. She snuggles up to El Iluminado, disturbing his sleep. He jumps up. He feels the moon on his face. He kneels to pray.

At the Werbenskis' house, the turtle that the cooks have been slowly mutilating to make delicious green soup (a dish fit for the gods) is also dreaming. In the dream, the turtle's pain—its left back leg and right foreleg are gone, next they'll cut off her other foreleg, then her other back leg, and finally her head, then they'll stew it all up together, using the meat beneath her shell for the soup on Sunday— morphs into a feeling like she's walking in the mud . . . a mud that covers her completely, eliminating the burden of being what she is, as well as engulfing her unbearable, gnawing pain. A pain you can chew like gum, gum that comes from the sapodilla, which the cooks cut out of the fruit to chew while they shell peas, pluck chickens, and remove the white pistils and green corollas from zucchini blossoms, making them sweet as sugar.

—

Mrs. Big's icaco tree also dreams. We won't go into detail in order to avoid the unpleasantness of the two cadavers' erections, which the tree cannot forget, transformed by them into something bestial.

And the shadow of Mrs. Big's icaco dreams, too. It's a more dignified dream than the tree's, but it, too, is saturated with violence.

The dogs dream dogs' dreams, resigned to be "man's best friend." This awakens them. They bark passionately without ceasing. The dogs barking in unison awaken the turtle, the icaco, its shadow, some of the cooks (interrupting their collective dream), Ranger Neals (who awakens if a pin drops), and Dr. Velafuente.

The roots of Mrs. Big's icaco tree don't know how to sleep, and therefore can't dream. Rigid, they extend through the muddy earth, thinking always of the Eagles because the Eagles are always going on about how "it's so important to defend our roots," etc.

Caroline Smith dreams of Nepomuceno as she dies.

Her dream seems bewitched. Nepomuceno guides her along a road, this can't be real. The tree's roots are exposed, hardened, challenging the wind. Its crown is buried in the dirt. She feels the rough, rocky road beneath the soles of her feet. Nepomuceno is carrying her. Caroline knows this road leads to her death, but she doesn't care. Suddenly, she is facing a door. She opens it. She can't pass through, she's dead.

Corporal Ruby dreams anxiously, for him eternity is drowning in a roiling river.

Sarah-Soro, in New Orleans, also dreams what the moon wants her to dream—its powers reach that far. She dreams about Moonbeam, the Hasinai Indian who's no longer with us. Scantily dressed, she dances on stage, never more beautiful. She speaks a few words in her native tongue, which Sarah understands.

In her corral, Pinta, Nepomuceno's horse, has a very strange dream: she climbs a ladder up to the fat white cloud that is looking down on her from the sky.

There, the magnificent mare dreams the cloud's dream: she's not made of flesh, not even vapor. She's just a color.

At her home in Matasánchez, Maria Elena Carranza is awoken from her dreams by a moonbeam falling across her eyelids. She gets up, feeling as if she's been illuminated. She looks out the window and thinks she sees the Talking Cross fly past.

"Sweet Jesus!"

She drops to her knees and begins to pray.

Three times Nicolaso has awoken to the birds' flapping, afraid there's a coyote, a fox, an Apache—someone who wants to steal them. It's just the moon making them stir.

In Bruneville, the moon shines on the Adventurer, who was formerly lying sick in the infirmary, but who has now fully recovered— he's handsome and well dressed, but there's something inscrutable in his expression; he's paying Mrs. Big (she's been drinking but can still attend to business) for two horses. He also buys a donkey to carry supplies (animal fodder, beef jerky, hardtack bread—nothing like the bread that Óscar bakes, but it'll last a long time) and water.

A cloaked figure awaits him beneath the icaco tree. It's Eleonor. They're running away together.

They ride, first along the road to Bruneville, then across open fields, for what's left of the night and well into the morning, until they find a place to rest, though they have stopped three times to give the animals a break. There's fresh water and trees for shade. While they ride he doesn't dream a thing. Eleonor dreams both when they ride and when they stop. Images come one on top of the other, flying through her head so quickly that she can't focus on a single one, but they make her happy, happier than she's ever felt before.

Glevack is with a lady of the night. Riding her.

Óscar's dreams are poisoned. First, the well where he stops to drink is full of cadavers. Then the meat Sharp delivers him is full of worms. Last, he offers Nepomuceno rotting bread. Instead of life, his bread bestows death.

No sooner has the sun appeared on the horizon than rumors begin to spread like wildfire through Bruneville and further north, and in Matasánchez and further south—distorted like Chinese whispers: rumors that Nepomuceno captured Bruneville dressed in a short cape thrown across one shoulder (a *manteau*), a high collar right up to his beard, wide breeches, tight socks, shoes with shiny buckles, and a wide-brimmed hat, his strawberry blond beard trimmed in a narrow triangle (the folks who said this also said that Shears behaved like a gentleman, an eye for an eye, while the really malicious ones said that Nepomuceno shot him just because he felt like it); rumors that the invasion was about a girl, identifying who the girl was, debating whether he kidnapped her or not, or whether they raped Bruneville's women. Someone even dared to say they used swords and lances and gunpowder to do unspeakable things to them. Someone else claimed that first they kidnapped the women, then they blew up the bridges (and that's really going too far, there's not a single bridge in Bruneville) . . . all sorts of crazy things. All the exploits of the Robin brothers mixed with the Coal Gang's and other bandits, even the pirates who used to attack Matasánchez and the ones who built Gálvez.

In the north they can't stop talking about John Tanner, the White Indian who's risen from the grave, going so far as to claim he came over with the Mexicans. In the south, folks who've heard of John Tanner claim that the White Indian defended the gringos.

In camp and beyond, folks sing along to their guitars, "Take care, Nepo, don't let them kill you."

Nepomuceno pays no heed to these rumors. But it kills him to think folks are going around saying he's a pansy, that he let them take Lázaro prisoner and didn't do anything about it.

Nepomuceno begins preparations for another attack on Bruneville, despite Jones's vehement opposition.

Óscar doesn't protest, he's paralyzed. He's heard that Glevack hid in his oven during the attack. That's too much to bear. He's a baker, a peaceful soul becoming a warrior, but his transformation is taking time.

From *The Rancher:*
  "Nepomuceno entered Bruneville with seventy-seven men
  (and women). Forty-four of these men have been charged
  by Cameron County Grand Jury; thirty-four are Mexican.
  That's not including Mexicans returning from the party,
  which made up the majority, and who, though they didn't
  exactly aid and abet them, acted the fool to provide cover
  for them.
      These seventy-seven people include the leading mem-
  bers of the Robins and the Coal Gang."

Moonbeam's funeral causes all sorts of problems in Bruneville. True, she was baptized, but they can't bury her in the Christian cemetery.

Funeral services are for honoring civilized Texans. So they decide to bury her with the Negroes. But if they bury her with the Negroes she won't be properly honored, and she certainly ought to be—she died defending Texas against the greasers; burying her with the Christians would be "the right thing," but it's not about doing "the right thing," it's about maintaining appearances and (as the mayor, Chaste, emphasized) "civilized society."

After a lot of talk, they don't even give her a pine coffin. They wrap her in a sheet they found who knows where—it's contemptible. They toss her in a hole without so much as a prayer. Minister Fear, who baptized her, should have been there but . . . Fear won't leave the house because he's crestfallen, he's been cuckolded.

As for Caroline, they couldn't give her a proper burial. She committed suicide. They buried her in a nice coffin, on unblessed land.

Chief Little Rib—chief of the Lipans—hears the news from a messenger. He consults the shaman. Case closed: all commerce with Bruneville is suspended until things calm down. The shaman adds, "You can't even do business with them when they *are* calm."

At the watering hole where the Adventurer and Eleonor have stopped, he lays down to sleep. Eleonor sits down to think. She loses track of time. She begins to fall asleep, too. The Adventurer awakens. He grabs one of her legs, then the other, removing them from her skirts, and falls onto her, whipping his hard dick out of his pants. One, two thrusts. What a relief! He couldn't wait a moment longer—he thinks, satisfied—it's been so long since he had a poke, *And this ain't no weapon to keep holstered.*

He puts away his weapon. He gets up. Without turning to look at Eleonor he goes off to look for brushwood to build a fire, he's hungry.

Eleonor looks like a ghost. All her fragile beauty has disappeared. She doesn't dare cry. She doesn't even dare look at the Adventurer. She hardly dares breathe. Now she does look like the honorable wife of Minister Fear.

She tries hard not to dwell on what she's feeling, *That was so horrible, so empty, how can it be . . .*

Nepomuceno and Jones are sitting down, writing, though it's really just one of them who writes, Jones is the only one holding a pen. Óscar stands beside him. Even the noonday sun doesn't lift Nepomuceno's spirits. The paper reads:

"My countrymen—I am moved to speak to you by a sense of profound indignation, the affection and esteem I hold for you, and my desire that you should enjoy the rights and protection denied to us, violating the most sacred of laws.

"Mexicans! When the State of Texas began to receive the recognition accorded to it by its sovereignty as part of the Union, bands of vampires, disguised as men, arrived and scattered throughout the State, with nothing other than corrupt hearts and perverse intentions to their names, laughing heartily as they foretold the pillaging and butchery dictated by their black hearts. Many of you have been imprisoned, hunted and chased down like animals, and your nearest and dearest murdered. For you, there has been no justice in this world, you have been at the mercy of your oppressors, whose fury toward you grows daily.

"But these monsters consider themselves justified because they don't belong to La Raza, who, according to them, don't belong to the human race.

"Mexicans! My part is taken; the voice of revelation whispers to me that to me is entrusted the work of breaking the chains of your slavery, and that the Lord will enable me, with powerful arm, to fight against our enemies, in compliance with the requirements of that

Sovereign Majesty, who, from this day forward, will hold us under His protection."

The Two Eights, Pedro and Pablo, lead the first operation. For three nights they steal boats from anywhere they can (mostly from Bruneville, but they bring some small ones from the little docks in Matasánchez and its neighboring ranches as well), they take them to the Old Dock in Matasánchez, and there, with the help of Úrsulo, Connecticut, and a group of peasants who have supported Nepomuceno from the very start, they hide the boats on land.

Guitars, violins, and voices rise in song to Nepomuceno on both sides of the river. *Because he's a wealthy rancher, he comes from good seed.*

Something is giving Nepomuceno terrible insomnia. He thinks of calling Jones and using the time to plan (or add to the proclamation—but it's already so long that Juan Prensa has had to fetch extra reams of paper—it looks like they'll have to fold it: "Maybe even stitch it"—"No, don't stitch it, this isn't woman's work,"—"Then bind it like a book,"—"Fine, but . . . everyone needs to read it! Not like the Bible or some boring romance for women!"—"Then shorten it, Nepomuceno, don't keep adding to it!")—but he doesn't call for anyone, this anxiety he feels can't be shared . . . He thinks of La Desconocida, he'd like to call for her, for a brief moment he's pricked by the needle of desire . . . but that would be beneath him, that woman's for lovemaking, not forcing . . . besides, she's not the filly he wants . . . what he wants is *his* woman . . . *his* wife . . . here . . . the only one who knows how . . . Isa . . . despite the fact he's furious with her—how could he not be? She really screwed things up riding into town like that . . . Who in their right mind walks straight into a lion's den?

The clouds are solid and white against the dark blue sky lit by the moon. The same moon, sick and tired of bursting with light, causes wolves to dream about the pleasure of sinking their fangs into a cow's flesh, bloody meat.

Telegram: "Minister Fear is moving immediately. Stop."

Another, from Mexico's central government to Matasánchez (which lie far apart, that's why there are so many complaints from the Far North, "They don't even glance in our direction"): "Don't let Nepomuceno break the law."

The telegraphist is being run off his feet and he's feeling low. He's tired, "Everyone takes me for granted."

From a conversation in Bruneville, in Spanish: "From now on, have no doubt, Nepomuceno himself will make sure the law is upheld, time's up for the gringos." "La Raza's hour has come."

On the fourth day Nepomuceno's men fill all the boats to the brim. Once more they mobilize at night.

Carlos the Cuban, along with three other Eagles, takes Mrs. Big's Hotel by force. They take up positions at the windows, waiting impatiently for the signal—a flare on the river—to fire at the U.S. troops who are guarding the dock, fast asleep in their uniforms.

Nepomuceno's strategy bears his trademark: catching the enemy off guard. The U.S. troops aim their guns at Mrs. Big's Hotel to respond to the shots that have left two of their men wounded. Meanwhile, their backs are turned on Nepomuceno and his men.

They soon arrive at the other side of the dock, where they're least expected.

There are hundreds of them aboard the boats, vessels of varying size—canoes and skiffs that people on both sides of the river use for their daily errands, some of which are well-kept, others half-rotting rafts. Some (the Mexican ones) have their names painted in bright colors: *Lucita, Maria, Mama, Petronila,* and Dr. Velafuente's *White Lily* (which is one of the finest, he uses it just for sport fishing, a luxury he seldom indulges in, and the occasional family outing).

The flare has also alerted Nepomuceno's men who are waiting further inland for the sign to charge in on their horses.

Nepomuceno's men begin firing from different vantage points.

It's worth taking note of the skill they display on the water (they've grown up alongside the river or by the sea, they may as well have been born with fish tails). The mermen attack the U.S. troops from behind. They don't hesitate, the goal is to kill as many as possible.

If the cowboys weren't so adept at handling horses, they wouldn't have been able to guide them toward the crossfire. They deserve recognition too. They arrive at Mrs. Big's when the field of gringos' cadavers is ready to be harvested. Riding atop their mounts, followed closely by their comrades who run and yell, they burst into Bruneville. Bang, bang, bullets fly left and right, it's a real shoot-out, a veritable hail of bullets.

Luis, the distractable boy who carried Miss Lace's shopping baskets, is hit—he doesn't have any baskets now, but he pays for them. The bullet enters his mouth and lodges in his head.

Without pausing, Nepomuceno's men gather on the dock, board their boats, and "Adiós, amigos gringos, we're outta here."

In addition to the dead, they leave pages printed with another proclamation scattered in their wake and a message at the foot of the Town Hall steps: "This is a warning. Return Lázaro to us within two days or we'll be back again every third."

Sid Cherem, the Maronite who sells cloth at the market—and who's diverted some of his orders to the encampment at Laguna del Diablo to support Nepomuceno's men without getting directly involved— had been prepared. He got up on the roof terrace of his house. He lay down with his rifle so no one could see him defending Nepomuceno if it became necessary.

Dan Print, who's been living it up (every time he goes to the Café Central, he stays longer) and hasn't returned to work in his room at the Ángeles del Río Bravo, hears news of the attack from one of his informants. "Now that's news!" He awakens Matasánchez's telegraphist, saying it's urgent, asking him to send a report about Nepomuceno's attack without delay. He ends his message with a note that's almost longer than the message itself: "The recent disturbances on the banks of the Rio Grande were initiated by Texans and carried out by them. This Nepomuceno and the majority of the bandits who support him are citizens of Texas . . . Very few Mexicans from the other side of the river, if any, have taken part in these disturbances."

Eleonor escapes from the Adventurer after several encounters similar to the first, him taking her mechanically and quickly, without so much as looking at her. She mounts her horse and heads off without a destination. The stars watch over her.

On the day of the attack, she arrives at the Aunts', the ranch of the Amazons. They welcome her with open arms.

When he reads the telegram in New York, Dan Print's editor answers as follows: "Where is your article STOP The clock is ticking STOP Thanks for the news STOP I want more."

After the attack, Nepomuceno and his men (both mermen and cowboys) return across the river, but they don't disembark at the Old Dock. Fearing an ambush, they look for a landing further upriver; though there's nothing even resembling a dock, the tide makes it easy to disembark. The Kids' Brigade ties all the boats together—forty-seven in total, a rosary of vessels—and lets them go. They have allies on the lookout at the Matasánchez dock, they won't miss them.

By the time Nepomuceno and his men arrive in Laguna del Diablo, negotiations between the mayors of Matasánchez and Bruneville have already begun.

By the next day Lázaro's release has been agreed upon. An official messenger goes to Laguna del Diablo to tell Nepomuceno.

The atmosphere in camp is tense. It's not like a party anymore, rather a military outpost.

"There's no date set? Go back and tell them they can count on my compliance once they give me a date."

"But the mayors are the ones setting the conditions."

"What conditions? This isn't a prisoner exchange. They kidnapped Lázaro, I want him back."

"You can say that, Nepomuceno," says Jones, "but according to their laws, Lázaro is a prisoner because he broke the law . . ."

"Their laws . . . their laws . . . they can take their laws and go to hell! They can stick 'em where the sun don't shine!"

Jones ignores this outburst, but everyone else present is taken aback.

"So now what?" the messenger asks. "What should I tell them? They're waiting for an answer."

"Tell them," Jones speaks up in response to the messenger, "that Nepomuceno accepts the truce but that they have to tell us when they're going to set Lázaro free, and it should be sooner rather than later. This truce isn't indefinite."

"Give them one week," Nepomuceno says, coming down from his cloud of fury.

"One week."

"We'll write our response down for you," Salustio adds sagely.

The horses Nepomuceno's men used, all of which were stolen, have been left at Mrs. Big's Hotel—they haven't even had time to rebrand them (though some have been rebranded before)—and there are a few mustangs and mavericks among them, too. No sooner have they freed themselves from where the Mexicans hitched them than Mrs. Big asks the first cowboy she can find to get some help and round them up. She plans to sell them. She's decided to leave town with the money.

In the Bruneville town papers there's an article about Nepomuceno, preceded by a letter from the editor:

"To the Mexican residents of the State of Texas:

"The arch-murderer and robber has been induced by some inflated coxcomb to allow his name to be put to the following collection of balderdash and impudence. We shall not inquire now who wrote it, but it certainly was no one who has the least acquaintance with American laws or character. We invite the attention of the people abroad to his pretension that the Mexicans of this region (we suppose he means from the Nueces to the Rio Grande) claim the right to expel all Americans within the same."

Some excerpts from the article:

"He claims to lead a secret society, organized to this end. He modestly describes his fellow villains as virtuous, especially courteous, pure, and good-humored. This is what he says about himself and his followers, even after stabbing and shooting the dead bodies of the Smiths' daughter, Caroline, and three of our own men, Mallett and Greer and McCoy, who were killed in the fight he and his men started . . ." and "His men survive by stealing horses—that's always been their livelihood. They've escaped justice with the help of perjurers. They broke into the jailhouse, stole the mail . . ."

Stealman orders Chaste, the sort-of mayor, to ship a new boatload of crazies across the river, in response to the damage and the losses incurred (in theory) by Nepomuceno's raid. He writes that it's more critical than ever to keep Bruneville free of burdens on society.

On the barge we recognize some characters: the priest Rigoberto—they say he's crazy because he falls asleep all over town (and because they want to get rid of the Catholic priest) (this recommendation also came from Stealman, via telegram: "Don't forget the guy who's always falling asleep")—and Frank, the run-speak-go-tell (since Nepomuceno's attack, two things have changed: he's been sleeping in the streets and folks have gone back to calling him Pancho Lopez, for the gringos if you're not white, you're Mexican whether you're a Texan or not, and regardless of your accomplishments). (In the jailhouse Lázaro still has enough heart to sing, although he doesn't have his violin:

You ain't Frank anymore,
Panchito, the gringos saw right through ya.)

De la Cerva y Tana's "emissaries" arrive in Laguna del Diablo: three Pueblans who are "ambassadors" for the federal government, dressed in stiff black suits totally unsuited to the climate.

The message they deliver is that the mayor wants to see Nepomuceno.

"Tell him he's welcome to come here."

They explain why he won't, why he must go to Matasánchez.

"And why should I go, if he's the one who wants to see me? Tell him he's invited for barbecue and sotol."

The emissaries explain it's a goodwill gesture, just to establish their friendship. Et cetera.

Nepomuceno has a word with Jones and Óscar. They decide he'll go.

They arrange the day and the time with the emissaries.

The word is that the Indian settlements are all gone, broken up, but here and there a few camps remain, existing in uncertainty. Some of the ones who are encamped receive the news of Moonbeam's death and burial. That the greasers killed her, and her death should be avenged. But the fact the gringos have put her in the earth without ceremony is even more unforgivable.

The Hasinai make a journey to Bruneville. They plan to present themselves "to the chief" and reclaim the body. The conna (the tribe doctor) and caddi (their chief) lead the way. Along the journey they dance for ten nights—their funeral rite—around a ball of straw attached to a long pole.

They also carry the coffin for their tribeswoman, it's as big as a cart.

They dance again on the riverbank in Bruneville, carrying an eagle's wing in their hands. They hail the fire as they dance around, spitting their tobacco into it. Then they drink a scented potion that makes them drunk.

That's how the U.S. scouts found them. They didn't even wake them, they killed them while they slept.

Six weeks after Nepomuceno's attack on Bruneville, eight pistol-packers approach the Bruneville jail at a quick trot as the afternoon ends. From a distance, judging by their clothes and their demeanor, they look like cowboys, which is to say, Mexicans. But they're not. There's Will, the Kenedys' Ranger, and Richie, who works for the Kings (he's the king of the kiñeros or reyeros), the rest aren't on anyone's payroll, they're guns for hire. All eight are cut from the same cloth. They stop about two paces in front of the door and form a semicircle. Shouting in English, they demand the prisoner Lázaro Rueda. They call for "The Robber" to be handed over to them, and, in pseudo-Spanish, they add, "The Bandito."

In response, Ranger Neals orders the jail door to be locked and barred. He shuts himself in with his men.

Ranger Richie approaches the window at the side of the jail and stops. The semicircle rearranges itself.

Lázaro asks his unlucky jailer to give him his Colt, they have it right there, "So I can defend us." He's certain they'll break down the door. As if to confirm his fears, a bullet zings through the high window of his cell and lodges in the wall about a palm's length above Lázaro's head.

Ranger Richie dismounts. He sets fire to a rag soaked in turpentine and blows on it.

The sopping rag flies through the cell's high window.

With his free hand, Lázaro picks it off the floor. With no fear of scorching his fingers, he puts it between the cell bars so it doesn't go out.

"Give me a stick or something! Anything, a pole, a rod, a piece of metal!" Lázaro begs the jailkeeper. He wants to use the fiery rag to defend himself.

Big kids, little kids, old folks, even women are thronging around the jail, some crowd together behind the horsemen, others line up behind Richie. In silence. Awaiting the inevitable outcome: Lázaro will come out that door. Or else they'll burn him up inside. The folks surrounding Ranger Richie help him soak more rags in turpentine. Then they toss them in the air and set them alight with shots from their pistols; some catch fire and sail, burning, through the window. Some catch fire and slide, flaming, down the stone wall.

"Whose idea was it to not build the jail out of wood?"

The jailkeepers reinforce the door. Lázaro insists, begs, "Give me my Colt!"

Another rag falls at his feet.

Mr. Wheel, who drives the cart, the one with the crabs, appears behind the horsemen, chewing tobacco and blinking, his eyelids like butterfly wings. He's the one who wears the sheriff's star on his chest now. He shouts:

"Ranger Neals! Open this door and I mean now! I won't let anything happen to one of my men. Open the damn door!"

"I take orders from Stealman!"

"You know he ain't in Bruneville!"

Ranger Neals thinks it over a couple of times, but quickly. Things are getting ugly. If he doesn't comply, they might treat him like he's just another greaser.

Lázaro keeps saying, "Give me my Colt, for pity's sake, for the love of God!" He understands exactly what's happening.

Ranger Neals's moment of indecision causes cart-driver Wheel to back off; he makes himself scarce; he leaves the same way he came (the relatively new sheriff's star doesn't embolden him much), but with a more decisive step, muttering about fetching some tobacco.

Wheel pokes his nose into widow Rita's tobacco shop and leaves in a hurry without buying a thing. He walks in silence to his office, where he locks himself in. His heart is in his mouth. He's terrified. He watches from his window, blinking, his nerves on edge. Frozen like a statue, he watches the doors of the jailhouse open wide.

One of the riders dismounts. He puts his reins in the hands of some kid, maybe his son; he walks, composed, toward the door.

The other riders dismount, too, gracelessly, but in unison. They file through the doorway. The new sheriff, cart-driver Wheel, leaves his office and heads to the jail.

Lázaro Rueda sees the riders enter, his eyes are riveted. Without his Colt, the only thing he has is the rag burning at his side. He thinks about throwing it. Whom should he chuck it at? He recognizes a few of the violent, cruel-hearted ruffians, two of them rape Mexican girls, more than two have been called kiñeros or reyeros.

Lázaro can just see—and hear—that behind the men there's a hoard of gringo Texans.

He doesn't lift the rag. It's futile, and besides, that's not what he's made of, he's no fire-starter, no murderer. Lázaro has never wanted to harm a soul. He throws the rag on the floor and extinguishes it with his boots—a gift from Nepo in better times.

Someone squats, picks it up and blows on it, someone else grabs Lázaro by the neck and stuffs the hot, smoking rag down his shirt, sparks and all.

The rag burns him a little. It's bearable. It's not searing. The pain reminds him: "You are Lázaro Rueda, you were born in the south, you have been a cowboy forever; you've been in the valley of the Río Bravo since the beginning of time."

On the other side of the river, Nepomuceno has entered Matasánchez with a small party of his armed men, not the thoughtful ones.

They've come to Matasánchez for an appointment with the mayor.

They go straight to the Hotel Ángeles del Río Bravo, the best one in the region. They'll spend the night there. Nepomuceno says he doesn't want to, because that's where his wife is staying, and he's still mad at her, but the truth is that he very much wants to, he misses her and knows that they'll spend the night talking and hugging and kissing as only widow Isa can.

But first, something cold to drink at Café Central. He doesn't have to wait for a table because they have reserved two for him. He sits at one, alone. His men sit on the benches in the plaza facing the café.

A regiment of soldiers in parade uniform marches in the plaza.

"What's the parade for?" asks Nepomuceno.

Doctor Velafuente shrugs at a nearby table. "They've been here three days, Nepomuceno, as soon as the Angelus is about to start, they march from one side of the plaza to the other. Who knows what they're up to!"

Then the news arrives, like a fuse about to be set alight, they come shouting into the café:

"The gringos are trying to take Lázaro Rueda from the jailhouse."

Nepomuceno feels a thick, viscous anger.

The church bells ring. Noon. The ringing freezes Nepomuceno's soul. In a few minutes he's supposed to be at the mayor's, that's what he's here for, to speak with him; "Take it easy," Nepomuceno says to himself, now more than ever he should be at one with his compatriots. He makes a decision: the mayor can wait, he should go to Bruneville to protect Lázaro. He makes a sign to his men, but they can't see him, the parade is passing between them.

In the jailhouse in Bruneville, Ranger Neals orders the cell to be opened. In a half second he forces open the handcuff around Lázaro's wrist,

"I was a locksmith before I became this unlucky wreck of a man."

He hands Lázaro over in silence, while the masses outside shout insults. "Greaser! Greaser! Dark-skinned idiot! Coward! You damn Mexican!" No one calls him Lázaro. No one attempts the "R" in Rueda.

Among those who have crowded into the jailhouse are Miss Lace, Mr. Chaste (the pharmacist), Mr. Seed from the café, and Smith, who once played cards with Smiley: all faces he knows but are now unrecognizable.

They drag him out. He would have preferred to walk, but they don't let him.

Blows rain down on him; anyone who can reach him lashes out, beating him. Nat, the messenger, takes the Lipans' knife from his pocket and cuts off one of Lázaro's fingers.

Mexicans lock themselves inside their homes.

Cherem goes up on his roof deck, armed with three shotguns. Alitas goes up to his.

The other Eagles do the same.

Carlos the Cuban sets off a rocket from the roof of his guesthouse. It's a sign for Nepomuceno. The Mexicans keep their fingers on their triggers. There's no way to stop the crowd that has Lázaro, they're on the other side of the jailhouse.

Sharp, the butcher, distributes six sharp knives to the crowd, "For the brave among you."

They slice whatever they can reach off of Lázaro. There is screaming and laughter, celebrating the slaughter. They drag him to the Market Square.

From there a few of the Eagles can see what's going on. It's a solid mass of people, women and children. They hang Lázaro from the only tree with a chain.

"What should we do? Shoot into the crowd?"

The Texans start a fire at Lázaro's feet. Shears, the carpenter— bullet still lodged in his chest, like a chrysalis, an incipient butterfly, as if it doesn't bother either him or the bullet to live like that, as if his heart were a shell, resting in his body, his gimpy leg—joins them, his eyes bugging out of his head in excitement. The new sheriff, Mr. Wheel, the cart-driver, is already among them, celebrating.

"Nepomuceno should be here any minute."

Another rocket.

It all goes so smoothly it looks like it's been rehearsed. They begin to roast the victim. They didn't use rope to hang him because they didn't want to set fire to it. He hangs there, burning. The smell stirs up the crowd. Music. Dancing. Clapping.

Before the first rocket even goes up, Nepomuceno rises from the table.

The waiter is holding the glass of horchata he was about to serve, "Good and cold, just how you like it."

The left flank of the regiment makes a half turn toward the café. They aim their guns at Nepomuceno. The right flank makes a half turn to the right, aiming at everyone on the benches, Nepomuceno's armed men and one hapless passerby.

The regiment of soldiers storms into the café. The mayor De la Cerva y Tana is right behind them, with the "emissaries" who visited Nepomuceno's camp.

The room at the Ángeles del Río Bravo will remain vacant tonight. They take Nepomuceno and his men prisoner without firing a shot.

"We have orders from the capitol, Nepomuceno."

Without further ado, a detachment of well-armed men, all in high-ranking uniform, accompanies him to Puerto Bagdad. They embark immediately for Veracruz in a naval vessel.

The widow Isa will spend the night without her husband, as well as the remaining (three) nights of her life. It's the second time someone's heart has broken with grief for Nepomuceno—not including Caroline, who couldn't face life without Moonbeam. Isa will die because it was one thing to know he was alive, albeit with another woman (which was, truly, quite cruel), but something else altogether to learn they had buried him alive, what a horror, because from Veracruz they took him to Mexico City, straight to Tlatelolco prison.

Pinta, a lonely mare, now free like a man, bucks anyone who tries to mount her.

She hasn't lost her beauty, her bearing.

She won't let anyone so much as touch her. No rider can even saddle her, she knows full well that she belongs to Nepomuceno.

There are those who'd say her story resembles the one Soro-Sarah made up about Cliquot, because only Nepomuceno will be able to ride her again . . . If we ever doubted who was more human of the two, the horseman or Pinta, there's no longer any question: locked up like a dog in Tlatelolco, Nepomuceno doesn't even know where he is, he's lost everything, he's a shell of his former self.

—

While they burn the body of this gentle, noble cowboy who sang and wrote songs and was easygoing and owned no land and had no interests other than caring for herds and pleasing his masters—he thinks:

"Ay, Lázaro, you won't survive this! You'll never ride again or lasso a horse or a cow by the tail, you won't go to the mountains, you won't eat carne asada again, you won't sing, you won't play the violin. You're going the way of the buffalo (and you were never that majestic, what a fearful creature to behold, when they stampeded, the earth trembled). You're no longer what you used to be, you're nothing, but these are your last words:

"I want one thing to be absolutely clear: I'm no troublemaker. Leave me out of your fights, your complicated entanglements.

"And I mean it. I get what happened with Shears (I admit I was wrong to get drunk) and now this—my wrist in a handcuff, how could something so unlucky happen to me?

"I didn't come into the world looking for trouble, I went to the jailhouse because Nepomuceno asked me to fetch Ranger Neals. But Neals had flown the coop, the coward.

"What I remember is that Urrutia called me over to the cell, I went to him, he spoke to me softly; I'm old and I don't hear so well, so I went a little closer, and he grabbed my wrist . . . and chained me to the bars.

"That's why Nepomuceno's men left without me. They tried to come break me out of there, but it didn't work.

"And the rest was fate, wasn't it?"

In Lázaro's head, in his last trace of consciousness, a violin plays, and he hears his own voice, singing what was perhaps his last song:

Ya no suenan sus cascos
tic tac toc,
Pobre caballito muerto!

✴

Fifteen days later, after Nepomuceno's camp disbands, in Matasánchez, Juliberto, a cowboy's son who learned the violin by listening to Lázaro play—he left Bruneville "to come live in Mexico, I can't take the abuse over there anymore"—plays under the arches of the Café Central. He sings:

"Ya no suenan sus cascos . . ."

A boy stands beside him, watching. He's one of the kids from Nepomuceno's camp—he carries Lázaro's violin in one hand, he grabbed it because it was there for the taking; he's come to watch Juliberto and learn how to play.

The Mexican federal authorities believe they've done the right thing. If they hadn't taken him prisoner, Nepomuceno would have launched more attacks, destabilizing the region. Because Nepomuceno was determined to avenge Lázaro Rueda. And he would have published more proclamations—four, five, or six more—with the help of Jones, in both English and Spanish.

Nepomuceno's imprisonment shakes the region more than Lázaro's lynching (he was neither the first nor the last Mexican to meet that fate).

But not the whole region.

Turner (who spoke English with a Mexican accent and ate tortillas instead of bread) celebrated his eighty-fourth birthday at his country house in Galvez, as if nothing had happened. A sumptuous feast followed by an open-air dance, they put a thirteen-foot agave with gorgeous foliage in the center of the patio and adorned it with Japanese lanterns to illuminate it.

Juan de Racknitz, German captain of the Mexican army, founder of Little Germany, got himself seriously drunk while he listened to the musicians and watched the girls he had paid to dance.

Lawyer Stealman, who is deeply involved in the region, despite the fact he's been in New York trying to get the false property titles for Padre Island completed, spends the day triumphant. He's finally received an affirmative response from the governor on another topic that doesn't concern us.

The Robins realize that their profits could grow if they change their line of work. They ply judges with bribes using the money from their heist on a San Antonio bank. Suddenly they are owners of hectares and hectares, yet they continue stealing livestock. They dispute with the rightful owners, accusing them of theft, and by using judges, lawyers, and witnesses—they were well trained by King, who had taught them himself—they became wealthy without so much as dirtying their shoes. Surely that's a better way to make a living.

Much later they became respectable. Instead of people calling them "The Robins" they become "The Robin Family"—Texan aristocracy—but the blood of thieves, not nobility, still runs in their veins.

Don Marcelino, in his search for specimens for his plant collection, has extended his territory, going so far as to use a cart to cover more ground. He enters the northernmost point of the Huasteca region by foot.

Old Arnoldo's tug has run aground on a reef. The sea there is a transparent emerald green. And it's there that the soul of the old captain who steered it for decades awakens. He's never been happier: here the sea is really the sea, sunsets open the sky's jewel box, the seafoam white as heaven. This is eternity.

AUTHOR'S NOTE

That's where our story ends. But others continue:

Nepomuceno spends a tiresome, filthy spell imprisoned in Tlatelolco.

The children, the Kids' Brigade, doesn't break up, despite the absence of Nepomuceno and his camp; they learn to live along the banks of the river by stealing from ranches or wrangling stray livestock.

The gringos kill all of the Rodriguez brothers' pigeons, but they don't punish either Nicolaso or Catalino.

When Catherine Anne Henry's novel is published in New York, the critics describe it as Shakespearean, pondering the depth of its psychological dramas and the universality of its characters. One writes that Catherine "is on par with George Sand and George Eliot." The novel is a smashing success, everyone is talking about it.

La Desconocida leaves with Dan Print—or Dan Print with La Desconocida. They don't cross through Indian Territory—they're crazy in love but they're not that crazy. They take a steamboat to Galvez and another headed to New York. En route, Dan Print finishes his story, "The Proclamations of a Great Man." He delivers it to his editor, who hates it and requires him to make so many changes that ("Thanks to these New York expurgations and embellishments") Nepomuceno morphs from a hero into a petty thief (the article is finally entitled "The Robin Hood of the Frontier"); the editor is happy with the title, but the journalist can't stand it; publication is a success; the Henrys and the Stealmans pay for it to be reprinted as a pamphlet which they give to all their family and friends for the following reasons: Catherine admires the journalist's writing; Sarah appreciates its portrayal of Mexicans; the Stealmans admire and appreciate everything about it except the title, but that was easily fixed—in the reprint he becomes "The Red-Headed Bandit."

Carlos the Cuban moves north, the Eagles no longer mean anything to him, and the only thing he really cares about is his country's independence.

La Desconocida and Dan Print get married, infuriating the journalist's mother.

When Snotty figures out how to escape from La Plange (with some of the negatives of the photos of Nepomuceno), he joins the Kids' Brigade, and a photographer is born, one who doesn't earn a living off of weddings, funerals, and baptisms, but a top-notch photographer whose name we won't utter here so as not to tarnish his reputation with his boring past.

Marisa, Nepomuceno's daughter, doesn't handle the loss of her father well—she loses her marbles.

—

Don Marcelino shows up again in Matasánchez lugging a trunk full of specimens, treasures from Huasteca for his plant collection.

Nepomuceno escapes from Tlatelolco to take part in the American Civil War. With the help of his organization, the steadfast Eagles, he aids the despised Confederate slaveholders, helping them sell their cotton and slip it past the Union Navy's blockade (they have a plan in mind and need the money to execute it).

The Civil War heralds Bagdad's moment of glory; its population reaches fifteen thousand, as steamboats laden with contraband cotton leave for New Orleans, Havana, New York, Boston, Barcelona, Hamburg, Bremen, and Liverpool.

Nepomuceno, wealthy once more, organizes and equips an army and fights alongside the Yankees. The Eagles serve as crucial spies and guides in plotting against the Confederates, who lose the war.

After the war Bagdad loses its splendor, as Confederate commerce is halted. Mexican governments try and fail to revive it by making the port a military bastion.

Stealman, King, and Kenedy (the cotton plantation owner), some other slaveholders, and two Comanche chiefs (whose names I can't recall) are invited to live in Brazil by King Pedro. The Brazilian monarch offers them extensive land and credit to facilitate their moving to his kingdom, where they can own slaves without any restrictions whatsoever (in lieu of livestock, he promises them slaves, he's interested in cultivating crops, not animals). King Pedro even sends a boat to transport them—he wants to found a slaveholding republic on Brazilian territory, to stimulate the economy. King refuses the Brazilian king's offer (he's interested only in livestock, not cotton or tobacco or any other crop, "If it don't moo or neigh, I don't like it, not even beans 'n' chickens"—although on the matter of chickens—and pork, which gets lumped in with chicken—it's not strictly true). Stealman doesn't accept the offer, either, because he already has one foot firmly planted in New York. Everyone else boards the boat, including the two Comanche chiefs and their tribes—they're good at growing crops and they're good with slaves, too. Mr. Blast, the freebooter, goes with them, embarking on yet another failed enterprise.

Carlos the Cuban arrives in New York, where we lose track of him, all we know is that he joins a group of Free Cuba activists.

The Coal Gang pulls off a major heist, which entitles them to the crown formerly held by the Robins.

The Mexicans take Nepomuceno prisoner once more.

Dozens of Confederate parties escape to Mexico. Most are penniless, their possessions have been taken, stolen, they've been tortured or humiliated; the ones who are killed by thieves' knives are the lucky ones. The Confederates are met at the Mexican border by civilians in uniform who pretend to guide them, most obligingly, giving them the runaround, leading them to and fro until they hand them over, exhausted and shoeless, to rebels in Veracruz, where most of them are executed for their role in the North American invasion or for mistreating Mexicans in Texas; although there are some Mexicans who, after thoroughly abusing the Confederates, send them back to their homeland, naked and starving (and barefoot, too).

The last of the camels dies.

———

The Eagles make up songs mocking the kiñeros and the Secret Circle—who have become more aggressive with the Mexicans, but still don't despise them as much as they do the Negroes. The Eagles call them "the square circle." They go around the Café Ronsard muttering to each other without anyone having the faintest clue what they're talking about. Nowadays the Secret Circle call themselves the Kuklos (which is the Greek word for "circle.")

Sarah-Soro foolishly moves to New Orleans (it would have been so much better for her to end up on the Aunts' Ranch, but no). She marries and publishes a pretty good novel, *Cliquot*. Her husband pulls a fast one and disappears to Tumbaco, Ecuador, with everything she owns, overshadowing the newly published novel with this scandal. Sarah turns to drink and becomes the laughingstock of New Orleans; few people take pity on her, and she dies in the street, a disgrace, not at all like a Henry.

Nepomuceno manages to escape from prison again and joins Benito Juarez on the border (there are letters to prove it), counting on the support of his Eagles. Yet again he is taken prisoner by the Mexicans.

In 1867, the year Emperor Maximillian is executed in Mexico, a hurricane smashes into Bagdad. The storm, which is eighty miles wide, hits Mexico after landing on the Texas coast. In Bagdad, the storm drags ninety refugees on the steamboat *Antonia* five miles inland; when the storm subsides, the refugees on the boat discover they are far north up the Río Bravo. "Everything was lost, nothing was saved, not even our supplies," wrote one resident. After the hurricane, hunger destroys Puerto Bagdad. The *Tamaulipas #2* rescues one hundred and forty residents, possibly gringos, taking them from Bagdad to Bruneville.

—

Once again Nepomuceno escapes, this time to support Porfirio Díaz on the frontier. And once again he's thrown behind bars. While he's imprisoned, he proposes to the young woman who does the laundry at the jailhouse. He's put under house arrest in Azcapotzalco, where he spends endless days in isolation. He dies. And his only honor is that, perhaps on account of the corridos about him which are sung to this day (his name has become legend), a crowd accompanies him to the cemetery in a handsome white coffin sent by Don Porfirio. (Nepomuceno's soft-skinned cadaver is hopping mad: "This color of coffin is for a child, not for a courageous man like me!")

CODA

The Saints were greatly displeased with La Desconocida's flight and her deplorable marriage. Doing everything within their powers to demonstrate their displeasure, they appeared on the southern bank of the Río Bravo.

They had grown fond of Magdalena. Especially Saint Agatha (holding her two perfect breasts on a platter), Saint Lucia (with her eyes on a platter), Our Lady of the Holy Conception (standing on the heads of three cherubim), Saint Margaret (barefoot with her crozier at her side), and Saint Cecilia (with her violin, identical to Lázaro's, or could it actually be Lázaro's and the saint is making fun of the cowboy for not being worthy of the instrument?).

Ringing bells, cymbals, tambourines, and Saint Cecilia's violin all accompany singing and swaying (which is both modest and virginal). It's such a din that it's impossible to transcribe a single lyric or exhortation—it's impossible to make out the words in all this racket. "Tower of ivory, pray for us"—that much is comprehensible, but no more, because their anger makes their words unintelligible.

Are they angry that La Desconocida left for Texas, which isn't Catholic? That she ran off with a gringo? Or are they mad because he's unbaptized? Or because he's a penniless journalist? Who knows. It's probably some combination of all these things. *What a waste,* they must have thought, *she had the makings of a queen and she chose to be a commoner, a peasant, another starving soul lighting fires, poor as a church mouse!*

Characters

(in order of appearance)

Sheriff Shears—Bruneville's sheriff, a carpenter's apprentice

Don Nepomuceno—landowner turned hero by circumstance

Frank—a Mexican run-speak-go-tell, formerly known as Pancho Lopez

Stealman—Bruneville's "developer," a New York lawyer

Sharp—the butcher

Señora Luz—the cook at the Stealman's home

Mrs. Lazy, aka Elizabeth Stealman (née Vert)—Stealman's wife

Doña Estefanía—Nepomuceno's mother, nicknamed "Nania" by her
    father

Alitas—the chicken vendor

Frenchie—seed vendor

Cherem—cloth merchant

Miss Lace—works with Judge Gold

Judge Gold—who is no judge, that's his nickname

Luis—skinny kid, carries baskets

Sabas and Refugio—Doña Estefanía's older sons from a former marriage

Judge White—Bruneville's judge, "Whatshisname"

Nat—a messenger

Glevack—immigrant, ex-friend of Nepomuceno

Mrs. Big—owner of a hotel beside the river

Olga—a laundress

Minister Fear—bereaved of his first wife and daughter, Esther

Eleonor—Fear's new wife

The Smiths—Fear's neighbors

Moonbeam—slave at the Smith's, a Hasinai Indian

Lázaro Rueda—the old cowboy, plays the violin and composes songs

Caroline—the Smiths' daughter, in love with Nepomuceno

Strong Water—arrives with Blue Falls to sell goods, a Lipan Indian

Blue Falls—arrives with Strong Water

Chief Little Rib—chief of the Lipans, only mentioned by Strong Water and Blue Falls

Jim Smiley—a compulsive gambler

Roberto Cruz—the leather merchant who everyone calls "Cruz"

Sitú—the artisan who decorates belts

Perla—girl in charge of Cruz's house since his wife died

Óscar—the baker

Tim Black—the free Negro, the wealthy Negro, owns land and slaves

Joe Lieder—German kid, the Lieders' eldest son

Don Jacinto—the saddler

Peter Hat—"El Sombrerito," Austrian who owns the hat store

La Plange—the photographer

"Snotty"—his assistant

Bill—works at Peter Hat's store

Michaela—Peter Hat's wife

Ranger Neals—oversees Bruneville's prison

Ranger Phil—Texas Ranger

Ranger Ralph—Texas Ranger

Ranger Bob—Texas Ranger

Urrutia—sells runaway slaves

Herr Werbenski—owns Bruneville's pawn shop, also sells ammunition and firearms

Lupis Martínez—Lupita, Werbenski's wife, sweet Mexican woman

Aunt Lina—Lupis's aunt, famous for her iguana stew

Santiago—the fisherman

Hector—the cart owner

Melón—Santiago's son

CHARACTERS

Dolores—Santiago's daughter

Dimas—Santiago's son

Tadeo—a cowboy

Mateo—a cowboy

Mr. Wheel—the cart's driver

Lucrecia—the cook at Mrs. Big's hotel

Perdido—kitchen hand at Mrs. Big's hotel, a ragamuffin

Flamenca sisters—whores at Mrs. Big's hotel

Clara—Cruz's (the leather merchant) daughter

Sandy, Eagle Zero—Nepomuceno's spy

Hector López—a Brunevillian cart owner

Leno—desperate gambler who never says a peep

Tiburcio—old widower

Captain William Boyle—Englishman visiting Bruneville

Rick—sailor

Chris—sailor

Doctor Schulz—German, one of the famous Forty, helped establish Bettina, a colony named after writer Bettina von Arnim

Engineer Schleiche—German passenger, assistant to Prince Solms, godson of the Prince of Nassau

Kenedy—owns the cotton plantation

King—a pioneer, became rich in Mexico

Father Rigoberto—Matasánchez's priest

Jeremiah Galván—owns a store by the river

The Robins—four brothers; robbers

Matasánchez—settler who got rid of the Trece brothers

Trece brothers—two arrogant pirates

Nicolaso Rodríguez—dove-keeper

Favorita—Nicolaso's favorite dove

Aunt Cuca—aunt of Nicolaso and Catalino

Catalino Rodríguez—Nicolaso's brother, also a dove keeper

Lucha—kitchen girl at Aunt Cuca's

Amalia—kitchen girl at Aunt Cuca's

Doctor Velafuente—Aunt Cuca's husband

Isa—Nepomuceno's wife

Rafaela—Nepomuceno's cousin, his first wife, who died in childbirth

Jones—a runaway slave

The Carranzas—adopted the orphan Felipillo Holandés

Felipillo Holandés—nobody knows he's a Karankawa

Laura—Felipillo's neighbor, had been an Indian captive

Don Marcelino—the plant collector

Petronila—one of the Flamenca sisters

Roberto—Jones's friend, one of the runaway slaves

Pepe—the bootblack

Domingo—post office clerk

Doña Tere—sells quesadillas on the corner in Matasánchez

Lolita—Doctor Velafuente's sister

Don José Gómez—De la Cerva y Tana's assistant

Goyo—the barber in Matasánchez

Green Horn—a Comanche imprisoned at Matasánchez jail

Captain Randolph B. Marcy—one of the good gringos

Pepementia—a runaway slave

Lawyer Gutiérrez—Green Horn's lawyer; Magdalena's husband

Carvajal—Nepomuceno's political rival

Don José María de la Cerva y Tana—Mayor of Matasánchez

Francisco Manuel Sánchez de Tagle—central governor

Mi Morena—a passenger pigeon

Wild Horse—Mascogo Indian chief

Juan Caballo—leader of the fugitive African slaves

Parcial—Juan Caballo's pigeon

Lucie—Gabriel Ronsard's mistress

Gabriel Ronsard—owner of Café Ronsard in Bruneville

El Tigre—runaway slave captured by the Comanches

Noah Smithwick—Texan pioneer who leads slave-hunting parties

CHARACTERS

Bruno—the Viking, the Coal Gang's leader

Pizca—Bruno's right-hand man

Pierced Pearl—Bruno's captive

Bob Chess—a "real" Texan

Rawhide—newest Kwahadi

Chief Smells Good—Kwahadi chief

Sky Bullet—a Kwahadi shaman

Penny—the Kwahadis' only messenger pigeon

Teresita—lives on the Aunts' Ranch

Peladita—lives on Aunts' Ranch

Ulises—ill-tempered Mexican whom Peladita pines for

Steve—a tameme that carries a basket of goods on his back

Nemesio—Galician from Puerto Bagdad

Charlie—recently arrived in Bruneville

David—comes from a poor family that puts on airs

Old Arnoldo—the barge captain

Lovely Teresa—only has eyes for Nepomuceno

Mr. Chaste—Bruneville's mayor and pharmacist

Mr. Seed—owns Bruneville's corner coffee shop

Alicia—Captain Boyle's Mexican wife

Dry—a teetotaler from the Temperance Society; Walt Whitman's character, his real name is Franklin Evans

Esteban—Nepomuceno's man

Fernando—Nepomuceno's man

Connecticut—a madman

The Scot—another madman

Carlos—the Cuban, Eagle One

Dimitri—the Russian

Wild—the buffalo hunter

Trust—Wild's man

One, Two, and Three—Wild's slaves

Patrick—sells persimmons, Irish

John Tanner—the White Indian; a ghost

Toothless—the old beggar

Alice—John Tanner's only white wife

Old Schoolcraft—in charge of driving the Indians south

Young Schoolcraft—his brother, murdered

Skewbald—afraid of John Tanner's ghost

Chung Sun—Chinese settler in Bruneville

Dr. Meal—Bruneville's doctor, away in Boston

Rebecca—Sharp's sister

Silda—a friend of Rafaela, Nepomuceno's cousin and first wife, who died of a broken heart

El Iluminado—Guadalupe, also called Lupe

María Elena Carranza—found and adopted Felipillo Holandés

Rafael, José, and Alberto—Maria Elena Caranza's biological sons

Polca—possibly Felipillo's birth mother

Milco—her husband

Lucoija—a beautiful warrior, possibly Felipillo's birth mother

Copete—Felipillo's favorite bird

Lucía—Laura's aunt, kidnapped and taken to the Chicasaw camp, refuses Nepomuceno's help

Chief Buffalo Hump—Lucía's husband

Juan Prensa—the printer

Mr. Ellis Producer—brings the circus to Bruneville

Father Vera—Matasánchez's Catholic priest

Fidencio—Josefina's grandson

Sombra—his mule

Loncha—deaf old cook who worked for Doña Estefanía

Magdalena—La Desconocida, Gutierrez's wife

Blas—Urrutia's man and friend of Bruneville's crappy mayor

Josefina—old cook at Gutiérrez's house

Mr. Blast—a wannabe freebooter, a privateer by occupation

"El Loco"—sleeps beneath the eaves of the main entrance to the market in Bruneville

CHARACTERS

Doña Julia—citizen of Bruneville
Señor Bartolo—store owner in Matasánchez
Tulio—the ice cream man in Matasánchez
Doña Eduviges—customer in Señor Bartolo's store
Juan Pérez—the wealthy, unscrupulous, Indian trader from Mexico
Lupita—his sister
Ludovico—gunman and an excellent cowboy
Fulgencio—cowboy
Silvestre—cowboy
Two Eights—Pedro and Pablo, Arnoldo´s assistants, the "mermen"
Ismael—cowboy
Patronio—cowboy
Fausto—cowboy
Güero—cowboy
Steven—kid who's friends with Nat, Dimas, Dolores, and Melón
The Lieders—German immigrants from Bavaria
Lopez de Aguada—port captain
Julito—young man from the dock
Úrsulo—the river-watcher, owner of *Inspector*, the canoe
Mr. Sand—the Englishman, travel companion of Chung Sun
Roho, or Rojo—their slave
Lieutenant Governor, Captain Callaghan, McBride, Pridgen, Senator
Matthias Ward—guests at the Stealmans' party
Catherine Anne—a novelist from the Henry family, author of *The House of Bouverie*, elder daughter of Sarah and Lieutenant Ware
George Henry—Catherine Anne's crooked grandfather
Sarah—his daughter, aged ten when he died
Lieutenant Ware—Sarah's' second husband
Georgette—Sarah's younger daughter by Ware
Sarah Ferguson—Georgette's oldest daughter, named after her grandmother, aka Sarah-Soro, author of *Cliquot*, raised by her aunt Catherine Anne after her mother's death
Tela—Doña Estefanía's childhood pony

José Esteban—Nepomuceno's older brother, son of different mother

José Eusebio—Nepomuceno's older brother, son of different mother

José Hernández—foreigner at the Café Ronsard, author of *Martín Fierro*

Frederick Cannon—gringo who raped Josefa Segovia

Josefa Segovia—lynched by the gringos

Judge Jones—people call him Busy Bucks, former judge in Bruneville

Shine—a customs agent

Señor Balli—Mexican rancher murdered by settlers who wanted his land

Platita Poblana—silver smuggler from Puebla

Blade—the barber

Josh Wayne—a Café Ronsard customer

Mr. Dice—speaks to Minister Fear in Café Ronsard

Pepe—the corn-on-the-cob vendor

Lastanai—friend of King's

Pierce—owns the most successful cotton plantation in the region

Richie—King's son, king of the kiñeros/reyeros

Neil Emory—owner of Cliquot, the horse in Sarah-Soro's novel

Gwendolyn Gwinn—Cliquot's winning jockey

Juliberto—a cowboy's son

Sila—Juliberto's wife

General Cumin—leads the Seventh Cavalry Regiment

Captain Rogers—punctual captain of the *Elizabeth*

Urzus and Captain Bouverie—characters in Sarah-Soro's aunt's novel, *The House of Bouverie*

Fragrance—a Tonkawa, General Cumin's guide (or scout)

Owl Woman—Fragrance's mother, a captive French woman

General Cumin's wife—accompanies the general on his campaigns

Eliza—slave of General Cumin's wife

Hidalgo—the Rodríguez brothers' best pigeon

Pajarita—their most trustworthy pigeon

Dan Print—young New York journalist

Mr. Pencil—painted Elizabeth's family portraits

CHARACTERS

Rafa, Doña Llaca, Aunt Pilarcita, Don Isaias, Don Cesar, Lucita—relatives or neighbors of the Aunt who tells a story about a Comanche raid

Five Yampariks—Joe's kidnappers

Corporal Ruby—U.S. soldier

Metal Belly—a Yamparik

Marisa—Nepomuceno's daughter

Mallet, Greer, and McCoy—gringos killed in the clash with Nepomuceno's men

Ranger Will—works for the Kenedys

Rita—owner of a tobacco store

Turner—old man who has his eighty-fourth birthday party in Galveston

Juan de Racknitz—German captain in Mexican army

King Pedro—king of Brazil

Acknowledgments and Homages

This book is full of homages: to Juan Nepomuceno Cortina, the Robin Hood of the frontier (the character of Nepomuceno is based on him)—from whose proclamations I quote directly. He was born on May 16, 1824, on a ranch that was called Carmen back then, not far from where Brownsville is today, when the region was still Mexican. Self-taught, he was educated at home and never attended any educational institution. The son of landowners, he accepted American nationality when Texas was annexed, believing that would preserve his rights to his property, which were threatened. He became the leader of La Raza (the Mexican Americans) after the beating of a cowboy that is fictionalized here. In 1859, Nepomuceno launched the Cortina Wars and occupied Brownsville, a city founded on land that legally belonged to his family.

Other homages: to the Percys, Confederate authoresses from whose lives and works I have borrowed liberally—if not necessarily faithfully (I've turned them into the Henrys). To the popular narrative poem *Los Comanches*, from which I drew characters and lines of poetry. To *Martin Fierro* and its author, José Hernández. To the stories of captives from the Far North. To Camargo, Matamoros, and Brownsville (Matasánchez and Bruneville are created in their shadows). *The Great Theft* also invokes characters from the works of Mark Twain, Walt Whitman, and several films. It would be impossible to cite every reference, quote, homage—Jerry D Thompson's masterful biography of Nepomuceno, as well as Nicolás Kanellos's rich works,

333

were indispensable; the work of Josefina Zoraida Vázquez as well as her generous assistance; the writings of Bertram Wyatt-Brown on the Percys ...

To Juan Aura, whose verses about the sound of a dead horse's hooves I borrowed.

Finally, I wrote this novel with a grant from the Fondo Nacional de las Artes, as a member of the Sistema Nacional de Creadores.

To everyone, thank you.

Carmen Boullosa is one of Mexico's leading novelists, poets, and playwrights. She has published nineteen novels, two of which were designated the Best Novel Published in Mexico by the prestigious magazine *Reforma*. Her second novel, *Antes*, won the renowned Xavier Villarutia Prize for Best Mexican Novel (1989). Her novel *La otra mano de Lepanto* was also selected as one of the Top 100 Novels Published in Spanish in the past twenty-five years. Boullosa has received numerous prizes and honors, including a Guggenheim fellowship, a LiBeratur and the Anna Seghers Prize (Germany), a Casa de América (Madrid), Rosalía de Castro (PEN Galicia, Spain), a Jorge Ibargüengoitia, José Emilio Pacheco, and an Inés Arredondo (México). She is a Distinguished Lecturer at Macaulay Honors College, City University of New York. Her books have been translated into several languages. She's a New York Institute for the Humanities Fellow, and her archive is held at the New York Public Library (NYPL).

Samantha Schnee is the founding editor of Words Without Borders, which has published 4,500 writers from 140 countries since the online magazine launched in 2003. She began working with Carmen Boullosa in 2006 and since then she has translated Boullosa's novels, poetry, essays, reviews, and a screenplay. Schnee is the recipient of a 2023 National Endowment of the Arts Literature Fellowship to translate Boullosa's novel *El complot de los románticos* as well as a 2024 Berlin Prize from the American Academy in Berlin to translate Basque author Irati Elorrieta's award-winning debut novel, *Luces de invierno*.